DEAD AGAIN

DEAD
AGAIN

Fred Wellner

FIELDSTONE PRESS

Frontispiece: Angel from a headstone
in Oakwood cemetery, Syracuse, New York.

Dead Again
was designed and composed in 10/15' Sabon
in-house by Field Stone Press.

To my brother Doug

FRED WELLNER is an artist, writer, and a student of Religion and Philosophy. He is the author of *SYN,* also by Fieldstone Press. His upcoming projects include *Green Man,* a complete novel written online every day for a year on Publishers Marketplace as an experiment in discipline, *Cutting Through God's Backyard,* a somewhat heretical roadtrip through the Old Testament, and the *Native Sun* trilogy, an epic of science fiction connected with *SYN.*

Baleful eye
Inward monster of the deep
You know nothing
And everything
All that water and unable to drink

DEAD AGAIN

1

Everything changed. A searing, blinding, fiery flash, a thunderous roar truncated in the fraction of a second, and then naked. The overpass cutting across Route 96 in New Jackson City was clogged with traffic just before the event. In the distance, over the rooftops of cars and trucks, past the renegade Harley Davison still defiant in the absence of a summer sun, lights flashed in a slow officious staccato. There was no way on God's green earth of knowing why things were snarled up. They just were.

The answer should have been clear to him by now. Recent news stories threatened. Warnings everywhere . . . why should it be any different in his city? If they could hit Pittsburgh, or Hampton, why not here? Someone, somewhere, should have seen it coming. It all had no business seeming fuzzy to him, but it did. And where were his clothes? He shivered, suddenly conscious of the pavement pressing against his face, chest, and legs. The chill of a sun-warmed autumn day on his back brought a thousand tiny points of skin to a confused state of pleasure and discomfort. He became distinctly aware of a strange, vacuous feeling underlying everything, elusive in that he couldn't zero in on its source, but peripherally its presence could not be missed or mistaken for a passing memory. In the mere absence of what was missing, it hurt. But even that pain felt like a distant ghost. That hurt too.

Next to his face, within six inches as a matter of fact, was a license with his photograph. The words next to it spelled out Jorj Tory Watchman. Underneath were separate lines. 2100 North State Street, New Jackson City. A smear of blood blotted out the state and zip code. He could read most of the rest. Sex: M, Eyes: HA, HT 6-00, Class: D, another crimson stain and finally, EXPIRES: 02-20-10. There were, of course, numbers, codes, and the like, but they were unimportant now. That much he guessed.

Something of a shadow passed his thoughts, memories from a distant where and when. His work, livelihood, everything he knew and was, looked back on him from above and then slowly winged it's way westward towards the inevitable path of the sun. Like his long-departed father, anything he set himself to do, he recalled, he did, so long as it didn't involve much commitment or more money than he typically carried in his wallet. Though he could not remember exactly what he did for a living, he knew that much about himself. And there were faces that appeared in his thoughts . . . people he must have known, had to care for, or be cared for by. He quickly found that he could not place a name to any of them. But he knew where he lived, or thought he did. And he knew what he was driving before . . . Shit! What an accident, he decided. Ripped his clothes off and blew them away with his brains. Shouldn't he be pushing up daisies? Yet here he was.

For good or ill, the matter of this wielded no power over him anymore, at least none that he could see. He rose to his elbows, his knees, and then his feet, not tiredly but with a confused weariness. Above him, what should have blocked out the overseeing sun was the absence of a highway overpass, its rubble scattered in a harsh knot of concrete, metal, and mangled vehicles. His own, no more than twenty two feet away sat nearly sideways and angled up as if ready to take to the air. Of course it would go nowhere now and never would again until this wreckage was cleared away. It, like its crushed peers, was beyond repair.

He staggered up to it, turning his disjointed walk into a normal stride as soon as he realized his odd, misrepresentative steps were not true to his apparent good health, and climbed carefully the three boulder-sized slab sections to the edge of his broken, Deep Forest Green Jeep Wrangler. No more 'Jeep Waves' for Johnny, he thought dryly. The door hung open, stuck where the twisted metal imprisoned it, never to function properly again. He turned his head to the spectacle below and around him, aware that there were no other bodies. Indeed it seemed as if this catastrophic bridge collapse was not new. Weeds grew up through many of the crevices, scorch marks— he regarded them for the first time with a sudden inescapable 'ah-hah' notion—were wind-abraded. He let his eyes drift off to one of the concrete supports, the one to his right. It was wide and oblong, sectioned off in thick segmented layers. Spanning the full breadth of it's inner face, the one directly facing Jorj, was a rectangular, maze-like piece of graffiti accomplished in an unassuming flat white spray paint. Underneath it were two words. 'Dead Again.'

Unhurriedly, he reached into the jeep and took out a dusty black gym bag, still hanging from the emergency break where somehow the carrying strap miraculously caught. After a brief visual survey, he descended to the road, littered and deteriorated as it was, and rifled through the contents of his possession. His hands, strangely cleaner than he last remembered them being, extracted a pair of jeans, a wrinkled khaki shirt, and a hat, all of which he immediately put on. After searching in vain for socks, finding a broken watch, and an address book, he closed up the bag and shouldered it, but not before casting the watch aside. Like the jeep, its days of service were over.

Questions abounded, and he should have wondered greatly at his own acceptance of facts as he presently saw them, but all such things were put away when he heard voices. An instinct in him, perhaps the one in all of us that prompts us to seek others of our kind when we are compromised, started him walking in their direction. They would know what happened and why he found himself abandoned, healthy, and alone. Of course they would.

But then the emptiness clutched him again, and an even sharper instinct made him duck down in a clump of weeds behind the crumpled remains of a red Buick. Shatterproof glass fragments crunched under his feet, cutting the undersides minutely. He shifted to a bare patch of earth and waited. The voices drew near.

"Yeah Bob," one said. There was an oddly familiar sound. Yes, a bolt was thrown back. Something else cocked. "We started getting a few here the other day. Pretty certain we got 'em all. Can't be sure though. Never knew one to straggle far behind the others in such a wreck."

The crackle of static. Semi-intelligible words followed. Something about 'Got what we need for now.'

"I'll look around a bit more with Tom here. He might see something I don't. Jeezuss it's cold." He paused and then continued. "Just as soon get inside. I don't care what you say Rick. You got June. I got January...LATE January. Three years of that IS hell! Out."

Two men came into view. One white, one black. Jorj remained still. Weeds were mostly what blocked him from sight. The white guy wore Bermuda shorts, red ones. An off-white muscle shirt hung loosely over his thin frame, giving the impression of a reasonably fit man with expectations far exceeding reality. The hunting rifle he carried was only marginally ready for action. Apparently he didn't honestly anticipate problems. Next to him was his opposite in many ways. The black skin of the second man's face was mostly obscured by sunglasses, the kind popular with skiers, and a pitch-black pull-over hood. A thick thermal jacket, gloves and green camouflage pants served most of the rest, with sturdy hiking boots on his feet to complete the need. Thick puffs of frosty air plumed sideways when he exhaled. He truly appeared as cold as he felt. "This is bullshit," he muttered.

"You could be Freddy," Bermuda shorts replied. He got it in a downpour. Never sees the sun. A miserable turd."

"Fuck you July!" Frosty walked off. He didn't look like he was coming back.

In fact neither man returned once they departed. Jorj took note that men with guns dressed in such a bizarre fashion were unlikely to be very amiable towards strangers. Getting shot didn't suit him, though he wondered where it would put things. He wondered on a lot of things just now.

He decided to trail Bermuda Shorts and Frosty. They seemed about as likely to inadvertently surrender information as anything this moment, being the only other humans he'd seen so far. In his bare feet he could move pretty silently, though it hurt to step on sharp rocks and there were several times he was forced to duck behind a bush or stranded vehicle, there being plenty of those anywhere there was a road.

The odd men were too far away to hear much of their conversation. It didn't appear Frosty liked Bermuda shorts very much. Probably not at all. Mostly B.M. just talked.

When they came to a bridge, the two men stopped and so did Jorj. The uncertainty was nearly overwhelming. If two guys with guns, dressed for every meteorological eventuality, were afraid, well Jorj guessed he would trust them. So far nothing was what it was supposed to be. Waking up naked in a pile of catastrophic rubble only served to amplify this fact.

There seemed to be a debate at work. Should they cross the bridge? Or should they just skirt the hundred miles or so around it to some marshy, trickling stream that helped to feed this swelled section of the Metoak river? Jorj filled in the voiceovers. He actually had no idea what was being said except that neither man ahead really wanted to cross the river.

But they did. Jorj bid them ado. He didn't have to cross the bridge. Contented for the moment to watch whatever happened to them commence, he sat down on a concrete barricade next to a construction site. Once a bank was getting refurbished, parking lot and all. The project never got off the ground for some reason and things just lay where they left off in limbo.

Weird.

About halfway across the bridge two clear shots rang out. They did not originate from either weapon belonging to the weather twins, and both men ahead of him fell over looking pretty dead.

In the backdrop of this, on the other side of the river, hills rose up far more persistently than behind. Lights popped on some of the larger ones in long strings, betraying ski resorts. The evening light was dimming everything else into an orange-purple sunset. Odd, Jorj noted. Hardly the time of year for Valhalla Slopes or Boarding Heaven to be open. His eyes scanned around for awhile, curious as to who guarded the bridge, and then, not seeing a damned soul, gave up the search. Time to go elsewhere.

Nothing was open and that was not surprising. There was no one manning the local Burger Flip, not a soul at the Jolly Bagger. He felt sort of hungry too, and sort of not. Okay, he decided, wondering why the thought didn't occur before. Home.

No one was home at his second floor 2100 North State Street Apartment. A good thing considering he lived by himself. Of course there wasn't any furniture either, and that was bad. No CDs, no DVDs, no refrigerator or television. No neighbors either, but upon closer inspection of three adjoining habitations, their things were unmolested. He could fix that.

He flicked on the lights at Sol Blum's place next door, made a brief search, and determined no one had been there for quite some time. Dust lay moderately thick on things, but not so much that it was disgusting, just a nuisance. He'd explain to Sol, if he ever saw him again, that the circumstances warranted invading the old gentleman's apartment.

The first thing he checked, once the rooms were identified as vacant, was the refrigerator. It still hummed along nicely as it probably had the last time Sol used it. He found some steaks marked December 2nd and fried them up until all the pink within them was gone. A further search brought forth a bottle of Castle Red and together they sated his appetite, sort of.

When he awoke many hours later on Sol's couch he felt pretty much the same, but it went below his radar. Eggs and juice turned up for breakfast. The bread was moldy so toast was out. Jorj found some undersized dress shoes, crammed his feet into them, and went out to see what was what.

It didn't take him long to find entertainment, if you could call it that.

Screeching its tires, a silver SUV crashed diagonally into the driver's side door of a vintage, faded-red Ford pickup. The latter rebounded, spinning 180 degrees before skidding to a stop. Jorj didn't physically see it but he heard the tragedy very clearly, even knew the color of the vehicles. He'd figure that one out later.

Odd . . . he hadn't noticed it before, *but* there was one of the wrecks, like it had been there for three years. The driver's side door of the pickup creaked open on rusty hinges. Someone, a man, uttered an epithet from inside and promptly fell out, naked and unaware that he wasn't alone. He coughed twice, sat back on his bare ass and looked around him, a terrible expression of annoyance on his face.

Jorj studied him a moment. The lad was about his own age. His reddish hair as unkempt as his defunct pickup. There wasn't much meat on the man, the angles of every joint sharp enough to kill anyone unlucky enough to bump into him by accident. Jorj would have bet his last meal that this guy was a smoker. At any rate, he didn't look like much of a threat, not that Jorj was concerned. He could handle himself alright. As a matter of fact, the poor sap likely could use a hand. He slid unnoticed back inside, and found a pair of navy blue dress pants, an ugly but serviceable powder blue sweatshirt that belonged to Mrs. Logan upstairs—she was eighty last time Jorj checked—and a pair of work boots from her son's apartment next door to that. A pair of socks, some underwear from the same dresser drawer, and he was set. In a flash he was back outside. Red hadn't moved.

The newcomer noticed Jorj easily enough as he stepped lightly down the apartment building's front steps. He thought about getting up and then changed his mind. The man had clothes and they might be for him. "Who the fuck are you?" he asked as Jorj approached. He had to at least set an impression just in case.

"Your tailor," Jorj answered easily. "Show some respect."

"I'm naked. How much respect you think I got on me right now?" The answer came in the clothes that fell at his feet as he was getting up. He considered them a moment and then grabbed the pants, watching Jorj even though there was an easy seven feet between them. "You pick these yourself?"

"Yeah. It was the best I could do." Jorj smiled. Even with his life turned upside down, he loved a good joke.

"Liar…but thanks, I guess. They'll do for now. You didn't tell me your name."

"That's right," Jorj nodded. "Guys with clothes on get to introduce themselves last."

Red paused, frowned, and then zipped up his fly. "What the hell. Doesn't really matter anyhow." He stuck out his hand. "Name's Dennis. Dennis Brinks. You can call me either or in combination, I don't care. Just leave 'Asshole' for when I deserve it. What's yours?"

Reluctantly the hand was taken. One never knew where such things found themselves before the shake…or after. "Jorj

Watchman. I'm pretty sure the only part that matters here is Jorj. You can work with that." He pried his hand away.

"George, huh?"

"Jorj. J-O-R-J. Just like it sounds."

Dennis put the rest of the clothes on, grimacing at the granny shirt. '#1 Grandma' was plastered on the front in tacky pink lettering. "The chest is a little stretched and it smells like vaporrub. You know how to pick 'em George."

"Jorj."

"Ah, yeah. Well thanks. Maybe I'll have a look-see for something better now. No offense."

"None taken."

Dennis started off towards another building. "Hope there's something left," he remarked. "At least something in my size." He turned abruptly, facing Jorj who fell in beside him. "Who do you work for?" His face looked suddenly very angry, even suspicious.

"Me." It was a simple enough answer, and an honest one.

"No, no, no," Dennis held up his hands, two primary fingers and thumb prominent on each one. A grin that was neither friendly nor amused split his unshaven face in two. "Everybody works for someone." He looked up and left as if an answer were waiting to be plucked out of the sky, and then darted his eyes back at Jorj. "Theo? No, I've never seen you in his crowd. Benedict. You look like someone he'd scoop up."

"No Theo. No Benedict. Just me."

"Look, whatever you guys want, I don't have it."

"What?" Jorj now began to reconsider this new acquaintanceship. "I know you don't have 'it.' Not unless it's in that truck back there, and I doubt 'it' is." *Should he tell this guy he didn't even know what he was ranting about? Eh, let him rant a little more.*

"Funny. Very funny." Dennis started walking again. "You couldn't even bring a few more guys to at least make it look like I'm a challenge? How'd you find my place anyhow?"

"Your place." It should have been a question, and Jorj knew it, but it came out as a tired statement.

"Yeah, man. My Kamaloka Crossroads, portal, keyhole, pinhole, Kharmic funnel…you know what the fuck I'm talking about."

Okay, enough of the charade. "Honestly, I don't."

Dennis stared at him like he had three heads. "What are you, a newbie or something?" A light bulb blinked on above his head, flickered for a few seconds, and then stayed lit. "You just got bagged, didn't you? I mean for real. This is your first time?"

For once Jorj didn't know what to say. The Red-headed bastard had him at a loss.

"You're a fucking virgin!" It couldn't have sounded any more demeaning. "A goddam cherrypie!"

Jorj did the only thing he could have under the circumstances. He hit Dennis Brinks squarely in the jaw with a solid right. Dennis hit the pavement on the opposite side of his face with a cataclysmic smack. It was about as lucky a hit as anyone could hope for, except that it was a little too lucky. Dennis lay there very still.

"Dennis," Jorj coaxed. "C'mon, I didn't hit you that hard." He knew it was a lie…well an exaggeration anyway.

Nothing from Dennis. Not a peep. Jorj closed his eyes and growled out a sigh. Nice. Not a good start, he thought miserably. He was about to open his eyes and see if the little smart-mouth still breathed when a distant creaking door interrupted Jorj's stunned attention. He turned.

Quite a ways back, the rusty red Ford vomited a second time. Dennis Brinks tumbled out in a tangled pink heap, angry but ready to deal. "What the fuck did ya do that for?!" he complained forcefully as his new acquaintance walked back to meet him.

Jorj, feeling a little better now, shrugged involuntarily. He really didn't have a good answer.

Dennis did. "Oh, you ab-so-lutely work for Benedict!" He shook off the frizziness he felt whenever he came through. "That's right up his alley!"

"Look," Jorj tried to explain, totally flabbergasted as to why the actual irrationality of the moment didn't phase him one bit. "You've got this all wrong."

"Oh do I?" Dennis exclaimed. He was getting his second wind back. "You think I'm a Cambrian man or something?"

"Cambrian Man?"

"NEVERMIND!" Dennis' frustration was showing through the thin veneer that was his patience. "I'd like to get through the day without another horse's ass telling me something I know is BULLSHIT!"

They stood staring at each other for another thirty seconds before Jorj spoke. "I need a cup of coffee."

"How about a beer?" Dennis asked carefully, his words slowly pronounced.

"Lead the way." Jorj paused and then added. "Clothes. I should find you some clothes." He did an about face, unsurprised that Dennis was not lying on the asphalt where he had knocked him cleanly to. Nothing surprised him much today.

Next door to Finnan's Threads, a small shop Dennis considered his own private clothing stash, was the Riverside mini-mart, most notable for the fact that it wasn't on the riverside but in fact three blocks away from it. Jorj ducked in and grabbed a dusty, un-refrigerated bottle of 7-UP with the date stamp of January 15. No telling whether it was January past or future. The year was worn off. He unscrewed the top and took a long pull before catching his breath. By the sun it was only midday, but the chill was lessened for it. He was unclear whether he was just not as thirsty as he thought, or if the soda lacked something. Eh, he thought, he wasn't a big fan of soda anyway. Too much sugar. He took another swig and stepped outside the mini-mart's front door.

Across the street, North State Street to be exact, was Mike's mechanic Shop. Always a 'Mike' wherever there was a car being worked on, Jorj noted, wondering why that was. It was a yellow building, made of brick, with the paint peeling away from the brick in hand-sized patches. There were two garage bays on the left end, one with a cracked window pane, and a front door next to a dirty nine-pane window on the right. From the bay with the cracked glass came a distinct crash followed by the ring of a tool sliding across a concrete floor. Faintly visible through the dirty film on the glass of the left bay was the blur of a red sports car, a BMW possibly.

"Ready?" It was Dennis, now the proud owner of a pair of jeans slightly too big, a belt to hold them up, a blue t-shirt, socks and white, geeky-looking canvas sneakers.

"Sure," Jorj answered, playing eye tag with the garage bay door and its red sports car. "We've got company." He nodded to the shop and raised the bottle to his lips for one last swig before chucking the bottle in an over-filled recycling bin.

"Forget it," Dennis said quickly. "I want to introduce you to a friend of mine." He whipped out a 45 and pointed it right at Jorj's face. "Jorj, meet Clint."

The target of Dennis' affections froze in mid step. "I thought we were going for a beer," he remarked uneasily.

"Depends on how much you hold a grudge."

"I'm pretty forgiving." Jorj answered, trying to smile.

"We'll see." Dennis' hand tensed slightly. "Meet me back at my truck and I'll buy...for real, okay?"

"Huh?" Jorj frowned, puzzled. Logic told him he should feel relieved. He didn't feel relieved. "Where are you going?"

"I'm not. You are."

The crack of a fired 45 caliber slug split the air. As it slammed home into Jorj's skull, spoiling everything between his eyes and messing up his day worse than before, thunder roared in, gravity sucked him down, and suddenly he was flying. He landed with a thud. Blackness, and a horrible headache teamed up against him and then there was nothing but the feel of cold asphalt against his skin. He opened his eyes and spied his Deep Forest Green Jeep Wrangler perched in its odd parking spot, nose pointed at an angle towards the sky. "Shit."

His clothes were gone, leaving him shivering in the suit he was born in. Was he mad?" he wondered. If so, he was disappointed. He always thought going mad meant that everything was hunky-dory because you wouldn't even realize or care when things weren't right. Of course he cared very much at the moment that he had no clothes, and that his Jeep was not drivable. He still owed over a year on the damned thing.

And then there was the little problem of being shot. Yes, his memory couldn't be faulted. He thumbed the space between his eyes, feeling no scar, no pain. Well, he thought angrily, he *did* get shot, at point blank range too. Okay. One thing at a time.

He rose to his feet and clambered up to the Jeep. The driver's side door, bent unnaturally on its hinges, neither opened nor closed. He reached in and flailed his hand around. No bag. That meant a lot of bad things...well, just one at the moment. He climbed down and surveyed his surroundings. Lots of junk cars, the shattered overpass, and that stupid graffiti on the bridge support that read 'Dead Again.' What the hell did that mean?

At some point he started walking, not realizing that he had done so until well past the opening steps. He knew where his feet were taking him. Bullet or no bullet, there was going to be a reckoning. No one shot him and got away with it. As soon as these thoughts passed between his ears he rolled his eyes, realizing how dumb it sounded. Was he that much of a lunatic to be thinking revenge when the existing picture was so much bigger? He shrugged impulsively. If he was a lunatic, he was certainly in the right place for it.

The red Ford was right where he last saw it. The door hung open just enough for someone to get in if they wanted to. He didn't. He stopped at the edge of things, not ready to commit to coming out into the open. Dennis likely still had that gun. Instead, he snuck over to a side street and came up on the other end of North State Street where he thought he saw a few shops just before he got capped.

The front door of Finnan's Threads had a bell attached to the top to let the former owners know when a customer walked in. There was no one to greet him when the bell jingled so he took it as a good sign. He needed clothes in a hurry and had no means or intent of paying. The pickings were slim. It looked like someone had wiped out everything even close to his size, at least on the racks. He ran down the aisles to the back. A door marked 'employees only' filled a narrow wall space, sandwiched between a rack with a few women's sweaters on hangers. He tried the knob. It was locked. Without knowing why, he looked left and right before kicking the door in. It gave at the expense of his foot's well-being. The pain, he decided, would pass. He'd check back later to see if it agreed. In the meantime, he entered past the ruptured portal and flicked the light switch. Nothing happened. Fortunately there was some light entering through the open doorway and he could see inside a short distance. There, on a table surrounded by pulled-back chairs, were three boxes. He rushed up to them and opened the first. "Jeans, all the same size: 36-30. Unimpressed, he opened the remaining two. White T-shirts and mixed socks, respectively. "God this sucks, he mumbled," but it beats being naked." He dressed himself quickly, noticing a locker off in one corner next to a vacuum cleaner and a small cart filled with cleaning supplies. The former he popped open, after finding it lacking a padlock, and found cases of toilet paper stacked all the way to the top. Any space that could take it found the odd roll stuffed in to fill it. Gold, he realized…no, better than gold. He shut the locker and exited the room, regretting the need to break the door down. This *was* a safe place, well, not an easy place for someone to get nosy. Of course it didn't stop a naked man, but that man was desperate. Desperation wields its own power.

Behind the check-out counter, in a corrugated cardboard box, he found a roll of duct tape, not the kind of thing you'd expect in a clothing store but it wasn't alone in being out of place. In the same box was a hammer, a sawed-off shotgun, a box of shells, a map of New York State, matches, a lighter, three packs of cigarettes, and a half bottle of Jim Beam. All he wanted for the moment was the tape which he took over to the front door. Carefully, so as not to make it ring, he taped the bell and it's clapper together with a single, torn-off piece. Sure, he thought idly, he could have just ripped it down, but he might want it there another time, like if he had to return. The previous owners weren't the only ones who might want to know when someone was entering their store.

Shoes would have been nice, but this was not a shoe store. What footwear existed was for women. Nothing fit him and even if it did, he wouldn't wear it. He wasn't that desperate anymore. He lifted his left foot, tugged off the sock, and repeated the exercise with the right foot. Might as well save them the wear, he realized. When he got some shoes they could go back on. He put them in his back pocket and left the store by way of the front door. The bell obeyed him nicely and kept its mouth shut.

There, in the middle of North State Street, was Dennis, still palming the 45. Looking gravely disappointed, he waved it idly at Jorj. "Did you break my door down?" He didn't wait for an answer. Instead he pointed the 45 right at Jorj, but not in a threatening manner. "My shirts! My jeans!" He paused, gazing at the feet below his pilfered items. "At least you left my sock stash alone."

Jorj smiled tightly and turned, pulling the socks, still hanging out of his right back pocket, into view. "No I didn't."

Dennis put his left hand over his eyes and then wiped it away slowly, deflated. "If you had just asked…"

"You shot me," Jorj replied, the tension in his voice quite apparent. "I thought maybe you'd say no."

"I shot you for two good reasons."

Jorj blinked. He wasn't going to ask, but he guessed he was going to hear the answer anyway.

"You one-punched me," Dennis said with an I-told-you-so tone. "That wasn't nice, especially since it killed me. I lost valuable clothes that time too."

"It was an accident."

Dennis let that one pass. "I did you a favor. That was the second reason…to do you a favor."

"Favor?!" Jorj took a step forward, eyeballed the big pistol, and took the step back. "You call that a favor?"

"Sure I do," Dennis smiled, guarded friendliness creeping back. He approached until he stood on the sidewalk not five feet away from Jorj. "Now you know what to expect when you get killed. It's important, especially since there are a lot of people who might just try to make that happen."

"Like you."

Dennis huffed. "Fine." The pistol spun in his hand until he held the barrel. He extended the handle to Jorj. "Want to shoot me? A show of good faith. Just so you know you can trust me."

Jorj stared at him a moment. Reluctantly he took the 45 into his own right hand, hefting its weight, feeling its balance. Dennis looked for all the world like a picture of trust. His hand offered no resistance when relinquishing the weapon. The guy was smiling like an idiot, content that Jorj would give it back. Bygones were bygones.

Like a bolt from the sky, Jorj raised the 45 and put a fist-sized hole in Dennis' chest. The shocked expression on Dennis Brinks' face plummeted to the sidewalk, revealing an exit-wound in the man's back the size of a basketball. Calmly, even leisurely, Jorj walked the short distance over to the red Ford pick-up truck. From deep within Mike's mechanic shop, something crashed and a tool slid along the floor. He glanced at it distractedly but didn't break stride. In less than a minute Dennis groaned from inside his truck and slid through the open door out onto the road. "Are we even yet?" he asked. The fight certainly sounded like it had gone out of him.

"Yeah, I guess that about does it." For a guy without a pistol permit, he sure was getting the hang of this, Jorj mused with a little satisfaction. "After we get you some clothes, can you take me to a shoe store?"

The clothes were easy, although Dennis winced when he saw the 'Employees Only' door. He shook his head through the entire ordeal but said not a word. Jorj, perhaps because he felt sorry for popping the man off, offered the pistol back. It did belong to Dennis after all. The latter gestured to the locker. "Underneath the toilet paper. I'm sure you saw it earlier."

"I did," Jorj acknowledged and hid the weapon away.

"We'll stop at Dimby's." Dennis announced, getting his second wind back. "There's at least three pair left there that I know of."

Dimby's wasn't a shoe store. It was a dark blue colonial-style house on Peat street that once belonged to Theodore Dimby, current self-proclaimed 'Baron' of Pratt's Crossing, about 2 miles west of New Jackson City, of which he was mayor. They entered through the cellar door and went up from there to the first floor, dodging the cobwebs.

"He never comes here himself," Dennis explained, "but he doesn't like others trespassing. I've never seen that he has the place watched so I rob it from time to time. He has an old pair of Addidas in his closet. I think they'll fit you. The Nike's are mine."

They made the theft clean, snatching the shoes and nothing else. Dennis told him he considered Dimby's more or less of a last ditch storehouse. "Break glass in case of emergency," he quipped, laughing at his own joke. Of course none of the windows were actually broken.

"About that beer," Jorj reminded him as they strode down the driveway from the side door of Dimby's.

"West Side Tavern," Dennis said casually. "My friend Nick runs it." He paused and glanced sidelong at Jorj uncomfortably. "Don't shoot him, okay? He's a decent guy."

"Why the hell would I want to shoot him? And with what? I left the 45 under the Dead Sea Scrolls."

"Look," Dennis went on, "all I'm saying is that he's special. I'm pretty sure that if he gets killed, he won't come back."

"What makes you think that? His feelings hurt that easily?"

Dennis gave him a sharp disapproving look. "He says so, and I believe him."

"You also gave a loaded gun to the guy you just shot. Not that I mean anything personal by this, but that's not too smart."

"*Well Nick is.*"

"Nick."

"Nick DeMoss. He's really old. You won't see it right away, but if you spend any real time with him, you'll know." They came to a red door in a green-trimmed beige, single-story building with a wide, low-pitched roof. "Here we are. Remember what I said."

"Sure thing." Jorj marveled that Dennis went ahead of him, not even concerned that Jorj could hit him from behind, or just leave. He was either naïve or he just didn't care. Either way was bad by his book.

It was a lounge atmosphere, low lighting, browns and reds for the furniture and carpeting, tarnished brass fixtures, and an off-white tiled ceiling. Paintings hung on the walls, landscapes mostly, along with some blown-up photographs of Bavaria. Jorj knew this because one in the lobby had a caption which read: *Bavaria.* It looked pretty much like the rest of them. Even the paintings looked like Bavaria. Mountains and castles. If this place couldn't provide a beer, even now, it was sad.

A lone, dark figure with longish hair sat in a booth near the back, casually sipping a drink from a short glass. There was no ice in it, but he probably wished there was. To Jorj, he looked like the kind of man who put ice in his drinks. He was well dressed, probably in his fifties, although if someone said sixty-two, it wouldn't have surprised most people. He reminded him a lot of Willy Nelson, only without the bandanna. A cigarette burned in a green plastic ashtray at his elbow. When he saw them approach from the lobby, he plucked it up, took a long drag, and set it back it it's notch. The smoke drifted out of his nostrils in wisps before he blew the rest out of his mouth in a cone of thick gray haze. "Good afternoon, Dennis." He spoke leisurely. To Jorj's ears he sounded just a little bit tired, but amiable enough. "Who's this with you?"

Dennis smiled, genuinely pleased to see his friend. "Nick," this is George…" His smile faded while the pulleys of his mind creaked suddenly to bear on old, frayed ropes. His smile returned almost immediately. "George Watchman."

"That's Jorj, with a 'J'." The owner of that name extended his hand.

An amused expression appeared on Nick's face. He took the hand and shook it slowly, gripping it just firmly enough to command respect, and then released it. "Not too many exchange the pleasantries these days," he remarked. "That marks you as new. I'd watch that from now on."

"I will," Jorj said, nodding curtly. "Consider that my last shake. This town's a bit more lawless than I remember it."

"Eh," Nick shrugged, picking up his cigarette again. "I wouldn't say lawless. We have laws, they're just different than what you're used to." He eyed Dennis for a second. "You helping him out, are you?"

"He needs a friend." Dennis let his own eyes drift towards the bar.

"Of course, go get yourself a drink. The beers cold too if you want some." He turned again to Jorj. "Thirsty?"

Come to think of it, he wasn't. He wasn't hungry either. In fact, the one thing he was noticing with growing certainty was that he wasn't much of anything. He felt kind of empty inside. "Uh, yeah. I'll have a beer if you don't mind."

"Not at all. Dennis! Give him something in a tall bottle from the cooler, will you?"

"Sure thing," Dennis answered. A sealed door opened and closed. The sound of a compressor mingled the air in-between.

"Have you met Theodore yet?" Nick asked, saw the head shake, and then shook his own in response. "I don't suppose you've met Benedict, either, or Daniel, or even Kathleen? The woman you can trust, when you do meet her, but I dare say I'd watch most women you meet from now on. We get fewer women than men and they tend to be worse…have to be, I guess, though I think they'd be nasty anyway. It's the nature of why we're here and what we are."

"And where is that?" Jorj asked.

"That, my new friend, is the million dollar question." He crushed out the cigarette that burnt nearly to his fingers and replaced it with his short glass of amber liquid. "I have my suspicions, useless as they are."

The sealed door opened and closed again. Glass clinked in the background.

"Useless?" Jorj prompted. He found listening to the old man was enjoyable, or at least intriguing. He had a way of sucking you in."

"I'm still here." Nick raised an eyebrow and pressed his lips tightly together, pondering the whiskey swirling around inside the glass.

"Ah," Jorj, nodded.

Dennis returned with two bottles of an off-brand beer Jonah never heard of before. 'Texas Red.' The crimson bull's head against the black background of the label proclaimed a promised boldness. Jorj didn't hold his breath. He knew where promises got you.

Jorj took his beer in hand and blew the mist from the long brown bottle's mouth. The usual satisfaction he got from that small act wasn't there. He took a sip and turned his attention back to his host, a wry smile poised gently on his face. "What's everybody do around here besides die?" Why was he not bothered by that question. The preponderance of madness was not far from his thoughts.

Distaste arranged itself like an intricate web over Nick's features. His eyes, bright within their wrinkled wreathes, flicked to Dennis for an explanation.

"It's pretty much his experience today."

Further explanation demanded itself.

"Uh," Dennis took on a slight stammer, "I shot him, he shot me. Pretty much the rest of the day was spent clothes shopping."

"Hmm." Nick regarded Jorj with an air of disappointment and raised his short glass to his lips for another sip.

"What *do* people do around this town?" Jorj asked when he didn't see an answer forthcoming.

Nick sighed and slid his ass around to the end of the booth. With an effort, encumbered more from the age of his soul than of his body, he stood up and faced Jorj. "Nothing worthwhile, I assure you." He started walking off in the direction of the coatroom.

Jorj's gaze followed him until he saw what had to be the reason for his abrupt departure. About fifty feet away, next to the coat room, was a small rectangular sign extending out from above a door to the side. On it was the word 'MEN.'

"Nature calls," Nick echoed Jorj's thoughts. "Dennis, see if Franklin's in the kitchen, will you? We'll be getting the usual crowd in soon."

Jorj turned to Dennis, aware that unseen, Nick was even now pushing against a heavy wooden door into a tiled room of porcelain urinals and hand-crank towel paper dispensers. "Usual crowd?"

"It's one of the things we do here," Dennis explained with a sarcastic smile.

"I don't get the humor."

Dennis shrugged. "Gotta check on Franklin. Stick around, have a seat, and enjoy your beer. I'll be back in a sec."

While Dennis wandered off to the kitchen, behinds a set of double doors just left of the bar counter where it took a short turn towards the back wall, Jorj took a stroll down the aisle. He noted with amusement that everything was in its place, the salt and pepper shakers, the condiments, napkins, menus, plastic stands holding the nightly—and probably unchanging—drink specials. Everything just like normal, as if he could eat, pay both for meal and tip, and go off home without getting shot and waking up naked under a demolished overpass. An angered sigh hissed passed teeth he didn't realize had clenched and he whipped around sharply. There was Nick, ten feet back up the aisle, standing with his hands in his pockets, a cigarette in his mouth, observing him patiently. "How long you been there?" Jorj asked, debatably trying not to be rude.

"About five seconds," Nick replied with a dry smile that came at some effort. "Why don't you have a seat and tell me a little bit about yourself Mister…Watchman?"

"Jorj is fine."

"Okay Jorj," Nick returned to his former place in the booth and relaxed a little until he noticed his drink lying low on the level. "Dennis!"

"Geez!" cried a voice, muffled behind the double doors next to the bar. The doors swung open and hung for a second as an angular, red-haired head popped out between them. "What's up Nick? I'm watchin' a pot in here for Frank!"

"Well, what's he doing?"

"Peeing."

"Oh." Nick waved him off and roused himself. "Never mind. Go back to it. I'll serve myself."

Dennis rolled his eyes and shook his head. In the next second the doors were closed and he behind them again.

The creases between Nick's eyes deepened into a double furrow and his head took on a kind of comical tilt. "Sorry Dennis," he murmured loud enough so that Jorj would not miss it. He took his drink to the bar and raised the partition so that he could pass through, setting his drink on the counter first. "How's your cooking skills?"

"My what?" the question took Jorj by surprise. He heard it well enough and grimaced that he did what he hated other people doing. "Uh," he recovered himself, "average, I guess. Why?"

"Just wondering." Nick found a bottle on a shelf behind the bar, read the label and put it back. He picked another and unscrewed the cap. "They find a lot of the booze with the seal broken, the bottles half full or less. We try to keep like kinds mixed together. Sometimes," he sighed a little at this point, "they get lazy, or sloppy. I hope this is good stuff."

"Who's 'they?'"

Nick looked up at Jorj a moment and then filled his glass to the three-quarter mark. "The scavengers. Most work for Theodore and Benedict. Others come in from farther out. We get a few independent contractors too, but they take a risk doing business with us."

"Why's that?" Jorj wasn't certain whether he was merely trying to be conversational or was sincerely interested. Not that it mattered so far, he acknowledged.

"Theodore wants order, and good clean business," Nick answered amiably. But you haven't met him yet so you wouldn't know."

"Theodore runs New Jackson City."

"You catch on fast," Nick laughed quietly and with good-natured sarcasm. "They're regulars here. Tonight he and his 'cabinet' will be coming for their weekly meeting." He took a sip, smiled with relief, and continued. " "I'll be putting them up in the east wing for the night."

"This place is a hotel too?" Jorj was surprised and wondered how much he sounded so.

"Not originally, but we reorganized."

"Couldn't they just stay anywhere?" Jorj really didn't understand any of this. "I mean, the city's wide open. There's got to be…" He stopped short.

"Nicer places?" Nick shot him a raised eyebrow. He gave Jorj a second to hide his awkwardness and continued. "Sentimentality's a funny thing. Theodore likes this place. I guess he used to come here a lot on the other side. And, if I do say so myself, we *are* the best in town."

"But why do they stay overnight? It's not like they need a designated driver anymore, right?" The questions were half heartedly asked. Jorj turned peeling the label off his beer with his right thumbnail. He'd always done that at some point when he had one. "Why not just go home afterwards?"

Nick turned his head to the window. Red and orange were spilling onto everything. The shadows were taking on a distinct purplish-blue. He took another sip of his drink, a small one, and let out a quiet sigh. "What did you do on the other side, Jorj?"

"Drove a flatbed for a building supply outfit...Blackwell's. Heard of them?"

Nick shook his head.

"That was just money, and not much of it." He tipped his beer back and let the last of it slide down his throat, foam and all. It was kind of unsatisfying, but habits were habits. Before he set it back on the bar with its label half pulled away, he shook it slightly and raised both eyebrows at Nick. "Got another?"

The old man half smiled and took the empty from Jorj's hand. "We almost never run out." His smile turned sardonic, even a little grim. "See that stool?" he indicated a red vinyl seat with chrome legs three spaces over to the left of where Jorj stood. The rest of the stools were black leather with dark-stained wooden legs, and they had backs. The red one did not.

"How could you miss it?"

"Well"," Nick gazed at it through his long eyebrow hair and then back at Jorj. "Don't ever sit in it."

"It's special...Theodore's?"

"Not Theodore's," Nick replied dryly. "Sonja Fries choked on a peanut in that chair."

"And if she dies..."

"There she is," Nick raised an eyebrow and the right corner of his closed mouth, "naked as the day she was born."

"Doesn't sound too bad for the guy sitting there," Jorj observed, eyeing the stool.

"You haven't seen Sonja."

"Ah." Jorj watched as Nick set a new beer in front of him. "Happened much?"

"Numerous times."

They let the subject die a quiet death.

"I guess you find this all a bit puzzling." Nick glanced out the window again. There was more purple on things than red, and almost no orange. He seemed a little on edge.

Jorj sucked in his upper lip and stared off at nothing for exactly three heartbeats. "Curiosity and ambivalence are fighting over my brain right at this very moment," he replied, "assuming I still have a brain."

A rare moment of amusement, genuine humor, momentarily erased lines of tension on Nick's weathered old face. "You do, Jorj, and that's why I haven't kicked you out onto the streets yet."

"Come again?" Jorj made no attempt to hide his confusion.

"Why don't you step into the kitchen," Nick said casually. He was looking out the window again. There was a mixture of relief and tension in his posture. "Have Dennis introduce you to Frank. Help them out if they need it. Mostly," and here he turned to face Jorj with the most business-like of friendly smiles, "stay out of sight. I'll put you up for the night and feed you if you do these things for me. What do you say?"

"I, uh…" Jorj cut himself off as he saw several large cars, all of them black or gun-metal and top of the line, pull up outside. "Sure. I'm sure we'll talk more later."

"Of course." Nick closed and opened his eyes deliberately, still smiling. "Best be off."

Franklin Wells was a fat man with few words, so few in fact that Jorj was still waiting to hear one. The off-white, stretch-fit hat on his head, covered his near-baldness neatly. He wore it more to keep himself warm than to keep the stray hairs from falling into the food. His age could easily be placed at about fifty years, but even sixty was a reasonable guess, for the hair of his eyebrows and armpits was all gray, the shades just differed in places. He kept the short sleeves of his tee-shirt rolled up past the shoulders. Jorj really wished he'd roll them down, but that wasn't going to happen, not while the man worked. The dirty white apron caught all manner of the evening's labors, lending him the look of a painter, and perhaps he was, in his way. Whatever his shortcomings where hygiene was involved, he knew his business in the kitchen. Whether he was stuffing mushrooms or creating ruffled garlic potatoes with chive and rosemary, he made the work look easy, the final product beautiful. Fighting off a nagging trace of ambivalence, Jorj ran the tip of his index finger through some cake icing when Frank had his back turned. It was sweet, but lacked the intensity he felt it should have had. It wasn't the icing though, and that was the problem. It was the place, or worse, it was himself.

Dennis was quick to pawn off the dishwashing on him, but it was something he could do, and in another incarnation, one still in high school, he'd operated the steaming, double-hooded dishwasher in a restaurant named the Kuntry Kottage. It was a name that kept the locals busy when they weren't shoving down hash browns or returning under-cooked eggs. While Jorj cleaned the bigger pots by hand, Dennis went out to take drink orders. It must be a full day, Jorj noted wryly, when you could died twice and still be nice to customers, that is assuming Dennis was polite.

He could hear them all gabbing it up out there. The intercom ran one way in the kitchen. If Jorj guessed rightly, and he would put money on it, whatever was said in the common area was piped into other places too, like Nick's office, wherever that was. There was something about the old man that didn't exactly put Jorj on edge, but it made him pay attention. And he was sure Nick never missed a thing himself. Whatever the old man might say, he heard more. Jorj had to do a rewind to see if he'd said anything stupid, revealed too much. 'What could be dangerous,' he pondered? Lots of things. The trouble was in not knowing exactly what mattered here. Of course there's been no discussion into the manner of his own demise. Somehow Nick stayed off that subject, though they'd get around to it eventually. The place would remain a secret. That, he decided, was a must. They all had to know that little unwritten rule. Knowing someone's . . . Kamalaka crossroads, as Dennis called it, certainly carried power. The obvious aside, there had to be other rules. At the moment he just didn't know what they were.

Jorj took his time with the pans, for they made too much noise against the stainless steel sides of the rinsing sink. Even Frank took care not to out-do the intercom. The conversations in the other room were still in their infancies, guests were yet arriving.

Dennis popped in between orders and identified some of the voices for Jorj. There was Thomas Francesco, once on the state legislature of New York, now a lawyer of sorts for Theodore and the Cabinet of New Jackson City, population numbering at best little more than a thousand by some of the idle supply and demand being discussed. Amazingly everyone followed a loose form of law, mostly involving trade. Another prominent citizen present was Anthony Scalatto. He ran a crew that kept lights on where needed. Frieda Mueller was water commissioner. Jack Rinaldo was Chief Constable. Henry Hooter was trade commissioner. Then there was Big Al Frazier. His appointment was unofficial, but few would ever argue what his duties were: protection.

There were other cities than New Jackson City, a great many of them. In fact, no one knew the extent of things, only conjecture. On a break, while everyone stuffed their faces and downed wine and spirits, Dennis poured out a few more facts. No planes flew, ever. No, that was not entirely true. But it was rare. There was enough ordinance floating around to discourage such modes of travel. Cars were dangerous too. The routes between New Jackson City's Inner Circle District and places like Dimby's were well guarded. The cars themselves were virtually bullet-proof. RPGs were another matter, but there were the Rights of Retaliation, laws that encouraged documenting 'new immigrants' and keeping an eye on things in general. If the wrong people blew up, etc., other things would too in adjoining cities. "It happened before, some time back, and it got real bad," Dennis pointed out. "No one wants to go through *that* again."

"What's the difference?" Jorj asked, realizing the stupidity of the question almost immediately. "No one really dies."

Dennis' face looked stunned. "I thought you were smart." He threw the towel that was in his hands on the counter and went to the fridge, opened it, extracted a Dr. Pepper, and closed it again. With a quick twist he unscrewed the top and raised the bottle to his lips, draining half in a single pull. Sweat was rolling down his cheeks and forehead from all of his running around. "All we have around here is stability and profit...whatever you consider the latter to be. It equals motivation to keep your sanity. Every time someone gets popped off, he loses. Get popped off too many times, you don't return." He took another draught, gasping at the end and wiping his mouth with the back of his hand. There was a scuffing noise as the skin rubbed against his unshaven face. "That's reason number two why the population isn't out of hand."

"What's reason number one?" Jorj asked, leaning back against the counter. About three feet away Frank was smoking a cigarette. A short stack of ash tumbled from the end of it onto the floor. The old man dispersed it with the tip of his right, flat-soled work shoe.

"Lots of people don't come here in the first place," Dennis answered, pulling out his own pack of smokes. "Take that demolished overpass that appeared the other day..."

The double doors opened and Nick appeared between them, straddling the line between bar and kitchen. "Dennis! Tables need bussing!" He withdrew immediately, the doors closing behind him. His laughter permeated them as he greeted Theodore on his way to the men's room.

"Fuck!" Dennis rolled his eyes and put the cigarette he'd extracted back in with its mates. "See ya later." He snatched up his towel and went back out into the common area.

Jorj looked over at Frank. "Busy night." The other stared dumbly at him for a second and then looked away, the smoke from his near-spent cigarette adding to the haze he'd created near the ceiling. Jorj nodded blankly and went to the doors, pushed the left one open a crack, and peered through the seam.

Even here, where very little seemed to matter anymore, the status quo on aptly-named Old Earth, ruled. These bastards still chose to wear suits and ties, Jorj noted with irritation, like the old power symbols would carry their asses through the rough times. But they were patterns, and patterns also governed this Twilight Earth. He found himself wondering with some discomfort if they also had adjusted so quickly. Did the hollowness of their new existence so quickly dull the memories of home?

They all sat at a table, or covered connected tables, off to the right of the bar. A handful of armed men in charcoal gray suits blended in with the perimeter, speaking into small ear-mounted devices and occasionally peeking out windows. One came through the kitchen--the intercom dutifully went silent--looked around, and disappeared through the back door where Frank and Jorj dragged the garbage cans to the dumpster just before full sundown. Frank locked the door immediately afterward. Now they just watched and kept automatic weapons handy. It was amazing anyone could relax around them, but they did.

To the right of the empty seat on the far end was the one named Thomas. He didn't like 'Tom.' It was always Thomas. He looked stuffy at first glance, but then something about him, and Jorj couldn't place it, made him think otherwise. Perhaps he was just disciplined, something Jorj took to his own way but resisted when it was pushed upon him. Thomas looked for all the world like a quiet, no-nonsense man, but it was noted by the balding Henry Hooter that the lawyer already had several drinks in him.

They all did. That was plain. Dennis kept a running count on the kitchen chalkboard. It wasn't the kind of thing anyone but an unrepentant alcoholic could place pride in. And it bordered on alcohol poisoning by Jorj's standards, for at very least

Thomas lacked the weight to absorb so much booze. Then again, he thought quietly, the beers he drank earlier lacked much past that initial blanket of calm. Something about the whole thing deeply disturbed him.

When Theodore returned, Jorj understood why he was the leader. It wasn't that he was a big man. In fact, he wasn't. Nor was he small. It was that he exuded confidence, and that said confidence bore no hint of malignancy. There was an intelligence on his face, in the eyes mostly, that commanded a special form of charisma. He was not loud, nor boisterous, and he watched everyone, though you had to look closely to see this, and Jorj did just that. The man was a bean-counter, but not an anal-retentive one. Unlike many accountants Jorj got to know over the years, something odd for his previously nomadic lifestyle, this Theodore looked fully in possession of a creative twist. So why, Jorj wondered, didn't Nick want him to meet this man?

He felt a tug on his shirtsleeve. It was Frank. Those old eyes stared at him like a mole, but the wiry finger of his left hand pointed to a sink filled with dishes.

"Right," Jorj sighed. "I'm on it." He took one last glance through the space between the doors and saw Nick, his right hand resting on Anthony Scalotto's left shoulder. The two were exchanging easy words. Through the intercom, Jorj thought he heard the word 'Ogam.' It was meaningless to him, as was everything else in the jumble of conversations. He turned back to the dishes and Frank's smoke with dull tiredness. Through the single kitchen window, well to the right of the sinks, past the back door and on the same wall as both, he saw how utterly dark it was outside. But he saw something else too. He paused over the dishwater and then walked to the window, feeling a slight draft as he passed the back door. In the distance at the edge of a large parking lot some three hundred feet away, give or take, was a handful of people around a barrel fire, their open palms and faces to the wavering orange light. They were all dressed in black. In particular he noticed a young woman, maybe in her mid to late twenties, short, punk-style—or Goth—jet-black hair on one side of her head, long hair over her face on the other, and she wore lots of leather. As if reading his mind, she turned her face and looked directly towards his window. "Who are they?" Jorj asked.

Frank strode over and abruptly pulled the shade down. He poked a finger into Jorj's shoulder and nodded at the sink, never speaking a word. Jorj regarded him a moment, weighing his annoyance against the consequences of ignoring the old man and rolling the shade back up. Later, he decided. He was tired and really needed time to think. It was a lot to absorb, the events of this day, and it was all just starting to catch up to him. He started longing for the sweet oblivion of sleep and then realized with a shadow of horror how un-sweet the darkness would be in this Twilight Earth. Was there another version darker still, he asked himself silently? Would he see it in nightmares, or worse, in reality. His hands dipped into the dishwater, steaming from the heat, after he walked the short ways back to the sink. Frank lit another cigarette and began peeling potatoes. Maybe, Jorj suddenly considered, the answer to his prior question was precisely why Frank did not speak.

2

It was decided by the great minds of New Jackson city that there was a slight but persistent problem with their neighbors. In short, there existed a disconcerting reluctance of late to trade goods, and what did cross the accepted borders generally did so to the advantage of everyone but the people of New Jackson City. The reason for this did not escape the likes of men like Theodore, or Thomas Francesco. They knew well enough where the matter of un-cooperation resided. South of wherever, probably Pennsylvania by the most credible accounts, someone stirred the pot of trouble, sparing only they who fell into line with their goals, choking anyone else went their own way. The means employed killed no one outright, for dying was so temporary these days, save for the 'thin' ones. But madness was always around the corner, and the line that needed to be walked was narrow. That line was paved, brick by merciless brick, with the patterns and trappings of Old Earth.

If Mammon called to man on Earth that once was, then his was a confusing cacophony here on Twilight Earth, where beauty was dulled, and brilliance dimmed. For the double hunger within could not be sated anymore, nor could it be ignored. Its gnawing teeth were the distraction to clear consideration.

Even among those souls of a moderate disposition, indifference laid desperate hands upon desire in a constant death struggle that saw no foreseeable end, no light within the tunnel. One had to wonder at first that it was manageable at all, but then again, if another way existed, it was quite out of everyone's grasp, for all were caught in the same web of nerve and callous.

Before Jorj went to sleep that night, in a room he had to share with Dennis, an incessant practitioner in the art of snoring, Nick made all of this very clear. "Better to know the devil exists, and ward him off," he advised, "then to close your eyes a free man and wake up in chains of madness." Jorj was grateful for the old man's wise consideration, but it didn't help him sleep any better.

He remembered reading a book on folklore once when he was younger. It used to be believed that sorcerers existed and that they sold their souls to the devil in order to attain their powers. The sorcerers inevitably realized the wisdom of 'finding God' at the end of their lives, but by then it was too late. In the darkness, night after night until their graves took them all, gnashing and clicking teeth kept them awake in the devil's anticipation. He understood it all now, even though he was anything but a sorcerer. Dennis made sure, unwittingly, that demonic noise was amply provided.

It wasn't just him though. That was the real scary part. There were sounds, barely perceptible and murmuring, but he remembered them now. They were there the first time he woke naked under the demolished overpass of highway 8. They were there the second time too. He thought, if he chose to listen to them, he might be able to describe them, even single out their differences from each other, but he let them become background noise, for he was afraid of them. That is the other reason he could not sleep that first night, Dennis' snoring being the first. In the morning he found himself quite un-refreshed, but he could function. The night's hell departed, or at least retreated, with the rising of the sun. Not everything here was without hope, he decided, so long as the sun rose.

He took his breakfast out in the common area. Everyone else was gone from the night before but the employees of the Westside Tavern. Nick fried the eggs himself for Jorj, Dennis, and Frank, accepting only the latter's involvement in the rest of their fare. It was, Dennis explained, his tradition.

Whatever anyone worked out the night before, whether personal or bureaucratic business, largely was forgotten. Nick liked to know what to expect, and wanted witnesses among those loyal to him of anything relevant, but rarely was there any threat or otherwise direct connection to himself that needed to be addressed.

The proprietor of the establishment sat down last, once everyone else was served, at the head of the table in the seat occupied the night before by Theodore. Dennis sat to his right, Frank to his left. Jorj sat on Dennis' right. "Sleep well last night, Jorj?" He was smiling, but it was pretty clear he knew the answer, and that his was a joke, a rather grim, unfunny one.

"Probably as well as you," Jorj replied. He wondered if that were true.

"I sleep alright," said Nick. "Just like the dead." Nobody laughed. He bowed his head. So did Dennis and Frank. Jorj, startled at this sudden, unexpected piety, reluctantly bowed his, but he watched everyone carefully as he did so.

"God is an unbroken circle," Nick proclaimed in a clear, respectful voice.

"God is an unbroken circle," Dennis repeated, uncharacteristically reverent.

Frank made the cross over his chest with his right hand.

Amen brothers," Jorj added. Had he not died twice the day before, and had his sleep been better, perhaps his veiled disdain would not have flowed so close to the surface.

Dennis grimaced and picked up his fork. "Don't fuck with our prayer, man."

"A hand touched Dennis' shoulder. It belonged to Nick. "Jorj, we may not look all that spiritual most of the time, but believe me, we still hang on to the safety line."

"No offense," Jorj replied out the side of his mouth, " but you think God hears your prayers here in hell?"

Frank slammed his cup down, spilling coffee onto the white table cloth.

"This ain't hell!" Dennis growled. "What's with you anyhow? Just eat your goddam breakfast."

"Where are we then?" Jorj wouldn't let it go. "Purgatory?"

Nick tossed Frank a napkin to soak up the coffee and stifled Dennis' next retort. "He has a right to want to know, same as we do." He faced Jorj sympathetically. "The trouble is, my young friend, that we don't have an answer, at least not a satisfying one."

"Why did you hide me from Theodore last night?" Jorj decided it was best to change the subject for now. He'd come back to it later.

Nick, having just torn off a piece of toast with his teeth, chewed slowly and swallowed. Before answering he took a sip of coffee and carefully wiped his mouth with his napkin. "Theodore is a man with many ideas, mostly good ones. His problem is that he's quite limited to one plane of thought. Also, and this sort of ties in here, he's not very religious . . . "

"Neither am I." Jorj cut in.

"Yes," Nick nodded mechanically, "but we are talking about Theodore. If you please . . . "

"Go on."

"He sees this all as merely another place. That's it. He gives no thought to leaving it, only to surviving, and holding power. There are other cities, Jorj, besides our own lovely one. Some of *their* leaders have less benign objectives than Theodore. In short, he has his sights on building an army for defense, perhaps even pre-emption. It's only a matter of time before things come to a head one way or another and he's beginning to show signs of desperation. He'd snatch you up in a second, use you to kill and control."

"And you care that much." Jorj knew there had to be something more.

"What I care about is that there are other deaths far darker than what you could ever experience here. Of course Theodore has no chance of success with the plan he has in mind, for the lack of permanency in death will lead us into chaos. We must leave this place, ascend. First we must discover how." He took another bite of toast and continued talking between chews. "I need people on my side Jorj. There is another way. It just needs to be found."

"Sounds like you're offering me a job." Jorj smiled skeptically. "What's the pay?"

"You don't get it, do you?" Dennis scoffed. "The man is offering you something better than a job." Nick kept eating but nodded in agreement.

"What's so special about me?"

"Very simply put," Nick answered with a smile. "You're off the radar. They don't have your name. That is useful to me."

"How so?"

"God," Dennis shook his head, "think."

"Just a question, Son of a Ford." Jorj pushed his plate away. He wasn't very hungry, in fact not at all.

"Son of a ... " Confusion gripped Dennis momentarily and then broke like a sheet of ice. "Ha. Ha. You better not ever tell anybody you saw that! You're the only one who knows besides Nick and Frank, and Frank ain't talkin'."

"Theodore keeps track of everyone he's catalogued," Nick explained casually, his eyes telling Dennis to shut his mouth. "He won't notice when you come and go, as long as you don't attract attention."

"And you want to send me ... "

Here Nick leaned back in his chair, satisfied. He was winning this one, as he knew he would. "Not just yet, Jorj. You can pair up with Dennis for awhile. Let him show you around."

"What if we're stopped?"

"Then we're stupid," Dennis cut in. "The idea is *not* to get caught nosing around."

"You died yesterday," Jorj pointed out. "How'd *that* happen? Part of some master plan?"

Dennis' face contorted into a goblin grin. "Accidents happen."

Jorj put his face in his hands and shook it gently in disbelief. "You must have some idea . . . a lead to follow, or you wouldn't be going to all this trouble."

"What trouble?" Nick shrugged. "You work for me, as long as you like, and I give you a place to stay among people you can trust. It is a fair bargain."

"Okay." Jorj pulled his hands away from his face. "Tell me about the barrel fires, and the people around them, and why everyone else I've met or seen so far doesn't go out at night?"

"Tonight," Nick replied, wiping his mouth one last time and then throwing the napkin on his empty plate. "Over dinner." He looked out the window nearest to their table. What's it look like out there, Jorj?"

Jorj turned, puzzled, and followed the old man's gaze. "Sunny, a typical day in . . . " He frowned and looked back at Nick. "Why do you ask?"

"No need to be alarmed. As I said, you can trust everyone here at this table." He continued to gaze outside. "Sunny, did you say?"

"Yeah," Jorj affirmed. "Sunny."

"Good!" Nick's smile was genuine. "Give thanks for that! Best be off, eh Dennis?"

"Should we clean up first?" Dennis began to take up the plates.

"I'll get them," Nick stood up, taking the plates from Dennis' hands. "Show him around the better parts of town, especially the campus." His smile broadened. "Introduce him to Father Tierney. He'll keep our secret."

"Aye," Dennis nodded. "We'll stop there after a few other places."

"Avoid the bridge." Nick's tone was firm.

"Of course," Dennis rolled his eyes. "Like I'm an idiot?" He took a last gulp of orange juice and rose to his feet. "C'mon George. Places to go and people to see."

"That's Jorj."

"Right."

They walked out the front door of the Westside Tavern and paused on the sidewalk. Dennis let out a terrible belch and smiled proudly. "You think you know this city, huh?"

"I did once."

Dennis nodded slightly, squinting in the morning's early light. "Forget what you knew. It's all changed, baby."

Their way took them up Myrtle street once again, retracing their steps of the day before. The passed by Mike's mechanic shop. Again there was a crash and the sliding of a tool on the garage floor. Jorj stared at the closed bay doors suspiciously as they passed by on the opposite side of the road.

"Forget it," Dennis said impatiently, reading his mind. "We've got a few appointments to keep."

Jorj gave the shop a last look over his shoulder as they neared the truck of Dennis past and inevitable rebirth. He considered asking Dennis about it and then changed his mind. The dork wouldn't say anymore than he did yesterday, which was nothing. Instead he considered the rusty red pickup truck, door half open, and then a revelation struck him, though there was no obvious connection. "No birds," he remarked.

"Huh?"

"No birds." Jorj pointed all around him. "No crows, no pigeons, no gulls. What's with that?"

"No souls," Dennis smiled sarcastically, turning around and walking backwards for a few steps so he could face Jorj. He nearly tripped on a crack in the sidewalk and wisely returned to the style of travel favored by millions.

"Or maybe they all go to heaven." There was no visible trace of jest in Jorj's voice. "Generally speaking, animals are better than people."

Dennis sighed. For once he didn't know what to say.

When they passed a few more blocks they entered what used to be commonly called the 'university area.' It meant more old houses, fewer businesses, and unique places , most of which Jorj wouldn't see that day. They crossed over Stockholm and under an arch made of red stone, each piece rough-cut but precisely seamed with it's neighbor. Inscribed in big Romanesque letters was the word Mosswood. Beyond was a huge, wooded cemetery, it's tombstones and mausoleums riding hills and valleys in a sea of green. Almost immediately Jorj sensed something unique about the place, though just how unique he had yet to fully appreciate. But there was plenty to see on the surface. According to Dennis, no more than three roads led in and out. There were paths in addition to the road, too narrow and overgrown to allow for vehicles, and it was one of these that he intended to take once they were further in. "A body could get lost in this place," Dennis remarked as they passed one of the hundreds of very old, and very large mausoleums. "You wouldn't catch me hangin' around here after dark."

"You go out at night?" Jorj inquired, not really believing that the other man did.

"No," Dennis immediately responded. "I don't."

The dirt road turned left at a cannon and the statue of an elk. "You'd think only rich people get buried here," Dennis said as he pointed to another statue, a towering angel, hands splayed outward as if in appeal. Time had turned it's former bleached marble surface into something macabre, so that the angel neither instilled hope nor trust in the object of its adjuration. "That was the case one time, but in other parts of the cemetery there's some pretty cheap-ass markers. See that?" He pointed to a silouetted hill in the far distance that poked out from the trees. There was a small stone cross at the top.

"I see it."

"This place has a friggin' pyramid. There's a big stone chapel at the far end too. Once," and here his voice became noticeably lower, "Theodore's boys cataloged the city in photographs. They gave up on that place. It cracked every lens that accompanied a snapped shutter. That's the word I got."

If not for the events of the day before, Jorj might have thought Dennis just a superstitious fool. He didn't think so now, at least not the first part. The jury was still deliberating the second half. "We going to go see the pyramid?" he asked, mildly hopeful.

"Maybe later," Dennis answered. "Business first."

They skirted a low hill, it's peak flat and ringed with markers as if it were a miniature Stonehenge without the crosspieces at the tops of the stones. Halfway around they broke free of it and cut over to another dirt road, and then to a foot path that ran through some trees. Through the leaves ahead, Jorj thought he saw the glint of chrome and a headlight. "Parking lot?" he asked.

"Forestry school, where the 'stumpies used to take their classes." Dennis looked above them and squinted. "How's the weather?"

"Why does everyone keep asking me that?"

"Is it sunny?"

"Yes," Jorj answered impatiently. "What's the deal?" His thoughts resurrected Frosty and Bermuda Shorts. A light bulb blinked on somewhere nearby. "You see something different."

"No, actually," Dennis remarked almost happily. "It's sunny alright." He turned, looked back behind him one last time and stepped up to the end of the path. Casually he peeked through the leaves and then, satisfied, pushed through. "I hate hoofin' around with some guys," he added on the other side. "There's this one guy who never sees the sun. On a day like today he'd be soaked clean through. You can't hand him anything made of paper."

"Freddy."

Dennis stopped short. "You know Freddy?" He asked suspiciously.

"Nope," Jorj shook his head. "Heard two dudes talking about him yesterday. They didn't know I was nearby."

"What did they look like?"

Jorj leaned back on one foot and hung his thumbs off of his jeans' front pockets. "One had a parka on, a big black guy. The other was a skinny little white guy in red shorts. Ring any bells?"

"Oh yeah," Dennis nodded. "They work for Theodore. Headhunters. Whenever something new shows up, like the collapsed overpass . . . " A strange light entered his eyes and he smiled, "That's it, isn't it?"

"Wazzat?" Jorj kept an even keel, but he didn't like where this was going.

"That's how you died, when the overpass collapsed."

Jorj sucked his front teeth a moment while staring at Dennis. "Whatever you say. So Frosty and his buddy were looking for victims."

"Frosty . . . " Dennis grinned. "I like that. He wouldn't, but I do." He studied Jorj's expression and the grin relaxed. "Fear not, man. I'm not one of the ones you have to watch out for. Stay away from . . . Frosty," Here the grin returned, "and his buddy. Bad mojo, both of them, especially the skinny one. Nick thinks he works for Benedict, you know, duel loyalties. Don't trust him ever." He started walking again, keeping to building edges. His vigilance notched up but his mouth seemed far from distracted. "Frosty would be okay if he didn't die in the middle of winter. That fucker's got one nasty disposition. I can't blame him, but I stay out of his way. You should too."

"I intend to," Jorj agreed.

A road slipped up the side of a hill in between a campus lot with a guard shack and a large brick building with a curved wall running alongside the road. A ways up and to the left, opposite from where the road turned, sheltered wooden stairs ascended in stages towards more brick buildings high above. Dennis gestured towards it. "'Summit of Zeus,' 'Pantheon Hill.'" He laughed suddenly. "For such an un-ivy-league outfit, they sure had big dreams!"

"You go here?"

Dennis' laughter subsided and he grew quiet. "Yeah, I went here, for a couple of years anyway. Wasn't my gig." He hiked on up the road along the curved wall. "C'mon."

The road leveled out once it split between woods and tennis courts. There was a softball field nearby, on the corner opposite several houses by what must have once been a busy light to their right. "What a stupid place for that, huh?" Dennis pointed at the backstop. "Wonder how many windshields got smacked in the summer time by foul balls."

Past another guard shack they crossed over a patterned brick three-way intersection to a corner next to a large, semi-modern brick building, built much more recent than the ones they'd just left. To the left there were other buildings. The shadows in between them looked chilly. "I should think to grab a jacket at some point," Jorj remarked, catching himself starting to shiver a little. Once the day warmed up it wouldn't be so bad, but he remembered the weatherman on the radio yesterday saying it was forty-three degrees, and it felt it.

"We'll see what we can do." Dennis paused and then led on along College Ave, one of the main streets bordering the Quad. Sykes Hall was on their left. They passed it and cut left again once they reached the bus stop, climbed three steps between some untended shrubs, and entered the east section of the Quad. Jorj didn't need Dennis to tell him what was what. He'd been here before too, or at least a place just like it. To the immediate right was the business school. Adjacent further in was Alliance Hall, one of the oldest, and largest examples of architecture, and once the self-styled United Nations of the university. Past that, the observatory, now dwarfed by it's neighboring structures, protected a telescope within a small, modest dome of iron and copper.

To the left, an administration building, all brick and boring, laid out it's two stories like multiple shoeboxes put end to end, then kicked in the middle and finally once on the far end for good luck. Rising above and behind it, built with no more concern for integration than the administration building, was the Geology School. But it was larger, and therefore commanded at least a modicum of respect. Rising even beyond this was the Coliseum, a sports arena that used to play host to the only team that ever did New Jackson City right: the NJU Thunderheads, champs of the 1968 Nor'eastern College Conference. Jorj smiled to himself when he saw the big block building. The only reason he knew that bit of lost trivia was because his Dad, once a point guard for the team, never let him forget it. This wasn't a sports college, he acknowledged, however much some once wanted it to be.

Straight ahead, with the crimson Frankenstein castle of the Reiss School for the Visual and Performing Arts hovering in the background, was a large domed building of brick and granite, Whoever designed it assuredly had the Roman Pantheon in mind. This was the humble sounding, but quite un-humble looking, Concord Chapel. Dennis jerked his right thumb directly at it and said, "The Padre's in there."

A wide sidewalk cut through high grass where surely on Old Earth it was a well-manicured carpet as green as an emerald. Now a low wind rustled it with an almost unbearable loneliness. Not even a rat could be heard to challenge the gentle but persistent breeze.

"You have wind?" Jorj asked Dennis.

"Yeah, I got wind."

"Seriously?" He didn't think he could ever be sure with this guy.

"Seriously." He stopped abruptly and faced Jorj. "September 28th, 2002, okay? It was a mild day, but breezy. Exceptionally warm. No rain." He smiled exaggeratedly and moved on. "Oh, and there was a small accident. One fatality."

"Traveling with you is looking better than I thought it would." Jorj noted the insulted expression on Dennis' face. "No, really," he corrected himself. "I don't think it rained the day I died, at least around here. I guess we'll see different clouds but no real surprises, eh?"

"Uh huh. I get your point."

They mounted the big marble steps leading up the front of Concord Chapel. The rare crack gave sanctuary to a lone bit of alfalfa, something that somehow mingled in the tall grass behind them. Three long strides, skipping steps in between, took Dennis to the top, a concrete platform guarded by six massively tall pillars of Greco-Roman style, spaced evenly at the very front, supporting a roof which was itself connected to the front of the main structure, above which was a silver colored dome. Below and protected by it were old double wooden doors in the shape of an arch with its stained glass windows. Jorj took the steps one at a time, vaguely admiring the ivy that crawled up the farthest pillar on the left and the corner where it met the roof. Dennis pressed his hand to a circle branded to the front of the right door, little bigger in diameter than his splayed fingers, closed his eyes for a full heartbeat, and then held the door open for Jorj, who caught the big brass handle with his own right hand. Dennis motioned him through and then followed behind, casting a quick glance about the quad before shutting the door. By contrast, all on the other side was dark as a tomb and barely warmer than the outside.

They stepped within and closed the door, letting their eyes adjust to the gloom. The lobby bore two wide staircases, one to the left and one to the right, presumably leading up to the balcony which overlooked the sanctuary from the rear. The right staircase had an electric chair lift for the elderly. Unless the electricity worked here, it was a safe bet the lift didn't work anymore. The place was as silent but for the two men's own noise; like a crypt, but free of dust. Someone, undoubtedly the vicar, was a dedicated polisher of woodwork and brass fixtures.

The darkness was oppressive, and the air felt heavy, charged with poised electricity. From everywhere at once rumbling came and went, dull at first, then demanding before it died away. Instinctively Jorj looked behind him but the windows of the door, made of stained glass, merely appeared dulled in color and rather unimpressive but what they added to the gloom. He glanced at Dennis with veiled alarm, spoke no word, laid a hand on the big brass handles, and swung the doors wide open.

All of the Quad was bathed in sunlight and caressed by the same light breeze as when he passed the hallowed portal. Yet it was not entirely as before. Superimposed against the wispy October clouds, like ragged ghosts from a dark childhood nightmare, translucent, boiling storm clouds raced across the otherwise pleasant sky. Something flickered in the east.

"Shut the door." Dennis had not yet sounded more serious. "Shut it now and don't open it again until we're ready to leave."

Jorj glared at him and then let it swing to so that it latched with its mate. Another slow roll of thunder came and went. Even the floor reverberated under their feet. "What's going on, Dennis?"

"It's usually not this bad, man." He turned and gestured Jorj to follow. Directly ahead and opposite from the front entrance were two heavy brass doors with cut glass windows in them, threatening the two men with deeper, darker shadows. Dennis made as if to lay hands on them and then withdrew. "The balcony first," he decided, his voice heavy with dread.

They ascended the stairs warily, Jorj no less than Dennis. Mid way a landing gave them a place to pause, to reconsider. They did not. Instead, the way took them to the right and higher still until they stood beneath an archway, carved of a single piece of white marble. Neither touched it nor marveled in the least. Past it another, smaller set of stairs, wooden and well-worn, continued up and to the right one more time. They followed it to a large landing, the balcony, which overlooked an ornately decorated sanctuary, dimly lit by candle light. There were perhaps three hundred candles, all of them in the choir loft opposite the balcony, burning in melancholy attendance for God knew what. Jorj looked to the far end of the balcony and noted stairs going down. Of course he knew where they went. Escape routes were always good to be aware of.

At the foot of the choir loft, before the pulpit even, was a man, strange to their eyes even in the near darkling play of light and shadow. He wore black, the black tee shirt and pants of a more modern, informally-clad priest. A white collar peeked out underneath his chin as he lifted his face towards them. As quiet as they tried to be, he had heard the creaks of the floorboards beneath their feet. A black patch covered his right eye. Jorj thought his skin looked mottled, but it could have been a trick of the bad light. In his hand was a knife, small and reflective. Next to him was the chair he was about to sit down on. Not once did he speak.

"Hey Padre!" Dennis called out. His voice, bearing a noticeable edge of uncertainty, echoed disagreeably with the silence of the sanctified chamber. A moment passed by as he eyed the knife, and the creaking pulleys of his brain turned their frayed, dried ropes. "Whatcha doin'?"

"Dennis." The voice was almost monotone, but for a trace of concern. "You should leave."

"I brought somebody to meet you, Padre . . . a friend."

"This is not the best time."

Dennis frowned, looked over at Jorj as if for support, and then back at the priest. His Adam's Apple rose and fell. "There's a better time?"

Another moment passed and then the priest made his reply. "Who have you brought with you, Dennis. Did Nick send him?"

The small foothold in their conversation bolstered Dennis' courage, or his resolve. "His name is Jorj . . . and yes, Nick sent him . . . or rather, he sent me to introduce him to you.." He turned again to Jorj, motioning him to speak.

For his part, Jorj was still very uneasy over the effect on 'his' weather. One could even say he was a bit rattled inside, though he showed no outward signs of it. "Hi." He waved half-heartedly. "Nice day, huh?" It seemed a stupid thing to say, but humor, as dry as it was sometimes, was a handy tool.

The priest smiled a little over this. It was but a thin smile, and he alone knew it was there, but it caused him to incline his head slightly in Jorj's direction as if to listen better. "You are new here."

"Everybody tells me so."

"Well, Jorj," The priest continued to not quite look his way, "I have a bit of advice for you."

Jorj waited.

"Don't ask people you meet here how they died. They tend not to like that."

"I'll bear that in mind."

For a moment the silence that followed gathered discomfort to itself. The priest seemed to waver, indecisive over some internal debate. Finally he spoke. "'What is your weather?' That, Jorj, is an acceptable question."

"Sunny, but with a chill." Jorj knew it was a rhetorical inquiry but decided to answer it anyhow. "But you knew that." God help him, but somehow he could sense that the priest did.

"Good day to you, Jorj," The priest turned away, as if he were going to ascend to the pulpit. "Dennis, please give Nick my regards." His right hand, the one which held the knife, disappeared from view in front of the priest.

Everything rumbled low.

Dennis' hands gripped the railing of the balcony and he rocked forward a few inches. "Padre!" he nearly yelled. Then he recovered himself and spoke in a more controlled tone. "Jorj . . . he tells me he wishes to know a bit about the bible." He shot his companion a desperate expression then drew an index finger across his own wrist.

The priest paused. "I am afraid I am somewhat inadequate these days as a teacher, much less a proper shepherd. I'm sure Nick can tell him what he needs to know."

"C'mon Padre!" Dennis' voice was rising in pitch again. "No one gives communion like you do! Nick can't do that!"

"Nick knows the Talmud. And surprisingly his knowledge of the New Testament surpasses my own." The priest shifted back on his left foot. "You know he is special."

"He says you are too, Francis." It was the first time Dennis referred to him by a real name. "He wishes you'd come out from this . . . "

"This awful place?" The priest turned his head minutely and listened. When no answer came but Dennis' unsteady breathing, he continued. "I have a secret for you. It is not the place that is the problem, Dennis. It is me."

Jorj moved to the stairs but Dennis caught his arm. He mouthed the word, 'wait.'

"For twenty years I served the Lord, five of them spent here, in this great hall of stone." He swayed subtly. It was clear now that his emotions were near the surface. "I have to ask myself Dennis, and perhaps your friend can answer this for me, him being so recent from a warmer world, why do I find myself abandoned?"

"Abandoned?" It was Jorj who spoke. "I don't know about you, Padre, but I never heard the old man's voice in *my* head. Not once, at least not before my . . . unexpected demise." He started towards the stairs again. Dennis did not attempt to stop him this time. "What I have experienced in the past day and a fu . . . " He checked his tongue, considered caution, and tried again. "If that thunder on *my* sunny day isn't God trying to get my attention, then I don't need a priest. I need a psychiatrist."

The priest still hid the knife. "Please go now, both of you."

"I would like to be baptized," Jorj announced. "Before I go, I would appreciate it if you would baptize me."

"It is not so simple as that," the priest replied, his voice gathering tension. "I could go through the motions, but they would not convey the meaning you seek. Do you not see that there is only darkness to be found here?"

"Please," Jorj asked again, standing at the top of the stairs. "If you do this for me I will leave you in peace." He heard Dennis gasp and looked. The man looked positively upset. Jorj looked back at the priest. "What do you say, Father?"

A silence hung in the air worse than a scream. Dennis planted his left foot on the rail, prepared to jump down. Then the priest gave his answer. Come down here before me Jorj."

Without even a backward glance at Dennis, Jorj descended each step of the staircase as casually as he ever would have back on old Earth. Dennis watched from the balcony for a second and then, once he heard the soft pad of Jorj's shoes on the marble tiles below, he took to the stairs himself, a trifle hurried.

The priest took his position by the baptismal urn and waited for Jorj to approach. The knife was still in his hand, but it was more loosely held now. He switched it to his left hand and with his right uncovered the urn to reveal a shallow bit of cool water within. "Jorj," he said quietly. "God is an unbroken circle. Come kneel before me."

Jorj walked the remaining seven steps until he was within easy arms' reach, noting now that his earlier assessment of the priest was at least partially correct. The man's face was mottled with the scars of a horrible burn on his right side. Some of the hair bordering his forehead would never grow back. The man's left side appeared less damaged, more normal. The left eye, patch-less unlike its mate, was filmed over so that the pupil and iris were obscured by a translucent white. The man was not only blind in his right eye, but his left also. Jorj put on a convincing, good-natured smile. "Thank you father." He bowed his head reverently, counted to three, and brought his right fist up hard against the padre's chin. Immediately he stepped in and disarmed the priest before the man could completely collapse. "Sorry, father. I never hit a man of the cloth before." His words fell on inattentive ears, for the padre was unconscious. Jorj threw the knife out into the pews off to his left where it clattered on the marble tiles beneath them. For that moment he faced the balcony as Dennis came running up. "Feel better?"

"Is he alright?" Dennis blurted out. "You killed my ass with one of those mitts yesterday."

"He'll be fine. What should we do with him?"

Dennis knelt beside the priest and cradled the man's head. Hastily he adjusted the patch properly over the priest's right eye. The uncovered left was fluttering open, the man's lips beginning to form sounds. "Take him back to Nick, I guess. He sure as fuck can't be trusted by himself anymore."

"What's the big deal? I mean aside of the obvious. He'd come back."

"Not the way you think," Dennis warned. "See those burn scars? Those happened last time he bought it . . . three years ago, when he tried to save a friend of mine from a house fire up on Eukert street, back when Theodore was more lenient about who lived where. My friend never showed up at his usual. The padre died too. He came back . . . to his starting place, but looking like this. He's the exception to the rule. What happens to him stays."

"Yikes."

"Yeah," Dennis agreed, gathering up the priest in his arms. "Yikes. Help me up with him, will you?"

They got him out the front door and Dennis took a moment to rest on the steps. The priest was coming around slowly. All around them, wraithlike storm clouds dimmed and unsettled the brilliance of Jorj and Dennis' fine autumn day. Thunder rolled and boomed as if on the horizon.

"I don't like this," Jorj remarked, "Not one bit."

"You're not supposed to," Dennis retorted. "That's the whole point."

"What? God's punishing us or something?"

Dennis' face was a study of reluctant, irritated acceptance. "Yep. Something like that."

"Crap." Jorj scoffed. "All of it. I didn't do anything to deserve this place. Did you?"

"I'm here, bud. We both are. Can't argue with that."

"Your capacity for eating shit amazes me, Dennis." Jorj turned his face towards the east. "You really buy into all this religious mumbo jumbo, huh?"

"Are you blind? Look at the goddam sky!" Dennis sat the priest up. "He needs some water."

Jorj turned, gave the front doors to the chapel one unhappy glare, and started towards them.

"Careful," Dennis cautioned.

"Of what?" Jorj's imagination could go a lot of places. He wanted a little more definition.

"Anything . . . you ain't in Kansas anymore."

The minute he re-entered Concord Chapel he noticed a difference. It wasn't relief exactly, but he didn't expect any of that. What he saw was the sun shining through the stained glass windows of the front doors, brighter than before. Spurred on by this he marched up to the double doors ahead, seeing for the first time through their cut-glass windows that beyond them a hallway led directly to the sanctuary. His hands found the latches and released them, swinging the doors open. The air was different, touched by just a trace of mold and dust. The basement must be nearby, he realized absently and plunged through the open portal, his feet hitting the crimson, low-pile carpet with confident strides. He was formulating an idea about this place, not just the chapel but everything else too. There was a lot of thinking to be done, he decided.

There was plenty of water in the baptismal urn. It crossed his mind to look for a faucet but if he was any judge, this water was fresh. The priest, any priest worth his salt, would change it every day, and the day was young. Besides, however tempting it might be to explore the doors in the back to either side of the choir loft, he had no intention of doing so without light, and he was not about to go with just a candle. He made a note to extinguish the three hundred or so of them before leaving.

The water was contained within the urn by a very shiny brass bowl. It looked a lot like the collection plates stacked neatly off to the side, but smaller, and without the cross-embossed red velvet inside. He lifted it carefully from the urn and set it on the chair at the base of the pulpit. Candles, he remembered.

It took him three minutes to douse them all. Only afterwards did he see the snuffer. With a mental shrug he left the choir loft and took up the baptismal bowl. The sanctuary was darker now, although the sun did a decent job of lighting his way back. By the time he opened the front doors again he had most of the water he started with, having only slopped a little at each set of doors.

"Is that what I think it is?" Dennis asked suspiciously. It was odd seeing him in the light of such a biblical sky. Lightning flashed in the eye of the sun, A thunderhead collapsed under its own weight as another one bubbled up nearby, and both in a sea of tainted cobalt and white horsetails. Angry clots of bloated rags threatened all with a rain that would never come.

"You bet." Jorj grimaced. "Want to go get water yourself?"

"Not a chance. Hey Padre, drink up." He held the bowl to the priest's face but found it pushed away.

"I don't need any water." The priest glared up at Jorj with one sightless eye that was not quite on target. "You broke my trust."

"You'll live." Jorj's patience was wearing thin again. "Think about killing yourself again and I'll have to break more than that." He relaxed when he recognized his own arrogance. "Look, you had a knife. Dennis . . . "

"I know what Dennis thought," the priest replied bitterly. "I asked you both to go. What I do has no bearing on you or anyone else."

A thought occurred to Jorj suddenly. "Why did Theodore allow you to live here?"

"I'm a priest. Where else should I be but a church?" His voice was cold.

"He scares the crap out of Theo," Dennis corrected. "No offense Padre."

"We should go," Jorj remarked, scanning the overgrown campus grounds carefully. "I thought I heard voices."

Thunder rolled, hit the horizon, and boomed back. Three seconds later the sky flickered. The sun was as pretty as ever.

"Voices, huh?" Dennis cocked his head to listen. "Which direction?"

"Not sure. Could have been a trick of the wind in the weeds."

"Alright. Best not take any chances." Dennis helped the priest to his feet. "Padre, Nick's going to want to see you."

"I assume I don't have any choice."

"None at all, Padre. But we'll fix ya a nice lunch. How 'bout that?"

Father Francis looked a beaten man. "Lead on." He took hold of Dennis' arm and waited for the other to begin walking.

There wasn't much discussion on the way back to the Westside Tavern. Moods were mixed, and whatever dark turmoil the priest carried with him could not be dispelled. Dennis found it easiest to keep the chatter down and Jorj preferred to mostly ignore him when he failed. Father Francis stayed silent once they started walking. He was in his own world, his own thoughts. What he heard, if he heard anything at all, didn't noticeably register.

Myrdle street looked unchanged with the exception of the weather which was at best schizophrenic. Almost to the heartbeat of seeing 'Mike's Garage,' something crashed within it and a tool clanged across a concrete floor.

"Take the Padre back, Dennis." Jorj switched his path in the direction of the mechanic's shop with the red sports car in one of the bays. "I'll be along in a bit."

"Hey!" Dennis protested. He felt some irritation that Jorj gave him an order but he shrugged it off. "You don't want to go in there, man!"

"I don't want to be here either," Jorj shot back, "but see where we are?" He picked up his pace as he crossed the street to the other sidewalk. It was late afternoon and the sun threw shadows before him arrogantly. A word or two poised on the tip of his tongue but he chose silence, his attention becoming consumed by what lay in front of him.

Some wisdom he still possessed, even though he'd died and murdered twice in as many days. When he considered this later, he chalked up any wisdom on his part to these very events. The very best teachers were sometimes the most brutal. Thus he approached the car shop from the front office corner and not the bays, though he stood a better chance of seeing something through the dusty glass of the latter.

The front window of the office carried an aged coating of dirt and was covered over on the inside with advertisements, thus they were useless to look through. After listening, he tried the small front door and found it to be unlocked. On a count of three, he started to open it slowly, winced when it creaked at the hinges, and flung it open in a change of tactics. No one was inside. The place was filthy, and the stained, worn-out carpet and tacky paneling only magnified the very un-feng shui attitude of the room. An old cluttered desk, grease-stained on the business side, kept a swivel chair in its pocket. Sitting on a pile of invoices was a ring with two keys. On the wall to the right before the desk was a poster for 'United Sparkplugs.' A small three-inch tear spoiled the bottom left corner. In the back of the office, to the left of the desk, was a door leading out, as the sign 'employees only' seemed to suggest, presumably to the garage. Immediately behind the desk was a bathroom, its door half open, revealing a toilet and sink within.

Jorj stepped up to the door on the left. It was a plain, cheap-ass, thin-paneled hollow door, nothing exceptional. A child could put their fist through it with no problem. He listened a moment and placed his hand on the loose door handle. Just before he turned it, something beyond crashed, quite loudly and something else, likely a tool, slid across the concrete floor with a ring. Jorj's adrenaline spiked. His heart pounded hard in his chest, pumping blood and emergency chemicals to all points of his body in readiness for danger. Still, he kept his hand poised on the handle and did not turn it. There was another sound, a gurgling, maybe even a gasp.

Now Jorj turned the handle very gently. The hinges of this door did not protest, as did the other. In one swift move, he stepped through and entered the garage area.

There were two cars in the shop. At the far end was a small fiery red sports car, probably of late-model Japanese make. Closer still, about six feet away from the office door in fact, was a dark maroon Camaro, big and old from the days when heavy cars with big engines shook the road beneath their wheels. The front passenger-side corner lilted and Jorj's eye followed it down in horror to the *reason why* almost as soon as he came in sight of it. The front, right wheel and tire were off and a hydraulic jack, not the final word in garage safety, lay on its side at an odd angle a mere foot and a half from the rim, partially underneath the car. Pinned beneath the rim, barely bestowing a gurgled hiss upon the air, his eyes glazed and half closed in slow death, was a large, hairy man, his chest horrifically caved into a purpling depression in the shape of the rim's edge. Blood seeped up both from beneath the rim and from the man's lips, some of which trickled to the grease-stained concrete. His left hand lay out towards Jorj, half-open and slightly elevated on the attached elbow from the floor, and his face, under the wheel well, was peppered with flakes of rust. A foot strayed out from beneath the passenger-side door and twitched sharply.

"Sweet Jeezuss!" The witness himself gasped and backed away reflexively. Now it was all clear to Jorj the meaning of the sounds that had so distracted him for nearly two days. He hurriedly turned back into the office and jumped as another crash resounded, followed by the familiar tool sliding across the greased concrete floor towards the far end of the garage. On the desk, through the office door, Jorj spied the set of keys he'd seen earlier. In three steps he took himself to the clutter of disorganization and laid all four fingers of his right hand upon them. His thoughts were only now catching up to his feet as he ran out into the garage and circled around to the driver's side door, hoping and praying, without taking the time to look, that the keys weren't for the red sports car.

Of course even if they were, the thing might not start, but it probably would. The naked guy was likely working on the brakes when the jack collapsed. Jorj shook his head violently as he jerked the door open and clamored into the driver's seat. What the fuck was the guy thinking? A puny little jack in a professional garage? He plunged the key into the ignition. It stuck at first. In his hurry he hadn't taken care to slide it in correctly and it was in at an angle. He tugged. For a second it stuck but then suddenly pulled free. Jorj took a breath and slid it in slowly, relieved when it it fit perfectly. With a quick twist of his hand he turned the key. The engine turned several times and then roared to life. A tape in the tape deck—the car's age showed itself—played Willy Nelson's version of *What a Wonderful World* in competition with the failing muffler. Not missing the irony, Jorj gunned the engine twice and then felt an abrupt disorientation, followed by a lurch, a crash, and the sliding of a tool across the floor.

Unperturbed, the engine still rumbled, the music played on. Through a vent, carbon monoxide seeped in unpleasantly. Jorj threw the Camaro into reverse, looked behind him, mostly out of habit, and floored the gas. The garage bay door smashed out ahead of it, torn off its track. Tension springs, now released from their shackles, flung themselves about with dangerously wild abandon. On the right-hand side of the bay, where the Camaro lacked a wheel, the frame track and surrounding wall was pushed out where he'd dragged the right quarter panel and bumper through it. He brought the Camaro to a screeching stop on the asphalt outside the bay and held his foot on the brake. Before him, in the garage beyond the broken and scattered shards of glass and twisted aluminum, the naked mechanic lay mutilated in a huge pool of blood, ripped hideously from his chest to his jewels and beyond. Jorj closed his eyes and killed the engine. After a second he had the presence of mind to throw the car in park. Still he refused to open his eyes.

A blood-curdling scream rent the air in the hollow of the garage, echoing as you might expect it would. Jorj's eyes blinked open with it. Where the once gruesome carcass of the mechanic lay was now a whole man, naked but otherwise physically in one piece. He did not stop screaming.

It was with a mixture of relief and dread that Jorj opened the driver's-side door and stuck his left foot out onto the pavement. His reluctance to begin the next necessary step clung hard to the old chevy. A cell phone would be nice now, he thought, yeah, a cell phone. He would call Dennis and Nick, say 'come clean this up.' Of course he couldn't do that. A curse escaped his lips and he hoisted his unhappy frame the rest of the way out.

Another crash sounded, but this time it was different. A set of metal shelves fell over tumbling plastic quarts of 10W30 onto the floor. The mechanic had worked himself into a fetal position against the wall in its place and, quite subconsciously, was working his way towards the office door, gathering every bit of grime to himself along the way. The man was a big ugly side of beef, with a head like a potato, an observation accentuated by the crew cut of dirty brown hair. On his left biceps was tattooed 'USMC.' His right forearm sported an inked-in naked woman. The faded look of both tattoos betrayed the passage of time. Likely the man was in his early fifties.

Jorj shook his head again and ambled towards him, taking care as he stepped around the glass. The man was near the door now. His eyes, when they showed themselves, reminded him of a panicked horse. At least they no longer had that glazed, dying look. Jorj was thankful for that. It was a disturbing sight he didn't want to see again.

"It's okay." He tried to sound casual, reassuring, but to his ears it was the most foolish thing he could have said. Of course it was not okay. Nothing here was. You try dying over 200 times a day for God knew how long, he rebuked himself under his breath. If this wasn't hell...

But this one hell was over for the mechanic. Another had to be dealt with. The thought of it both sickened and angered Jorj more than he could accept at once. Feeling like an overstuffed suitcase of emotions, he sat on it all in order to deal with the business at hand. He could tell those responsible later.

As soon as the naked mechanic caught sight of Jorj, he grimaced, all screaming reduced to moaning like a deranged animal, and clumsily fled, crawling on his hands and knees to the office. He was out of sight no longer than 2 seconds when Jorj heard the bathroom door slam shut. The moaning worked its way into an uncontrolled whimper, a disconcerting sound from such a big man regardless of his predicament.

Eventually Jorj wound his way into the office. The shadows were growing longer outside. He figure there was at least an hour and a half of good light left though so he didn't feel the need to push things along. Instead of disturbing the man in the bathroom right away, he studied the paperwork on the desk, remembering absently that the keys to the Camaro were still in the ignition.

Several invoices had a scrawled set of initials 'BM' in the box marked 'service representative.' Certain words came to mind, in his warped way of thinking, but he shrugged them off immediately. He scanned the desktop a bit more until his eyes caught the business cards. "Bill McDonough," he spoke out loud, unmindful of the man behind the closed door.

"Whu…wh…what do you want?" the voice came obviously from the bathroom, a fragile shell of the normally baratone one the man took for granted.

Jorj looked up, suddenly recalled to the fact he was not alone. "Bill? Is that your name?"

"Uh…uhhuhuhuh…" he began wailing again. It was clear he was in no control of anything yet.

"Bill! Biiiilll!" Jorj applied his best 'get a hold of yourself voice.' It was an arrogant, simplistic move, yes, but he had a crude, triage-style plan in mind. "Where's Mike?"

The wailing died quietly to a whimper again. "M-m-mike?"

Alright, Jorj thought quickly, you've got his attention. "You got real lucky, guy. That Camaro almost nailed you good!" Jorj let the words sink in and then added, "It's not my business why you're naked and all, but if you can tell me where your clothes are, I'll get them for you."

"Uh....uhhh" The wail was starting again.

Jorj cut it off abruptly. "Look, why don't you clean up while you're in there. You got pretty filthy. I'll check around here for your duds."

"M-Mike...h-he don't work here no m-more."

A pause. "Well...whatever," Jorj called back. "Clothes first, then I want to talk to you about that red sports car in the other bay."

Silence from the bathroom.

It was a start. Jorj hadn't much to work with, but it was something. Keep the man confused on trivial stuff. Keep his mind off the bad stuff. And by no means let on that he died. Not yet. Maybe not ever.

After some searching he found a pair of navy blue coveralls hanging up on a hook in the garage, dirty and frayed, but serviceable. Above the left chest pocket was a patch with the embroidered name 'Mike.' "Mike doesn't work here anymore," Jorj mumbled and took them down from the wall. He didn't find any shoes, and didn't expect to, so he wasn't disappointed. Quietly he returned to the front office.

"I found a bottle of vodka in the garage," he lied. He'd sort it out with God later. Right now, Bill needed a cushioned explanation, even if it was false.

Silence, then, "I-I d-don't drink." Jorj could hear him shivering behind the door, could even hear him pacing in the tiny, four-foot square room. "A-a-alcoholic. Q-q-quit last year."

"Looks to me like you started up again. Here. I found Mike's old coveralls."

At least half a minute dragged by and then, after some fumbling, the door opened a crack. One eye peeked out, wide and fearful. "Who the hell are you? I never seen your face before."

Inspiration is a wonderful thing sometimes. Jorj could have kissed it were it tangible.

"Do you really want to know?" Yes, Jorj mused, inspiration is sweet. It's just that little detail of making it one with reality that's the tricky part. He wondered how vulnerable this guy was…enough to take the bait? He didn't seem too bright, and he doubted that whatever the man might once have been, that was all gone now in the brain department.

A hand reached through the space between door and door jam, grabbed the coveralls from Jorj's clutches, and retracted sharply. Immediately the door slammed shut as if to punctuate an unvoiced retort.

While he listened to Bill slide one leg in at a time, Jorj studied the rest of the desktop that he'd given only the precursory glance of earlier. The name plate in front read Mike Chezky. There was a small double picture frame, folded in slightly so that it would stand upright. Within it were two photos, the left one of a girl, probably less than ten years old, the right one a boy of maybe thirteen. No wife. Divorced? Probably. Both children were dark haired and smiling. Neither looked like Bill, the man in the bathroom. The fact that they weren't screaming might have had something to do with that, Jorj noted. He did think, though, that they were not his kids.

Jorj considered opening the pen drawer of the desk and then changed his mind. About that time the bathroom door unlatched and drew back part way very slowly, unsurely. The hand that still clung to the inside handle quivered slightly, but it was clean. The face above, sprouting out the open collar of the blue coveralls like a fearfully uncertain spud looked drained of pretty much anything but wanting to go home and curl into a ball. But there was a sliver of life behind the haunted eyes, and mental gears, hand-cranked by goblins of confused and worried curiosity, turned slowly—but they did turn.

"Why are you still here?" His voice came past the lips slow and numb. The quiver, the stuttering, no more bothered to harass him.

Nick needed to take this guy in. Jorj knew that. But he knew that Bill, if that was truly his name, likely was not going to just follow him without a good reason, maybe not even with one. He decided to push through with his plan. "What I said before...about the booze...it was bullshit."

Relief and alarm crossed swords on the other man's punch-drunk face. A trace of anger, too stupid to realize it should hide with his other emotions, betrayed itself. But his words still came halting and slow. "I told ya I didn't drink no more."

"Yes." Jorj pursed his lips, paced across to the other side of the room, and pretended to study the Union spark plug poster. "You did say that. Tell me Mr... McDonough is it?"

"Maybe." Shock seemed not to have dulled every sense.

"Whatever," Jorj replied quietly. This was a mixed bag, he told himself. The guy wasn't screaming anymore, but now his guard was mustering itself. Better play this well and lay it on thick. "I'm going to tell you something. You won't believe me, so you'de better do something for yourself first." This was a gamble and he knew it, for what he had in mind was untested. "Pick up the phone."

Bill McDonough stared at Jorj like a neglected potato, all eyes and nothing behind them.

"Pick it up Mr. McDonough."

Something inside the blown bulb rekindled itself. Bill looked down at the phone on the desk like it was an ancient artifact, stared at it dumbly for another few seconds, and then reached for it slowly with his left hand. His fingers, stout and calloused, fumbled with it until they found purchase. As he brought it up to his mouth and left ear, he let his right hand dangle abandoned at his side. He seemed awkward even standing idle. "No tone," he murmured and raised his eyes questioningly to Jorj. "How come?"

Relief commended Jorj for a worthy gamble. "Bill," he began, taking a careful yet not un-casual tone, "the city's been evacuated. You will find, once you go out that door—and you will go out there—that everyone's gone. Left town on the last bus."

Bill's eyes shifted past Jorj, through the open front door and at the window he couldn't see out of. A furrow emerged between them as he tried to comprehend this new piece of misinformation.

"There's been an accident, a chemical spill." Now the real bait...the lure to get him to Nick's place. That old bastard would know what to do with this guy, how to keep him from losing his sanity. "I'll explain more in awhile, but first I need you to come with me back to the shelter."

It wasn't clear whether Bill believed him or not, but it sure looked like he wanted to. He let the phone drop from his hand onto the desk and came out from around it, not stopping on his way towards the door. At the threshold he paused, but then continued on through. Jorj followed him out, keeping a respectful distance. Suddenly he wished that he wore something besides a plain white t-shirt.

Bill stood at the curb, looking left, looking right. It was true. There was not a soul to be seen. He seemed not to breath, but his breaths surely came and went shallowly, gathering strength each time. "Is that why I didn't have no clothes on?" he asked, scarcely audibly. Cringing horror crept back into his face. "No one did nothin' to me, did they? I mean, while I lay there all naked and all?"

"No one around to do anything to you," Jorj reassured him. "I can tell you more at the shelter. I want you actually to see someone there who can tell you more than I can. He has authority, you see, that I don't?"

"Y-you don't look so official to me."

The stammer was returning. Time to ease back on the throttle, Jorj acknowledged. "I'm with the Red Cross." He smiled with fake certainty. "Really."

Confusion hovered on Bill's face and became replaced by an increasing awareness of what he thought he understood was happening but really didn't. He half turned to the right and took in the maroon camaro with its mashed-in passenger side front fender and the remains of the garage bay door that preceded it. "I'm in trouble. I'm in a whole lot of trouble."

"We just need to get you checked out." Jorj said, keenly aware that he had no radio, no credentials, nothing even remotely connecting him with anything official, and hoping like hell it didn't occur to Bill that anything about him was amiss. Perhaps, he hoped, everything else that was wrong with this place would do the job for him, that and the fact that this guy was a few matches short of a pack.

Bill turned back to him, that dazed look on his face again, and nodded, first just a little, then with more vigor. The shadow of a telephone pole stretched across his legs. "Okay."

The solitude of the next few blocks between Mike's Garage and the West Side Tavern only served to solidify the sham. There was not a soul, not a car, no working street lights…nothing at all that said people lived there. Jorj was sure he'd seen one or two movies with this effect, but somehow it didn't catch him the way it did Bill. And he wasn't convinced it said as much about the big man as it did himself. And that, in its own unsettling way, bothered him considerably.

So what would he say to Nick, he wondered? 'Hi Nick… here's a guy who died approximately 288 times a day—he did the math in his head—and don't you dare tell him.' Or 'I lied my way through his psyche so he wouldn't freak. Now he's your problem.' He would be Nick's problem too. There were reasons why, that he considered totally justified. But that would wait. First get Bill standing in front of Nick, without Dennis opening up his mouth, or Frosty and Bermuda Shorts showing up, a doubtful but reasonable possibility, or anything else mucking with what he had accomplished here. That's all he asked for the moment.

Whatever Bill might have been on old Earth, he was a broken man in the Twilight. Jorj realized this early on. If the man could be built up again, it wouldn't be overnight. Hell, he laughed bitterly inside, it was all still a gray fog to himself, and he only died twice, only got here the other day like a foreign refugee on Ellis Island.

The West Side Tavern no longer had a sign out front. Nick took that down a long time ago. He'd made changes over the years, for it was years he assuredly spent under its roof, and to some degree it looked less like a bar than it once had. But a bar never entirely loses that look, or that feel. It was a point not lost on Bill. He stopped in the parking lot and shook his head. "Uh-uh."

"C'mon in Bill," Jorj motioned with one hand. "This is the shelter. It's safe."

"I don't drink no more."

Jorj sighed impatiently. "You don't have to. I just want to have you checked out. It's for your own good." How many times had his parents said 'for your own good?' And how many times had it made a difference? Still, it was the way of things here.

Bill shook his head.

"Look," Jorj placated, "You need to get checked out. The chemicals might not be out of your system yet." He paused. An idea occurred to him. "What if you went buck again? You don't want that do you?" It was like talking to a big dog, only one that understood English and could pound him into a pudding.

Bill glowered uncomfortably. Once, Jorj noted, he must have had one hell of a drinking problem. And it seemed now, even at his best, that he was none too bright, even on old Earth.

Jorj held the door open, saw Dennis through the glass of the inner doors and frowned. "Nick," he mouthed.

Now Dennis saw Bill and made towards the door. Jorj's face turned angry. When Dennis pushed through, the former stopped him in his tracks with a glare. "Nick," he repeated, his voice terse. "Get Nick now, will you please?"

The word 'please' hardly undid the effect of Jorj's tone and expression. Dennis hesitated, glanced at Bill standing bear-like out in the lot staring at his bare feet as if for the first time, and then nodded. "Be right back. The man's on the shitter but I think he's almost done."

"Great." It was more than Jorj wanted to know. He turned his head and smiled amiably at Bill. Bill stared back dumbly.

The next time the doors opened it was Nick who opened them, dressed smartly in a dark suit. He looked tired, but curious, and even a bit surprised. "Who have we here, Jorj? I don't recall seeing him around before."

"He's a victim of the chemical leak. Apparently he didn't evacuate the city like everyone else." Jorj turned and smiled again at Bill, motioning him over. "Bill! This is Nick DeMoss. He runs this Red Cross Shelter." He saw peripherally that Nick turned a sharp glance his way, but at least the old man didn't contradict him. He turned back to him and half winked, knowing that the action was unnecessary. "He doesn't want to come in…it's the booze. He's a recovered alcoholic, I think."

Nick took in a sharp breath and let it out slowly. Ever watchful, he regarded the newcomer. Bill met his eyes and then slowly ambled towards them, his face a blank slate.

"I hear we're supposed to get a storm this evening," Nick said with a cautious smile. I hear a trace of thunder from time to time." He stood with his hands folded in front of him. They remained thus as Bill stopped three feet away.

"I don't see no Red Cross," Bill mumbled. His head was lowered a little but his eyes were straight forward. He was taller than either Nick or Jorj, but not by much. The main difference between them, physically, was that he was built like an enormous tree trunk. They might as well have been saplings.

"We don't put out a Red Cross," Nick explained. "Isn't that right Jorj?"

"Not anymore," Jorj agreed. "Not since…"

Nick stepped up and placed a hand gently on the side of Bill's head. Bill pulled back at first, but then relented. Nick had a natural way of gaining trust. The hand shifted so that his thumb could lift each eyebrow as Nick looked into the pupils. "Jorj, would you be so kind as to get me the med kit? Dennis will know where it is."

"Sure thing." Jorj went into the tavern and returned within a matter of minutes, bearing a simple metal box, painted white with, yes, a red cross on the outside. He made sure it faced outwards so Bill could see it before setting it down on the sidewalk to open it.

"I would like the flashlight first," Nick remarked. He had been taking Bill's pulse and looking at his watch, an older wind-up model that he wore on his wrist. Once the flashlight was in his possession he returned to looking at Bill's eyes, chiefly the pupils, flicking the light in and out of their dark centers. "I've informed our new friend here that we do not serve drinks at the Red Cross." He paused and regarded Jorj with a half smile. "Would you have Dennis make up a bed for our friend. Even though he appears to be over the worst of it, I've convinced him to stay with us for a few days until we know that he is completely over the effects of the chemical spill. Please make sure everything is spotless." He placed special emphasis on that last word to ensure Jorj made no mistake about his intent, then, casually, he raised eyes raised towards the sky. "Looks like rain."

"Rained all week," Bill remarked colorlessly. "The weather guy said today was just gonna be cloudy."

"The weather guy's outta town now, Bill." Jorj smiled at him and went back inside.

As soon as the door closed behind him the thunder rolled quietly around him. He did two things. First he yelled for Dennis, and Frank. Only Dennis responded, and that only because he was right there in the first place watching out through the blinds of one of the big front windows. Second, he surveyed the room, setting his sights lastly on the shelves behind the bar.

"We've gotta put all the booze out of sight...now!" Jorj threw himself behind the bar and began stashing any visible bottle underneath it or on the floor. "Get the Padre to the window, will you?"

"What? Why? He's with Frank in the kitchen."

"Around the knives?" Jorj stopped for a second, incredulous.

"Frank's quite capable," Dennis retorted. "What gives?"

"The thunder?" Jorj's sarcasm was as thick as he was serious. That guy out there isn't the brightest bulb in the box but..."

"Gotcha," Dennis was off to the kitchen.

Jorj was half through when Dennis returned, leading Francis the blind priest past the bar to a booth near the front door. The angels bowled more heavily now, as if the fates of their very souls hinged upon the outcome of their game. Dennis poked his fingers through the blinds and looked out. Both Nick and the big guy next to him were looking up. It was a good sign.

"Good Lord!" The priest made the sign of the cross over his chest.

"What's the matter Padre?" Dennis looked concerned.

"There's a man outside…how…how awful!"

"Huh? How did you…"

"Dennis!" Jorj called out from behind the bar. He was almost finished, at least for the immediate need. "Nick asked that you make a bed up for Our new guest. He'll be staying."

"What is he, an alcoholic or something?"

Jorj stopped and shot back a look that carried an equal measure of anger and disdain. "Yeah. And if he asks, we're the Red Cross, this is a shelter, and there's been a chemical spill. He missed the fucking evacuation."

"Is this a joke?"

"The only crappy joke is that no one ever helped him before today." He went back to putting the rest of the bottles out of sight. For good measure, he took down the electric St. Paulie Girl sign behind him and stashed that on the floor at the opposite end from the kitchen.

A light clicked on over Dennis' head and his tone became more subdued, even respectful. "Okay. Watch the priest then, will you?"

Jorj came around and took his place at the booth as Dennis passed him on his way to where they kept supplies. He did a quick scan to make sure there was nothing the priest might be tempted to use against himself and relaxed when he saw only the napkin dispenser and the condiments. No one, to his memory, ever successfully killed themselves with one of those. At the moment though, it didn't look like the priest had that particular sin on his mind. A different kind of trouble was throwing shadows across his features.

"They have touched him."

"Only Nick," Jorj replied. "He needed to look him over. And if he asks…"

"I wasn't talking about your bit of well-intentioned play acting." The priest folded his hands before his face, making a steeple with his index fingers and touching them to his scarred upper lip. The front door opened. Bill came in first. "You should ask Nick about the night folk, Jorj.

"Why don't you tell me?"

"Who said that I would not?" The priest smiled grimly, knowingly.

As Nick entered, he regarded the priest and Jorj amiable, but in a business-like manner. "Francis, this is Bill McDonough. He's been through some troubles. Could you sit with him for awhile?"

"Yes, of course, Nicolas."

Jorj removed himself from his seat opposite the priest so the burly mechanic could replace him. Quietly he and Nick removed themselves to the far end of the dining room.

"An accident." Nick produced a pack of cigarettes and offered one to Jorj after taking one himself.

"We're the Red Cross," Jorj pointed out. "Remember?"

Nick frowned.. "Yes. How right you are."" He replaced both cigarettes into the pack and put it away. "He spoke to me a little of nightmares, of being crushed endlessly." Nick tisked. "I suppose you saw his point of entry and all that?"

Jorj narrowed his eyes. "Yeah, I know where he'll turn up next time. I say we blow up the car…burn it, sink it to the bottom of the…"

"It's done." Nick sighed and gazed across the room at Bill. The big man was listening silently as the priest, uncharacteristically animated, relayed what was most likely his version of God's word. "The car is out of the equation. He told me it rolled out into the parking lot, crashed through the garage bay door."

"Something like that."

"You did a good thing, Jorj." Nick smiled respectfully at him.

"Somebody had to."

The frown returned. "Don't be so cold about this. There are other factors of which you have yet to learn."

"Like the night folk?" Jorj folded his arms now. Anger began to bubble to the surface. From one side of the building, thunder rolled to meet the other.

Nick stared at Jorj in silence for a moment. "Who told you of them? Dennis? The Padre?"

"Does it matter?"

"I'm going to need to have a talk with Dennis."

"It was the Padre."

"Then I'll need to speak with him." Nick's face darkened somewhat. "You should learn to walk before you run, Jorj. This is not Old Earth."

"Yeah, I keep hearing that." Jorj unfolded his hands and started walking towards the hallway which led to the room he shared with Dennis. "And I should wait at least an hour after I eat before swimming. Whatever."

"Where are you going? There are still things I want to ask you."

"Home."

Nick glanced out the window. The sun rested on the horizon somewhere to the west. There were too many buildings in the way to allow more than long shadows and streaks of orange. And then there was the ozone green tint of Francis' troubled existence. "You are home, Jorj."

From down the hallway came an angry response. "My home. My apartment."

Nick waited until he returned with his few personal effects. "It will be dark very soon." His tone was quite serious. "It would be better, much better, if you wait until morning. I strongly advise it."

"If I followed the advice I've gotten so far around here," Jorj said with bitter sarcasm, Bill would still be struggling vainly for that last heartbeat, and that breath he just couldn't quite catch anymore. See ya around Nick." He slid past him and made for the front door. "I'll be in touch."

He might have tried to stop him, but the waves would upset too many boats. There was Bill to consider, and the Padre. The man, who in a single day brought two needy souls into the sanctuary he'd created, was leaving. And he was not unjustified. They were too cautious for God's work.

Nick felt a pressure rise in the left side of his chest. He rubbed it, feeling strength drain from him suddenly, so much so that he was forced to sit down in a nearby booth and recover from his sudden fatigue. No one had noticed and that was good. This would pass like the others, but he knew he was running out of time. Jorj was an unforeseen hope to him, and the man was just now pushing open the inner front doors to leave. What had someone said to him once in the long ago and far away? 'The wind goes where it will, and though you hear it, you cannot tell where it was or where it will be at any given future. So it is with a man's spirit...his soul.'

After awhile, the pressure eased, but he still felt weak. Dennis entered the room and approached him. The latter was struck by the ashen pallor of the former. "Again? I'm getting the doc in here tomorrow."

Nick smiled uneasily at Dennis. "I'll be fine." He waved off a further comment impatiently. "I think it would be good to have Bill share a room with the Padre."

"The Padre needs to be watched."

"I don't think so." Nick gestured towards the front of the dining room. Bill was a perfect listener.

"Oh," Dennis nodded. "Should I have Frank fix them something to eat?"

"I think that would be nice for all of us," Nick replied tiredly. "Set five places tonight."

Dennis turned to go and then stopped short. "You mean six." He still looked over Nick with concern. He was getting the doctor tomorrow whether Nick wanted him to or not.

"Five. Jorj has left us."

"Will he be back?" Dennis looked sharply out a window. The sun no longer cast even the slimmest ray. Everything was that twilight purple of neither nor. "Jeezuss! Where's he going?"

"I'm not sure he knows, Dennis." He let out a sigh. "Please pull the shades. I think it is time."

4

The sun dipped into the ocean of the far western horizon, immediately denying its waning gift of heat to the land until the next morning. For some, that gift would be miserly indeed, yet others would take for granted the warmth bestowed upon them for no other reason than the timeliness of their demise. Such was the fairness doled out upon the inhabitants, the squatters, prisoners—whatever one wished to call them—of Twilight Earth. For Jorj, evening brought back the chill of morning. As the first stars began to peep out in the fading blue above, he became resolute in his decision to find a jacket to wear.

This was the time when shadows ceased lengthening and began to meld with the landscape. Jorj was glad to get away from the priest's biblical weather. Frankly, he found himself acknowledging, the whole bit should be a dream, a weird, hallucination brought on by the fever of his injuries inflicted from the accident at the overpass. That's what it should have been, but he knew better. He also shouldn't be taking this so evenly, but that, too, was not to be made sense of.

He supposed if he had much family left, or if he had a significant other, or real prospects back on the Earth that was, he might panic, rage, even cry. If that's what the response should be, then he wasn't playing by the rules. Things were as they were. He couldn't change that. What mattered was what to do next, and of that he hadn't a real clue beyond the jacket, food, and sleep. Up ahead he saw Dennis' truck and smiled an empty smile. His apartment was across the street from that. If Dennis choked on a chicken bone and keeled over tonight, he could crash at his place. It was just a short walk.

Before he approached the scene of Dennis' accident, he saw her, out of the corner of his eye. She stood in a shadow of a three-story building with a brick façade, the third story being set back and consisting mostly of the attic. It was, in fact, a house converted into a pro shop some years ago, at least as he remembered it. And there she was, until he turned his eyes directly upon her. The second he did that, she was gone.

Trick of the light? He didn't think so, not where people got offed and then came back like Lazerus without the kind but beckoned help of the Lord. No, he decided, she was there, at least for a moment. He stopped in his tracks. "Hey! I saw you, ya know!" No answer. He shrugged and continued on towards his apartment. Enough of the games.

What was the big deal with them, he wondered, these night folk. Nick could have just told him, buy he didn't. The priest could have been straight too. Dennis never mentioned them... or did he. Jorj couldn't remember. He placed his hand on the handle to the front door to his apartment building and swung it open. Darkness waited for him just beyond but he feared it not. He plunged through with only minor, common sense, precaution.

He ascended the stairs deliberately, tired but not willing to cave to fatigue's demands just yet. He wondered if any of his neighbors had guns, and why their stuff was there when his was not. The thought of dying slowly, and people's potential to exploit the nature of this 'Twilight Earth'—the term fit—began to erode his cavalier attitude somewhat. Bill McDonough' in right mind, would argue that perhaps he was not as cautious as he should be. But fear was something to watch out for too. Fear compromised men' actions, subdued the demands of necessity, and ultimately threatened acceptable solutions. Just ask ol' Bill about *that* one, he mused bitterly.

He reached the next landing and went straight to the nearest apartment that was not his. Without knocking—for who could be there now?—he turned the handle on apartment 3A, the son of Mrs. Logan. What was his name? Chad? No one was home, so far as he could see, nor had been since last he entered it two days before.

Dark apartment. It might have creeped him out, had he cared about things like that, but he never did. Ghosts, denizens of the dark, demons, all of these were a fantasy to him, always were. Muggers, rapists, murderers, now these were people to fear, for they were more than real on Old Earth. He was sure they were here too, but they weren't horror material, just dangerous people.

Once he'd checked each of the two bedrooms, kitchen living room, and bathroom, making sure he was absolutely alone, he tried the lights. They didn't work. There was no hum of the refrigerator, like in Sol's place downstairs. He had half a mind to check and see if that one was still running, but he knew the answer already. Of course it ran. It wasn't dependent on the local power station. Nothing here was. He wondered whether starting up the local power station would screw with the power supply in a bad way and decided it was too complex a question. Let Theodore's eggheads work that one out, if he had them. All he wanted right now were a few simple things until morning. Warmth, which would mean going down to Sol's apartment, a dependency he supposed he could get used to, and some food.

He left Chad's apartment unlocked. Later he would return and scavenge. On an inspiration, he went down to the front entry of the apartment building, intending to lock the outer door. That was when he remembered he did not have the key anymore. Another item he'd have to look for. Mentally he began building a basic list of things to gather. This was his building now, as far as he was concerned. Let Frosty, Bermuda Shorts, or the shadows converge on it. With a little preparation he'd be ready. Such was the confidence he tried to instill in himself, knowing that he would not be staying long, that real security would come on the road, and ultimately finding a way to a better existence where people stayed dead or did not die at all in the first place. That empty feeling took root in these thoughts and flourished. It would not do well for him to relax too long, he realized.

Of course he was right. Sol's apartment ran quietly on the electricity it had in the back where and when. The refrigerator hummed nicely, although some of the food within it was questionable. But that was the natural way with refrigerators.

Jorj searched until he found a cheap duffel bag, a flashlight, and the apartment keys, the last item being the best find for the short turn. Immediately he descended the outer stairs and locked the front door. He followed this up by checking every apartment, room by room, until he was absolutely assured of his solitude.

In Chad's apartment he found a shotgun on a wall rack in the far bedroom. The guy was a deer hunter, and had camouflage, bright orange hats—Jorj tossed them aside—and a box of deer slugs on a shelf in the closet. He took the gun and shells, putting the ammunition in the duffel.

"You won't need those, you know."

He whirled. It was a woman's voice, a young woman's voice. "Who's that?" He heard the edge in his own chords and stifled it, choosing instead to scan the room sharply. A light outside the window, in the apartment parking lot, caught his eyes, and he went to the glass, steaming it with his own breath. Like he saw the other night, a barrel fire burned, only no one stood around it this time.

Every room in Chad's apartment he rechecked, finding no one. There was nothing to indicate anyone entered or left, for the door was closed and he'd heard no sound from that quarter. "Okay, ghost," he called out. "Want to talk? Show yourself."

The ghost, real or not, didn't seem to desire conversation.

Jorj went to the window again. The barrel fire still burned, casting a wreath of wavering stars on the pavement around its base where rusted holes let air at the burning material within. His eyes unfocused for a second and then he saw her, the girl from the street, reflected in the glass behind himself. This time he only smiled, but it wasn't a pleasant one. "I guess if you're going to off me, this is the right time...the best time, because you won't get another chance. If not, why don't you take a seat on the bed. It's not a proposition, by the way." He saw no change in her expression before she receded into nothingness. Turning, he found no one there. For a moment he watched the door, but knew it had nothing to do with her appearance. He turned back to the window and saw that there were four people around the barrel fire, three men and two women, one of them the girl with the smile. She turned her face towards his window casually, but made no reaction other than to simply watch. After a few heartbeats she turned back to the fire, her palms open to it. No one spoke a word to another.

Silently he pulled away from the glass and made a decision, though how wise it was he didn't know. That, he would find out within the next five or ten minutes.

After a moment's hesitation, he left the shotgun on the bed with the duffel and exited the apartment. What he wanted to do, to find out, didn't need a gun, and if somebody wished him ill, well, they seemed capable of reaching him without exposing themselves to his kind of danger. Whatever game was at play here was of another sort altogether.

He left the building with the keys in his left jeans' front pocket, the only thing he felt important or of real use to him now, and shut the outer front door behind him. He paused, withdrew the keys, and locked up, for this didn't call for carelessness, and pocketed the keys once again. That done, he made a bee-line for the barrel fire.

Three steps in he saw it, warmly lit in orange and yellow against the darkling colors of the night, without a single soul around it. The shadow people were not there, or chose not to show themselves. He approached it anyway, for perhaps they would return, and warmed his hands by the dancing flames.

Someone had busted up a shipping pallet, actually a few of them, and it was these that burned within the rusting 55-gallon drum with the holes near the bottom. The fire hissed quietly, popping off a spark periodically on business of its own, on a level entirely unaware or uncaring that human hands sought the warmth it provided or the company of those that brought it into existence. A part of Jorj found the familiarity reassuring, for since his childhood he loved fires, and drank many a beer around them with friends back on Old Earth. Here fire knew not the slippage between the planes of existence, or the demented politics of Heaven and Hell that strove to influence those who were marooned on their unpredictable shores. In this place, fire was simply fire.

"He is either foolish or brave," A older male voice spoke out of the shadows. Jorj did not turn. He'd learned that such reactions were unlikely to matter just now. Instead, he ratcheted up his peripheral senses. They would serve him far better.

He is not like the others," A child laughed. "I like him." There was something altogether too seasoned about the child's voice. It both disturbed and encouraged Jorj.

"He is a new immigrant," A female voice corrected the child. This was the woman who spoke to Jorj earlier, in the apartment. "He does not understand their fear. Perhaps he can be taught the way of the road."

"All can be taught that," a mocking male voice replied.

"All can be forced down it," she again corrected. "There is little use in that, except to terrify."

"Exactly." It was the mocking voice again.

Finally Jorj turned. It was slow and steady, displaying no elements of impatience. There was an expectation on his part, misplaced, but harmless, of facing his observers. He was, of course, disappointed. A wind blew through the parking lot, not heavy but persistent, causing the flames to gutter and cling greedily to the skeletal wood within the barrel. Down the street,

under the shadow of the moon which slyly poked out from behind a ragged cloud, a shadowy figure stood leaning against a
dormant, possibly dead lamp post. It was a man, Jorj thought,
by the posture of the individual. He wore a long leather coat
that matched the night. His hands had it pulled back so they
could hang from black front pockets by the thumbs. Jorj smiled
thinly, both at the irritated observation that the night seemed
to breed denizens in black leather, and that this was the mocker.
He nodded, acknowledging the other, and slid a quarter way
around the fire so that he could keep his eyes on him. For the
other's part, he seemed either uninterested or unappreciative,
for he turned and walked away in the opposite direction, quite
unaffected by Jorj's curious stare.

A voice next to him, to his left, spoke up immediately. "Got
a light?" It was the child.

"Don't smoke," Jorj replied. "Neither should you." It occurred to him that there was fire right before him. He turned
a critical gaze towards where he thought the voice came from,
sensing he'd been the butt of a joke and saw a half-sized character across the parking lot drinking a beer. It was a boy, by his
best estimate, dressed in overalls, a corduroy jacket, and an old
leather chauffeur's cap. The imp tipped the beer in Jorj's direction. Jorj made a welcoming gesture. He didn't intend to leave
the fire just yet.

The child only shook his head and smiled. There was more
to that smile than a 'how do you do' Jorj noted distrustfully.
He turned and looked down street. The child's friend was gone.
When he looked back, so was the boy. .

He waited. They would return, come hell or high water. If not,
they wouldn't have bothered with him in the first place. At least

that was his going theory. But they did return in the form of the girl, a young woman really. She said nothing, though she watched him from a dark corner across the street. He watched her in detail, such as the darkling shadows afforded, and something else, a sort of second sight he was just learning to understand. She was slight, and not overly tall. Her eyes, though large, were so in a pretty way, and he knew that they could suck him in if he let them. That was part of her magic, such that she had. When she slipped back into the oily blackness of the night, he realized that another had approached from behind. It was nothing that he heard. He felt it, and the feeling did not bring him comfort.

As he turned, he saw peripherally something slink to the left and blend with the shadows. It didn't surface again, but he knew it was still there, for its presence hovered, ungenerous in the declarations people usually offer to show they're not a threat, or that they unabashedly are.

"Enough of this." Jorj was losing his patience. "What do you want?"

"What do *you* want?" a voice, disembodied, quite possibly in his mind, replied.

"Talking's a start."

The presence shifted unseen. There was nothing that betrayed discomfort with itself, or uncertainty. Quite to the contrary, it bore itself with extreme confidence. It noted approvingly how Jorj was not afraid of it, but that he watched its area warily, mostly for his lack of understanding. Had he knowledge of it, true knowledge, he might have run all the way back to his apartment and locked himself behind that front door he deluded himself into thinking would keep out the night, but he didn't. He only watched.

"Tell me about this road," Jorj said coldly, "and why some-one wants me to learn it."

Laughter rippled through him down to his bones, even into them. It was not kindly, and could even be described as clinical. Whatever the source, it regarded him with no more respect than a dog, or a gopher, but that he provided it with something desired. And he couldn't imagine what that was. He only half sensed the intentions Surely, by the time he caught on to things, they were already in motion.

He was about to speak again, to say that he wasn't anyone's dog, or their gull. Something, however, caused his tongue to stick, to stop with unfinished syllables still attached to its moist, glistening, spongy surface, where they soon after died the death of neglect. Afar off, through the forest of shadows, past buildings and trees, he heard the mutterings of dissatisfied souls, and the inability to slake that was the nature their hollow cries let slip into the night. At that moment, he caught his first inkling that he might have stepped too far, and what Frank sought to separate him with a simple pull of a shade.

Alas, it was too late.

The voices departed. With them, the inky black existence faded from his awareness and his vicinity. Only the fire remained, a staunch friend in a place where all other light, save the fickle moon, fled from millennial hours aforetime.

Footsteps took him by surprise as soon as he heard them. They touched pavement rapidly, springing away from it like it burned beneath them, and perhaps it did, for the fire of a pursuer was hot upon them. Jorj turned his head towards them, his arms raised in readiness, hands balled into loose fists.

Something, on a far wind that dipped quite suddenly, echoed into Jorj's mind these words:

For every truth, there is someone trying to cover its light. These days if they cannot cover it, they will redefine light as darkness. All such criminals of humanity share the same gravity, though they will tell you that the point on the globe from which it pulls them somehow characterizes the degree of their righteousness. Only unchallenged bias will let them into your heart.

What such wind words had to do with a chase, he hadn't the slightest idea, nor if the two were indeed related, but he did not take the time to attempt drawing a connection. Besides, he was surprised yet again by another specter of confusion, or rather two of them. Not much more than vaguely human blurs of light, two figures flew past him from the southwest, apparitions through which the darkness held little power of penetration. He stepped back, unmindful of the barrel fire, and brushed up against the hot, rusty metal. Only when he felt the burning of his backside did he step forward again, and even that was an unconscious act. His eyes were still glued to the fading phantasmal forces, lost to him in the slipstream of overlapping realities.

This way.

One of the voices, perhaps the child's, maybe the mocker, grazed his mind. 'Absurd,' he thought back. Which way? And why?

But he knew. The nudge was there. Go downstreet, towards the turn off to the West Side Tavern. His head swam. The dim light of the moon, held at bay by the firelight, condensed the darkness beyond into blurred shadows. His judgement seemed impaired. Was he actually considering following the direction of a disembodied will? If not, then why had he come out at all? Why did he not stay indoors like the others, cowering behind the patterns of Old Earth, behind window shades, and men with guns and expensive suits? Or behind his pilfered shotgun?

His friend, the fire, could not stop him, for he did not even offer it a second glance, did not ask its advice. It burned on behind him, the top portions of pallet wood crumbling hot coals into an arcanely transformed ruin beneath, spitting tiny sparks out of the air holes near pavement level. Jorj entered the darkness like a fish tossed up by a wave and retrieved by gravity into the cold, murky depths of a bottomless ocean. Unlike said fish, this was not his home.

His walking seemed more like floating to him, for his feet felt light on the pavement, and he was hyperaware of almost every movement his body made, as if he walked on stage before a crowd of thousands...no hundreds. Perhaps not even that many could pull themselves away from their predicaments to watch. One could shut out the hundreds and thousands in any case. But it wasn't the sense that there were watchers that affected him, it was the place itself, and the unnaturalness with which he fit into it. More frightening, for that much he felt coldly now upon his soul, was the surety that given time, he would adapt, become familiar, and even be accepted into this strange new piece of real estate.

He'd almost lost his nerve, considered returning to the barrel fire with every intention of recalling reality, *his* reality, whatever that was, and clinging to it until there was no question but that it would stay. Instead, he turned left at a 4-way stop, northwest onto Peat street, marveling at how dark the city was even with an occasional moon slipping free of the grasping clouds that floated above, each one a single gray ship in a lost Spanish armada.

There came up behind him footsteps, many of them, an unquestionable army of unfettered, determined relentlessness. His head cocked to the left, face tilted towards the road, ears listening for signs of himself becoming the target of their attentions. It was clear after a second that he was, at very least, in their path. With discretion, he veered off to the right, first to a sidewalk, and then into a yard, and finally to an alley between two old, once-proud, west-side houses. They marched by like ants, invisible, giant dog-sized ants with high heels, dress shoes, military boots, everything a foot could wear. The road accepted them all with equal indifference. Jorj looked hard. In the untouched ether, he saw that it was not entirely so. There were hints of things, glints of metal, of jewelry, patches of color that emerged and receded from the darkness. If he stared hard enough, the color lingered, the glints and gleams tarried. At the last second, the one he knew would suck him in, he turned away, shutting his eyes tight. The crowd passed on. Echoes drifted into the hollow coldness and eventually dispersed. He thought, finally, that he was alone.

When something rustled in the leaves less than ten feet away, deeper into the off-road property, he whipped to face it, his skin tingling in a cold sweat, his hands up. A shadow moved off. It too, had watched the crowd, or maybe it had watched him. He didn't know.

Jorj waited awhile longer, lingering where he had as safe a spot as any, unmolested for the time, knowing to step out, to move on, could offer no equivalent guarantee. The wind blew through his white t-shirt in earnest, and he gave thought to the houses he stood between. He could have brought the flashlight, he realized, and inwardly chided himself for not doing so. The coward surged within him and he abandoned the idea of breaking and entering. This was not his where and when. The rules did not favor him. Besides, his head was beginning to clear and cowardice seemed more like common sense with every breath. Like a rat, he'd followed the soundless flute this far. It was time to go home, or at least his version of it. Carefully, with an eye to things waiting in the shadows, real or phantom, he stepped back out onto the sidewalk.

Behind him, the wind gusted, belching swirling leaves out of the alley so that they flew around and past him in a cloud, a murder of crows as his father would have said. On the flat gray of the street, the moon cast each one in shadow. Jorj could almost hear their caws, the only sound of true cynical laughter in the bird world. They knew what their lot in life was, and that of their Earthly masters. While they paid the price up front, their eyes watched humanity piss its fortune away before the bill was due. Theirs, Jorj knew in those shadow-swirled seconds, was a cold humor. The crow-leaves flew off hither and thither, leaving him alone in the moon-speckled shadows.

He faced south east. The first and closest of the four corners between Peat and North State Street was a five-second walk. Easy. Go to it, turn right and just keep on walking until Dennis' truck, abandoned to decay in the middle of the street, looms into view. Just before and to the right of that is the barrel fire. Go to that.

His inner voice gave the directions but the flute, silent in its lure, played on once again. As it could not, or would not, be denied, neither did Jorj's feet seek to do so but turned in the direction of the lilting medley, to follow the doppelganger-lark's song. And while the soles of his shoes gently padded cat-like towards the West Side Tavern, his insides stirred, shivered even, for he could sense the abandon, uncharacteristic for him, and he powerless to stop the puppet manipulations of his circumstances.

Before it came into sight, he heard the music. When he rounded the building that blocked his way, he saw light, big and yellow, beaming sheet-like from the windows, all of them, and not a single pulled shade to be found. The lot was full, and so were the seats within. Around the bar, a throng milled, mingled, gabbed away, a drink in every hand or nearby, cigarette smoke piling on within three feet of the ceiling. They must be choking to death in there, Jorj observed. But if they were, they didn't seem to mind.

Remembering the other night, he wandered to the right side of the building, where the kitchen door opened out onto the parking lot. He'd check in with Frank and see what was up. Then Frank would ignore him and Jorj would have to wait for Dennis to pop in so he could ask him instead. That was the plan.

With more caution in him than he immediately understood the need for, he approached the door from the shadows, avoiding the yellow light that spilled forth in a long, skewed rectangle. He could see plainly five individuals. Two white men and a black man, each of medium build and middle age, worked the pots and pans. A young buck banged pots noisily in the dish sink, and a rotund woman with sagging forearms kept the butcher block busy, her hair netted up tight on her round head. An unpleasant odor of cooking meat clung to everything, an inexplicable thing to Jorj for he was not repulsed by the idea of a good hamburger or steak. He shrugged mentally and then realized that he had the black man's attention. The man stared at him for a second or two as if Jorj was a ghost, and then called to the fat woman who took one look at the stranger outside their door and immediately approached it, still carrying the butcher knife in her right hand.

"A bit late out for you, ain't it? Now what do you want?"

Jorj stepped back three feet further into the shadows of the lot. "Frank. I'm looking for Frank. He works here." He suddenly wondered if his words spoke true.

She stared suspiciously, her grimace doing nothing to beautify her needy appearance. Something came into her eyes that Jorj didn't like. "Frank Wells?"

"No," Jorj gambled. She was too smart to offer the right name the first time. The name 'wells' was bait. "Not Wells."

"Then who, honey. There's a lot of Franks that come through here." A smile, artificial and only the mask of a bad actor creased her plump face.

A change in tactics. "How about Nick. Nick DeMoss. Is he around someplace?"

She put her fat right hand to her primary chin. "Let me see, tall fellow, medium build?"

"Wrong." In the space of a heartbeat he heard a twist of gravel behind him. What a sloppy bastard he was, he cursed himself. Just in time he whirled and dodged a baseball bat aimed straight for his head. It was the youthful dishwasher, a lad with murderous intent. A second swing immediately prepared itself but Jorj was no longer an easy target. In the fraction of a second, he closed, checked the nearest arm holding the weapon of choice among sports aficionados and criminals alike, thereby halting the blow, and smashed his right fist into the boy's chin. It was a quick, clean stroke, but the boy was no Dennis Brinks. He staggered back, dazed. Jorj pressed forward and grabbed the bat, twisted it, and wrenched it away before the dishwasher could collect himself. His next move was to finish the fight but footsteps behind, lots of them, had other ideas. Instead he bowled the young man over and ran on past, hopping a picket fence, clamoring over the top of a chain link one, and falling hard on the other side. His pursuers were persistent and the sounds of their chase bore no signs of stealth. With as many as Jorj guessed there were, at least a dozen, they probably felt they didn't need it.

He scrabbled to his feet and took just a second to get his bearings. A dozen or more people fanning out were going to cut his chances of escape thin, and he knew it. Worse yet, by climbing the fence, he'd neglected to take into account what the fence was for. He was inside its enclosure. All the others had to do was run around it and surround him. And most were doing that even now. The remainder, three burly men, were cursing to themselves loudly as they climbed over the fence with less finesse than Jorj. It was only a matter of time.

He still had the bat, and he also mastered his wits. The third thing he counted in his favor was the house and the big maple trees around it. A stand could be made, and a stand he would make.

No time was wasted trying the lock on the back door. The only key that would suffice in a time like this was the baseball bat. With the first blow he knocked out the window and with the second he cleared the glass shards away so that he could reach in and unlock it without cutting his arms. The lock twisted once and the door was free. Then the first ascended the back steps. Jorj turned and brought the bat down on his head. Unlike the dishwasher, he didn't miss.

It was a good bat, this confiscated item. All wood, not aluminum, it let out a crack like it was sending the ball out of the park. The big man went down in a heap, never seeing the face of the man at the plate. His compatriots who approached hesitated. One called out to him.

"You got yerself in a heap o' trouble, boy!" No doubt he thought himself clever, thinking that words would delay, buy time, sucker Jorj's guard down. Yet the object of his words was no longer there. No melodramatics could stop Jorj's sense of urgency, or his common sense. The big idiot out in the yard shrugged and started up the stairs casually. No need to hurry, he realized. Where could this stranger go? Then he stopped and grimaced, realizing what the house was that he had entered.

Jorj slammed the door shut behind him and locked it. Not an entirely worthless maneuver. Putting your hand into the dark to unlock a door when you knew no one expected it was not a big deal. Now it was a big deal, at least to the perception of anyone with intelligence.

His epithets hurled out the gaping maw of the destroyed backdoor window and landed on the two large men. They stood on the back steps, one behind and left of the other, in mud-stained suits, the jackets ripped in key places where they'd either stretched arms too far or snagged on the chain link fence. Neither man was anxious to be the first to try the door.

Within the house, the darkness ended abruptly. Still watching out the back door from the shadows of the inside, Jorj saw the faces of his pursuers emerge clearly from the darkness, monstrously scarred, hideously malignant in their inner character. The lead one smiled goblin-like and started up the stairs, no longer concerned. Jorj turned and retreated further into the kitchen, where he'd entered, crossed out into the dining room, now turned into a medical macabre of gurneys and amputees, still twitching in the darkness, and came face to face with a man in a bloody white smock. He held a cleaver stretched before him, pointing it at Jorj from a distance of six feet. At the moment the back door banged open, Jorj swung, not at the knife, but at the head behind it. Having gambled correctly, his stroke removed the grisly doctor from the inconvenience of existence. By the time he turned to face his new threat, entering the dining room cautiously but not slowly, Jorj was only vaguely aware that the body which hit the floor by his feet was no longer there.

There were two of them here, both considerably bigger than himself. It was then that a hoarse voice, like from a crypt, rasped out in the absence of vocal chords, a desperate plea. "Kill us."

The first of the hulks moved forward. Jorj grasped the corner of a gurney, bandaged, dismembered body upon it, and lurched it in the way before backing off. He took note of the second hulk backing into the kitchen. He would either get a knife or try the other door, to flank him from another direction. Quickly he moved to cut him off as the first pushed through the obstacle in his way. In that moment he pressed an inspired move forward and swung a well-placed blow on his closest aggressor. It was not a fool's move for the other had in that moment let his guard down, his size, and the fact that he was not alone, no doubt at root. The window of opportunity did not go to waste. As the hulk raised his arms to stop the blow, perhaps even thinking to seize the bat, his ribs opened wide to receive the last home run of the night.

Jorj was no weakling, and his ability to find momentum when needed did not let him down this time. The hulk was just a man, after all, no matter his size, and each rib thus touched, collapsed inward and broke. Jorj didn't wait for the punch line but leaped around the stunned monster who, now deflated, backed against a pantry, knocking over tools of the grisly trade practiced here. The monster was out of the running. A door creaked further in from where he'd come and he knew it was the other, seeking the flank.

His breath came hard now, and his heart raced. Adrenaline pumped through him, wearing on his body, pushing his mind to quicker decisions. His eyes met one of the gurney victims, did not question the why, but trusted that which could only be transmitted in the fraction of a second through the most primal of human contact. The bat raised and fell, again and again, meeting the eyes of each, seeing the agony, and the gratitude. He knew why they were here, had figured it out between the kitchen and this moment, and after the last one left the world, pain smote his left forehead, a sharp impact that staggered him, dropped him to his knees, and plunged him into darkness. The bat, having hit singles all the way to the end, fell from his lifeless hands.

He watched it all as if for the first time, and then slipped into an understanding of sorts. Whatever he at first thought, it was wrong. He'd not been struck by the other man, not been caught on the flank, having abandoned his own safety for the sake of stopping the horror done in this house. The impact had come from something streaking out the barrel of a pistol, light caliber but close enough range to penetrate flesh and skull density, dealt by a hand with enough steadiness and skill so that it would find its mark easily. The grinner behind that barrel froze in his tracks, not quite aware of what he had done, only the success of his intent. That is why, when finding a large kitchen knife thrust up under his ribs, his expression of total surprise could not have been more genuine, or the finality of it more acute. Some things were not his to take.

"Come away from this place." It was her voice. Jorj heard it plainly, though he did not see her. He wondered at it for a moment, and then decided that there was another thing that warranted his attention. On the floor, his own body lay prone. He did not find himself drawn to it, but in staring at it the pull began.

"Come away with me. Follow my voice. Do so now."

He looked away. The pull ceased. There was something in her voice. In the apartment of Chad Mezler on North State Street, she first announced her presence to him, though he'd seen her once before, in the parking lot next to the West Side Tavern, the good one. This was another Earth, he understood, but the voice was the same as before, a link back. In his troubled, confused state, he turned to it. Then he felt another tug, slight but persistent.

"Don't pay attention to anything but my voice," she said quickly. There was an edge in her tone, an urgency, and it bothered him. "Follow my words to the street. You will see people, but they will not see you. Nothing they do can harm you. Do you understand?"

He nodded, though the sensation of it was watery, intangible.

She hummed now, something simple, and nothing he'd heard before, though it was pleasant enough. Such juxtaposition of contrasts, a disembodied musical voice against the backdrop of blood, darkness, and gloom, carried him out to where the low slung moon wavered, his own swimming through a sea of murky possibilities. He was instantly reminded of the priest, how his own imprint overlaid others. At that moment, he struggled to see his moon more clearly, to help it emerge from the others before and behind it, and the overarching cloud cover.

The humming ceased. "That's good," the voice encouraged. "Don't stop doing that, but you must hurry with me. My time is short." She took up her wordless song again, leading away to the corner. Jorj followed, keeping the moon in his sights. It was easy to do until they turned onto North State Street, for once there, the buildings to his right swallowed it up. Dark blue no longer, the sky winked out its stars one by one. The drifting path to Dennis' truck was slow. At first he could not see it, just bare road ahead. He thought maybe he'd been led down the wrong street. In that moment he looked again for the moon and found it between two buildings, partially obscured by the trees beyond. It was clearer now, more his own. He turned his eyes back and there was the crappy Ford pickup truck, closer now and catching the first of the predawn light. To the right of that was a barrel in a parking lot, smoke lazily drifting out the top, no hint of flames within. He made for that.

"I must leave you now," the girl announced with obvious regret. "Beware of Jed. He is near. I cannot stop him."

With that, the sun peeped its unstoppable edge over the horizon. Jorj's head swam and then gravity turned him over onto his stomach and chest. Cold pavement touched him everywhere the Earth hugged. Once again, he was naked.

His first breath of air was sweet, even for Twilight Earth. Compared to the other place, one step closer to hell than he liked, this was heaven. Of course it was not truly, but it was better, and did not offend his senses so.

Three minutes later his bare feet padded coldly by Dennis' truck on his way across North State Street. He crossed the sidewalk between himself and the front door to his apartment building and ascended the steps, tired and still trying to sort out the night's confusion. At the top landing, a concrete slab worn smooth by feet and rain, he stopped. On the front door, nailed deep into the wood so that any loitering wind should not blow it away, was an 8 x 10 piece of white paper. Upon it, written in the strong characters of a man's hand, were these words:

> Who knows where each leaf blows
> Under the thistle moon
> Every one dries a different curl
> To ride the omen all alone
> And if they tell you, falsely tell you
> You are we, and we are they
> Just remember, they fall before you
> Into graves of deep disdain
>
> Is there something in the sunshine
> That marks us for our day?

For we buy it hook, line and sinker
And then we watch for a refrain
Because our hands hold onto nothing
Our dreams are filled with holy words
That speak of riches, endless riches
As we hang in trees being eaten by the birds.

"You have chased the night, Jorj," a man's voice spoke with confident amusement, "and it has found you."

Jorj turned but it was gone. The sun's first rays were reaching out, stretching towards him king-like. He waited for the voice a moment longer and then went inside, his mind full of things he needed answers to. The fact that his door was neither locked nor closed eluded him altogether as he reflected absently on Martin Luther's fate.

5

That day he drank. He could have said it was not to get drunk, that he just needed to tranquilize himself after the bad night he'd had. One might have excused him under these circumstances, if one knew his circumstances. Of course none of this mattered, to him or anyone else. This was Twilight Earth, if to no one else but its inhabitants. Even drinking held little escape. In such a place, one could only become accustomed to the numbness, the callous, the extra step away from what idiots called heaven. And that, more than anything else, was the greatest threat one could have.

He was surprised when Dennis came by. Even more surprised when he refused to answer the skinny bastard's persistent knocking. After everything he'd been through, he still carried the grudge that Bill, if no one ever told him, and maybe if they did, would never carry, though he had every right. Instead, he drank from Chad's collection of warm beers, beers of the world. The man was a collector, and Jorj, the spoiler.

He wondered if Dennis read the poem someone else had written, and if he credited that piece of macabre nonsense to himself. He should have ripped it down and he knew it, but he just wanted clothes at the time, not to straighten out the world.

Through the course of the day, around eating, pissing, and filling his bloodstream with warm, crappy alcohol, he thought about the girl. Not necessarily because she was a woman and he a man, although there was always that. She saved him, helped him find his way back. Hadn't she led him away? She was certainly with the others, and they played a part in his wandering off. Wasn't she at least partly responsible for his own entering into that Nether Earth, or whatever the place called itself? It sure wasn't here. That West Side Tavern was not Nick's. No way.

A lunch of crackers and cheese wiz left him marooned in lethargy, but he managed. Thoughts of those poor bastards missing their limbs and wanting to die kept regurgitating. At times he considered Bill's plight, to have a lie stand in the way of possible madness, and he wanted to cry in anger. But he drank instead. What kind of god, he wondered, let this happen? But he knew he didn't believe in a god, at least not anymore, and certainly not the one who managed puppet strings in the Arab, Old, and New worlds, completely fucking off Asia. That, he decided, was utter nonsense designed by a partnership of ignorance and stalwart political organization through the centuries. He wanted no part of that.

It didn't help him any though, considering that it left a colossal vacuum in what to think of it all. Let the priest have his cathedral of gloom, with his hopelessness and suicidal solutions. He'd have none of that. Nor Theodore's cracker barrel war planning. They could fight for the crumbs of humanity's future all they wanted on the floors with the dogs until they all became the same fucking animal for all he cared. There had to be something better. If there was, he wanted to find it.

Later the light began to settle. He threw the sliding glass door of the front balcony open and looked out beyond it to the street and the parking lot left of that. The barrel waited like a good soldier, but it needed wood. He could provide that, he decided.

In Chad's front closet Jorj found a Carhartt jacket, frayed at the cuffs and collar, but serviceable enough to keep him warm. He put it on, finding it slightly large—Chad was a big man—but that was okay too. Better large than too small. Tomorrow he would find a pair of shoes that fit exactly right, and jeans, underwear...the works. For now, he made do.

In the back lot, behind Mike's mechanic shop, was the back lot of a small-scale construction contractor. Jorj picked out three pallets, mostly overgrown with weeds, and hauled them one by one to the barrel where he broke them up and shoved what he could inside. What would not fit he made a loose pile of nearby. It wasn't neat, but let the ghosts complain. Let the night folk cry big sloppy wet tears if they could. They'd get over it.

He hunted further around the neighborhood. Wherever the people, in their long, dark leather, got their wood, it wasn't close by. He wondered if they imported it from their half-light travels. If so, it was mighty kindly of them to burn it here. Of course, he didn't understand any of it, only that the night folk intrigued him. And if they led him off again, he decided, he'd kill every last one of them.

Until they did that however, he wanted to find out more about them, what they did, why they avoided the light, or why it did not permit them entrance into its world.

In the evening hours, specifically the last one, where twilight formed a thick, hazy line with the night, he lit the wood ablaze, starting it with old, out-dated newspapers, laughing bitterly over the fact that every issue in them mattered not a jot, and waited for his first contact. He was not disappointed, nor did he have to wait long.

First it was the boy who appeared, at the far end of the parking lot like before, the little smart-ass he liked and disliked, he who threatened to be a trust-breaker, and a future friend. A bottle wrapped his fingers around itself. The kid needed someone watching him, Jorj mused, a good guide. When the cigarette came out, he could only laugh, for here nothing like that mattered, and he was a fool to think otherwise.

Across the fire from Jorj, a man smiled thinly at him. He was here the other night, Jorj noted, the guy with the long leather coat and the close-cropped brown hair. Wasn't he the same guy? He was no older than Jorj, and probably a little younger, but he carried himself like an old army sergeant. He also lit a cigarette from the flames before him, heedless of the flames which danced over his skin. It was obvious that he did not care.

"Jed." Jorj wanted that out front.

The man laughed, but any sound was lost to them both.

"Not Jed," a female voice...the female voice, answered from behind. "We don't allow Jed to come among us."

Jorj sighed and looked hard at the man across from him. "Does anyone ever talk face to face around here?"

The smile on the other flat-lined. He raised the smoke stick to his mouth and dragged long and meaningful. Jorj saw a long scar extending from the man's left temple to the other side of his chin, cutting right across the bridge of the man's nose. It was thin and pink, not a stitch mark upon it. Up to now he never had this close a view.

"Knife slash," a male voice explained, though the cigarette was still in his mouth, and smoke still filing down into his lungs like a chimney in reverse. "Missed my eye but found my heart on the next stroke. Lucky me, eh?" The man had brown eyes. Neither of them regarded Jorj.

"Telepath?"

"Jeezuss!" His voice again. Angered? annoyed? It was tough to say.

"Sorry," Jorj conceded. "I'm new at this."

"You wonder about us." Her voice again.

"Would you please come to the fucking fire?" Jorj nearly shouted. "I don't like disembodied voices unless I do the disembodying!"

"Crude." She came nearer. He didn't see her yet, but he felt her. "You certainly are a bloody man. Quite capable."

Jorj's face reddened. "Not before I came here, goddamit! I do what I have to now."

A silence reigned. The man across the fire, took another drag and regarded Jorj a moment. Suddenly he was gone. Just like that.

"Wow." Jorj acknowledged sarcastically. "Mysterious. What are you guys."

"Who are we," the female voice corrected irritably.

"Whatever."

A sigh, perhaps no more than the wind. "Like you." Her voice lost some of its edge, less of the harshness. "After last night, you should know. You straddle the horse with both legs now."

"Come again?"

Silence. Then...

"How confused the immigrant is," she nearly laughed, the sarcasm, thick and sad, spilling from her like syrup. He dies into his world, his Twilight, and then dies in the night, and he asks us who we are."

"You died at night." Jorj extended it as a statement.

"Bingo!" The child's voice, though it was excruciatingly thick with arrogance, and bitter amusement.

"And you are stuck there." Again, Jorj exposed his penchant for the obvious.

She appeared to him then, at his left side, staring gently into the fire, pretty but for the left half of her face. He could barely see it but she'd been in a fire. The scars said so. Her hair was black, and it might have been dyed that way, but Jorj didn't think so. Her sadness ran deep, overpowering any anger within, no matter how potent, and he knew she was not to be trifled with once her ire was up. She was of that distinct nature.

A tattoo ran along the inside of her right arm, a dragon wrapped around the Christian cross, the two locked in bitter struggle, one of movement, the other immoveable. Over her hand was a black lace glove with the fingers cut out. Between the first and second was that damnable returning cigarette, smoldering relentlessly away, the last years of a lost soul. "However little it matters in the long run," she said to him quietly, "what you did last night was humane."

"It was barbaric."

Silent at first, she responded finally, never taking her eyes away from the flickering tongues of heat. "As you said yourself, you did what you had to."

"So I did." He joined her in her fire vigil, wishing he'd brought something down to eat or drink, glad in a way that he had not. He wanted to say how awful it was, that what was practiced on that side was an utter abomination, but it didn't need to be said. It was a waste of time here to banter the obvious.

"I would show you more."

He looked at her again, and she was gone. "Why?" he asked the darkness, but she did not answer. The boy and the man, they too, were both away from him. It was some hours later before the fuel was spent, turned ashen without glow. By that time he'd gone inside, to the apartment once occupied by a man named Chad, now just another space with things in it.

No more phantoms disturbed his night. No notes from Jed waited for him in the morning. It was as if he was given time to digest what he'd seen, and what he'd heard. In the morning, after a few hours' troubled sleep, he lay in bed, watching as the sun entered through the window and crept over his new 'life.' Somewhere, in a place he could not fathom yet, the woman of the night wandered in her own soul searching, perhaps wondering about him, perhaps not. But he, Jorj Tory Watchman, had difficulty releasing his thoughts from her.

He spent that next morning moving furniture and food from the various apartments to his own, a fairly easy task considering it was empty. What he wanted, he took. No one was coming for them now. Not Chad, not Sol, nor Chad's mother. The Hildebrandts, sole occupants of the fourth floor, would never miss their many canned goods. Jorj cut into the wall of the living room and built a hiding place for them that afternoon, leaving enough space for a few other essentials someone might find worthy of stealing. He covered it over with a flat screen television. If it didn't work, he reasoned, they'd leave it where it was.

It was about mid-afternoon when another knock sounded downstairs on the front entry door. Jorj eased the glass balcony door open quietly and padded out onto it. When he looked over the railing, he saw that it was Dennis. He let him knock some more, let the man's frustration build, and then tossed a penny down so that it bounced off the top of Dennis' unkempt head.

"Why didn't you just answer the goddam door!"

Jorj tried to smile but couldn't quite find it in himself. "I want to be alone. What's so tough to figure out about that?"

Dennis squinted up at him, not because of the sun but because of the angle he cranked his head at, and maybe, Jorj realized, his eyesight wasn't all that perfect. "Nick want's you to come back. He wants to make a deal with you." He put one hand in his left jeans front pocket and ran the other through his red hair. "He also said to say he was sorry about Bill. If he knew, he would have done something about that." Dennis waited and then added. "C'mon man, open up."

"Tell him I'll think about it," Jorj replied impatiently. "Tell him also that part of the deal is that he comes clean, about everything."

"Can I come up?"

"No."

It did Dennis no good staring up at the balcony. Jorj had gone back inside. After a minute or so of loitering, catching sight of the burn barrel and wondering about that, he turned, descended the front steps, and walked off, casting barely a glance at his nigh defunct pickup truck.

One more night, Jorj decided. He wasn't giving up the apartment at any rate, but if he hooked back up with Nick and company, this would be his outpost, his way station. He just needed to stock it better.

About a quarter of an hour passed when he heard voices down in the street. They appeared to be arguing, for the pitch of one rose and fell while the other, though keeping his own voice low, hardly lacked for anger. Jorj stepped up to the wall adjacent to the balcony door and peered around the edge of the glass. Some thirty feet from Dennis' truck, on the far side, Frosty and Bermuda Shorts stood facing each other, the former with a rather large pistol to the latter's forehead, pressed so tight that Bermuda Shorts teetered back on his heels. Needless to say, Frosty looked pissed, and it was his voice that ran low, like a troubled engine.

"Go ahead, ya icy-souled bastard!" Bermuda Shorts' sharp retort to something uncaught by Jorj was a nervous one. "I'll be back!"

"In the alley?"

B. S. stiffened noticeably.

"Yeah, baby! Didn't think I knew yer hidey-hole, didjah! I got my people waitin' there."

"You wouldn't."

"Oh, cut that melodramatic crap with me, man!" Frosty's words came out in thick, short puffs of steam. "How long you known me?"

"F-Five years now...no six!"

"And you still don't think I'd..."

"Ok! Ok!" B. S. shook uncontrollably. It was easy to see that he was trying to hide it but failing miserably.

"Try it one more time," Frosty ordered with mock amiability. "How much does Benedict know?"

The answer did not come immediately which was most unfortunate for one of the men in the street. In a flash, Frosty pushed B. S. backwards and shot him in the right knee. A stifled groan squirted out past the latter's lips, culminating in truncated gasps. "Theo! He know's Theo's dead...dead and gone, alright you bastard?" His voice echoed dramatically throughout the barren neighborhood.

Another shot cleared the skies, the bullet passing within inches of something more valuable to Bermuda Shorts than his obnoxiously well-tanned knee. "How long has he known? And call me a bastard again, you'll see how surgical I can get with my rounds."

However many times B. S. might have been shot in the past, he didn't show signs of becoming accustomed to the pain, or threats thereof. His gasps slid into groans, partially of pain, partially of fear. "Since yesterday afternoon." He grunted out at last.

Frosty calculated silently. "He'll be makin' his move in that case." The icicles adorning his words broke off and pierced B. S.'s soul, dragging him down further into his fear of Frosty's malice. All his animal noises lulled suddenly. He stared up at his long-time partner bleakly, no words on his barely parted lips. Frosty continued. "So what to do with you." It was not a question, therefore B. S. didn't bother offering up an answer. Rather he reconciled himself to thinking a way out of what he, personally, would do. His shivering stopped. Perhaps it was shock, maybe that calm which rolls over certain individuals when faced with the final hand to play, when they've only just looked at the cards. Frosty noticed. When he smiled, it was truly terrible. "And you still think we're that alike." Yet another statement. "You can't get into my head so you play yourself." His words were reviling. "I was never like you. People say I'm a bad mutha fucka," he said this with an obviously intended ghetto slur, "but you're fuckin' sadistic. You killed Theo, didn'tcha? Didn'tcha!?" He yelled the last one. The vein in his right temple pumped hard, always a sure sign he was near the end of whatever he was at.

"And what was he to you?" Bermuda Shorts croaked the words out like evil toads, his own anger overtaking his fear, his loathing of himself and his situation. Somehow, and to Jorj it seemed strange that it should be so, the hatred in his voice ended there. What the man harbored for or against Frosty was akin to regretful respect, and a clinical death wish no different than he would have wished on anybody with the power of his life or death in hand. "He was on the out and you knew it! No way he'd sign a pact, not that one!" He grit his teeth and swore, the pain in his knee spiking after a savage kick from Frosty's right boot.

In a low, even tone, barely loud enough for Jorj to catch, the black man, bundled up in his ski jacket, still pointing his heavy pistol just south of B. M.'s gut, uttered an epithet back. "You just blew every chance we had for somethin' better! Don't know WHAT Benedict's people paid you, but I guaran-damn-tee you ain't gonna git ta spend it!"

"I told you what you asked!"

"That's why I ain't gonna shoot'cha." Frosty tisked. "A shame too. I gotta be a man of my word, even if I was only thinkin' it. No, I ain't gonna waste the bullet neither." He saw something in B. M.'s face, or maybe his posture, and then shook his head. "You may well wish I had before the night's out."

Bermuda Shorts held his damaged knee with two bloody hands, his lips working in a silent mumble. He began to shake his head. "No," he whispered.

"Oh yeah," Frosty replied. "I'm gonna let the night judge you. Gonna tie you up and you can sort it out with whoever shows up first, the Good Lord or the bad, bad devil. The latter might have offered you a contract too, if you hadn't already signed one." He waved the gun at Bermuda Shorts. "Get up."

"But my knee…"

"I don't care 'bout your damn knee! Git up on your good one or I'll blow that one out too and make you crawl. Use it or lose it."

B. S. glared but he did get up on his left peg. He wasn't steady, but he stood before Frosty in hunched defiance, waiting for the man's next move. Blood seeped pretty steadily from the wound, and began forming a small puddle around his right foot. His face looked ashen. "I'm gonna die again!"

"You will if you don't sit down soon and tie that thing off." Frosty motioned him off to the curb. "Git over on that storm drain grate." While the other half hopped, half limped, he produced a pair of handcuffs with his left hand and threw them on the asphalt within a yard of the steel grill by the side of the street. "Soon as you sit your ass down, fix your left wrist to a bar.

The injured man sat down awkwardly, wincing dizzily at the pain of his wound. Quite against his will, at the direction of another threat, he did the deed. Frosty promptly shot him in the right tricep. B. M. cried out and then clamped his mouth shut, moaning behind his teeth. Whatever words lay behind those perfect ivories would likely get him killed, and he knew Frosty's closest men too well to want to take his chances with them for a easy return.

"There now!" Frosty grinned, his own teeth, white and crooked, beaming back like a broken fence. "Ain't that just a fine thang!" He could speak all 'white' when he wanted to, but that cliché pigeon slang was expected, and kept white people off guard most of the time and added that touch of dramatic flare.

"You're like him."

The voice broke over Frosty like a hammer, mostly because he wasn't expecting it. He spun, the pistol, no longer needed to keep the tormented B. M. in check, pointing outwards in the direction he thought the voice came from. "Who the fuck's talkin'?"

Jorj stood on the balcony, shotgun in hand, loaded, and beaded on the wintry-dressed man below. "Kill him now or I will, after I kill you." It was an even shot probably, deer slug against a pistol at this distance. He doubted Frosty would care to chance it without at least exchanging a few words. He was right.

Both men faced each other, the one below lofting his pistol at the one above who he saw quite clearly now. "What's he to you?" Frosty shouted. "You one of Benedict's boys?" His eyes flicked left and right. Mostly his ears perked for other outsiders.

"Nope." Jorj's voice carried pretty good from the balcony and he found he liked that. "Just don't like torture."

"If you wuz listenin', you know what he's got waitin' for him back at his startin' line."

Jorj frowned. "I know what he's got waiting for him after dark." He paused, then added. "I don't think you do."

The man on the storm drain was half out of it all, half listening, half conscious, half alive. But he lifted his voice to be heard anyway. "I'll deal!" he cried out. "Cut me a fucking deal!" He began to cry for real, like a small child. Once, Jorj recalled, he had a teacher who had a phrase he liked to repeat to his kung fu class. 'Fatigue makes cowards of us all.' It was a lesson about staying in shape, but the deeper meaning was self evident. Everyone has a bottom. Bermuda Shorts found his. There were some things he would not announce, even to death. To Frosty's nose, it was self evident, and he found the odor vile enough to let it distract him from the man on the second floor balcony with the hunting rifle.

Frosty's real name was William. His parents thought naming him that was a funny thing at the time, cute even. It was not surprising, in their juvenile, stoner way, that they should think so, considering that the shared last name was Bender. Willy Bender, he mused. Haha. His old man lasted just long enough to name his son something stupid and then get himself shot on Fifth Avenue in New York, right on the steps of Saint Thomas' cathedral. His mom, last he knew, in that oh-so-long-ago, was still doing time for pulling the trigger. As a matter of fact, he was on his way to visit her in the pen when he, himself, got capped off. What a world. What a life.

It wouldn't do to ask him why it was that the smell of Bermuda Short's offal reminded him of Theodore. Maybe he didn't know himself. Assuredly he wouldn't have told anyone regardless. The fact served itself and nothing more. He didn't even think that he could have been more angry than he was at that very minute, when he looked into the eyes, those cold blue eyes, of Kevin Spencer, the man who died in Joo-ly, but he was wrong, oh so wrong. The fact was that he hated weakness with such a mean streak that it put him in a murderous mood. That a man, any man, could soil himself out of fear so raked at his good senses as to push him right up to the edge of his patience. He leveled his pistol at B. M.'s head and spat over his right shoulder onto the street. "I'll deal with 'Hero' later," he mumbled, just loud enough so that his partner of five years could hear. "This ain't for you!" he yelled loudly, so that Jorj could hear him well. "This is for me!"

He pulled the trigger once and lowered the gun, turning as he did so. "There! Ya happy?" Before the last word left his lips, he raised the pistol again and fired three more shots, even as he dived behind Dennis' pickup truck for cover against return fire. Two of the rounds hit the outside of the apartment complex. The third shattered the window behind the balcony where the interloper stood no more than thirty seconds before.

By then, Jorj was at the bottom of the back stairs, cursing over the physical damage and irrevocable loss of anonymity his hard built sanctuary now suffered. He kept his word by not shooting Frosty, but the feeling that whatever wisdom existed for it still danced out of reach could not be shaken. Dennis didn't need to warn him about the man being dangerous. It was obvious from the first.

He eased the back door open, slowly at first, and then enough to allow him an exit. Outside was the back alley, all gravel, a couple scraggly city trees, and weeds. The sun no longer sprinkled on any of it now, pointing to late afternoon. In the shadow of the next building, he crept out, keeping the shotgun ready, hoping he wouldn't have to use it. Adjacent to him was a large three story house, four if you counted the attic which promised a fourth tenant to the slumlord crafty enough to dodge city regulations. Around the edge of its own parking lot yard was a low, crossed-wire fence, painted green presumably to help it blend in, and propped up by long, narrow, metal stakes. He raced through his options, at the same time remembering what happened to him the last time he hopped a fence. To go around either side of the building meant possibly running into one of Frosty's bullets. Of course the man might also have backed off, but more likely he was working his way towards him, in which case he needed cover where he would be able to eventually have a way out of the neighborhood. He might have stayed in the apartment, he realized, but buildings have their disadvantages too, mainly in the ease with which one can watch the entrances, especially if they can call in friends. Jorj didn't know what Frosty's resources were at present, but it was plainly better to be mobile. He made his choice and clumsily hopped the fence. The rest was easier than he expected, which was troubling in itself. He had a destination in mind, had one for a day or so which led back to Nick's place, that weird little way station called the West Side Tavern. It just came a little too soon. If he wasn't careful, he either wouldn't make it, or he'd have a shadow, neither being an acceptable outcome.

His decision to take back yards and alleys to Mercer street at the other end of the block, he considered the best. Cross over, take another block or two out of the way and then circle back, that was the plan. But he hadn't yet stepped out into the open of that once busy byway when he heard shots. Instinctively he ducked down and rolled to the side, changed position, and peered out from the corner of a house turned store front, turned abandoned, hollowed-out ghost. It occurred to him that nothing flew by him even close. At that moment, he heard someone shout. It was Frosty.

"Ya missed! But I got one o' your boys back a-ways. Got another one on the run, too! You lookin' ta tangle wit' Mr. Bender?"

"Give it up, Willy!" A voice, deep and rough, called back. It was all business, not an ounce of humor or banter in it. Jorj darted his eyes around. Assuredly the owner of that voice, if he had friends, would be fanning them out into flank positions. He had no desire to be caught in them, and as a matter of fact, thought it a good time to depart. Let this bunch have their party to themselves if they wanted it. But then he heard something that glued him in place, forbade him to leave until he understood what it was that echoed across the wide expanse of Mercer street. "You know what we can do, to you and for you. Theodore couldn't stop us. Neither can his friend Nick. You've got a reputation that's attractive to our organization, but not if you force us to do bad things to you first."

"Don't know what you got against Nick," Frosty shouted. To Jorj's ears it seemed that he was a little closer than before. "He's just an old fool with a good restaurant. As for Theodore, that's a different story. He's worth taking your head off slowly, with a dull knife!"

"Bravado, Mr. Bender. But I think you make your position quite clear."

Noise rustled to Jorj's right, from behind. He turned, leveling the shotgun as a man in urban fatigues came into view. The newcomer carried an automatic rifle and harness for his extra clips, but nothing else. Clearly he didn't see Jorj, which was very bad for him. All that the former needed to pick a side in this little war was to hear that these were not Nick's friends, and that by inference, they meant to off him like they did Theodore. With one sharp movement, he picked his target and let the rifle speak. A single word of death and rebirth connected one to the other and the creeping man, geared for war as he was, fell by the same sword, his right eye competing with his brain for the biggest mess award. Jorj ran up to where the man fell, to make sure he was dead, and found only the broken branches and blood.

The voices fell silent, each certainly making rapid battle judgments, connecting them with each other. Jorj fell back and circled right, wishing he, too, had some clothes that didn't stand out so much. That very thought made him collapse to the ground and remove the white t-shirt, wondering why it was that luck allowed him the first drop. He grabbed a handful of mud from the bank of a narrow side yard that adjoined a driveway and smeared it over his back, chest, arms, and face. It was ugly, but better than creeping along like a flashlight at night.

He thought, too, that an automatic rifle would be handy. But such things could not be taken off of dead bodies here. This world was an open graveyard, but the corpses didn't stay down long, and they left absolutely nothing that they carried behind. Jorj didn't even try to figure it out. That was way back on the list, behind Dennis spilling out of his truck and after Frosty's winter coat in the fall.

Mercer street had few buildings that were of any use in a real gunfight, and none close by. All were pretty much of the same height, and close together. Unless someone was stupid enough to cross the street shooting, they couldn't see much. Worse, once someone saw you at a window, and Jorj knew this from his demolition days, the walls around it would fall away like paper, unless you happened to pick one of the crappy houses with asbestos shingle, but that was a gamble too. Still, he found, once he picked up his own rifle and moved along, that every building drew his eye.

More gunfire now, to his direct left. Semi-automatic rifles reported, one after the other. Again, none followed in his direction, though he did hear their ricochets, and some of those found their way nearby. Frosty was out-gunned. Jorj might not, at another time, have cared what happened to the man, but circumstances put it plainly to him. If Frosty bought it, then it was just him…him against an unknown quantity of well-armed men. And then there was Nick, and Dennis, the priest, Frank, and Bill. He had to warn them.

But there was a connection between Frosty and Nick, too. They both knew Theodore, sure, but the other speaker out there lumped them together, triangulated Theodore and Nick with Frosty, as if there was more of a relationship there, and Nick's being consequential enough to spill blood over.

"It doesn't have to be like this, Willy." The speaker, alarmingly near, went informal again. He was playing good cop. Amazing that the bastard could switch roles so easily, Jorj noted irritably. "We're taking this piece of real estate soon enough, and when we do, you'll turn up sooner or later…or run off as best you can." It was a taunt, one for which the time of reply was over for wise men.

Silence. The time for giving away position was over, at least for Frosty, and Jorj approved. The speaker, however, had yet to get the point. Did he have that many men to cover his folly? Or was he that arrogant?

"You have no men anymore. Theo's core has been infiltrated and rooted out. We know who's with us and who..."

It was unclear to Jorj at first why the voice ended abruptly, but then, not at all to his liking, he understood. A large man had emerged within sight of him, some twenty yards distant, dressed in urban fatigues like the other Jorj shot, and had his rifle pointed at him. A bullet cracked the sky and pieced Jorj's left calf, passing clean through like a fiery lance. Had he not moved, it would have sent him back to the overpass, at least there was the good possibility.

His pant leg blossomed with blood, and the irony did not escape him as he limped maniacally into cover that it was the first time he'd been shot without fatality. As soon as he felt pursuit was not instantaneous, he started unthreading the shoelace of his left sneaker. He was no medic, in fact knew next to nothing about emergency treatment, but the specter of blood loss putting him in the hands of anyone he didn't already know had him tying a tourniquet within thirty seconds of freeing the lace. Then he had to move, his senses that strange mix of adrenaline-induced clarity and the fog of reality, when you know that something very, very bad needs to be dealt with, and there is no alternative but to act.

The big man would come from a side intended to herd Jorj towards his own men, something the latter expected. For the moment, Jorj found himself at the back corner of a delivery van parked at a closed loading dock behind a low brick lock-smith shop. He'd made it that far without a shot fired, but if these men had any training at all, which was more than Jorj acknowledged in himself, they'd be on him soon. Then he had a thought, a risky one, but maybe not the worst under the circumstances.

Sixty feet away was a box truck backed up to the loading dock of another building. 'New Jack Dairy' in Bright yellow letters on a sea of rolling green grass adorned its broad sides. The lettering, as best as could be described, was made to look like Swiss cheese. It would suffice, he decided, though he needed to address a more immediate issue. Blood saturated his jeans, even with the makeshift tourniquet. In a few places it even formed small puddles on the pavement. If his pursuers looked around carefully at all, if the leisure was there, it would give him away. He couldn't tear off his shirt to staunch the wound because he left that article of bright clothing behind. He'd have to risk it, he realized, because time was the one thing he had very little of.

He scanned around him and then limped the distance, dizziness beginning it's unwanted courtship. It would have to wait. What he would have liked was for them to come right along, but this wasn't nearly that lucky, nor so clever. At the box truck, with his exit path picked out in advance, he fired several rounds at the gas tank on the delivery van until it turned into a fireball. Shrapnel answered sharply the invitation, very nearly making Jorj a casualty. He was on the move almost as soon, keeping his head down, hoping the unexpected blast would distract and confuse, and that the cloud of smoke would draw more eyes to it than his change of direction as he made his final bee-line for the tavern. A few blocks was all he needed to reach it.

There was gunfire again, and lots of it. But it still was not directed his way, something that greatly mystified him. As he crept into a hedge, closely hugging the adjacent building, he understood why. The West Side Tavern was in view, currently being shot up gangland style from the front. He could easily see snipers training their rifles on the back exit. Whatever chance he had of warning the others within was gone. His options changed immediately. He'd never find Nick, Frank, or the Padre, but he could find Dennis and Bill. How he'd explain to the latter his naked return to the garage could be figured out later. He couldn't even get close to him now, not with all the goons. At a rough survey which hardly told the whole picture, he counted at least eight men, all in urban camouflage, well-equipped, and disciplined in their murderous actions. As much as he wanted to shoot each and every one of them, he chose retreat. At least if he could stay alert, and not lose too much more blood each time he eased back on the tourniquet, he could break into another house and see to his leg wound, maybe hole up for a little bit before looking for Dennis. The dizziness was getting to him. He couldn't ignore things as they were too much longer.

Of course, the sound of gunfire, and the destruction of the West Side Tavern, drew what attention he had left away from his normal caution. When he felt a hand on his shoulder, one intended to hinder his immediate turning around, and the ice-cold barrel of a pistol pressed against his kidneys, he realized almost at once what Frosty's voice began to explain, and decided it best to hear it out.

"As you know, Dyin' don't mean much around here for most folks." The voice was Frosty's, talking low and quick. "Now a hole on the old pee-filters...that's a different story. Some prefer the stomach, or the intestines, but it don't matter. You get my point, dontcha' Mr. Watchman?"

Jorj tensed, but only momentarily. He wasn't doing well to begin with. He nodded once cautiously in the affirmative.

Frosty continued. "Shouldn't leave your wallet around. Someone might pick it up. Might know where your place of reckonin' is." He sighed, or maybe it was a laugh. Jorj couldn't tell. "They be done soon makin' a mess of things. You want ta' live, you come away from this place wit' me. If I thought you wuz wit' them, I'd a hurt you bad, but you ain't. So we go someplace back a ways, fix your damned leg, and you can tell me what you got goin' on wit' old Nick. I'll let you keep that redneck piece o' shit but the second I think you might get funny I'll hurt ya. Understand?"

Again, Jorj nodded, but he felt less together than he had before. The adrenaline wasn't keeping pace with shock. The rifle, clutched so tightly before, was slipping from his grasp and finally fell to the ground. When the blackness came, it was not heralded by the appearance of Night folk, it announced itself by releasing him from his own resistance to gravity. He leaned forward and hit the ground head and knees first, rolling to his left side thereafter.

"Shit!" Frosty squatted next to him, checked his pulse, and shook his head. "You almost gone, Mr. Watchman." He glanced up and around, noting that the gunfire stopped, followed by stray tinkling of shattered glass. "No sense wastin' things, though. He patted Jorj down hurriedly and recovered the box of shells for the shotgun. These he snatched away and then, after tucking them in a coat pocket and recovering Jorj's gun, drew a large buck knife from his belt. "See you soon," he quipped and severed Jorj's moorings to this spot. When all that was left was the blood, pooled like crimson paint on the soaking dirt, Frosty shook his head again. "Amazing!" He up and left immediately, taking with him Jorj's few possessions, and deftly avoiding the men with the high-powered assault rifles. The time, he realized, had finally come for plan B.

No one knew where Theodore might show up. To Benedict, that was unfortunate, all the more so because one of his moles went against orders and shot New Jackson City's mayor instead of taking him prisoner. It was a simple thing really, to just capture the man, to grasp the concept that killing him let him get away. Then also there was the possibility that it was deliberate. Perhaps a better deal, as unfathomable as it might seem, was put on offer and duly accepted. He, Benedict, would probably never know. The mole, quite aware of his mistake, did not allow himself to be captured, choosing suicide instead. And now Theodore was on the loose and there was no one to punish. What a crazy world.

Tomorrow, maybe the next day, he would make the drive, pay the pretty little town a visit. Tonight he had something else in mind, something he'd only toyed with until now, and one didn't play lightly with such things unless complete confidence in one's abilities was assured. He was fairly so. Everything needed to be perfect, so his scavengers did not participate in gathering the things he needed. He searched and found them himself, along with a personal guard, of course. One could never be too careful. So he recovered only the very best, and it took time, for supplies depended on the immigrants. They were unreliable at best. Still, it was only a matter of time. All things come to those who search diligently.

He was something less than an artist, which, though not a crucial thing in itself, would bear future consideration for improvement. Finesse impressed the powerful. Making that impression would have obvious uses down the road. For now, more utilitarian methods would suffice.

Upon the floor of this very dark room, every surface blackened by soot and charcoal, was a pentagram of silver, poured molten into an etched path and then cooled with holy water so that it should never be disturbed by mishap, nor crossed by anything untoward. Much depended on its integrity, and accidents would certainly flirt catastrophically. As he already acknowledged, everything had to be perfect. That could never be stressed too much.

Benedict sucked his teeth, trying to remember what was still missing. Yes! Of course! The honey. One did not catch flies with vinegar. It was amusing, how books of myth and wistful pagan pseudo-histories put such emphasis on virgins, and the sacrificing of their tender, pale flesh. What rot. Virgins had hope when they died. What did his flies care for hope? What did they even know of it? It was pain that attracted them, and despair. The pitiless distortions of one's soul against their will, the abasement of the proud, and ironic control...THAT was honey! Filling the ranks of the damned was honey. Filling it so full that it burst the seams of...well, best not think too hard on that. Such paths were always tantalizingly entrapping. And were not all the flies spiders, in their way? Preying on each other, the strong, as is always the case no matter which side of the fence you straddle, winning out? Sitting on top of the damnable mountain?

Of course it was. That is precisely why the very best honey came from the mountain top. Abasing the highest, or as close as could be gotten on short notice, was honey enough. Theodore would have been a very sweet temptation for the discriminating fly, or spider. In lieu of Theodore, there were others, enough so that he could do this again and again. As much as need be, so long as he was careful. The far flung souls, lost to God's radiant light, were not forgiving. Only their sadism aided them in withstanding the pain of turning. But they did not consider any trade equal to it, and if one let his guard down around them, even for a second, regret would not pay the bill. And blood? That would just begin things, for as he knew, there were far higher prices to pay in every world…even heaven.

Before the unhappy victim was brought in, Benedict spent considerable time in the construction of an altar. It wasn't that he worshipped what he planned to invoke, quite the contrary, but an appeasement needed to be made. He had no more desire to love or serve the thing than he did to follow its path to hell. That didn't mean he couldn't flatter it, feed it, and ultimately milk it for his own needs. The altar would serve that end in part, though the victim would not be upon it but rather within the five-pointed silver star. The honey had to feed the thing, but the thing could not be allowed past the boundaries of the silver lining.

The altar itself consisted of stones, one placed upon another, in rival of God's own in Testaments past. Oil was poured over them, and then blood, the latter for blasphemous effect. Maybe it mattered, maybe not, but with proper blowing of his own horn in this regard he just might touch on a visiting appreciation for irony. It certainly couldn't hurt. Besides, such things could be fine tuned, for this was but the first of what he expected to be a useful, and frequent engine of oracular endeavors. The thought stirred him to action.

Dressed as he was, in black pinstripe suit and red tie, he bore the appearance of a corporate Baron more than he did a summoner, at least by lay standards. But this was not the Middle Ages, nor the First Dark ones, though, he conceded, it could be argued that they were the Second. He looked as powerful as he could on this 'Twilight Earth' as most came to call it. Power was what mattered, and he never lost sight of that, not even now as he lit the first sticks of incense.

He wanted to start out small, but not too small. As an important person, and he was in his growing circle of alliances, he knew better than to crash his way into the top. Always have an 'in' to grease you through, to pave your way with solid words, brick by brick, so that when you finally reach the serpent's head, it does not bite you. That is why he chose to call first on one of the Nameless Ones. He first encountered them on dreamwalks, where there still exists a thin but protective membrane separating the worlds. Like everything in the darkness, they were dangerous and cold, but unlike other forces deeper than they, intelligence did not seem to be their strength. If one was cautious, listened with skepticism, and placated liberally, there would one learn things barred to others. If he was very lucky, one might open the door to a more powerful spirit of darkness, one willing to forge a mutually agreeable business relationship. A thin, gloating smile lifted the corners of his lips, minutely but unmistakable. Let the greater men come to engulf the land.

Let even the inevitable nuclear fire fill all the valleys with new immigrants and their ruined houses, turning this world into a radioactive nightmare of torment, death, and rebirth. He, Benedict, would be gone by then, on his way to other worlds to do as he would, dodging hell and skirting Heaven, delaying indefinitely any form of retribution natural law decreed to await him. He would deny them all.

7

'Not again. Oh dear God, not again.' That was his first thought. His second was the total absence of clothes, and the chill of the air creeping across his bare skin towards evening; cold, impersonal answer . . . yes, he was here at his starting place once more. He remembered bleeding. Had he bled to death? Very likely. Things were rather dark at the end. Staying alive was unfortunately more difficult than he expected. His tough, calloused right hand went to his throat, an act that surprised him. Everything seemed in place, though he couldn't think of a reason why it should be otherwise. The hand dropped to the calf of his left leg. It felt good compared to what he remembered. No wound, no blood, no worry.

When he rose to his feet, still somewhat in a confused state, he became suddenly conscious of his vulnerability and took quickly to the temporary cover of some rubble and the light blue remains of a minivan wreathed within it. There was a light jacket, mostly dark blue nylon with a thin cotton lining, dirty and draped over the passenger seat, well within reach through the distorted door window, the glass of which lay partially inside on the heaved floor and partially under his brand new feet. He took this, prying it carefully from its pinched place between the bent roof and the passenger seat, and tied the arms around his waist silently. The former owner must have been a large person...extra large. It was a good thing, considering. He was duly thankful.

He crouched again and listened. Off a ways, and not too far, something disturbed a metallic object, like a hubcap. It was short, and muffled, but unmistakably not the wind, and as far as he knew, rats weren't a part of the local geography. It was obvious he was not alone.

This was the second time he returned to find someone else in the area. Perhaps this was an appropriate time to break out the paranoia, he nodded inwardly, marveling at the fact that he wasn't worried, hadn't been for days. Of course there were things to be concerned over, once he thought about it, and memory slithered back into place. Nick and the gang weren't bad people, certainly not deserving of the Swiss cheese they got turned into. And didn't Dennis say Nick might not come back? Or might not be able to? That, he decided, was too bad, for even though he had his gutlessness about him—Bill came to mind—the old guy brought an order of the kind even the officials seemed to appreciate. So, Jorj reflected in that blink of an eye, if he wasn't worried, he might at least start to be motivated towards that end.

Through the weeds, over the rim of the concrete wreckage, he spied a familiar face, one with a winter hat and sunglasses to cut the glare of snow Jorj would never see. The face was in profile, eyes unseen turned away as evidenced by the angle of the head. The man was listening as intensely as Jorj. If he found his wallet, his driver's liscence, he knew the spot of return, the Kamaloka Crossroads, as Dennis put it. Jorj bet he didn't even know what that meant. Probably heard someone else say it and latched onto the phrase. Whatever the case, this was it and Frosty knew where to find him from this point on. Jorj silently cursed himself for being such a stupid asshole. Information was important everywhere. Naked or not, back from the dead or not, that wallet should have gone with him, to be burned in the barrel or some other fire of cleansing. Now he was rooted out, or could be, and there wasn't a damned thing he could do about it.

Unless, of course, he never got caught. That would sew some doubt at the very least.

Steam vented from Frosty's nostrils. It was bizarre, seeing him standing in the waning October sun, dressed for winter fun, armed to kill, and seething like a dragon under all those thermal layers. The man grimaced, as if reading Jorj's thoughts, and brought his pistol into view from the other side impatiently. "Muthah Fuckah!" he hissed. "I know you're here! Don't be hidin' on me, boy! There's no time f'that now."

No time? Jorj smiled unhappily. What was there in this place *but* time? He was sure he'd never find Dennis at the truck now. The skinny shit was probably long gone, high-tailing it out of town for better pickings and less enemies. Poor Bill likely cowered in his garage, riding out the riot of noise a block and a half away. And Nick? Frank? Padre? Who the hell knew? Assuming they were minced up in that rejuvenated house of release they called home, and it wasn't reaching to think so, they could be anywhere. Jorj was on his own now.

Suddenly Frosty jerked his head to the right and ducked down behind the rear end of a fire-blackened Dodge Omni, flipped over like a turtle to expose its useless underside to the last rays of the sun. He crept to the left and then ran in the same crouch to Jorj's left, passing briefly in plain sight of the half-naked man before disappearing around beyond and behind. The bastard had his shotgun strapped across his back. How, Jorj wondered, coming close to the answer even as he asked the question, did Frosty manage to retrieve that from the black hole of death?

Whatever he thought, there were bigger considerations now. Weeds swished on the other side of the Omni and a camouflaged man came into view, crouched at the upturned front bumper and armed with a hunting rifle. He only paused a moment before moving on, following in Frosty's wake. Behind him on either side, keeping a flanking distance of twenty feet, were two others, one unseen but for the brief movement in the weeds and rubble, the other only heard in passing. None of them were exceptionally quiet, but they were somewhat so. Numbers were their strong point apparently, and the persistence they exercised in their attempts to reel Frosty in. Jorj supposed he couldn't blame them. From what he saw, Frosty was not the enemy you wanted lurking within your borders. And these borders belonged to Benedict now. The meaning of that was yet unclear to Jorj, but through the murk of what he didn't know, sun-lit rays of what he did boded ill. He, too, needed to find a better place.

When he heard no more disturbance to what had previously been the usual birdless silence, he crawled out on the balls of his feet and his fingertips, holding agility ready in case he should have to bolt. He did not have to. Taking the way opposite from the other instances of his Lazarus awakenings, he traveled under the ghost of the overpass to the other side. There was a neighborhood there once, a run-down one if he remembered it right, sandwiched between that section of the highway and the river. Now it was a graveyard of burned-out skeletons. No accident could have spread the kind of destruction Jorj stood witness to. Only an arsonist on the level of Robert Cobb Kennedy, that infamous Confederate firebug who almost burned down New York City during the Civil War, could have achieved such wanton ruin. It looked such an evil place that Jorj skirted it's northwestern edge until he felt it safe to part company and hit a better but more secluded part of adjoining town where he hoped to avoid Benedict's boys. It would have been apparent to any who saw him that there were things he needed.

It was a small, working-class type area he hit upon one block over from the burned out neighborhood. It took him exactly seventeen minutes, with the sun sinking fast behind him, to find an unlocked back door to a small, inelegant, post-WWII ranch house. The lights didn't work and nothing hummed, leaving him feeling slightly creeped out but brave in his nakedness. He truly hated this, starting with nothing, dodging thugs, and robbing abandoned homes out of desperation. And he didn't know but that there might be someone living here, or stopping by like himself, but he doubted it. In the reddish purple of late evening, he found candles in kitchen drawer, and a large knife in the one next to that which he set aside just in case. Matches took longer but he discovered these too in a wooden garden box on the kitchen table. Before he lit the candle, he snooped a little more. He knew that in this light, all a little candle flame would do is make him a fine target. He wanted to know for sure no one was here, and he could do that better on a level playing field. Quietly he untied the jacket sleeves, let his only clothes fall to the floor, and snatched up the knife in his right hand, blade down with the blunt edge snug against his outer forearm. It was a trick his brother showed him once, better for close fighting.

Each room of the house, save the basement, he checked this way, before all light was gone. He made up his mind that whatever was in the cellar could wait until morning, but a table in front of the door couldn't hurt either until then. The back door he blocked off too, with a stool and pots and pans stacked precariously, deeming a noisy alarm better than cutting off a potential escape.

Whoever lived here before was not his size, but was once. On Old Earth what he found to wear was fashion suicide. Fortunately he cared less for that than for regaining some sense of psychological security, such that it was, and staying warm. The house wasn't, being chronically unheated on the down side of the year. He couldn't think of a safe way to make it so, at least until morning if he chose to stay a few days and search the basement. That was unlikely too. He had to stay on the move until he got out of New Jackson City, or made peace with the new landlords, and that was the least likely prospect of all. What he found he wanted now, and it surprised him, even ran a chill down his arms, was to visit the burn barrel outside the West Side Tavern, or in the parking lot of his 'old' apartment. He suspected it didn't matter so much the where. They might even find him. It was this thought that unnerved him mostly, for the girl, the woman, had helped him, but the others he wasn't so sure of. And then there was someone who the night folk called Jed. Jed was a poet…he stifled the next thought. Jorj was sure Jed knew what he was.

Once he secured the house, and had something to eat from the skimpy can cupboard—an opener was another valuable find—his real thoughts, the ones lurking in his dark, leisurely recesses, began to unfold in a relentless wave. He realized now how truly alone he was, and that it took a mass murder, however temporary in nature, to point out this elusive but simple fact. In the morning he would look up Bill. The idea crossed his mind to go and seek him out tonight, but he rejected it out of hand. The nightmares of this Earth, Twilight Earth, were not given to Mother Goose. They were quite real unfortunately, and Jorj lacked the confidence to handle them half as well as he did last time. And *that* had killed him. It would have gone very much worse but for the Goth chick in the black leather. He owed her a thank you at the least, something he did not recall telling her during their last chat, such was the shock that coursed quietly through him at the time.

The thought of Dennis, pointy-chinned, scraggly, bad-complexioned man of the fringe, sent him searching for something to kill the knot in his stomach. Not a beer in the place, he lamented, not even a stashed, dusty, half bottle of wine. When he spied the cliché portrait of the bronze Euro-Jesus, it made sense. Probably Methodist, he mused, or Presbyterian. Most Catholics—and they would have wine at the very least, had the man hanging from the cross, a gruesome way, in Jorj's opinion, to pay tribute. And that with all mention in the good book about the evils of graven images notwithstanding.

Oh well.

Every candle he could find he brought to the kitchen. This totaled nine, meaning that once they were gone, they were gone. The night, not one to care much for the plights or inconveniences of others, would take as long as it desired. Jorj hoped that in the end he would not be left in the dark. It wasn't so much that he was afraid of demons and ghosts, though he had no doubt but that they wandered where they would, and likely nearer than he wished. No, it was the thought of losing the anchor of a focus, something as simple as a tiny flame. As long as he had that, he felt mastery over the night. The darkness could drown him, and if he chose to listen to the growls and barks of the souls on the other side, he feared they might suck him in. He knew without even considering it that 'his' choice very well might not be his own. There were things about what one does that defy explanation at times. It was a most disconcerting idea, but every ounce of curiosity carried a pound of compulsion for him, and he dared not invite it.

He was never clear on when he dozed off, never would be, but he knew that it was the fifth candle that set the house ablaze by means of the window curtain. It was a clumsy affair, and one he wasn't proud of. His disregard for basic fire safety was blatantly at the root of it all. Somehow he knocked the candle over and with it touched the whole mess off. It was a wonder, he would recall later, that the smoke never killed him. Coughing, crawling, he exited through the clamor of falling pans out the back door and onto the lawn, watching the windows in their orange, dancing glow. He could not think anything other than that he was indeed the biggest asshole he ever knew.

"Nice," a voice, male and self assured, commented to his right. "If you build it, they will come...isn't that what the man said? Or was it 'if you *burn* it?'"

Jorj lurched left, even as he faced the voice. He still held the knife, something that he hadn't even noticed until that moment.

"Who's there?" He growled, seeing nothing but that which he saw before, and certainly nothing that should own that voice. "Show yourself!"

"Haha!" The child, the boy with the beer from the other night, emerged at the edge of the yard and stopped, still thirty feet away. His features seemed vague in the growing amber glow. "You oughta be in pictures! That's the most overused line in the world, man!"

Smoke swirled in orange plasma on the bad side of the window. Hot tongues licked greedily through the ceiling into the attic crawl spaces. This one was going to go up fast. Jorj wondered absently if the nearby trees would die, or whether the adjacent houses would catch. He didn't want firebug status on his conscience. He regarded the imp tiredly, impatiently even. "I was thinkin' of you guys tonight. Fire wasn't part of it though."

"Your party man."

"Where's your third?" Jorj wished he knew her name and made it a point to ask her the next time they talked.

"Gret?" It was the older male, still unseen. "She'll be along."

Jorj moved to the back edge of the property. If this torch hadn't attracted attention yet, it would, and soon. He wondered who else besides himself and the night folk would come out tonight, braving the dark and its nightmares. "I'm going for a walk."

"Sure you want to do that?" The child grinned, he seemed unafraid of the Inferno unfolding next to him. His every feature on one side blazed forth in detail, sharply contrasting his shadowed half. His was an Irish face, round in places and freckled, his eyes, mouth, nose, all arranged simultaneously in angry, jovial intensity. One could trust him probably only as one trusts a raven to steal. Jorj saw no apparent evil in the boy, but such things are not always intentional. Still an enigma to the man, the boy grinned wider. "Last time it didn't go so well."

Indeed, things also did not go well for the little, one-storied structure. For the fire, everything was progressing just as it pleased. It's tastes became more refined, sampling of the Formica in the kitchen, plastic tub surround in the bathroom, and the asphalt roof shingles wherever little yellow wavering leaf blades poked through. Colors rarely found in the natural world of combustion, greens, blues, spoke of consumption better off not inhaled by mortal lungs. Jorj left the yard entirely, turning his back on the conflagration and his own culpability at once. Immediately something inside the house exploded, sending Jorj to the clay-like mud where the back yards intersected. "Jeezuss! What kind of Christians…"

"Don't judge!" The imp cautioned loudly, never losing the dignity of self-control. "You killed four people in how many days? And one of them twice."

"Hey!" Jorj found his feet again and rattled out to the street on the block over, in front of a white house that looked a lot like the one he was in the unintentional process of burning down. His ire was up again, partially from fatigue, mostly from events. "The rules were written long before I got here, shorty!"

When the child laughed, Jorj noted, there was an air of condescension, no hint of a care to anyone else's impression. It was the dry, animated smirk of a seasoned adult. "There ain't no rules *here,* Jorj, just bars and broken glass." It was unclear which 'bars' he intended, and he wasn't going to elaborate.

Even through his 'new' shirt and jacket, the dirty aluminum siding of the house Jorj leaned against felt cold. In contrast to the heat of the fire he just left, radiating in every direction not immediately stopped by mass, it felt sharp, even here on this dead plane of existence. That, he realized suddenly, never let him down in the sensory department. Everything else could be dulled, mostly was so, but chilled unsettledness was as keenly felt as the air outside a newly plundered womb, and about as satisfying. Good thing crying wasn't his thing, he brooded.

That the child even spoke got by him almost unheeded. It wasn't so much what he said that kept his attention from totally wandering off, it was how he said it, and he made a conscious decision to listen better the 'what' of the words the little bastard spilled out into the night. Let him play. Jorj knew what that was like, to be used, toyed with by others. He considered this situation to be a little more open, though, and that had its merits. "You two bound to that fire?"

"Us two?" The older male hadn't spoken in a few minutes. It took Jorj off guard.

"That's what I said."

"Depends on where you're headin'." This time it was the kid.

Jorj started walking down the street, away from the river and the charcoal neighborhood to which he could hardly be self-righteous anymore, and towards a four-way stop where he intended to turn left. I want to find...Gret, is it?"

"Greta."

"Alright," Jorj continued. "I want to see her. And I also want to get a look at, possibly in, the West Side Tavern." He spoke low, even though the child maintained a distance of at least thirty feet, something that still remained a mystery to him.

"I'd be more concerned with your immediate situation." The man was back again, this time walking beside Jorj. He stopped to light a cigarette. The flare of a match lit the serious architecture of his face up like a bonfire before a pagan totem. The dark eyes that regarded Jorj through the shredded plume of sulfur and wood were cold, out not malignant. "Yeah. That's what I'd pay attention to if I were you."

Jorj glared at him a moment and then turned his eyes left, distracted by the laughter of the imp. The urchin walked along through the front yards, pulling from a flask every now and then. That's what I'm doing now," he answered, turning to see the man at his side no longer there. His anger erupted. "Je-ezuss! I wish you'd cut out the shadowy business!" Another chuckle escaped the child, but no words followed. Jorj stopped at the corner of Slyke and Eldridge, realizing he still clutched the knife, and not knowing what else to do with it, tucked the blunt edge closer against his forearm. He felt like a thug, even though there were no police to give him that contrasting effect. Slyke cut more or less east and west, with the latter dipping south also. He went left, following this southwesterly track, passing three more blocks before arriving at the one behind the West Side Tavern.

"Do ya think it's watched?" The urchin spoke in 'common smart-ass,' but Jorj found he did not mind.

"Likely, " Jorj mumbled back. He came to think that no matter how loud the night folk talked, or yelled, or not, they wouldn't be heard by anyone they didn't want to hear what they had to say. He, on the other hand, lacked that luxury.

"If they didn't find anyone inside, or at their places of return, they'd stake the place out."

"Presents a problem."

Jorj knew the man was at his side without even turning to acknowledge him. "You got a name? And don't tell me it's 'The Wind' or something like that."

"Sid," the child answered. "The name is Sid."

Jorj had another question, an obvious follow-up inquiry, but then another voice grabbed his attention, mixing in relief, tension, and something else akin to gravity.

"You won't find your friends tonight." Her voice struck him like an arrow, not from any intent on harm, but because it made parts of him a soft target, something he intended to settle with himself about later when his head was more clear . . . if it ever became so again. "But they are together."

"Greta!"

She continued in her clear, unhurried, cautious voice. "They hide because of the dark. Because of us."

"Then they are safe?" Jorj was almost jubilant on the inside, whatever his outer control might conceal. "All of them?"

"Even the simple one from the garage."

"Sweet Jezuss!" His relief spilled out into the night. He scanned the darkness until he saw her, two yards away under the shadow of a maple tree. "You've seen them then."

"I know they are safe."

"You haven't..." He stopped short. How she knew was less important than if she knew, and he didn't sense that she lied now. For some inexplicable reason, he couldn't imagine her lying to him in any situation, and again it caused a mix of unsettled feelings that others less trapped by conditioned manliness would call 'trapped butterflies.' He flung these feelings aside, angry that they trespassed upon the sacred ground of his self control. His jaw set itself with determined irritation and he trained his hazel eyes on her with an inner fire equal to the task. "Would you please come over here and talk to me like a real person. This shadowy crap sucks. I don't like it."

At first he thought she would fade into the darkness and emerge next to him. It was something he would have accepted, tolerated actually, but not welcomed. He was pleasantly surprised when she stepped out under the moonlight and walked over towards him with a sure and steady grace. It disarmed him to see her again, real and what seemed to him very tangible. Her raven hair, cut short on her good side, hung over the scarred half of her face in what suggested style, but in reality masked a self-consciousness he didn't expect, one she had not displayed before. In its way, it hurt him.

"Thank you," he said more congenially.

She met his gaze only briefly, choosing to land it past him for the most part. Though a calmness still radiated from her, underneath it was a tension, testing its restraints. Everything is going to change for you very soon," she told him, her words deliberate, independent of opinion.

"Everything already has," he replied softly. His tone carried a firmness that could not relinquish strength, but pulled short of assuming control over the conversation. He told himself that he could trust her now, and he intended to honor it. "The man named Theodore got knocked down today." He stopped, considered the probable time, and shrugged. "Or yesterday, however you want to…"

"Petty king, petty war." Her voice took on an edge of anger and breathed back heat. "Meaningless in itself but for the usurper's..." Now it was she who did not finish the sentence. She lifted her eyes to his. They were like wells of dark oil. As Jorj noted before, once one slipped into them, freedom from their viscosity became an almost extinct concept. "I said I would show you more. Do you accept my guidance?"

He was not ready for this. Fresh came his memory of people on gurneys, amputees silently begging for release from their lot, and of the demonic gathering in the West Side Tavern of another where and when. Was he up to another slipping between realities? He did not even understand this one. His escape from the elsewhere almost was not, and might not be again.

"I will not force you."

"I will come," he replied. "But I want to know why it is that you would show me these things, these other places."

"That is simple." She almost smiled...almost. "There is no other who will take the journey, and someone from your side needs to."

It left him puzzled still, but he conceded his fate to her care. "When do we start?"

"We already have."

The gibberish that hung in the background, that he ignored as much as he could, focused itself. He could hear a voice, a man's voice, distant but full of itself and its ambitions. Jorj could not place a face to it and concluded that it belonged to a stranger. Around him the darkness shimmered slightly and took on a tone of blood to its blackness.

"I offer this life to you, to do with as you see fit. Will you not parley?"

Silence reigned. Again the man's voice placated something unseen, once, twice, and more. There was the sense that this was but the middle of something longer, that ritual, in all the length of time that its name implied, was not a thing to be hurried. Inscense burned, and to all witnessing what was taking place, be they visible or no, the scent of it permeated, though to some it was a heavy thing, cottony and intoxicating. And though it was plain to some and suspected by others, when the new voice spoke, deeply rich and horrible, it took all by surprise but the speaker of that nether plane.

"This life hath no meaning to me. No value. What is thy sickness that thou shouldeth trade insult for boon?"

Another silence began, but very quickly the first speaker broke it, unsteadily at first, but with gathering momentum of self-control. "It is but a trifle, yes, but there is more. Should the main course be tasted before the appetizer?"

"Do not bandy foolishness with me! I do not endure the touch of your world but that there is the smell of death upon its future, far more than this miserable soul provides." A scream erupted, telling all, within and without, that the offering was at very least, considered. "I must know why, and when."

The invoker gathered himself. "You are far more perceptive than I expected," he lied. Indeed, he was surprised by what he suspected, and pleased with what he had so far discovered. "But the why and when are unclear to me. It may be that you and I are in seeking of it together, and mutually we may find it if you are amenable."

Something slopped, wet and thick. A hiss escaped a parted orifice. "Yet you confine this portal within a circle of elemental chains."

"Ah," the man conceded, "it is but a window for now. Let the door come later, when we have something more substantial to exchange."

As these things were said, Jorj's eyes turned towards Greta, seeking her own. He found them cast down towards the broken asphalt of the weedy lot adjacent they stood at the edge of. She seemed shaken, but kept her composure through it all. When he moved to speak, she placed the fingers of her right hand, tips up, over his lips, a soft gesture meant only to bar the sound of his voice. Her eyes, dark and deep, met his only briefly and her lips parted to noiselessly mouth caution. Over her shoulder, the imp child laughed quietly, holding his index finger over his own lips in an act of sarcasm. It was unclear to Jorj if he knew or even heard the beginnings of the unholy relationship on the other side of the veil. Even less a mystery to the man was whether or not the boy would care. He wondered why Greta kept his company. In the back of his mind, thoughts wandered to other questions, but then he was drawn back into the substance of the conversation at hand.

"What hast thou to offer that I cannot myself obtain?"

"I think a better starting direction to all of this is knowing exactly what you desire." The summoner became more relaxed in his business approach. It was familiar ground to him, after all. Surely we have on our side things you would have? But more importantly, and I think we can skip on to address it now without our wasting further your precious time or patience, there is this matter of death that you speak, that which has drawn you hither, and that we may, as I offered before, find profit in together where we might not through our separate efforts.

Silence, and then, "Speak on."

"I cannot say that I feel it as strongly as does your immense being, but I am aware that something impends." He lied, of course, but it didn't hurt to swell his own presence if he could.

"I wonder, though, if it is as secure in its inevitability as it first seems. There are many possibilities, as I am sure you understand. Might it not use some measure of security, that events might not teeter away from it, and therefore assure your feast, or whatever it is that you would gain from such a release of souls?"

In what at first appeared to be a discounting of the question, the creature from the nether planes of existence groaned out one of its own. "What is thy gain? That you seeketh the annihilation of your own people, doomed by fire to the outer cold of hell?"

This time, when the man spoke, and he did not do so lightly, knowing it to be more useful in this case than to lie, he told the truth. "Why I desire nothing more than to escape this world and move on where I will. Can you not see the immeasurable value in such a thing?"

His answer did not come in words, but in a sucking sound which lasted a full thirty seconds and then some. When it was over, the man sighed. "Well," he proclaimed loudly, his voice carrying the personality of a completely different mood, "that went rather better than I expected." A door opened, its sounds hollow in the expanse of the chamber. "Augustus! Prepare my limousine!"

All sounds faded to the souls loitering on the third block of Slyke. There followed a sense of relief overpowered by a secondary sensation of dread. "Alright," Jorj turned to face the woman. "I'm listening."

Her voice was broken, composure hanging on by its fingertips. "I could tell you much," she responded. Somehow all of this gripped her hard, in a way Jorj had yet to fathom. "How can it matter?" She seemed not to be so much speaking to him, as to herself, or another.

"There's no other way, Gret." Sid was there, smoking a cigarette not three yards away.

Jorj turned sharply at him, and then back at the raven-haired goth. "We're gonna burn, is that it?"

"It's-not-all-about-you." Her eyes turned on him, firm and dark.

"Tell him, Gret."

"No." She turned away abruptly. "He needs to see more, but not tonight. There is still time, and this can't be rushed."

"What can't be rushed?" Jorj was getting angry. "Look, if there's something you want me to do, you'd better tell me now."

But they were gone, Greta, Sid, the imp...Jorj was alone, just like that. "I hate it when you do that!" He yelled. If anyone watched the West Side Tavern, they knew he was there. It couldn't be helped now, he realized, not sure he even cared. He'd about had enough. There were things a man could tolerate, roads he would walk if given a reason. For some reason, everybody liked to keep him in the dark, with the exception of Dennis, and that man knew practically nothing as far as he was concerned. All the players kept their damned cards close. Well they could just...

...that was it. They showed him before. Maybe he didn't need them to do so now. He could walk the road, slip between the cracks, learn something more on his own. Sure he might have trouble getting back, and there were bad, bad citizens out there, but things didn't look too promising here if he stayed. And no one seemed too inclined on opening up to him in any meaningful way. He'd toss the dice. What was there to lose?

Slyke was a long, narrow street, dark, abandoned manufacturing shops on both sides, unlit for lack of electricity and someone to flip the light on. It was as good as any other, he decided and started down it in a westerly direction.

A breeze picked up, as it did every night the exact same way. He was glad for the jacket he wore, even if it was rather not to his tastes. It kept him warmer than without it, and that was enough for now. Overhead, the clouds drifted by, spent tissues, frayed clumps of cotton in a vast sea of moonlit black. Stars competed with the full orb for attention, neither realizing that there were few below who cared here on Twilight Earth. But Jorj was one of those few. If he had nothing else to cling to here, to link him back to what he thought he knew, however vague it resided within his memories, he had the sky and its many inhabitants. There was the Big Dipper, and Orion, and the Seven Sisters. There was always that one sister you had to look hard for, otherwise it looked like six. Tonight he had trouble finding her, as he would for the unforeseen future. She was quite shy in the silvery haze. Maybe the farthest, or dimmest sibling was afraid of the night, too, Jorj mused sullenly.

It was not so easy, he realized, this night travel. The last time it seemed so magical, dark and eldritch, forbidden but alluring in the way merely staying out all night is for children. But he was not a child, and he understood that well. First times didn't always have the lasting impact that one might wish, and his solitude, something he used to relish, was disrupted now by attachments he never asked for, and nightmares he didn't wish to be drawn into. In this light, or lack of, the night refused to immediately give up its secrets, forcing him to choose between abject submission to or outright denial of reckless fate. As Greta observed before, Jorj had much to learn. But he was not entirely without wisdom, and so he chose to merely walk the dark streets, until, in the last hour before the sun returned, Greta did also. She was alone, and Jorj knew she would not stay long. Nevertheless, being tired, and in a section of the city he neither recognized nor knew the way back from, he was quite comforted to see her.

He almost passed her, for she did not make herself seen so easily. She stood in the front archway of an old synagogue, its large wooden double doors closed tight behind her. When he spied her, he did not stop suddenly, nor was he startled, for he sensed her presence immediately. Casually, not wanting to reveal his pleasure at seeing her, he turned his path towards the nearly abandoned house of worship and came to a stop fifteen feet before the marble front steps. There he stuck his hands in his front pockets and waited, knowing she would speak when she was ready. He, himself, was in no hurry.

"You are one stubborn S.O.B.," she remarked, letting only a little lightness into her voice. Jorj suspected it was as much as she could bring to bear, and he quietly appreciated it being done on his account. "Did you really think you could find a way out on your own?"

"I thought I'd give it a try."

"And how would you come back?" There was almost a disdain about the way she phrased it, but it was not precisely so. What Jorj heard was a trace of disbelief lingering in her, and yes, something else.

"Concerned?"

She stared at him a moment, half of her face hidden behind a shoulder-length curtain of straight raven hair. Jorj knew what she was hiding, and wished he could tell her how unnecessary it was for her to do so. At the same point that he saw her close her small right hand into a fist and then flex open the fingers sharply, she spoke, subdued but clear. "Of course. Do you think I saved you last time on a whim?" She sounded almost angry, and maybe she was at that.

"No, I don't suppose so." His eyes cast to the ground between them and then he found himself taking a step forward.

Abruptly her next words carried a tone that made him cease his advance. "You will find the others at a restaurant called 'The Millhouse.' Do you know of it?"

"I'm afraid I don't." Whatever new feeling struck him just then, he hid it down deep, witless to the possibility that such things might be transparent to others. "I'll look it up."

"Nicodemus will ask something of you when next you meet," she continued in a gentler voice. "It is in your interest to follow his wishes," then she added still more softly, "and mine."

"Will I see you tomorrow night?" Jorj asked, the fullness of her words not yet upon him, but it was too late. The archway was empty, and the breeze that came and went swirled leaves through the threshold as if to give credence to the fact that she was gone. His shoulders slumped for a second, some bit of his sails becalmed, and then he shrugged loosely, reconciled to at least one bit of motivation. With something of a reluctant effort, he turned and bee-lined for a smoke shop he'd passed two blocks back. There he'd find a map, play a lottery ticket, and grab a bite to eat before the sun finally stretched its head above the eastern point of no return.

8

Only when Jorj had his fill of 'Old Timer' beef Jerky, some stale off-brand molasses cookies, and a "Cedar Springs' bottled water, none of which was especially pleasing to him, did a specific word Greta spoke come back to him. But he was sure he heard it wrong. Nicodemus? It was a jest, if anything, he decided, a name play. Before leaving, he picked up a newspaper and looked it over in the early autumn sunshine that beamed in through the big storefront window. The banner headline read, 'Mayor dies in freak hunting accident.' Below that, in smaller but still prominent type continued: 'Foul play ruled out.' Jorj gave the meat of the story a quick once over, skimming impatiently until he became bored with even that and moved on to the sideline. He used to read them first, even before the headline sometimes, because they highlighted world and national news. What was more important, or interesting, than that? The local construction deal that kept stalling? Or the increase in city real estate taxes? Local news might not irritate him any more than world or national news, but it was almost never entertaining.

A man got bit by a zebra at a zoo out west. There was always a weird story in there somewhere, but that was alright. Entertaining none the less. Another short patch of text dealt with the ongoing issues between the Jews and the Palestinians. Jorj tried to remember a time when they hadn't been fighting, or posturing before the whole miserable world. He supposed they were still doing that now. Then it hit him. He checked the date of the newspaper and it read yesterday's date. *Yesterday's date.* He took a moment to let that one sink in. Okay, another immigrant. So he wasn't the newbie anymore, not the 'Freakin' cherry pie.' He scanned the aisles again, having checked the shop out already just to be on the safe side. Nothing. Dennis told him to always travel on the 'buddy system,' that being yourself and your guard, which you never, ever let down. Jorj was working on that, though admittedly, he wasn't up to par like he knew he should be.

Well, he observed, one's 'guard' could mean a lot of things. He decided that this newspaper had just become drastically more important, and that maybe all of them had. His eyes started searching the rest of the front page. It took him about three seconds to find a story, lurking at the very bottom of the line-up, that mattered. It's title read: 'Fears grow over lost nukes.'

He froze at the sentence that followed. 'New Jackson police are currently cooperating with the federal authorities to track down the nuclear material missing from Fort Wick and, according to undisclosed sources, are confident that they will be found within days.' It didn't matter that later sentences played down suspicions of a local terrorist cell, or completely squashed rumors of a homegrown religious threat. Jorj knew better. His information came from the inside, and it did not unnerved him. The immediate implications were just beginning to form in his head, and other, more subtler ones had yet to break water, but one thing was clear. The city was in for a major upheaval. He needed to find the others quickly.

In the back room he found a duffel bag and proceeded to fill it. Several things in particular he made sure to grab. Newspapers, whatever food was decent and would last, flashlights, batteries, charcoal lighter fluid, lighters, these and more he stuffed into the satchel, realizing unhappily how heavy it was once he'd finished. It was a long haul to the place he needed to go. He considered trying to hot-wire a car, but he saw so few of these that looked in decent shape that he wondered that he could even get one that would start. And then there was the problem of drawing attention. If he didn't draw someone's fire, he'd likely lead them straight to the others, and he couldn't have that. He looked around a bit more until, in the miniscule car section, he found some cheap straps to convert the bag into a makeshift backpack. When he did this to his satisfaction, he hoisted it up and hit the road, turning left to reach the corner of Murdock and Fletcher, then turned left again onto the latter which ran parallel with his intended direction. Already he regretted filling the pack so well, but he knew they might need every bit of what was inside. No telling when they might strike it so rich again, and the store's merchandise wouldn't last forever. What didn't get pilfered soon would go bad not long after. If it was safe to come back, he surely would. That was, however, soon to be completely out of the question.

Wherever the sun touched the streets, mists rose like tendrils from a low carpet of fog. The dew was heavy each day, and would be, something Jorj made up his mind to appreciate, and not to get tired of, for it would always be there and he might always be here. The last consideration went against his hopes, but he had to face facts. There might be endless versions of existence. Whether or not he had a place in any besides this one remained to be seen.

The north side of New Jackson City was a lot like the west, now that practically all of the people were gone. Sure, more of the shop signs had Italian names, but the general makeup of the neighborhoods were still working-class. Old houses, converted to multi-family dwellings clogged the blocks on the periphery of small business main streets. What was missing, as Jorj noted on the west side, were all the cars. Even the small dealerships, with their crappy office trailers, had mostly empty lots besides. That, he concluded, indicated a strange puzzle yet to be understood. He didn't really believe that so very few people as he thought populated this city, or any other for that matter here on Twilight Earth, could or would remove so many vehicles as must have littered the streets at one time. Not that he minded so much. Gone with the missing cars was their pollution. He tried to remember what Theodore's parade of vehicles looked like. Were the cars a little the worse for wear? Did some have body repairs that couldn't entirely hide in the failing light of evening when the whole bunch arrived to stay overnight at Nick's for dinner? Were they, he asked in a moment of revelation, accident cars? Christ! He shook his head with the thought. The city should be full of slammed souls! But it wasn't. Hell, he realized at once, he saw more folk in the bad place, on the other side of night. Given the billions that split life before and after his own unanticipated end…the original one, none of it made sense. *Where,* he asked no one, *was* everybody?

An abstract memory brushed by him, looking back but not stopping. He recognized its face at once as what astronomers called 'the expanding universe.' The best explanation he ever read on the subject, and it was a rather simple one really, almost insulting but beautiful, was this: Fill a balloon with air, sprinkle it with dots, and then inflate it some more. The dots, as should be evident, grow more distant, each from its neighbor. Why that fact should nibble at his ankles so now was a mystery to him, but he couldn't deny that he smelled a connection, however much it might taunt him from the darkness of his own ignorance. Maybe Nick would have an answer. He seemed like the kind of man that was seldom short of such things.

Dansforth street was a wide thoroughfare lined with small shops, each something along the lines of re-upholstery or pizza. Trash blew by Jorj in the schizophrenic morning breeze, paper soda cups, faded newspapers, the odd fast food container, all of them as much a wanderer as himself. Only when the clatter of scraping paper products subsided momentarily did he hear something that stopped him in his tracks. There, riding on the magic carpet wind, was music, an Old Irish drinking song, he thought. There was something like,

> "They chop off our heads
> and we drink and we die!"

It was faint, but it made him laugh. Jorj realized then that he hadn't experienced mirth, real mirth, since before he first stood on two solid feet beneath the ruins of the overpass where I96 cut through Route 5. His light-heartedness becalmed but didn't entirely die, for neither did the song. He decided to follow it to its source. At the corner where Dansforth intersected Llewellen, outside Hank's Half-Price Book Warehouse, sat a long-limbed, gnarly tree of a man, barefoot, leaning back in a well-seasoned wooden armchair and smoking a pipe like he had all the time in the world. His faded straw hair was long, wild, and as scraggly as his extensive, goatish beard. A sort of floppy hat like the kind environmentalist hippies wear shielded his bespectacled eyes from the sun which had yet to cross them. On his tan khaki lap was an immense volume, at least five inches thick, opened to the middle. A leather bookmark lay neatly in the spine on the verso side. From within the store, clamoring out the open front, aluminum-framed glass doors, came the drunken Irishmen in sound, if not in spirit. Jorj even wondered about the latter. He stopped in the street to watched the man read, wondering if he should move on or give greeting.

"Grab a book and sit a spell." The stranger's tone was un-hurried, carrying that little hint of the aging academic without a real job but having pretty much a reliable opinion on any-thing of worth if you gave him the opportunity to say it. He didn't even look up as he spoke. "They're free."

"I really don't have the time…" Jorj began.

"Places to go, people to see," the man finished for him. "I know. Some patterns don't die with their owners, but what can you do?" He raised his eyes once, looked at Jorj for a second, and shook his head slightly. A small smile tipped the edges of his moustache and he returned to his book.

Intrigued both by the man and the general fresh air of the place, Jorj yet lingered a bit. His brows furrowed as he looked past the man into the store, lit only by the new morning shadow blue. Then something obvious dawned on him. "Electricity."

"Mmm hmmm. It's nice when you have it, though actual use still determines the true value."

"Right." He found that the smile he was trying to subdue would not go away. "Name's Jorj."

"Nice name, Jorj."

Slowly, in a mist of forgetfulness he would later puzzle over for days at a time, Jorj put his quest on hold, set his load down right there in the middle of Dansforth, and approached the sitting figure. "Whatever your name is," and he said this congenially enough," there's a man named Benedict who's decided to take this city by force. This probably won't be a safe place."

"Benedict?" The man looked up from his book and adjusted his glasses. "He can't touch me, here or anywhere else." He shooed away a phantom fly and went back to his book. "He is a nuisance though, but not to worry."

"You know him then."

The man in the chair sighed, yet still carried on the appearance of reading around Jorj's words. "I had the unfortunate experience of introduction and acquaintanceship with the man. Benedict has a rather magnetic personality of the worst kind. I make it my point to avoid him."

Jorj looked truly confused. "How do you expect to do that sitting here, old man?"

"That," the other returned somewhat sharply, "is my business." He jerked his left thumb over his shoulder. "Why don't you go on in and peruse the store. You might find something you've been looking for."

"Can't," Jorj replied, shaking his head. "I have…"

"…places to go, people to see. Yes, I know." The sitting man went on scanning the page in front of him. To Jorj it looked like the text upon it was written in a different language, in tiny, elegant calligraphy. "Suit yourself. Stop back later if you like. Bring some friends too. Something in there to interest everyone."

Jorj strode over to his bag and hoisted the back-breaker up so that the strap hung over one shoulder. "Never got your name."

Silence, and then, "True enough. Nice talking to you, Jorj." He looked up briefly, smiled, nodded his head in farewell, and dropped his eyes back to the page he was looking over so stead-fastly. "Maybe I'll see you around."

"Maybe." Jorj stared a moment longer, almost pressed him another time, and then shrugged the question off completely. Odd bird, he thought, but nice enough. Pretty decent actually. A regular genuine bit of self-assured sunshine. What he was doing on Twilight Earth only God, Bhuda, or Elvis knew. There had to be some mistake. With this and other unsolvable mysteries in mind, Jorj moved on, northeast on Dansforth until it turned into Alodi, somewhere near the 'Coliseum Bakery.' For what it might, or might not have mattered, he never noticed the change. One road seemed the same as the next.

Where Alodi crossed Thurber, some five blocks up from Hank's Half-Price Book Warehouse, the four corners created an interesting mix of shops. To Jorj's immediate right was Ike's artistic Tattoo, the name self-evident of the business intent. To the left, small and crammed in between a bank and a tenement, a tiny cop shop once did its part to clean up the neighborhood. Fat lot of good here and now, Jorj noted. The expansive front windows were all shattered and the glass on the inside covered most of the dark brown linoleum tile and the desk beyond. Here Jorj paused. Even in such sad shape, the place might have a thing or two of use. He quickly discarded the notion. Every time he put a gun in his hand it was trouble. Best to let it go for now. Kitty-corner from local police headquarters, once brightly lit, now dark as a pit, 'Heat of the Night' Video Rentals stood in the solid gloom of an adjacent building's shadow. Dennis likely would like browsing there, Jorj nodded to himself, even without what it took to watch what was inside. What irony, too, that it should be across the street from where the man was even now just stepping out the front door of another tall corner structure, stopping as soon as he spied Jorj. The painted wood sign above the round-topped, red wooden door read, 'The Millhouse.'

"Jeezuss!" The skinny redhead jerked back inside and yelled, "Nick! You were right!" The shade of the front window parted slightly and a familiar face appeared in the opening. A slow, casual peal of thunder rolled in as if on cue.

The reunion was an awkward one for Jorj, whose own father rarely hugged him as a child and who expected only such shows of affection from his mother. Even so, it was a wholly positive one for Nick and Dennis, if less so the others who were content to nod or shake his hand, something that suited him just fine. They sat him at a central table made up of smaller tables pushed together, joined with a large white cloth, and traded news and supplies, holding back little, although Jorj kept word of his night escapades to himself for the time. While everyone talked, he spread the newspaper out on the table and drummed his right index finger on the nuke story for Nick to read, meeting his questioning look with an expression of concern.

Nick's company escaped slaughter through advance warning. Whoever sent them word of impending doom was safely hidden behind a wall of vague answers and suddenly inspired questions. The important part was that by the time the West

Side Tavern got whacked with lead and steel, something Nick took rather well Jorj thought, they were safely setting up temporary shop at the Millhouse. Jorj's eyewitness of their former residence's demise was of particular interest to most of them, but strangely little was said in response to it. What brought Dennis, Nick, and even Frank's attention into sharp focus was when Jorj mentioned, in passing, the middle-age, professor-ish man he met outside Hank's Half-Price Book Warehouse. Immediately Dennis blurted out, "There is no such place."

Nick suggested Jorj produce his map, which the latter did immediately and spread on the table before them. "No Dansforth street, either," he remarked. "Interesting thing, that."

"It was there," Jorj insisted. "I read the sign, followed the map..." He looked more closely at the city layout. "I swear it was even on the map." When Dennis regarded him with patronizingly uncertain eyes, Jorj felt the urge to throw him through the front window, security bars and all. "Fine," he growled finally. "Don't believe me. It doesn't matter anyway."

"Oh, I think it does." Nick sat down in the chair next to Jorj, looking very tired. The man you said you saw, did he say where he was going, or what he was doing?"

Jorj sighed. "No he didn't. He just read, and spoke like I was distracting him, but he was friendly enough."

"Describe him again, if you would please."

Across the table, Dennis shook his head. "It ain't him, Nick."

"Him? Who?" Jorj was perplexed and irritable.

"Never mind Dennis, Jorj." Nick maintained a calm, persistence about him. "What did the man look like? And he didn't give you any name?"

"No name. Stringy yellow hair, and goatish beard dulled by his age, which I'd place his at or around fifty, small, wire-rimmed glasses, canvas hat and khakis like he just got back from the woods, or the university...and bare feet."

"Bare feet?" Dennis couldn't contain himself. "Hell, how many times..."

"Dennis?" Nick's tone never entered a mean field when he said what came next. "Please shut your mouth."

"No shoes," Jorj reiterated. "He seemed a lot more interested in reading his book than in finding something to put on his feet. And I didn't see any shoes at all other than my own." He stopped suddenly. "Why are his feet so important to you guys?"

"They're not, really," Nick said thoughtfully. "But he never wore shoes that I ever knew."

"Who didn't?" Jorj's tone was more demanding this time.

"Ogam," Dennis answered, sounding reconciliatory.

"Ogam." Jorj's was a reaffirmation of what he heard, audibly and without further words inquiring explanation. He expected his friends would supply that without any prompting.

"He was something of an enigma, I'm afraid." Nick shifted in his seat at the table, next to the head, for he never took that seat, ever. Out of habit he shot Dennis a glance and then almost immediately clenched his eyes to withdraw the unspoken request for a drink. This house was not stocked with spirits, nor much of anything else. Likely Dennis wouldn't bring him one anyway, given his health. It was good, he acknowledged, that Jorj brought some supplies to add to their own small store. Quietly, after a gentle pause, he continued. "Some thought he was a bum, homelessness being an old pattern with him. But he had a home, and that's something few people realized or really cared to inquire after. A bit of an eccentric, he was, but most truly gifted people are, and he was all of that." He raised his eyes gratefully, if not entirely satisfied, as Dennis set a glass of water on the table at his left elbow. It was the only thing they had in good quantity. "Thank you," he said.

"So, what's so special about this Ogam." Jorj leaned back in his chair and drummed his fingers on the armrest. "You guys seem pretty spooky on him."

"Nick raised an eyebrow and looked first at Frank, then at Dennis, finally at the Padre. He turned his gaze directly back to Jorj when he spoke. "Ogam wanted to find a way out of this world, or at least this incarnation of it. Most of us here saw him before he left, the Padre, and of course Bill, being the exceptions. He told us he was leaving in search of a place called Terminus."

"Terminus." Jorj rocked his chair on the back legs. "Never heard of it."

"Neither has anyone here. We don't know what he meant."

"Where did he dig in?" Jorj's eyes wandered habitually to the window but the shade was drawn. He didn't like that but thought he'd wait to raise the issue of not seeing if someone approached, evidenced by Dennis' surprise at his arrival.

"Padre knows, don't he?" Dennis was back behind the bar cleaning a few glasses and a plastic camper's cube.

"I've never seen it," the priest admitted with a touch of sarcasm. There was little resembling humor in his voice however, and the building rumbled in response. "I believe he took up residence in Fischer."

"The library." So many of Jorj's questions came off as restatements.

"Always was an appropriate place for someone of Ogam's disposition." Nick bowed his head in recollection. "Always reading, ever looking for something." He sipped his water and studied Jorj over the rim. After he swallowed, he grew more serious. "I know what you are thinking."

"I'm not sure you do."

Nick smiled. It was all business. "You can find his roost on the sixth floor of Fischer, but take the stairs. The elevators don't work." He held up a hand to silence Jorj's inevitable response. "I told you some days back that I might have a task for you, if you are interested."

The chair in which Jorj sat creaked loudly in protest at the rocking. He ceased it immediately. "What's the pay?" Half in jest, he managed a smile, but the meaning behind it was clear. Where was the incentive?

"Your soul, my soul, and that of everyone in this room, saved from the encroachment of hell." Nick looked very serious, but not exactly grim. "By your newspaper's account, and another development you don't as yet know, the clock ticks away irretrievably."

"Get to the point." Jorj's impatience was, by now, legendary. "I think we're crazy to stick around here longer than we have to."

"Crazy?" Nick pondered the question thoughtfully. "Let's just call it unwise to rush answers before we know what questions to ask. As to the point you push me towards, Mr. Watchman," he smiled, easy and confident, noting the angered surprise at the breached use of Jorj's coveted last name, "unless we find a way out of here, life as you know it is going to become considerably less tolerable, something I've suspected and you've come some distance to confirm. I haven't much time left, due to a bad heart, and you, Frank, Dennis, Padre, and Bill...you all have even less."

"We don't die," Jorj replied tersely, knowing how simple he made it sound, and how complicated the answer truly was. "We come back, remember?"

"You'll wish you could die." Nick took in the other man's gaze, met the deep black vacuum of the pupils, each funneling inward the gray waters of the surrounding iris. "You know it. I know it. Everyone here, except Bill," he nodded to a booth where the big man now snored peacefully, "unequivocally knows it."

"Why the hell do you need me?" He saw himself as callous in light of Nick's personal news, but he found it difficult to see what it truly meant. "Is this another form of hand-holding? Like when it took me to save..." he stopped short as Bill's snoring faltered and then slowly resumed it's long duet with the ceaseless biblical rumbling.

"What would you have me say?" Nick asked, spreading his hands, palms up, on the table before him. Everyone could see that they trembled slightly and Jorj felt suddenly cold inside. "None of us have figured it out yet, and there are a certain few who have had all the time in the world."

"Like Ogam."

"Maybe." Nick held up a finger. "He's onto things, but exactly what is unclear." He placed his right hand on Jorj's forearm, almost a fatherly gesture in its appeal. "You haven't had time to learn proper fear, and that is good. You act when you need too—when we failed to do so. That is good also. And then there is something more. Ogam somehow sought you out, even if it *was* just a dream."

"It *wasn't* a dream." Jorj was quietly adamant.

Nick sighed heavily, without dramatics. When his words came again, they were slowly spoken, but deliberate. "We're not asking you to hold our hands, Jorj. We're offering them to you, in the hope that you will offer yours. We need your strength to add to our tired own, to go the rest of the way with what some of us started a very long time ago. There is time for leaving, after we first find a few things out. It's doubtful that we'll ever get a second chance."

It struck Jorj as the most peculiar thing, this. He glanced at Dennis, expecting jealousy, or affront, but saw only agreement, sincere reaffirmation in the skinny bastard's eyes of what Nick laid on the table, belly up.

"I ain't got the brains," Dennis remarked, as if reading the other's mind. The way he said it suggested a fuzzy, honest humor in it all. "I just do what Nick asks, and I'm cunningly sneaky." He laughed. "See? Everybody's got their part in things. Now how 'bout you?"

"Frank?" Jorj just wanted the man to speak. He hadn't in Jorj's presence yet.

Frank nodded his solidarity with the others.

Now it was Jorj who sighed, reconciliatory in its surrender. "I'm going to disappoint you,"

"I think not," Nick encouraged him. "Let's start with what you already had in mind—and don't tell me otherwise. Sixth floor, but I didn't tell you to do it." His smile was faint and mischievous. "Ogam will understand as long as you don't loot."

Pessimism embraced Jorj's countenance, but he smiled back stonily. "Wouldn't think of it." He checked himself and added, "not unless there was something important."

By this time, it was almost mid-afternoon. There was time to reach the university on foot, but not to return by dark and search out Ogam's lair. Jorj knew this and accepted that it would be an overnighter. Dennis made up his mind to go with him and, if Jorj thought to protest, he decided against it. The company, and the extra set of watchful eyes, would be good to have along.

They left almost as quickly as they could put a few supplies together, mostly food and water, but also a small 9mm for each and extra clips, these being previously stashed away at the West Side Tavern before things went south. No one knew what they would find once they found Ogam's place, for Nick had only been there twice, and the others not at all, but any knowledge at this point was of value. Before their departure, Jorj woke Bill and had a small, private talk with him. The latter listened and then looked distressed, shaking his head at first but finally nodding, mostly with his head down. Jorj tapped the table between them, made a gesture of silence, and then clapped the big man on the shoulder. He caught up with Dennis outside and together they hit the road back on Jorj's cold trail.

"See?" Dennis parroted his earlier self once they hit the southern track of Alodi street. "No Dansforth street. No crazy bookstore."

"I guess I was lost then," Jorj stated dismissively, his eyes elsewhere than on his companion.

"I guess so. Look, it doesn't matter what you saw, dude. Maybe it was something...maybe you ate the brown acid and

God spoke through songs of drunken Irish..." He stopped suddenly, the smile falling from his face. "What?"

"You talk too much." Jorj pointed to the southwest. Smoke rose in the distance, a thin pillar of wispy charcoal-gray against the blue and purple-white of their shared, albeit asynchronous, autumnal sky. "What do you make of that?"

"Someone's having a campfire. How the hell do *I* know?"

"Big campfire. Looks like it might be on the other side of the bridge."

Dennis whistled. "Benedict's starting early."

"But why burn what he already has?" Jorj considered finding a higher vantage point and then dismissed the idea. There wasn't time. "Remember what I told you? What the guy chasing down Frosty said? Theodore's crew gutted from the inside out. Benedict already owns this place."

For a minute or two they stared in silence, and then Dennis, his ropes pulling hard on their mental pulleys, spoke the very name Jorj had been thinking of. "Theodore."

"It would seem so." Jorj sucked his teeth, thinking of how he needed to find a toothbrush. "Even so, it won't stop a thing. Benedict's real mischief isn't here."

"What are you talking about? He's invaded..."

"Forget this petty violence they call a war, Dennis." Anger tugged at Jorj's voice but he kept it on a leash. "And don't ask me how I know. If I'm any judge of things, you'll find out soon enough. For now, trust me. We'd do right to stay out of their way and not get distracted by what they have going on. It will only lead us away us from what's important."

They reached the campus just before noon. It took them another twenty minutes to get to the quad and from there it was just a few more minutes to Fischer library, an impressively large six-story box of windows and textured concrete, built in the late 1970s. The decision was made to circle around to the rear, skirting it in the narrow mid-day shadow of adjacent buildings. There was only one car in the back lot, a Volkswagen beetle in the handicap spot. It lacked the proper permit.

The glass doors at the back opened easily into what was once the heated, transitional area. The next sets of doors, all six exact duplicates of the outer ones, were less cooperative. Dennis licked his lips nervously and glanced at Jorj. "Glass breaks, right?" It was unclear the degree to which his sarcasm dripped.

"What amazes me is that they are still intact." Jorj studied them skeptically. Nobody in this town thought to loot the library?"

"Loot books?" Dennis was incredulous.

The head shook. The eyes rolled. "That's why you waited tables, Dennis."

"Not funny." Dennis' eyebrows formed a pair of crippled orange caterpillars. "It's not just slinging food anyhow. There's…"

"You see?" Jorj couldn't stop himself. Fatigue was kicking the crap out of his good sense. "We have here an impasse and you argue in defense of the restaurant business." He suddenly stopped talking. Both he and Dennis forgot their banter and listened intently, every muscle poised to exit in the fastest way possible, if need be, but held back by the oddity of the sound itself, for it was faintly familiar to them both, though they would never speak willingly of it after that day to anyone but themselves.

It grew from a faint dissonance to an alarmingly blaring one in a matter of less than a minute. Acorn street, which ran straight back from Bicham, the street running parallel to the narrow back parking lot, was separated by a park, itself divided by further intersecting avenues running roughly east and west. It was at the far northern end of Acorn, on the side that used to direct traffic towards campus, that the horrible reminder of every child's innocent summer evenings approached. To Jorj and Dennis, the very idea of such a thing where no child existed carried with it a certain blasphemy about it, and the threat of at best, insanity, and at worst, uninvited, gratuitous violence.

"Oh God," Dennis beseeched the curiously aloof Almighty, his mouth hanging open as the words tumbled out.

A cynical retort tripped and hung lifeless at the base of Jorj's closed, tightly-pressed lips. This wasn't the time for frivolous banter, How he knew was as cloaked as it was related to Dennis' sibling gut reaction to the distorted music-box that rolled slowly down Acorn street in their direction. All both men knew for sure was that the driver of that dementedly out-of-place vehicle was not selling 'Buried Treasure.'

Slowly, sensing a daylight horror that was inexplicable, both men resisted the temptation to meet each other's questioning eyes and instead turned with gathering speed toward the outer doors. When they pushed against them, in those fractions of seconds that slow time down so perceptibly, gravity dragged on them monolithically, for heavy glass doors rarely emphasize their weight but when they must be opened hurriedly. At the last, each man pushed past them, not waiting for full aperture, and split in different directions. Once done it was too late to change course. Jorj rounded the right side of Fischer Library, and Dennis the left, mounting the massive granite stairways that embraced the building's flanks, not stopping when they came parallel with each other out front, but racing hard and breathless across University Avenue until they reached the hill on the other side and the long, wide steps leading up to Language Hall, an old granite building with an imposingly tall, central, four-sided tower. Only for a second did they stop to catch their breaths, and then as one they ran up the stairs to the front doors, opening them wide and so hard that Dennis nearly yanked his right arm out of the socket. Later they would reflect upon the good fortune of the doors being unlocked. They immediately closed them and peered out the dusty windows set in the thick oak slabs, not even caring to check the shadowy space behind them. In their breathlessness, each man glanced at the other and began laughing uncontrollably. "Goddam, fucking ice cream man!" Dennis gasped. He sat on his haunches and clutched his chest, not from pain, but of habit when he was this tired out. "What was that all about?"

"Shit if I know!" Jorj tried desperately to sober up. He wasn't there yet. "Maybe the music? That freakin' out-of-tune music box on wheels just…"

It got louder, never having really vanished. Neither man laughed anymore. Sheer terror slid its tendrils in past their ribs and wrapped them around hearts caught in a sudden icy chill neither man could explain.

"This is stupid!" Dennis went into a poised crouch. Jorj noticed that the man trembled. "It's just a fucking ice cream truck!"

"Yeah, that's why we're hiding." His skin turned to gooseflesh. He started to speak again, to say something smart, but his tongue felt thick and his lips were numb.

Their own silence gripped them, all but drowning out the delirium chimes of the harbinger of frozen summertime spenders. Finally Dennis spoke, entirely subdued for the moment. "What should we do?"

Jorj's answer was a full minute in coming, an agony of delay for his companion. "Wait." He tipped his head thoughtfully. "We have guns, you know."

"You think they'll protect us from whatever that is down there?"

"No. Not really."

"I can't imagine what it is." Dennis' teeth were beginning to chatter uncontrollably. "This is freakin' whacky."

"Don't imagine." Despite his inexplicable terror, Jorj knew he had to keep his head, keep it for both of them. Dennis looked like he might fall apart any second and do something they'd both regret. He especially couldn't have the man split out the front door right now. They just needed to hide, to wait it out, whatever it was. "Do you remember when you first died?"

"What?" Dennis' eyes shifted in confusion. "Of course! Why the hell are you bringing *that* up for, now?"

"Just answer the question. What do you remember about it?"

Silence. Then he spoke, irritably. "I was confused, angry. Some asshole wasn't watching where she was going. She kept yammering on her cell phone and blammed straight into me. I was doing 45 miles an hour with my brake on when we hit."

Jorj pushed himself. He really didn't want to talk, but he kept at it. "You were speeding, then. God! You must have been doing over fifty before your foot touched the pedal. It's only a thirty zone, Dennis! What the hell were you thinking?"

"Me?" He was getting totally flustered now. "That bitch was the one who screwed up, took my life! You didn't see her car out there, did you? She lived! I didn't! You're blaming... what are you, nuts?"

Jorj forced a smile, as arrogant and self-righteous as he could muster. "What a reckless shit you are man! That poor woman was probably paralyzed. How old was she? I'll bet she had a family." His face managed an expression of anger-in-revelation. "Did she have a kid in the back? You're lucky you didn't come over to this side and hear the wailing of a freakin' baby. How could you live with yourself then? Huh?"

Forgetting everything else for the moment, Dennis grabbed Jorj by the jacket scruff and pushed him back against the adjacent wall with something of an effort. "No baby! No fat mama! She was alone yappin' on her silly cell phone! Probably to her boyfriend 'cuz they were gonna friggin' do it that night and I never will again without a magazine in one hand and my wank in the other!" As soon as he said it, he suddenly sobered up. Then, in an even greater change of expression, he looked up and to the side. "Jorj?"

Squeezed between the wall and the boniest pair of hands he ever saw in his life short of the skeleton in Ms. Martin's high school health class, the bigger man calmly found his voice. "Yes, Dennis."

"I don't hear the ice cream truck."

"No, Dennis. I don't either." His heart was still pounding, but the pace was slowing to something approaching normal.

"Did it park? Is it outside still?"

Jorj closed his eyes and counted to ten. "Do you feel like it's out there?"

"No." He paused, listening. "I feel a lot better, not afraid."

"You should be."

Dennis turned his face back to the man he still gripped by the collar, now drained of all passion and anxiety. "Afraid? Why?"

"Because you still have me shoved up against a wall, that's why. I'm restraining myself, but I don't know how much longer I can keep from sending you straight back to your crappy truck."

"Right!" Dennis released his friend, fingers quickly splaying wide in the air and retreating. "Sorry...got a little carried away." He took a step back. "Uh, what I said about the magazine..."

"Gimme a break, Dennis." Jorj pushed past him and went to the door, suddenly turning around. "Maybe we should give this place the once over," he said, inspired. "Since we're here."

"Why?"

Did you see what the building said outside, carved into the granite?"

"Dude, I was running, screaming like a little girl. So were you."

"I wasn't screaming." He frowned at the distraction. "And I saw what this place is...or was."

"Okay..."

"Language Hall. I thought you knew this place?"

"I was running...screaming..."

"Wasn't Ogam a linguist or something?"

Dennis crossed the central entry hall they loitered in and sat his bony ass on the third right wing step of an open split stair leading up. "He was an egghead, into languages, old civilizations...I asked him about Atlantis once and he just smiled. I think he thought I was being funny."

Jorj studied the open room a moment, noting how it was open all the way up to the fourth floor, and that the stairs looked as if they were designed with a military defense in mind. Of course they weren't, but it was good to note. "C'mon. It should only take a half-hour at the most. All we have to do is see if it looks like Ogam had a second roost here somewhere. Then we hit the library, okay?" He didn't even wait for Dennis' response but launched himself up the left wing of the stairs. "I'll start at the top and work my way down. You work you're way up, Dennis."

"You're not in charge, you know!"

"Okay!" Jorj shouted back down over his right shoulder as he turned the sharp 180-degree corner going up. "What do you want to do?"

"Work my way up!"

"Works for me!" In another ten seconds Jorj reached the top, found the right wing of the building, and started with the classroom at the far left.

He didn't need to look any further. His expectation had been that they would come up with a big nothing, that Dennis would complain for his wasting their time and they would go to the library late with nothing to show for it. It, fortunately, proved not to be the case. None of the student desks he thought to see, arranged neatly in rows and columns like vacant soldiers awaiting brains, were there. Jorj suspected they were stuffed into another classroom, stacked maybe, if Ogam was a neat freak, or piled in a haphazard clutter, if he was a distracted slob. Maybe they would find out later. For now, Jorj only entered within the spacious room and approached the single teacher's desk, ringed in tables and lit by a single lamp.

Lit.

It took him a full seven seconds for that to strike home. The building not only had power, but someone left the light on. He ran out of the room and down the hall to the solid wooden railing overlooking the front entry four floors below. "Dennis!"

Nothing.

"Dennis!" He started running down the steps and was half way down when his red-headed companion appeared from the left wing.

"What is it?"

"I don't think we're alone! Someone left a light on upstairs, and I found a room that appears to be what we're looking for." He produced his 9mm and clicked off the safety. "Better come up."

They searched every room from the top down, taking the emergency stairwells on each end of the building separately. An hour later, they were as sure as they could be that no one was in the building, which neither would guarantee. Even the basement got a once-over. Accepting it for what it was, they returned to room 64A, the one Jorj first encountered, and found that nothing was disturbed during their search.

"The book of Kells." Dennis dropped a dusty volume back onto the table he picked it up from. "What the fuck is a Kell?"

At the desk, Jorj rifled through the drawers, giving each one a quick, preliminary inspection. "Kells was a monastery in Ireland during the Middle Ages." Every word he spoke carried an air of distraction as his eyes scanned whatever his hands revealed. "That's where they kept that particular manuscript at the time."

"Great." A thought occurred to Dennis. "How do you know that?"

"I can read. Look at the back of the book."

Dennis picked it back up and flipped it over. "Oh. Thanks, Braniac. What exactly are we looking for?"

"Anything that looks interesting."

The problem was that everything looked interesting, at least to Jorj. The number of bibles surprised him, but considering that each was a different version, he supposed it shouldn't have. The *Qur'an* sat beside *The Bhagavad Gita*, the one tolerating the other's presence, the second entirely oblivious that it's existence was a blasphemy to the one. Good thing they were only books, Jorj mused, containing an eagerness within. They might kill each other if they were flesh and blood.

Suddenly Dennis gasped. He held up a book and shook it. "Jorj! Check it out! Edgar Cayce!" He immediately began thumbing through the pages. "Jeezuss Christ! I thought this was going to be a wash!"

For a second, Jorj looked up and smiled, then returned to what was on the desk. *Self-Reliance,* by Ralph Waldo Emerson lay atop *Relativity* by Albert Einstein, the two steeped in casual conversation. There was still reason in the world.

In the very center of the desk was another volume, unmarked, plain in its suede binding, each page opened to a work of simple hand-made paper. It seemed Ogam, or someone, was handy at more than just reading, Jorj noted appreciatively. But the pages were blank, at least all but one. In the very middle, a full forty-nine pages front and back, was a single page upon which was inscribed a circle in ink the color of Prussian Blue. There were no other markings, no notations, nothing at all to explain the uncomplex geometry of the endless line, perfectly rendered upon the rough-fibered paper. Jorj gazed at it for several minutes before placing it in his inside jacket pocket, a bare fit, but a fit none-the-less. Whatever its worth or unworthy, it intrigued him, and he thought it best not to leave it behind.

He also took the incense from the middle left-hand drawer, and the matches from the center one. Let Ogam come back. He wouldn't, and Jorj knew it, at least not in a way that he'd care what was left. How he knew that, he couldn't say, but the feeling was strong within him, and not one born of covetousness.

As a matter of going with the flow, he lit the candle on the desk, a big, fat, red one with three wicks. It offered a healthy glow, but only for ambience. The electric desk lamp carried the day as they needed so far for reading.

It struck Jorj that there were no books on language of any sort, an odd thing considering this was Language Hall. But perhaps he was reading too much into things, he acknowledged. What would this place have that Fischer Library lacked? It was, as he was forced to assume, just another place in which to work that Ogam liked. It could be that he had quite a few such places sprinkled around the campus, if not the city.

At one point, Jorj looked up to see Dennis sitting against the wide wall to the right underneath a window, *The Mote in God's Eye* clutched in his hands. By the thickness of the pages spent so far, Dennis was either wrapped up entirely in the story or he was jumping ahead. He suspected the former. It was an exceptional piece of science fiction, though he thought it odd to find it in the company of such spiritual giants as they'd found so far. Then he saw some of the other books, stacked crookedly or splayed on the tables by absent hands.

"The Bible According to Mark Twain," he murmured, a smile as crooked as some of the book stacks on the third table.

He turned back to the desk and picked up the *Tanakh.* "Ogam, what the fuck were you looking for?" He set it down and slid another book out from underneath *Futhark: A Handbook of Rune Magic.* It was a wide book, almost square, of the same shape, though not as thick, as his own, now lost, copy of *The Mustard Seed Garden Manual.*

"Scholar Warrior." He knew this one, had even met the author once, through his teacher, a man he expected never to see again. He flipped through the pages, remembering them, and smiling in reminiscence at some of the herbal concoctions, some of which he'd used more than a few times, others he never had the guts to try even once. Then he set it down. "I think we're done here, Dennis."

"What?" The man had been disturbed, it was painfully obvious. "Oh, man…"

"I ain't yer father," Jorj tipped in a hill-billy drawl. "Stay if it pleases ya."

"No, I'm coming." He rose stiffly to his feet and crammed 'The Mote' in his back pocket, probably pleasing Larry and Jerry, the proud parents of that auspicious volume to no end, had they known. "Find anything good?" He bunched his eyebrows, crossed to the second table, and pilfered the book on Edgar Cayce he looked at earlier.

"It's all interesting," Jorj replied, "but I can't take it all with me. I saw all I wanted to see. Let's hit the library." As an afterthought, he blew out the candle and turned off the desk lamp.

Fischer's front doors opened easily enough. By now it was past noon, and neither man felt like going around to the back, as planned earlier. If their panicked flight across the street, up the hill, and into Language Hall hadn't attracted attention, provided there was anyone on campus to see, then a short, unhurried walk to the big glass frontal entry wouldn't matter. Jorj certainly didn't have the patience to make a big deal out of it, and Dennis didn't care except that they got inside.

Within was pure spaciousness, much more so than the generously designed Language Hall. A wide central staircase spiraled up the six prestigious floors of Fischer, practically daring anyone who saw them to follow. In obscurity, but without neglecting their purely utilitarian nature, two elevators occupied a large nook, paneled in metal that tried to look like wood but failed in a way that still managed to not humiliate the rest of the building. On the periphery of the first floor, books filled shelves, while just off the middle, past the security check, a large counter station once kept librarians busy with students, tracking books, or reporting ones stolen, lost, or late. Now defunct computers formed a row past that, replacing the card catalogs Jorj knew as a kid. Which way served now, he asked nobody, knowing the answer already. What serves the time need not think of the future, for that will provide for itself, or not. If computers sat silent now and helped he and Dennis not at all, they, nor their installers, could hardly be blamed. Tables spread out to fill every other available expanse of carpeted floor.

"What do you think?" He asked Dennis. "Stick together? Pretty big place."

"Uh huh." Dennis was in awe, not from the books, but the size of Fischer's insides, and the wondrous daylight that filled it. Strangely enough, he had never been in here. "I'm with *you,* bro."

The sixth floor was not one of books in the conventional sense. It was one of large, windowless, private offices for certain retired professors with Emeritus status, clinging to the periphery of a long, narrow carpeted hall with paneled walls, separated from the stairs by another, less intrusive corridor with a front desk area. One of the doors of the inner hall actually did not open onto an office, but a conference room with a wide, oval table, presumably for the use of the privileged retirees and their guests.

It was upon this conference table that more books were laid out, with maps, both local and for farther afield, and reams of paper neatly stacked at one end. In the center of the far side was a comfortable, cushioned chair. Before that, on the table, was more paper, and plenty of pencils scattered about at the edges of what appeared to be Ogam's work area. Jorj flicked a switch by the door and fluorescent lights recessed into the ceiling illuminated the room. "Let's check the other rooms before we get too far here," Jorj called back to Dennis who looked over his shoulder from the hall.

They found his bedroom at one end of the hall. It was a plain affair. In one corner was a futon on a bamboo frame, blankets piled recklessly without even the pretense of looking organized. Next to that was a standard end table, probably dragged in from an adjoining office they had yet to look into. A lamp rested atop it, again of university issue, and a note pad. On the floor at its feet, below the note pad, was a pencil. Out of habit, Jorj picked it up and set it next to the small pad of paper, then, as an afterthought, he picked up the latter, turned on the light, for the shades were drawn, and inspected the first page closely.

"He wrote something down before he left," Jorj announced. "Can't make it out though." He held it up closer to the light. "Alright, I got three letters. How good were you at playing 'Jeopardy?'"

"I sucked, why?"

"7...P...G..." Jorj frowned. "There are other marks but..."

Dennis didn't let him finish. "Seven Pillars of God, and that's two letters and a number, by the way."

Pleased surprise struck Jorj, causing him to turn and regard Dennis with something closely resembling respect. "I thought you sucked at this stuff."

"I know the city. That's a bookstore over on Avery, on the east side. They sell mostly new age crap, incense, crystals, weird books. I used to live in that neighborhood before the rif-raf took it over, in a lower flat on Green street." He smiled nostalgically. "I haven't been back there since I had my little fender-bender." The smile faded as the sharpness of the memory decayed. "We're going there, aren't we?"

"Tomorrow, on the way back to the Millhouse. We're hardly done here." Jorj pocketed the slip of paper after folding it twice. "I want to find out as much as possible about 'Terminus,' provided we can find anything. The man was too cryptic for my comfort. I had the distinct feeling he was playing me."

Nothing more of interest was found in Ogam's bedroom so they left it to check the other offices. Dennis remarked that all of the name plates were missing from the doors. They both agreed that it reflected Ogam's claim to the place. That he took up such ownership cast a shadow on their undeniable trespass, but the task in their charge was an important one. Secretly, Jorj suspected Ogam expected them to come here and rifle through his inner sanctum. It was doubtful, in light of everything else they believed, that he ever intended to return.

As they anticipated, the remaining offices were either left as they were or used as storage. One such room was completely empty while another contained stacks of furniture and cardboard boxes filled with desktop nik-knacks and books of little intrinsic value to the philosophic mind. It was clear Ogam cared little for New Jack lacrosse, something Jorj did, back in days now gone. Eventually their path returned to the large conference room and its table of books and notes.

There were pages with all manner of things written on them, spread across the table. Some had drawings, likely in Ogam's own hand, strong and sure in stroke if not exceptionally skilled. Most of these were copied from books on archaeology, especially anything pertaining to gods. It seemed Ogam was something of a poet too, for there were more than a few scraps with verse, interesting, but not likely taken from any texts. They had a personal character to them, a similar style, and an unfortunate inability to stray far from cliché rhythm. One in particular caught his attention, for its column was tall and lean.

> The stone it grinds,
> Refining minds
> But even so
> In age it slows,
> Its spin decays

> At end of days
> And no more gold
> From strands of lead
> Within this land
> Of restless dead

Jorj didn't have the slightest clue what it meant. "Let's find a box and fill 'it.'" He looked across the table at Dennis tiredly. "Anything that looks creative and personal. If Ogam wants his stuff back he can come claim it at Millhouse."

Neither of them desired Ogam's bedroom to crash in for the night, choosing instead to scrounge for cushions and drapes for comfort, if such could be called that. Sleeping on the floor, cusions or no, was the province of the temporary, before a television, or shooting the bull with friends. Never had Jorj spent a comfortable night on the floor, nor did he expect this one to be any different.

Around 1:30, shortly after Dennis finally shut up, for the man seemed determined to talk endlessly once the lights were turned out, Jorj rose quietly and went to a window on the fifth floor, taking only a small flashlight and his 9mm. He knew well what he was looking for, but admitting that to himself was more of an effort than he was willing to acknowledge. He told himself, albeit indirectly, that it was his back, which never took well to sleeping on hard floors. And then there was Dennis' snoring, occasionally interrupted by bouts of talking in his sleep. Before Jorj could gain more knowledge than he really cared to receive, he made his decision and left the man to the dysfunctional inner workings of his troubled mind.

He had his own problems.

Restlessness was an animal whose hunger gnawed harshly at the soul. Ever since he first touched the night and walked its streets untethered, something within him burned with a fire. At first he thought he knew what it was, something arcane, primeval, dangerous. It was certainly the latter, but now it felt like something else, and he was drawn to it as a moth to flame, though he scarcely faced what he knew to be true. It was crazy, he thought, and ill-timed, misplaced, this driving force, but unstoppable. Without waking Dennis, he cast himself outside onto the dark sidewalks of the campus quad, against his good common sense and consideration for his friend's safety.

Once he crossed the street outside Fischer and rounded Language Hall, the latter's tower dark and imposing against the moonlit shreds of autumnal clouds, the vast open space of the quad sucked him in, for it was meant to do so, designed with an inviting purpose. To his right, drawing his eyes immediately towards it, Concord Chapel rested like a domed hulk, dark but its stained glass windows dimly glowing as if the very pieces of colored glass smoldered.

Padre? Jorj did not think Nick would arrange for the priest to return here, risking Benedict's new influence in the land. But then who? His bare feet started padding in a bee-line, crossing cold sidewalks and freshly cut dewy grass. The clippings clung to the soles of his feet and filled the gaps between his toes. Benedict, he decided in the unhurried portion of his mind, so often given to petty analysis, was a neat-freak...a control freak too, no doubt. In this case Jorj didn't mind. It made the walking easier, though to what he could only wonder.

The last time he was here, the sky blended with ominous clouds not his own, and thunder that belonged to someone else.

Such were not present now. Only the silence of the night, eerie in its lack of insect noises, or nightbirds, dominated. His bare foot, damp with the dew of wet grass, pressed onto the first marble step, cold and stark against the numbing existence that permeated Twilight Earth. He felt suddenly very alone out here, at the very edge of what he thought before now to be a meaningless temple. Someone lit candles within, he knew that plainly. As he rose, step by step, to the level of the large double wooden doors and then placed his right hand upon the cold brass of the handle, wrapping his fingers loosely around it and pulling neither too fast nor too slow, his heart picked up a notch, not from fear, but in anticipation.

The dream-like quality of the night was an intoxicant. There was simply no other description that fit. Fear of it, like Dennis, Nick, Frank, and yes, Bermuda Shorts felt, did not press its fangs to his flesh, despite his first experience with the darker versions of Earth and the demon souls which populated them. He wondered that maybe he was too dumb, callous, but deep down the truth spoke otherwise. There were dangers to respect, and to fear, true. There were also places not on any map, lamps covered that should not be so. The night, he sensed early, was not tamed by any man. For those who believed the day could take harness, the night scoffed, for the lords of light were merely too aloof to ward their backwaters. The night was for hunters, a test of what they were. Only the best, bravest or luckiest could hope to see the morning sun. The funny thing about it all was, that like any intoxication, once it set in, every man thought he contained all three of these magnificent qualities, regardless of his worth.

A congregation of ghost lights quivered on the ceiling of the sanctuary, mirroring the candle flames which sang their silent chorus of dimly warm illumination to the walls and pews, the pulpit and choir loft, and to the balcony in the rear. Jorj entered through the shadowy staircase to the left of this, vaguely aware that there were many places to hide if someone wished to. The likelihood of that seemed implausible. One did not light candles but that they intended for someone to come, or that they did not care who did, and Jorj was nearly as silent as the ghost lights upon his entrance. Yet if someone shared this cavernous house of worship with him, it remained for them to make their presence known.

Shadows danced to the music of the flickering yellow flames, and amidst them he entered the sanctuary, padding along the perimeter like a cat, watching everything. When he came parallel with the very first pew, at the front, he realized he was not alone after all. She was there, kneeling before the communion rail and a portion of the burning candles. Suddenly it all made sense. He made no attempt to hide his own presence. Instead, he managed a smile, though he knew she would sense that it did not come easy, and that he was unsure that it was the right thing to do. Still, he did so. For Greta's part, she did not return the smile, but neither did she frown. Instead, fingers small and fine guided the long ebony hair, pulled back behind one ear, down so that it covered the scarred half of her face. The sadness in her came out only through her eyes, and it dispelled the expression of pleasure on his face of seeing her again, if not the feeling itself. "I didn't expect you to be here." As soon as he said it, he knew that it was not true. Somehow, part of him had.

Her face turned away from his, back to the candles. The ambient glow spread across the exposed half of her skin, turning its normally delicate paleness a warm straw color.

When she did not immediately reply, he added, "You don't have to do that."

"I do what I wish." It was not an angry tone. It was matter-of-fact. "Why have you come here? You are safer in the library."

"I can handle myself."

A period of silence equal to several heartbeats stretched and then quietly broke. Still she did or would not look at him, the small multitude of flames holding her as if she were mesmerized by them. "You should beware of your overconfidence. It is a fair-weather friend at best. Did you learn nothing from the night?"

"I learned things fine." He studied her, considering how almost every time he saw her there was firelight to be drawn to. Then a thought took him in another direction. "I wondered how a blind man could light so many candles without burning the place down around him." He wanted to approach her, to kneel by her side. Somehow he knew enough to hold his place. Now was not the time to trespass upon her space, nor to seek an invitation. But this knowledge did not cause the urge to recede.

Her hands, gently folded upon her lap, tightened into themselves, something Jorj only just noticed. "You still have not told me why you are here."

Suddenly he felt slightly ashamed. He had indeed trespassed upon something. His hands found the end of the pew and he leaned his weight against it, more for security than any physical need for support. "I don't know," he said finally. "I don't really know. I just…couldn't sleep."

Now she turned her face to him. It seemed small and fragile in the glow. Jorj wondered for that millisecond if she was real. When her voice, poised, calm, and sad, spoke, he would never again doubt the reality of her existence. "Join me."

He was at first taken by surprise, the invitation entirely unexpected. Then, as if a force other than his own, guiding him where his own facilities yet struggled to regain autonomy, he shifted his weight away from the pew and silently closed the distance between them to within a few feet. He kneeled as did she, somewhat awkwardly, but then seeing her unspoken approval, relaxed and soaked in the subtle warmth of over two hundred tiny beacons of consecrated light. "I'm sorry if I disturbed you." He meant it, every word, though not for the chance to see her again. That he kept separate from his apology.

"It would be difficult to disturb this," she absolved him, her face again to the flames. "If you bothered me, I would not remain here."

They sat thus, in silence unbroken for a time he would later only marvel at, but not taint with a guess. It was a fair assumption on his part, that much of the time they spent thinking of each other, and what each must have within them to be here, both in the chapel and on Twilight Earth, the great mystery Jorj could only vaguely wonder at without becoming angry. He did not dive deep enough into the latter to raise the dark fire of his wounded sense of fairness. She did not deserve the shadow upon them, and he wanted to absorb her presence, her generosity at not turning him away or becoming angry at his intrusion.

It was she who eventually parted the gossamer strand that connected them, and he could tell that she did so reluctantly, but that there existed a need to. She still did not turn her face to his, keeping the scarred side well hidden and out of reach, as she did most of her soul, though tonight was more than she had allowed him to see thus far. "I will help you when it is time. Will you aid me when my need is upon me, Jorj Tory Watchman?" Her voice was small and still, or almost so, as if she were speaking to him through pure water from very far away.

"Of course," he responded without a moment's consideration, somewhat surprised at himself, but perfectly at ease. He saw suddenly that a tear, like a spherical diamond, lay gleaming against her cheek, at the end of a frail path just under her left eye. He raised his own heft hand and reached across to wipe it away.

"No!" Her voice was sharp but not loud. In fact it was barely above a whisper. She started to turn, a quiver so slight that if he were not expecting to see it Jorj would have missed it entirely, disturbing the calm waters of her quality. It appeared for that instance that she would meet his gaze, and he shivered inside, but then, like a shaft through his heart, draining it of all blood and life force, she was gone.

Gone.

It took a second to sink in. The flames wiggled, carrying on their own quiet conversations, oblivious to the ambushed wound of his unexpected solitude. When he found his voice, it was broken. "I'm sorry, Greta! Come back!"

She didn't. He hadn't really thought she would, yet he stayed there until the candles were truncated through the long hours.

His soul, filled with a leaden weight he never asked for, and that could not do aught but distract and slow him from what he had to do, fought against the need to leave, to return to Fischer before Dennis woke, or something found him in his sleep. The thought of him alone, unprotected by what his childhood protectors used to call the 'buddy system,' brought him heavily and sharply to his feet. Damn the candles, he voiced silently, retracting it almost immediately as a ghost of his thoughts recalled their source. Putting everything out of his mind except the single purpose of returning to his friend, he left Concord Chapel, crossed the quad, and rounded to the street separating Language Hall and Fischer Library. All was quiet, silent like a tomb. It was still at least a half hour before sunrise. In the chill of that span he did not shiver, though the exposed skin of his arms prickled with gooseflesh. He placed his right hand on one of the handles of Fischer's front glass doors. Then he stopped. "You are here still?"

The color of sadness, never entirely absent from her voice, seemed lessened in its depth as she replied to him. "Look for me tomorrow night."

"Where?" He asked the question vainly, knowing as he did so that this time she was not going to answer. His next breath came easier, if heavy and deep. The tug that opened the door pulled it wide and he slipped through easily, entering the darkness of Fischer and finding the stairs without incident.

When he finally found his sleeping cushions, and the drapes that were all the blankets he could find, Dennis stirred.

"Where the hell were you?"

"Thirsty."

Dennis stared through the darkness at him, neither man believing the lie, if lie it truly was, and then lay back down. They spoke no more that night.

Catching Willie Bender came as close as possible to the impossible. He was as fast on the fly as he was on his feet. When a window of opportunity was large enough to squeeze through, he did, because second chances were as rare as rain. On his day of reckoning, that meant something, for it was the coldest day in January of Old Earth, on his forty-third birthday, that the Reaper first caught up with him to blow out his candles. Ever since then, no one ran harder, faster, or smarter, until now. And no one ever tagged him with more than a bullet. The fact that he shook loose Benedict's cub scouts came as no surprise to him. Losing track of this Jorj Watchman was a disappointment he found particularly hard to accept, for two reasons. It meant that he'd have to waste more precious time turning over rocks, and that the man was either extremely lucky, or as apt in a pinch as himself. The latter could be good or bad, and it all depended on this Mister Watchman's disposition. Recently it came clear to him that the man worked for Nick DeMoss, a friend of Theo's. But he was new, real new...too new. Either Nick was a fool or he saw something no one else did. Theo trusted Nick, and that had to be respected, but a background check was absolutely in order for anyone new, tumbled regime or no. It troubled him because he thought he knew all of Theo's men, and Nick's—wrong on both accounts, and it was his job to know the lay of the political land. That was a mistake he didn't intend to repeat. The old man's mantra beat its nagging path between his ears.

> Know you friends.
> Know your enemies.
> Know your friend's enemies.

No more or less than that, he submitted bitterly, mentally pissing all over his failure.

Well, he thought, done's done. All business now as before. He lowered the monocular, rubbed his right eye impatiently, and joined the two again. Surveillance was a dry hag, but it had its place. Sure he could shake answers out of people, like that scrawny toothpick that Nick always had waiting tables at the 'Westside.' But answers weren't good enough. They had to be accurate ones, and most mutha's learn to lie real good when they got a knife prickin' their ribs. The best ones live. Nope. Trust the eyes and ears, nothing else.

But Willy wasn't tracking 'the watchman' as he now called him. He kept his eye on the whole bunch he helped get the fuck out of Dodge and into the Millhouse, the safe house, the place so safe that only he, until the time they moved into it, knew what it was. Nick's crew had no clue what they were sitting on top of. And they wouldn't find out either, for everything he put in there was safer from them than they from Benedict. It was a good long time since Willy Bender got knocked over, and he didn't waste any of his time in Twilight

Earth. There were things he hadn't even told Theo, and that was something.

It was clear to him for almost five months—every day the same cold bitch—that Nick played at something, but the old bastard was too sharp with his cards, however silent or stupid they might be. Now the man had a third, a fourth, and a fifth, but the last two didn't count either. Both were ruined in their own ways...liabilities. What made it all so damned frustrating now was that Willy needed people to trust, that's why he had to know about Nick, hence the watchman. As long as there was a sliver of doubt under his skin, he was entirely on his own, and a lone man could only stand so long no matter how bad-ass he thought himself.

He loathed the cold, and having the third-floor window open to allow his sound enhancer adequate unimpeded space to work didn't spark any latent love. A cold breeze struggled against the tacked-down drapes. It always won, he spat bitterly, always won in the end. For now it only pushed, chilled the room, laughed at him the same as ever. He could work with that. After so many years, any misery could be endured if the payback was right. Still, he took another slug of coffee, just to hedge his bets.

It wasn't always like this. Once, Willie Bender knew better times, far better ones. Even in the cold of January, eternally forty-three years old, shivering, angry, and focused, he could hear the crashing waves of the ocean, see the Golden Gate Bridge, and smell the perfume of a woman he'd never see again. His teeth clenched slightly, but still he smiled in spite of things. As that damned bastard partner of his pointed out to him just last week, or was it the week before? Things could be worse. He wasn't in Freddy DuPonte's soggy shoes, and considering the other sordid sides of a man unlucky enough to be killed on the rainiest day in New Jack's history, there were at least a hundred blessings to grab at.

Frank was out and about, but he usually left once a day, hitting a food stash someplace. God knew there were enough of those around the city. People shared, or used to, but everybody held something back for the rainy days to come. There wasn't a one who didn't think things would eventually get worse. For New Jack, everyone was right. It was about as bad as Willie Bender expected it would be, though sooner than he expected. Bad things never sent R.S.V.P.'s, even if you watched for them.

On two of the previous occasions, the big dummy went with him, always returning with a box or two in his arms, that in addition to what Frank returned with. Maybe they were digging in for the duration. Not a wise move, Willie 'Frosty' Bender acknowledged. Benedict would find them given time, and he had a dossier on Nick. He did on everyone who worked for his enemies, and his friends, such as they were.

He took a bite of a ham and cheese sandwich, surprisingly fresh, and compliments of a new store just opened up down city a ways. He always liked it when immigrants arrived at New Jack. They always brought something.

The front door of the 'Millhouse' opened. Frosty shoved the rest of the sandwich into his mouth and chewed it down to something manageable while he snatched up his monocular. He saw plainly enough without it that it was the idiot mechanic from Mike's, the local tragedy. Once he'd considered relieving the man of his misery himself, like 'the Watchman,' but there were other's who held an interest in him, night folk, and it didn't do to upset apple carts until they were all accounted for. Now he might never know what it was those bats went there for almost every night, thanks to 'you know who.' And probably he risked his black ass for nothing going out there those nights when he did, grounds for another grudge against the newcomer.

Through the single-eyed magnification of the monocular, Frosty looked Bill over for anything out of place, other than the man himself, who was pretty odd. Then, distracting him suddenly, the door, not fully closed yet, lurched open and there was the Padre, his mouth open in speech. Bill hesitated and came back until the Padre had a hand to his sleeve. Then, as one, the two went off down the street, out of sight past the angle of the window.

Well that left Nick, Frosty concluded. After a moment's consideration, he packed up a few weapons, nearby and ready for a quick move, and launched down the stairs and out the back door. Nick might be interesting when in the company of others, but by himself he could bore the pope to tears. Big lummox's and priests promised better entertainment. He cut through the alleys and parking lots, catching sight of them two blocks over and keeping a steady distance. The dimbulb would doubtless never notice, but the priest was a weird fuck, probably had good ears and one of them God's, despite his circumstances.

The two men in the lead didn't go far. On Katherine Street they came to a car lot, the small, dirty kind run by small, dirty men with office trailers, usually keeping a wad of green in their pockets for self-esteem. No man greeted them now, for the owner was long gone, one of the ones who didn't return after their first mistake on Twilight Earth. Frosty remembered him. A paunchy, self-important shit-head who couldn't keep his mouth shut, panicked at the wrong time—like there was ever a right one—and found his bullet. Now his parting gift was one of cars, crappy, rusty, but a past source of poor Theo's small, now confiscated fleet.

Bill and the Padre picked their way through the lot, past a Dodge Omni, three minivans of that characterless light blue paint job all the cheap ones had, and a brown Pontiac Sunbird, showing no interest whatsoever. Frosty watched as they stopped finally at a dark olive green muscle car, a 1970 Plymouth Road-runner, it's surface rust mostly on the roof and hood, though the bottoms of the doors were starting to bubble. Even through his monocular he could see that. Padre loosed his hold on Bill and placed his hands on the right fender, immediately dropping to the ground and sliding underneath. Bill released the hood's catch and raised it, staring dumbly down at the engine. Willie 'Frosty' Bender considered listening in with his electronic ear, but changed his mind. He wanted to listen for other things, considering the fact that he still had a considerable amount of enemies running around now.

Why was the Padre with him. That was an oddity, but then he almost laughed in spite of himself when he suddenly realized why. There was no way Bill would ever get under a car again. The Padre was his proxy set of hands to go into that dark place of death below. What a joke. What a goddam, dark-ass joke.

Yet it was also plainly evident to the angry man of winter that Bill's hands had not been idle, and that he had likely been coming here for the last two days, slipping out at least once without Frosty's knowledge. The black man's eyes narrowed at the thought, and then he smiled grimly, sarcastically. He was so paranoid of Benedict's men that this shouldn't surprise him. He couldn't keep track of everything at once. What was one dumb-ass slipping out when he had his attentions on other things, like pissing, or pinching off a loaf?

When it came to his strength, Bill's lack of mental prowess paled. So long as he didn't have to go underneath the car, which he didn't once, he worked as hard as anyone Frosty had ever seen, and with an art. Somehow, the dumb bastard found torch-es, tools, everything he needed, even an auto store which he left the Padre to acquire parts from three blocks away. It seemed once away from Nick, the good priest and the mechanic had an understanding, for by now Frosty noticed the protectiveness with which the others showed both men, only deeming them safe when in each other's company, and it wasn't a hard guess why they felt so, given what Frosty knew of both of them.

It wasn't going to be a whole lot prettier unless they got the car into a large shelter to paint it, but Frosty didn't think that was their point. They *were* going to leave, at least some of them. And this was going to be their chariot, fast, tough, and big enough to carry…he did some quick figuring. Hell, he real-ized. You could get all of them in there if you wanted to, maybe a couple more if you didn't give a crap about comfort. His eyes narrowed again as thoughts raced around each other. Okay. Good enough for now. He pocketed his monocular, briefly as-sessed his perimeter, and made an exit. He needed to do some thinking, and to do that, he needed to get warm, maybe even have a drink of something stronger than coffee.

The strong drink came, but it was brewed by the gods.

Willy crossed Second Tilbert street, not known on Old Earth for its culture, or its concern for worldly events, and

stopped at a minimart. There were still a few items of sustenance, carbonated sugar water, baked sugar carbs, gum. This
last he liked, knowing that it would rot his teeth if he ever ran
out of toothpaste, but there were so few things to enjoy now.

He entered like a cop at a bank robbery, pistol raised and
ready, checking every aisle, every place of potential trouble. No
one was there and it was good for him, good for whoever didn't
appreciate a gunfight. He was in no mood for distractions.
That's why when the blonde haired woman with the heavy bo-
soms entered through the front door, he didn't flinch from leveling his sights on the flat space between her ice-blue eyes. She
looked cheap, but standard in that hill-Billy, upstate model sort
of way—not much ass, or too much, pick one—and the hair
just a few years out of date. He could place a bet which lake
she had her camp at. The fact that she didn't look at all bewil-
dered told him everything he needed to know. "How many?" he
demanded, knowing exactly what would be her reply. He had
been through this once or twice before.

"I just want a pack of cigarettes, honey." She almost
laughed, and that would have been a bad mistake. Willie didn't
play games unless they were his. Her rules just might get her
killed, as he was sure they might him. But she knew something
of how these things worked herself, and so she restrained the
easy path to overacting. "The road's getting dry, if you know
what I mean."

"How many? I ain't gonna ask you again." Her ass was
definitely too big, despite what he used to think was acceptable.
Twilight Earth had that strange ability to affect your tastes, and
not in the way you might think.

She regarded him for a moment with an air of disbelief, and then shrugged. "Eight, maybe a dozen. I don't know. Whatever you want. Can I get a smoke now? I'm dying for one of those coffin nails." She realized as she said it that it was the wrong choice of words. The air hung heavy as they settled upon his judgment.

"Yeah, honey?" He smiled, far too old to buy her words at face value. "You know I could send you back to where you came from with one pull of this ol' fertilizer dispenser?" His face sobered. He knew where he was heading. The question was, where was she? "How many?" he repeated, both words fired with equal force.

Her eyes closed and she breathed once in, once out, heavy and deliberate. "You think I'm more scared of you than him?" Her eyes popped open, two cannons wide with nothing to shoot but their sincerity. "I know you. Willie Bender, Theo's man at arms, his security chief. You got a reputation for meanness, one bad ass mother fucker." Her hand, resting on the counter now, in full view of Frosty, squeezed into a fist. "He's listening. We ain't got a word he can't hear. So when I tell you he has my point of entry, I don't think I need to tell you what that means. You can hurt me, hurt me bad, but not as terribly as he can."

"Better leave now, bitch." Frosty had an idea, a terrible idea, one that even he didn't like much. "Take your smokes and get out, compliments of Willie Bender." His lips protruded just enough to suggest the anger he felt, the revulsion of her part in things, and at the one who forced her to play that part. "Take your goddam cigarettes, lighter, matches, donuts for your fat ass! Take 'em and get out!" To add emphasis, and something else, he grabbed blindly from the shelf behind him and threw the contents on the floor at her feet.

She stared at him like a deer into the headlights of an oncoming car, and then made to leave. Then, as he knew she would, for her kind never missed an opportunity, she hesitated, reached behind the register counter and grabbed several packs of Marlboro and one of those fancy torch lighters. Her eyes lighted on him for that brief moment of victory, the mouse who got away with the cheese while the dog cornered the cat, and fled out the front. He waited until she did the other thing he knew she'd do, and stepped up to the door, confident that if they shot him, it wouldn't be fatal. They wanted him alive.

The woman stopped midway between the store and the gas pumps beyond, unable to withstand the craving for a smoke. That much, as Frosty knew, had not been an act. As she fumbled with the lighter, producing at last a flame as blue as her Nordic eyes, Willie Bender aimed something special from his pocket at the gas pumps, fired from the launcher beneath the barrel of his semi-automatic rifle. The cigarette, he acknowledged, was just an effect that he could have realistically done without, but it was the irony that he wanted to shove in his opponent's face like a fresh dewy pile of dog shit. Even as he turned away, the grenade coming into contact with the gas pumps just past the significantly startled face of the urbanely-challenged blonde, he took a bullet in the last place he honestly expected too. As it blazed a pinstripe of pain into his kidney, his eyes rolled, not in unconsciousness but in bitter appreciation for the irony that the 'sharp shooter' missed, and that if the imminent explosion did not kill him, a war of pain would commence between this intrusion into his internal organ and his burning, glass-lacerated flesh.

And then, in a wave of hellish immolation, the mini-mart and all nearby went up in a fireball, consumed and smothered by heat and heated gases. Several blocks away, The Padre banged his head against the Roadrunner's frame, startled by the loud noise, and Bill ran behind a Ford Taurus, as if it would, could protect anybody from anything. The cloud of smoke that rose into the sky formed into a mushroom plume. Someone, nearby and in charge, shook his head, deciding to leave for Mexico, hoping never to meet any bad men. Like his predecessor, he had no place left in the service of the man who sent him.

There are things in life, any life, that resist tampering. Nature surely has intended it this way. Were all our parts and programs ours for the meddling, what a sorry existence it would be. And therein lies the problem. It *is* a sorry existence for many in life, be they human, or inhuman. The key to this significant failure is the word 'resistant.' The definition does not include 'impregnability,' or 'unassailability.' God, or the godlike, seem only concerned with reserving that for the province of the divine. Power must be maintained by the powerful, after all. With this in mind, one can easily see the beginnings of the trail to disaster and hopefully avoid it. But though hope springs eternal, its streams long ago cut channels in the rock of men's minds that seldom take them anywhere useful unless they are willing to sacrifice of their own.

Mankind is not good at that.

It is this detail that lay at the root of a specific blood-stained circle, and the conversations passed across that ring of silver from the star within. No man spends his own currency when another's will do, unless he be of exceptional metal. Even those who deem themselves so, and most of us do, are quite capable of rationalizing our way into someone else's wallet. It is an ugly thing, and not to accept as part of being human, but it is just that to those unwilling to change. And though most meander in some form of oblivion, willing to change in spirit but anchored to the evils of the body by five inch framing nails, others are more than aware of their state. They are willing collaborators with their dark nature, picking the fruit from their neighbor's grove by night, milking their cattle and then slaughtering the entire herd in their gluttony. The sins that they heap up are legion, and the day of reckoning put off again and again, until it is unclear if they will ever have the means to pay in full. For such, there would seem no salvation, no debt fulfilled, no equal weights and measure.

With God, or the godlike, all things are possible. But don't hold your breath. No one said probable. Furthermore, patience is a measure of the divine, but in such there is little accounting for the desires of man, but that God or gods turn a face for reasons entirely His or their own.

No one told Jorj these things. No one had to. If he filled his head with these and other like considerations, and did not expect great and good things, one would have to know him before finding fault, and in knowing him, what fault would they uncover? That he expected the worst of men, received that plus callousness, apathy, indifference to change, resistance to improvement, and only rarely, short-lived like a sunny day in Seattle, the surprise encounter of a good soul? The funny thing was that he didn't know himself. Memories of Old Earth slipped through his fingers every day—he couldn't tell you his father's name, though he recalled the face, and the good feeling he got from it. It stuck in his throat that his mother's voice was all that he had left of her. And life itself as he knew it? His

Twilight Earth apartment was bare. He had a wrecked jeep and demolished overpass to remind him, and the face in the mirror. About all he really had now was what he felt in his heart, whatever old experiences made it. He had that and his new friends, some of whom, Dennis being one, he felt he'd known all his life, and it was eerie, inescapably eerie.

With these thoughts churning inside him, he met the morning sun from the fifth floor of Fischer. There were times, this being one of them, when he felt he'd welcome the rain, maybe not so much as that 'Freddy' guy that Bermuda Shorts mentioned to 'pissed-off ol' Frosty' that first day of Jorj's reckoning with the Lord. But a little gentle shower would be nice for contemplation. Of course that was never going to happen, at least not here . . . not for him.

It was a morning like every other; sunny, cool, a slight breeze blowing, Dennis complaining about something. This time it was his stomach. After a while, during which he refused food, but took water to replace what he lost puking in the men's room, he admitted eating a *dubious pudding* from a machine in the basement. It wasn't bright, and he didn't argue when Jorj pointed this out to him, but it was pudding...chocolate pudding, sealed and without need of refrigeration.

"Did you look at the expiration date?" Jorj asked, finding it difficult to be sympathetic.

"Well, yeah," Dennis replied, not convincingly. "Sort of."

Sort of." Jorj blinked and waited.

Dennis swallowed. Jorj waited to see what would stay down, what would appear center stage. Things settled and the former found his words, rough and haggard. "You know they exaggerate." Another swallow. Jorj watched the lump rise and fall but said nothing. "They can't give you the exact date of… of going bad. Even if they could, they know someone like me might push it."

"Which you did."

"Right." Dennis' eyes glazed over and he got to his feet. "I'll be back." He was off at a run, hitting the door jam on the way out of the sixth-floor conference room and nearly spilling on his ass as he cleared the threshold.

For a minute, or almost, Jorj simply stared at the door as it closed slowly to. He understood why Nick wanted someone other than Dennis to do his important tasks. Twilight Earth had few enough people as it was. Good help, as the cliché goes, was hard to find.

They fully intended to leave Fischer and return to the Millhouse that morning. As things progressed, Dennis took a turn for the sicker. Jorj decided to stay another night and take care of his stupid friend. It was not something he did lightly, for Benedict's men might come around, but there was no travelling for two until both were well, and neither needed to get into a vigorous debate with the other as to why.

During the day, Dennis took turns sleeping and puking while Jorj kept him hydrated and tried making sense out of Ogam's notes. The books they could read later, as time allowed. It was Ogam's head he needed to get inside now. And he kept thinking about the bookstore, Haydon's Half-Price Book Warehouse. What did the woody straw-head tell him? That he'd find something there he was looking for? 'Bring some friends too. Something in there to interest everyone.' It was an invitation, but it was more than that. It was also an expectation. They dicked around in his leavings when he already told them where to go...except that the place, according to Nick, Dennis, and yesterday's 'eyewitness Jorj' held an address on a street that didn't exist. There was, in fact, no street named Dansforth in New Jackson City. And, to make matters worse, where Hayden's should have been, on the corner of Alodi and Llewellen, was a large thrift store, an empty one with a disheveled overhead sign out front.

He stared at a slip of paper with eight words printed in Ogam's curiously-styled hand. They sat atop each other in a single column:

Time

Elysium

Reality

Manna

Immortality

Nirvana

Utopia

Shangra-la

A wish list. Jorj grimaced. A funny mix of words. One or two of these words clashed, in his estimation, but who was he to argue. Idle thoughts from an idle mind? They meant something to Ogam. He almost threw the slip into the cardboard box he had sitting on the conference table, ready to be packed and carried as soon as they could get the fuck out of Dodge, as soon as Dennis got a handle on his stomach, but then folded it once and crammed it in his left front pants pocket. It was just a small torn piece of note paper, after all, too easy to lose in the shuffle of books and things. Likely it's importance, or lack of, would escape them all in the end, he admitted.

Evening brought Dennis no closer to eating, but at least he kept water down, and that, Jorj acknowledged, was progress. He did his best to let the man sleep, and even found an MP3 player with weak but serviceable batteries to help him relax. Beethoven wasn't what Dennis would have picked, but then again, he chose a bad pudding for his dessert the night before. This is what he needed now, and Jorj couldn't escape wondering that he found it in one of the offices, in a desk drawer by itself, with only furniture in the room besides. Had they found it earlier, Dennis most surely would have wasted the batteries by now.

While Dennis slept, about mid-evening, Jorj descended to the basement, flashlight in hand, and found the suspect snack machine, pulled away from the wall and slid sideways. Dennis never broke the windows on these things when the coin-op would do, a surprisingly wise move for someone like him, and likely not discovered on a lark. This was the case now, except the evidence trail led to the reminder that there was no electricity, for the back was dismantled with a hammer, screwdriver, and pry-bar, leaving the glass in front intact. It was clear that Dennis, not one to waste an opportunity he couldn't later screw up, cleaned out every morsel within the machine. Jorj rolled his eyes, realizing his miscalculation, and ran the 7 folded flights to the sixth floor.

He found Dennis sitting up, unwrapping a package of snack cakes. Immediately Jorj dropped to his knees and slapped it out of the man's hands. "Don't *even* look at me like that!" he barked in response to Dennis' startled, glaring reaction. *"Little Debbie* will whup your butt asshole! We lost time because of you. Should I carry you back? Over my shoulder if I have to? You *better* not make me regret taking care of your sorry ass!"

"Jeezuss Christ, Jorj!" Dennis edged back away several inches. "You don't have to get all prehistory on me! I'm feeling better, and I got hungry."

"So you're going to roll the dice again with the bakery from hell? Maybe I should just call that ice cream truck back!"

Dennis stopped in mid retort and frowned. "That's not funny. And this isn't from the machine. It's from home...Nick's."

To Dennis, Nick *was* home, all the home he had in Twilight Earth. Jorj noted that with some empathy and softened his tone. "But you cleaned out all the bad stuff. Let's separate it out...get rid of it before one of us gets someplace we'd rather not be."

"I didn't empty it out. I thought about it, but procrastinated."

Silence.

"Someone's in the house." Jorj rose to his feet slowly, taking in his own words. "It's not like we locked the door, or could have, but..."

"You think they're still here?" Dennis looked only slightly concerned. It was comforting.

"Big place, bigger than Language Hall. No way we'd find that one out if they wanted to stay hid, or jack us."

Again silence.

"You feel well enough to travel?"

Dennis shook his head. He did not stand with Jorj, and drifted his gaze over at the snack cakes, secretly grateful that

Jorj slapped them away before he could add more to an unwilling stomach. "My step mom used to make me broth."

"Go find your step mom then." Jorj grinned murderously. "And keep your pistol close. I'll lock the door behind me. If I don't give two short knocks with a hesitation inbetween..."

"It ain't you."

Jorj blinked and nodded once, slowly.

"Going hunting?" Dennis really hoped all would stay quiet, but he knew better than to expect it.

"Not really. Just gonna look around." He paused. "You come across any tools in your library wanderings?

"No." Dennis was uninvested in further conversation. Jorj thought he looked rather pale again.

"Okay, buddy. Just wondering."

For once, Jorj was apprehensive, and for more than the obvious reason of suddenly seeing interstate 96 again in the buff. The night was creeping on, dimming the natural light, preparing for the general coma some would collaborate with, and the several million darkling parties others would instigate. She would appear, somewhere near, and look for him. He preferred to talk to her alone, and alive.

His decision was not to go so far this time, to watch from the windows on the first level. Then he thought it a bad idea. The last couple of times he saw her she was alone, and there were no barrel fire to serve as a beacon. He had to go outside. There was something in the wildness of the autumn night, with the light breeze, and the moon's dance with the ragged clouds. Tonight he would ask her a frivolous question, simply because he had to know, and then he'd ask her a serious one, because if he didn't, he felt he might never get to again. If he was lucky, he deemed, she would give him an answer to at least one of them.

Feeling irresponsible nonetheless for leaving his sick friend to fend for himself, he picked his way down three flights of stairs, silent as a cat, and then stopped. Someone was on the first floor, flashlight in hand, rummaging through the books. Jorj went into a crouch and drew his 9mm. So far the flashlight, barely necessary in the waning evening light, was pointed down and away, but it could turn, along with the eyes of the dark figure wielding it, anytime. Worse, there might be more than one.

From three floors up, the window of vision between the flashlight and Jorj was narrow, widening the further the latter descended the square, spiraling staircase. Jorj watched only a few seconds longer and then made up his mind to proceed downstairs quickly to the first floor. He had sneakers on now, unlike the previous night, and he was keenly aware that his paddings were not completely silent. Yet the owner of that flashlight seemed not to have heard a thing, for it's subtle, focused wiggles remained as before. To add to this, more obvious than Jorj's footfalls, were sounds of books being withdrawn from the shelf and then thumped back in place, one after another in a hurried fashion. "What could this person be looking for? Jorj wondered as his distance to ground level closed. Then also, another might be curious to know, why were he and Dennis so interested in this place?

Once he was on even visual par with Fischer's new visitor, Jorj found his going easier, for the stairs, bare and hard, were replaced under his feet by carpeted floor. Better still, he made use of the many bookcases, tables and counters, enabling him to come within enough distance to see that the intruder, if such could be called more so than himself, was none other than Frosty, half naked and shivering.

Jorj realized he had more than one decision to make here, and depending on which one he went with, things could go several different ways. He had a vague idea at what happened, and that Frosty was alone. Somewhere, hidden in those books, was a gun at the very least.

One thing he remembered concerning their last encounter was that Frosty was 'enemy of my enemy.' Another recollection was something to the effect of his kidney being held hostage, since an immediate death wasn't the best deterrent in some cases. But there was also the impression that Frosty planned to see to his leg wound, an occurrence which was never to be, for Jorj's final memory was one of dimming light, and then it was all crumbled overpass and wreckage. The blood loss was more than he could handle.

He decided, reluctantly, to take a chance.

Stepping out into the aisle where Frosty busied himself with controlled ransacking, Jorj maintained a dozen feet between them and raised his 9mm. He picked his words carefully, knowing that his voice alone would turn on the other man's dangerous adrenaline. "Benedict sucks moose cock."

The effect was immediate, and entirely not what he expected. Frosty, as Jorj was to find out, was in some very important ways, like himself. One difference was in experience, which in regards to life on Twilight Earth, one Willie Bender enjoyed a surplus of. The flashlight spun away for the briefest of seconds and then jerked forwards, hurtling at Jorj with all the weight and mass that four D batteries could bring to bear. It struck the man in the elbow, and only because he slipped his face out of the path, but as it bounced away, the bigger man was on him, punching him in the face, grabbing the wrist that held the pistol, relentlessly gaining control of an out-of-control situation. Jorj fought back in the way that a strong, hardened man does, with near adamantine determination. Three shots fired, more to alert Dennis than to hit Frosty, and then the 9mm slipped away. With a last deliberate maneuver, he kicked it away, under a table, surrounded by a phalanx of chair legs. Like any good chess game, you either wanted the only queen, or denied one to both players. "You goddam bastard!" he yelled, reeling from another blow, fending off the clutch that sought his throat, and wrapping his own fingers around his aggressor's face. "I wanted to talk!"

His hand peeled away and an arm slid around his neck. Jorj wriggled out just in time only to find a second hold attempted. This one found purchase and took root. Within three seconds he found himself struggling at the mercy of Willie 'Frosty' Bender, the angry man of winter. He expected a warning, words, the jerk of an arm...something. Instead, the hold tightened on either side of his neck. He knew this move. God help him, but it was a sleeper. Then he remembered. Dying was an escape. Frosty, whatever else he might be, was not a stupid man.

His hands were tied when he came to. So were his feet. As best he could tell in the dark, for the last ambience of the evening sun was long since evaporated from the air, a lamp was missing its electrical cord. When he attempted to move, he realized, besides that his hands were tied behind his back, that they were also tied to his feet, and finally to a garrote around his neck which tightened every time he struggled. 'Jeezuss Christ!" His voice croaked low but carried for all the world in the silence as if he'd been shouting. The hardness of a table, large and wooden, announced itself from beneath his ribcage.

"He ain't returned yet." The voice carried a certain sarcasm, confident, but not overbearing. "I'd be mighty surprised if he answered you now, almost as surprised as I was to see your face around here."

"This...how you treat people who are on your side?"

"Funny you should pick sides with the man who tied you up." The voice moved out from behind him and circled around on his right side, coming to a stop somewhere near his feet. Better pick your friend's better."

"I could have shot you."

A flashlight blinked on, revealing Frosty's face, angry looking, but not angry. "You mean with this?" He held up the 9mm. He laughed suddenly. "I gotta talk to Nick. His hardware is ok, but he could do better. Some Muthafuckas out there wear body armor...all the freakin' time. Strange, terrible world."

"Could you untie me?" Jorj pushed his patience. There was nothing he could do but talk, unless he saw red, then there was no telling where things might go, but he could guarantee they wouldn't be in his favor.

Frosty pursed his lips and tapped the muzzle of the 9mm against them for dramatic effect. "God works in mysterious ways, Mr. Watchman. Anything's possible." The pistol and the hand that held it fell to his right side. "Question and answer time. You know how this works, right?"

His head throbbed. This wasn't going very well. "I think I do."

"Good." Frosty's face, hard-lined and lightly bearded, lost the rounded edges of sarcasm. "I'd like to think we could get through this without any more unpleasantness, but that all depends on you. What was your gig on the other side?"

"Gig?"

"Your profession, Mr. Watchman. What did you do...besides run a forklift?" Jorj's eyes unfocused as he searched the dark confines of his memories. Willie Bender sucked his teeth impatiently and then added, "I went through your wallet. There were, to use that dumb-ass cliché, irregularities."

"Why?" Jorj was dumbfounded. "Why would you possibly care?"

Three steps took Willie Bender level with Jorj's face. He grabbed the garrot and brought it tight, causing Jorj to gasp and glare. There was just enough air to breath...just. "Tell me Mister Watchman, why would a man like you, employed by Wayne's Wholesale lumber, be in possession of a radiation badge?"

Radia...I don't know what you're talking about!"

"Wrong answer!" Frosty nearly yelled, tightening the garrote another notch. "Search your stupid ol' SUV, muthafucka! Did you bother to check under the seats? You don't act so sloppy on this side. Cough it up."

Jorj met the other man's eyes, the glare replaced by a glassed-over stare. He was trying desperately to calm himself down, slow down his breathing and his pulse rate. "Gut me, kill me..." he gasped. "Whatever. I...don't know anything...about a radiation badge." Then he added, later he would be unsure why it came out the way it did, "Go ask Benedict...he likes to play with hot things."

"Now how you know that?" Willie Bender drew Jorj's face up closer to his own. "Best be truthful!"

"Untie me first." Jorj managed a smile, despite his miserable situation, remembering well Clint Eastwood in a Spaghetti Western in the long ago and far away. "Vinegar's for idiots."

This caught Frosty off guard, and his eyes widened in anger at first, then narrowed to frustrated and cornered understanding. With a spiteful thrust, he released the garrote and stepped back. "Play a player and you know what happens, Watchman."

With the garrote a little looser, he could gasp for breath better, and respond more confidently. "This isn't a freakin' game, jackass."

"Don't think I ain't still got the hammer." Frosty produced a knife, long, wicked, and sharp. "You're right. This ain't no game...but I'm still gonna take a gamble." He placed the blade, to Jorj's relief, between the restrained man's skin and the lamp cord and tensed it for a cut. That is where things froze in time, and then, as abruptly as you could imagine, lost any further momentum of hard-won intention.

Once the first blast had cleared the air of any uncertainty, and the second one followed up, spraying blood over Jorj's chest and the right side of his horrified face, All Willie Bender could do was mouth a lung-less word to reflect the bitter irony he must surely have felt, and then drop slowly and sloppily to the carpeted floor. From the direction of the stairs, something half slid, and half plodded down them. Jorj, still trying to gather his senses to the fact that the man that he had just rolled the dice with and won, for at least the short-term, now shivered naked in the snow and cursed his name, turned his eyes out into the dark. The flashlight which offered so good a target up to a few, shell-shocked seconds ago, was as gone as the man that was holding it.

"Anyone else around here, Jorj?" The voice in the black belonged to Dennis, not that Jorj would have guessed anyone else to be behind the two bullets hurtled like bumbling angels from above.

"No." It was all he could muster for the moment. He spat, tasting the salt of Frosty's brinish life wine upon his lips. After Dennis untied him, some minutes and banged shins later, he would peel his half-soaked shirt off and use the dry side as a towel. A quarter of an hour later, Jorj found a water cooler and properly washed himself up with soap from a second-floor bathroom while Dennis, still unwell, bantered behind a closed door.

"No," Jorj raised his voice impatiently. "I swear I won't tell him you did it!" A few seconds later, after wiping his face down briskly with a paper towel, he added, "He'll probably figure it out in time, anyway." He heard his friend choke and gag outside the bathroom. "I don't think he'll hold much of a grudge though...too much at stake now, and he knows it." He knew the last part was bullshit, but he thought it might ease apprehensions.

It was clear to them both that they couldn't stay much past sunup. If Frosty came back looking for Jorj, and the shooter, this was the obvious place to start. To Jorj, this presented an opportunity to slip out into the night, on the pretense that they move things to Language Hall until such time as they chose to clear out of the campus forever, for Jorj didn't expected either of them to come back. Dennis wanted no part of a night move, as his companion expected, so he crawled back to the sixth floor to sleep, leaving Jorj to hump the boxes over to the next building across the street.

Fortunately for Jorj, his jacket was still upstairs when he went looking for the snack machine thief. As such, it was spared the bath of blood that his shirt would never recover from. He wore the jacket now, outside, and was grateful for at least one layer between himself and the night's chill air.

What he had not forgotten, during all the time he was tied up, or after, was Greta, and now he kept an eye open for her, though he knew that if she wanted to talk, she'd make her presence known easily enough. So it was not until he was making his exit from Language Hall, having deposited all of Ogam's notes upstairs in the man's 'study,' that he saw her, sitting outside on the cold marble steps, waiting for him.

"Your hands were full," she spoke evenly. "I thought it best to wait."

"Thanks." He tone was crisp, though, in truth, not unfriendly. He stepped lightly down to the bottom step, her being on the third, and leaned back against the hard, lightly-carved marble railing, sticking his left hand into one bluejean's pocket, hanging his right thumb off the other. "Don't you ever get cold?"

"I'm always cold."

There was something in the way she said it that caused Jorj to shiver down to his soul. Nevertheless, he began to take off his jacket.

"No," she said calmly, neither looking at him or offering a gesture to go along with her singular word.

"It wouldn't do any good, would it?" She did not answer, did not have to. Jorj took no offense, chanced a feeling of pity, and discarded it, knowing that was something she neither needed nor desired. He looked away for a moment, noting Fischer's silhouette against the starlit sky and moonlit ragged clouds, studying the shadow that spread like an over-long drapery about the building, covering everything it touched in inky, bewitching blackness. "I'm leaving New Jackson in a few days." There was at least one more sentence he wanted to tack on, but he faltered, unsure of the approach, cursing the unlit runway of his intent.

She remained silent, more still than usual, instilling an air of expectation upon all around her.

"You need to come with me."

This time, to Jorj's surprise, she bowed her head. Her voice, scarcely more than a whisper, chilled him. "Everything has a time, Jorj. You can demand no more than can I."

"Why do you keep talking in riddles?" Jorj pulled away from the railing, standing firmly with his left foot on the second step, his right on the first. "I hate feeling like everyone knows something I don't, and that somehow I'm expected to know it just the same. I need more than that."

"You shall have more, Jorj Watchman, but you must be patient."

"Patient?" He found the night's events were starting to play on him, unraveling his composure. "How patient should I…"

Her hair, when she turned her face, only partially obscured her eyes, but not enough to hide what was behind them, the pain and sadness, the long endurance. It all stopped Jorj cold, stilled his tongue. "Come with me now, if you would unfold a secret long held." Her voice chilled him with its frozen beauty, put upon him a strange tension from which he could not easily release himself, and ultimately chose not to. "It binds more than you now know, and if you would walk this path with me, know that it is but the first leg of what I asked last night, that I will ask more, and that you have already given me your word."

"Of course." Jorj watched her rise gracefully to her feet and let her descend the three steps past him to the sidewalk before himself starting off. All of his former life was in recession, memories slipping away rain-like, yet he felt a familiarity about her presence that was unshakable. Questions, poised on his tongue were legion, but to puncture the pregnant silence of the night seemed a sacrilege, a crime he was unprepared to commit himself, at least not yet. He wondered why she was sometimes alone, and what she did when she was not seeing him. Did the daylight merely close the door between them? Or was it more potent to her, elementarily threatening?

She led him quietly across the quad, through the tall grass as if it was not there, and he found that it was less substantial with each step until, by the time they reached the sidewalk before the steps to Concord Chapel, his sneakers were wet with dew and grass clippings. He dared not look behind him for fear of losing her, but he remembered suddenly that it was cut the night before. His confusion slid to the side as she ascended the stone steps, each one taken with an unhurried care. At the top, she paused and turned to him. He brought himself up so that he stood but a foot away, wondering if, at this distance, he might be able to feel her breath on his skin, and waited attentively.

Her face inclined towards the great double doors with their stained-glass windows, and brass handles. "It is yours to open."

For a moment he stared at her, the gentle paleness of her cheek, the almond slant of her shadowed right eye partially hid just beyond the bridge of a small, elegant nose. He almost asked her the most obvious question for the present circumstance, and abruptly seized the handle to the door on the left, swinging it just wide enough for himself, and allowed himself to be sucked into the darkling shadows beyond.

It was dark inside no more. In fact, all was well-lit and much more inviting than he ever saw it before. The power was on, he realized, easily noticeable despite the ambient sunshine filtering in through windows just out of sight. He looked in amazement at an easel set up with large placard displaying the weekly and Sunday morning services. It was something he didn't notice the last time he was here, or the time before that. Somewhere, rumbling the walls, floor, and ceiling like the thunder, an organ played. He did not recognize the song, but that in itself did not surprise him. Despite its inescapable, impervious presence in western society, Jorj pretty much hated organ music. Still, this was different. It was out of place, and he had to wonder, for all signs seemed to point to it. Did Benedict install a new preacher? And if so, why? More obvious still, what of the sunlight? He turned and looked behind him. Outside was night. All was still. Greta, betrayed by smoke from her newly-lit cigarette, sat just around the corner on a granite side rail. Jorj turned again, facing the stark contrast of a sunny day church, not certain it was even the same one, and climbed the many steps on the right to the sanctuary.

Each royal-red carpeted step gave way softly beneath his feet, the blood of Jesus, plush and acrylic. He felt a little blasphemous thinking this, and regretted it, for Jesus, whatever his own personal truth, was a square guy by him. A group of well-dressed women appeared at the top, mostly middle-aged, oblivious at first of his presence, and then alert to his vagrant look and the tension he displayed when they came into view. They started down the stairs, their lively conversation suddenly becalmed. At first he kept that guarded expression on his face. He was, by now, conditioned to initial distrust. Then, and it came slowly with a subliminal realization, he smiled, but he knew it was plastic and was not surprised when it did nothing to alleviate their uncertain apprehensions. Politely he shifted to the wall and passed them quickly on the way up, almost hearing them collectively breath easier. Once he was on the upper landing and around the corner, he heard their voices pick up their former volume, though the tone was somewhat different than before.

Lit artificially from above, and naturally from without, the sanctuary was brilliant in its ambient glow, warded by electric circles of white translucent glass, each quarter edge adorned by a small golden cross, and the divine power of the sun, that ancient pagan god, through man-made, god-inspired, filters of stained glass. Below, business in aftermath of some extracurricular function, still continued winding up, the organist, a slightly overweight woman with large wire-rimmed glasses replaying a section of music after an abrupt stop, and a thinnish man in black, his back to Jorj, gathering up his papers plus a small bible which he placed in a suit jacket outer pocket. Here the newly-arrived man paused, unclear whether to enter or simply watch the rather pedestrian doings of two seemingly ordinary people. This, as far as Jorj could distinguish, was not Twilight Earth.

A decision was made for him almost immediately. The man in black turned, a curious look of momentary confusion on his now suddenly familiar face. Padre, without the sightless eyes, minus the scars, and bereft of all biblically endowed thunder. He bent to pick up a pen which had fallen to the dais floor, and then stopped, noticing Jorj for the first time. For three seconds he simply stared as one frozen in place, and then calmly retrieved the wayward pen. Once again, his eyes met those of the other, and then he turned and exited directly through the door to the right of the choir loft, leaving the distinct impression that he did so premature to his earlier intentions. Through it all, the organist kept playing, her glasses and chubby face, bathed in merciless fluorescence, pointed with absolute focus upon the sheet music before them. It was obvious to Jorj that he must follow. Greta did not lead him here merely to be an observer.

His walk was brisk but not a run. For good measure, he took the aisle between the pews and the right-hand wall.

The organist kept blasting the great brass pipes, and that was good, for it meant she either didn't see him, or did not care. Nevertheless, her skills did nothing more to dispel his dislike of organ music, god-inspired or no. The dark wooden door, carved and adorned with carefully sculpted molding, yielded to him easily, the tarnished brass knob unlocked and not even properly latched. Jorj passed through without hesitation, and found, out in the tiled hall on the other side, the Padre waiting for him, his bible clutched tightly to his chest as if it were a flotation device, and he alone on an ocean with no sight of dry land.

"Did you come back for it?" he asked, his voice struck in a defensiveness that was all too transparent. "You can't have it, you know. You've made your choice."

For the moment, Jorj was speechless. What could he say? He hadn't the blindest idea what the good father was talking about, other than the absurd appearance that they'd met before. But he eventually found some words, words which, under the circumstances, should have seemed obvious to him. "I just want to see it again." He watched as the Padre's suspicion mixed and transformed into uncertainty. "I need to know that it's safe."

"I assure you it's quite fine. "The priest made no move to acquiesce.

"Humor me, Padre."

"Padre?" The priest seemed irked. "Father Francis will do." He studied Jorj for several heartbeats. "I suppose it can't hurt." His eyes dropped to the clothes worn by the man before him. "I can give you something better to wear, if you wish, from our 'Giving Center.' It seems leaving your benefactors has put you in some straits, but I commend you for your sacrifice. God will surely bless you in time for your difficult choice."

This was worth seeing, Jorj thought, though he merely nodded, stone-faced. Please lead on."

Down the hall was a set of stairs, much narrower and less ornately somber than those leading directly up to the sanctuary on the other side of the church. They took these down to the first floor, entered into another hall, and descended an additional set of steps, leading finally into a smooth-walled concrete sublevel. Off the main room, beyond the pipes and conduit running like futuristic tubular highways across the ceiling, were three doors, two on the left wall, and one straight ahead. They took this last one. Beyond, a very short hallway continued, with another door on the left and another on the end. Again, they proceeded straight through into a larger room, cluttered with religious paraphernalia, most of which was only good for use at certain times during the year. There were two items in defiance of this observation. When Jorj saw the first, an old oak lectern with a bent gooseneck lamp on top, he didn't even blink an eye. It was the second that he thought odd, at least in a chapel, even in the basement tucked way in the back like this was. Not surprisingly, the Padre made a beeline for it. Jorj let him pull away the Christmas wreaths, brass menorah, and the large painted-plywood bake sale sign. Then he watched, quite intensely, as the priest moved to the handle end of a hot-dog cart and pulled it around to expose the stainless-steel door on the end beneath them. His face most grim, he opened it, revealing a white, propane tank. Carefully, as if he were handling the ark of the covenant, he withdrew it. In the shadowed recess beyond, something made of an olive-drab plastic rested, totally out of place, although, other than its appearance, the reason for this was not immediately clear.

"Are you satisfied?" the priest asked, not looking at Jorj. He kept his eyes on whatever it was inside the hotdog cart.

Jorj walked a little closer, noting the priest's discomfort that he should do so, intending to get a closer inspection. On the end of the object, its surface ringed twice below the lid with raised flatness, was a metal handle painted the same olive drab. Presumably there was one on the other end. There was no question but that this thing was military in nature. "What are you going to do with it?"

This provoked a sharp response from Father Francis. "Are you well? Do you remember nothing of our deal?" He stared at Jorj as if the man had three heads, and then sighed heavily, tiredly. "My friend will take care of it. He is in the government, an agent in the FBI. We have an understanding."

An alarmed expression lit into Jorj's eyes. "If the Feds are involved, they should be swarming this place right now." He wondered why the priest should wish to spare him trouble, and exactly what was inside that olive green case, stuffed deep within the hotdog cart.

"There is an appointed time for pickup." Father Francis paused and then added, "we've been through all of this. Are you having second thoughts? If so, I must tell you I cannot let you take it back."

The Padre didn't look like he could stop Jorj if such was the case, but the latter man held up his hand. "What is the agent's name?"

Another incredulous look. "I can't tell you that."

"But you trust him. He's shown you credentials."

"Of course." The Padre grew impatient. "Now I believe we are finished here. You should go."

Could he take it now? Should he? Jorj's grave apprehensions gnawed at his ankles. His thoughts wandered frantically, then, in a dark epiphany, pounced on a certain news story shared with his friends so recently at 'The Millhouse.' His racing mind seized upon the disembodied conversation between Benedict and his new business partner from the netherworld. "It's a nuke." He didn't mean to say it out loud, but he did so anyway, to the confused dismay of the priest.

For the space of several heartbeats, a silence, terrible and pregnant with revelation, boiled towards inevitability. Then, bending the silence in a slow, steady grip, until it snapped like hardened steel, the priest, his breath as unsteady as his hands now betrayed themselves, spoke almost viciously. "Get out. Go. I want you gone *now*. Do you understand me?"

"Tell me the agent's name, Francis."

"No. You will leave now!" The Padre picked up the propane tank, all caution on the cusp of abandonment, and replaced it within the hotdog cart in front of the anomalous object, immediately shutting the stainless steel door and clasping the handle.

At the moment when Jorj was about act on his decision, made with more spontaneity than forethought, someone small, and very familiar, spoke from behind him, startling both the priest and himself. "Father Francis? This guy bothering you?" It seemed like bravado, but it could just as easily be sarcasm. Coming from the night imp, now clean-cut and a model boy of no more than nine years, it was difficult to tell. His hair was dark, almost black, and freckles dotted his cheeks, new-fallen rain from a rusty sky. Behind the ice-blue eyes, and evidenced by wide mocking lips, an intelligence, keen and discerning, worked its own motivations. "His voice dropped to something more serious. "Should I get help?"

The lad was within ten feet of Jorj, a fact not lost on either of the two men in the room. To Jorj, grabbing him was out of the question, but the priest, as evidenced by the expression on his face, and the tone he took when answering, did not know that. "We're just having a disagreement, Richard." He struggled to maintain a level voice, to contain the shake within it. "What are you doing down here, child?"

"Margaret sent me to tell you that we're all back from our field trip." He cast an uncertain eye on Jorj. "She says she wants to talk to you just as soon as everyone is settled down."

"Tell her I'll be there…in just a few minutes." When the boy did not immediately move, he waved his right hand gently. "Run along now, Richard. I'll be upstairs quick enough."

Reluctantly, the boy turned and ran off through the door and down the hall. Father Francis regarded Jorj more calmly than he had before. "Are you going to hold us all hostage, now? Women? Children? I won't let you take it back, you know…not even for their sakes."

"I don't want it back," Jorj answered curtly. "And I'll leave it here, for now. But I don't feel right about this. I can't explain why. And I'll add one more thing. If your agent's name is Benedict…" He saw no sign of recognition on the priest's face and continued. "…or…" Here he realized that Frosty's real name was a mystery to him, as was Bermuda Shorts. Dennis never told him either. He sighed, feeling defeat and frustration. "Forget it." He nodded at the hotdog cart and then narrowed his eyes at the priest. "I hope you know what you're doing, Father. For everyone's sake, I hope you do."

"You came to me because I could help." Father Francis was not relaxed, but he felt that most of the threat from Jorj was over. "Let me do my part."

Whatever Jorj was thinking, he held his tongue on the matter.

He left the church the way he entered, making the disturbing transition between day and night, his soul feeling the shadow before his eyes could register the difference in light. He found Greta waiting, smoking a cigarette but with no apparent satisfaction. We are prisoners to our acquired patterns, Jorj acknowledged. He approached to within three feet of her, letting the doors swing slowly shut on their own, and stopped. "Why didn't you just tell me?"

"We believe our eyes and ears. Words are weak." She took a smokeless breath, held it, and slowly let it out, an exercise of self control.

"I'd believe you."

She regarded him with her dark eyes, her lips un-parted, and he knew what she did not need to tell him again. Some things could not be accomplished through words. In fact, speech had a terrible effect at times of allowing the mind to concoct fallacy, fantasy, and ultimately obstacles to true understanding. He was certain that in the truest existence, there were no words.

"Alright," he conceded. "Send me back to an earlier place. I should retrieve whatever it was that I misguidedly brought to the Padre."

"That is not an open door to you," she replied, looking away towards the north. "But I would offer you passage again, on another night, when I am less tired."

"There is an urgency..."

"Yes," she ceded, "but there is yet time, and timing. Return to your friends tomorrow." She brought her dark eyes to bear on him, inky almonds mysteriously charged, and all the horns of Jericho behind them. Softly, in a way that caused Jorj's heart to hammer recklessly in his chest, her lips parted to form one more sentence before she receded into the shadows. "Pick me up at the corner of Thurber and Alodi, midnight, and keep the motor running."

Jorj smiled, despite the fact that he was now alone. Let people say what they will, argue as they might, and kill each other for the sake of beliefs they cannot prove under a mortal sun or moon. A god existed in some fashion. Every now and then, he mixed a little good in with the bad.

12

His original plan scrapped, Jorj still implemented half of it. By night, he moved everything that was Ogam's from the sixth floor of Fischer Library into a first-floor classroom in Language Hall. He and Dennis would leave most of it behind when they returned to The Millhouse, but he kept his options open for the future.

Seeing little chance of ever getting to sleep that night, and unsure in such a version of Earth that it even mattered, Jorj undertook one more task. In the aisle where he'd first seen Frosty, there were many books, but there was something else, something the angry man of winter searched diligently for until he was interrupted. Jorj spent some time, no more than an hour, and eventually found a thick book, a box cut out of its center, and within it a 45 colt with a single extra clip. He pocketed both, considering it an even trade for his vanished 9mm.

After the first ray of sunlight breached the line barring yesterday from tomorrow, the ever-blue morning sky lit up and got busy for Jorj, rained mercilessly on Freddy, howled a cold January wind against the side of a pink house in a burned-out, working-class neighborhood on the east side, heaping only icy coals onto the soul of Willie Bender, and rekindled the most beautiful July day a traitor had ever known. God bless, the last one thought, far away and free for now, but the baddest men always got rewarded while the good ones...he laughed, sipped his coffee, and went for another swim.

Dennis felt better, not great, but well-enough to travel. Best of all, he wasn't puking anymore. His taste for chocolate pudding, whatever it was before, lay assassinated in the past, never to be resurrected in this man's incarnation.

Both men carried heavy packs, full of paper mostly, though there were a few essentials neither thought Ogam would ever miss. They left immediately, taking the shortest possible way back to the Millhouse. This did not take them on their previous route, that being traveled merely to point out to Jorj that there was no such place as Dansforth Street, or Haydon's Half-Price Book Warehouse. Their way lay along Columbus Avenue, and then to Teac Street which went on for miles, changed neighborhoods several times, led them past outdoor malls, vacant lots, and finally ended in a 'T' with West Ticket Ave, the butt of long standing jokes, teenage night-time races, and resultant speed traps, all of which were just a nocturnal echo on Twilight Earth. Going right, they veered left when the reached Umberland and slipped through a manufacturing district before spilling out onto Thurber, where was the Millhouse.

"What the fuck is that?" Dennis stopped, his feet glued to the road, his back hunched and sore under the weight of his burden.

"Looks like a car," Jorj replied, his smile widening as he saw the wide single air scoop in the hood. He crossed to the parking lot quickly, set down his bag, and bee-lined for the single driver's-side door. His left hand, poised but still, hovered just inches from the chrome handle as his eyes took it all in.

"Whose?" His companion's shout carried easily, followed by the plop of the man's pack dropping to the asphalt. A door opened nearby, just below the Millhouse sign that hung over it.

"Mine...I think." This time he let his hand close over the handle, depress the button with his thumb, and swing the door wide. It opened easily, with only a minor creak to the hinges. "It's got some rust, but so far...so good."

"Yours?" Dennis was still stuck on one word syllables.

"It'll be a tight squeeze. We'll have to just take the necessities, but this will get us where we need to go, I think." Jorj got in, sat down on the bench seat behind the leather-wrapped steering wheel, and placed his right hand on the 4-speed shift. He jerked his head around, noting the all black interior, relishing the smell of a freshly cleaned car that couldn't shake the pleasant smell of its history. Fuzzy green dice hung from the mirror. Jorj laughed at that, and then caught Dennis' expression. Evidently Jorj was behaving like a madman, and why not? This was a little closer to home. Not a one of them knew that his brother Doug once had a car just like this one, except that his was a deep blue...B7, if he remembered rightly. Like his brother's, this one had a black Go-Wing in the back, small and useless, but one that looked cool as hell. And this car would fly, not as well with six, maybe seven people in it, but it wouldn't be easy to catch.

He turned and kicked his feet out and onto the gravel of the parking lot, pulling the hood release and lurching himself back out again. Immediately he went to the front of the car and raised the hood. Bill appeared at his side, a look of pride on his face. Nick was at the door of The Millhouse with the Padre, both approaching leisurely.

"Nice Job," Jorj remarked, looking at the engine. "Very clean."

"440." Bill smiled dumbly. "Changed the air cleaner, plugs, gave it a valve job, tuned it up...the father changed one of the brakes lines for me." He suddenly looked away, embarrassed. "I don't go under there no more."

"The blind priest?" Jorj stopped and smiled amiably. "It's cool." He clapped him on the shoulder. "You did good. Thanks Bill." His face sobered. "Sorry I wasn't straight with you the day we met. You understand why, right?"

"Nick said things are different now, that we have to stick together."

"That's right. And we're getting out of here just as soon as we can...tomorrow, to a better place. We have to find another friend."

"Ogam."

"Yeah," Jorj studied the man carefully, wondering just what and how much Nick told him. "That's him. He's waiting for us, I'm pretty sure."

"At the bookstore."

"Could be." For the first time since he arrived that late morning, Jorj was aware of the priest's thunder rolling through his pleasant autumn sky. Vaguely he imagined listening to that indefinitely, trying to hear his tapes, or CD's, or whatever, over the ominous racket, and all the while seeing his sunny world glowing in that creepy greenish tint, boiling storm clouds superimposing themselves over partially clear skies. For those few seconds, he wondered why the hell he couldn't wake up. "It's a place to start, bud."

Clean clothes were found for them, jeans, t-shirts with irrelevant company logos on them, and fresh socks. Jorj took a bath, for the water was the only thing in the Millhouse that worked, and it was clear. He didn't question it, he just cleaned himself up gratefully, his hygiene being rather on the ropes of late. Frank found a barbeque and some pans, gathered up some canned goods, and went to work on their dinner, likely the last one in any real comfort for awhile, at least as far as any of them could foresee. Dennis, taking a hard lesson from experience, checked the date of expiration on every can and box.

While the charcoal fired up, Jorj pulled Nick aside, taking both him and the newspaper to a booth in the back. When they both sat down, Jorj with a beer Frank found earlier that day, Nick with a glass of ginger ale, they regarded each other with something of expectation. Jorj spoke first. He leveled with him about his night time excursions, who he met, and that they apparently had friends. He also confirmed the presence of a military grade weapon in their equations. Probably a nuke. The only thing he left out was how he knew, and his own, still mysterious, connection to it all. The business with the Padre would have to be sorted out separately first.

"We all have our secrets, Jorj," Nick said with a smile. You have yours, apparently, and I have mine, though I'm sure neither of us is as bad as we think others will see us." He sighed, stirring his soda with a swizzle stick idly. "I'm tired, more than you know. It's really amazing that I made it as far as I did. I should have been dead long before now, and I doubt I'd quite be up to the trip back if I chose to take it."

"How bad is it?" Jorj didn't care to mince words, and hoped Nick wouldn't either.

"I get short of breath sometimes. Occasional chest pains plague me, though if I don't get too excited, it's not so often." There appeared a bittersweet smile on his lips, and Jorj knew why, but he listened patiently. "I quit cigarettes, quit alcohol, try to get out for more walks, but it's only a matter of time. I'm not fooling myself. How long? Ask Dennis. He'll tell you forever. At least that what he tells me, as long as I clean up my act."

"Wishful thinking."

"Wishful thinking," Nick nodded, thumbing the back end of the swizzle stick like he would a cigarette over an ashtray. "I figure I'm not seeing my point of return tomorrow, if that's what you want to know. Past that…God's hands."

Jorj pushed against his own silence, grave and forbidding, until finally, almost unbearably, it gave. "I have to go out tonight."

"You want my permission?" Nick appeared surprised.

"No. Just letting you know."

"You trust them, then." It was clear Nick could not shake loose his skepticism. "How deep is your involvement with the woman?" It was a fair question.

A second passed before Jorj answered. "Not enough to cloud my judgment." He wondered if it was a lie, or at very least a form of denial. "She saved my life some days back." He left out the part where she allowed him to wander into danger in the first place. It was an accident, an unpredictable circumstance. Anyway, it didn't matter so much now. *He* trusted her. In a way, they needed each other too.

The afternoon sun was still high, keeping most of everyone's demons at bay. Nick betrayed little personal disturbance by Jorj's dabbling with the dark, at least for the present. How he might fair later, when the light was low, and the shadows cast by the fire they would surely sleep around danced their eldritch spells, who could say? Now was an hour of the sun, and under such, how could evil possibly raise a threat? The old man simply blinked once, slow and thoughtful. There really was nothing to say that might make a difference.

It was good to be together again, and funny how memory seemed so hazy on how only a few of them actually knew each other for more than a week. Jorj didn't miss the fact, but by now, he knew something more, that these men around him were his family, his brothers, his father, his uncles...only one seat was left empty at the table he sat at. There was no extra place set, nor a chair placed in waiting, but that was not his fault, nor due to anyone else's inconsideration. Through the banter, and the dinner conversations, he remained silent on the subject of his emptiness. Soon, very soon, and he did not know how he knew this, the circle would be complete, each place set, every chair filled.

Dark came hard for all of them. The Millhouse, no matter how secure they made it, or that it grasped at least a handful of familiarity by now for most of them, lay in a strange neighborhood, and New Jackson City no longer enjoyed the protection of Theodore, Nick's longtime friend. Benedict was Lord here now, though his reach had yet to properly extend itself. Jorj didn't share with the others what he had with Nick, that Benedict bridged a forbidden gap to the profane. They didn't need to know that. Sleep came difficult enough with the night's mutterings. The sun was away now, taking with it the fickle protection it offered earlier. For those afraid of the dark, and most sane people in Twilight Earth were, nighttime approached the dogma of the dark ages. A few even began to unearth the pagan bewitchments of glyph and ward, the success of which remained to be proven.

But Jorj was still largely unafraid of the dark, or the night, or of it's denizens. Fear, in his estimation, was a thing entirely different from respect. One was irrational. The other was not. He saw her from the parking lot, waiting on the street corner as she told him she would be. His first impulse was to walk to her, but he resisted this. One reason, and perhaps the most obvious one, was that she told him to 'pick her up' and to 'keep the motor running.' He doubted she was being anything but absolutely serious.

As expected, the driver's side door creaked when he pulled it to. Both that and the introductory unlatching of it echoed familiarly in the quiet of the night. She did not look, did not even turn her head his way, but he knew she paid attention. Her coolness was a telling thing, but so was their shared bond, and even their limited prescience, such that it was. When the keys jangled, he felt a silent thrill, and his skin rose in places so small and legion that he shook reactively. The engine started with a roar at the first turn of the key, and he noticed that the heat was on, though it would be a several minutes before the engine could fulfill its promises of comfort. Had Bill set it to position? Or the Padre? In a warped sense of nobility, he closed the vent, remembering Greta's remark about being always cold, even though on or off, it would physically make no difference to her.

Tires chewed gravel in his tear out of the parking lot. Once on the street he laid out a patch, at least ten feet long, before swinging the Roadrunner up alongside the closest curb at the corner of Thurber and Alodi. If Greta was impressed, she didn't show it. Jorj pulled up on the passenger-side door handle and pushed it out for her. "Hop in."

As soon as she was by his side, the hump in the floor between them, the door closed behind her. "Turn on the heat," she said quickly.

His hand automatically reached for the levers, already over to their proper position. Balking, he registered genuine surprise on his face. "I thought…"

"It's not for me. You'll be picking somebody up."

This stopped Jorj cold. "Wait a minute…"

"Drive, Jorj. There's little time."

"Who is it?" He seemed adamant.

"I'll explain on the way." She regarded him sharply, almost angrily. "You're going to save someone's life tonight. Please drive now!"

His foot hit the gas pedal even before he turned his face away from hers. "This better be good."

"This one works for the man named Theodore, your patron's good friend."

"'Worked,' you mean. Last I knew, Theo was out. Benedict's in."

She looked out her side window. Jorj glanced her way and saw her eyes in the reflection of it watching him back. "He still does Theodore's work. He fights the same fight, and manages daily to stay one step ahead of his adversaries, but tonight he will fail unless you help him in time."

"That's great!" Jorj grunted angrily. "I didn't bring a gun with me! How badly will I need it?"

"Not at all if you hurry." She pointed up ahead. "Turn left there and take your next right."

The Road suddenly came at them faster, slowed, and then the Roadrunner pitched Jorj into a hard starboard lean, noticing absently that Greta seemed immune to the current laws of inertia. He gunned the engine again until it made sense to pull back, took a sharp right, and blasted down an unnamed side street. "What the hell am I going to shoot back with if they shoot at me?" Adrenaline entered into his bloodstream in a steady drip, hypnotic and with a forward momentum all its own. "Use my finger for protection?" He made a mock pistol with his right hand, pointed it backwards, and went 'BANG!'

"Meep, meep."

"Come again?" He swerved onto an onramp and entered the eastbound stretch of Route 17, following the flick of her persistent gesture. "What's that? A cow horn?" What was he, he wondered, Dennis? Making dumb jokes just before going into danger? Then he noticed that she almost smiled...almost, but not quite. It was close enough for him.

"Your car, Jorj." She regarded him with those dark, crushingly beautiful inkwells again, forcing him to look away, suddenly silent. "It's a *Roadrunner*."

There it was, he realized. She'd made a joke herself, without even lifting the corners of her mouth. He let out half a laugh and raised a quarter smile on his right. "This is going to be one hell of a night, lady." Though he didn't turn his head, or tear his eyes from the road now, he knew her own yet lingered on him a moment longer. In an act of sheer cowardice, he found his lead foot, pressing his lips together to avoid speaking. What words banged at the gate now were better off unsaid while there were things to do, and questions to have answered.

They took the exit spilling into the burned out district. Jorj, having passed by here days before, knew this wasn't going to be good. "What's the guy's name?" The car fishtailed on a left turn and shot like a bolt of thunder down a wide open street that ran parallel with a battered old brick warehouse, no more than an empty husk now, it's many shattered windows staring down at them like hollow sockets lined with knives.

"He'll tell you, once you have his trust." She thrust her slender finger towards a side street, Milan Ave. There, house number 33. Keep the motor running. Go to the door, knock three sharply, three spaced, and three sharp again Then get back in behind the wheel as fast as you can."

"Just like that?" His sarcasm fell away as he pulled up next to a run-down, survivor of the fires, a house once blue, now only scarcely so underneath the baked-on coating of ash and smoke that clung to it like old paint. Greta was not in the car. He lurched around and looked in the back seat, knowing before he did so that she was gone. "Damn!" His hand found the door latch and pulled hard. A simple, quick thrust swung it out with little more than a high-pitched squeal to announce his presence. No time was wasted climbing out and running up the dirty walk to the rotted front porch. It didn't even occur to him that he'd left the driver's-side door open. Speed was what was called for now. His right hand balled up into a fist, the knuckles of which rapped out the S.O.S he'd been instructed to do. Then he ran like hell.

A fireball erupted somewhere to his right and behind him. When he reached the Roadrunner, the green finish now brightly lit and surreal under its temporary new sun, he clamored inside, shut the door, and blew the horn like he was trying to wake up God himself. "C'mon, damn you! Let's go..."

His jaw dropped even further than he thought it was already. A brown hand, extended from a parka, found the passenger door handle and made entry, its owner now climbing inside. Before his legs were even in the car, the man was yelling at the top of his lungs just like Jorj had been but seconds before, only in great plumes of frozen breath. "Go! Hit the freakin' gas!"

Like he needed telling. The open door had not slammed yet and Jorj was in the process of painting half a screeching donut on the road in front of the driveway. All legs in, the door pulled shut and the Roadrunner leaped away, a gazelle before the outstretched claws of a hungry lion. Several dark shapes appeared behind them, raising weapons, but by now they were veering out of sight as the Roadrunner turned the corner and ran back along the path of the abandoned warehouse. Two sharp, and very solid objects, hit the trunk before the Roadrunner fully rounded the bend, but nothing hit the gas tank, and both men, keeping it from the other, vented a hidden sigh of relief. Frosty covered his own with bravado.

"Not tonight, you bastards! Hahaaah!" He cranked down his window and spat, yelled a string of epithets, each one more creative than the last, and rolled the glass back up again. Then he turned to look at the driver. "You!" He seemed dumbfounded. "You?" For the first time in his life, Willie Bender was speechless.

"You're welcome, Frosty!" Jorj had no other name to call the man at his side so he stuck with the one that worked best for him. "Surprised to see me?" He realized he was still yelling and grinned fiercely, slammed the gas pedal to the floor, watched Frosty lurch for balance, and yelled louder. "Where to?"

"Where's Theo?" Frosty found his voice and raised it angrily so he could be heard above the engine's din.

"Not a clue!"

"But he sent you!" He sat sideways in the seat and glared at Jorj. It lost some of the effect when the car swerved and he pressed back hard against his door. It occurred to him that locking it would be the smart thing to do under the circumstances. In one quick stroke his right fist hit the button behind him.

Jorj laughed. A sharp turn took them north, on a road that strayed contrary to going home. "How well do you know the city?" He wanted to switch subjects, but he also didn't want to drive into another bad situation, or lead anyone back to the Millhouse. "Watch the signs. I'm getting us lost so that if anyone follows…"

"Yeah, yeah! Don't bore me with the obvious details." Frosty swerved his head right and left, catlike. "Take that street coming up on the right. When you get to the first stoplight, blow through it and then veer left at the fork." His face twisted into a question. "Who supplied the warning? That was way too close, so close it stinks."

"First things first," Jorj replied, spinning the wheel clockwise, fighting against the momentum pushing him into the door. He straightened it out and bobbled back into his normal upright position. "Where do you want to be dropped off at? You pick the place."

Frosty bit on one of the knuckles on his clenched right fist, all his mental pistons firing. "Goddam cold," he muttered. Always so goddam cold!" He pulled his hand away, the knuckle glistening with residual saliva. He wiped it on his pants twice. "Pull over. This is good enough."

"What?" Genuine surprise. "No threats? No question and answer session? Where's the gun in my face?"

"Later. Maybe. Stop the car."

By now they'd entered a commercial neighborhood, small businesses, nothing overwhelmingly corporate. The Roadrunner slowed and then came to rest outside Faher's Locksmith. Frosty yanked on the handle and pushed against the door. The lock held. Cursing, he pulled up on the slender chrome button and tried again, successfully making his exit from the idling vehicle this time. Before closing the door, he stuck his face in again and grimaced at Jorj. "Today's your birthday, Watchman. We're even."

"Steven?"

"Not funny. Theodore didn't send you, did he?" Frosty studied Jorj's silent face and smiled without humor. "That's what I thought."

It went against what he considered to be his better judgment, but Jorj forced himself. "Get back in. I have friends, a warm place to sleep."

"I know who you keep with," Frosty replied, a touch of vinegar in his wine. Jorj wondered just how much he knew, but held his tongue. The former rummaged his right hand into the mate pocket, shivering and tucking his arms in close. Snow appeared on the top of his tight carpet of hair like stars winking awake in an evening sky. "Wanna show you something, just so we're clear on things." Suspicion erupted on Jorj's already guarded features, and he was putting the car in gear when Frosty sat quickly back down in the passenger seat, 38 in hand and pointed straight at his vitals. "It's a small piece, but it does fine in a pinch. If I could stop getting killed, I might be more consistent in my firepower, but..." He smiled wickedly, Dennis's warning came back strong and clear in Jorj's ears. Then, just as suddenly, Frosty put the pistol away, opened the door, and stepped out. "I wanted you to know what I could have done, had I wanted to."

His foot pressed on the break, the roadrunner chomping at the bit, eager to fly, Jorj didn't smile, but his facial muscles hardened in that unique way that they did when only the strength of tautness would suffice to contain his reactive nature. He put the car back in park, wondering, still, if he wasn't crazy. The engine responded with a deeper, more even thrum, as if to say, 'It's all right Jorj. Just relax. Have faith for once.'

"Here's a bone for you." He said, an edge of tension still stubbornly refusing to leave his voice. "I don't remember jack shit about my past anymore. Not my mom, my dad, or any goddam radiation badge. You got something on me. If you've got more, I'm all ears."

Frosty stepped back, tall and straight. "Go home, Mr. Watchman. A couple miles up this road you'll see signs for Route 17 Westbound. You can take it from there. Tell Nick that Benedict will be in town tomorrow, with all his toys and friends, some of them new to the game, from what I hear. He's a bigger player now. Tell Nick to watch himself. Do just that, Watchman." He slammed the door hard, turned, and ran off down the alley between Faher's Locksmith and Nachman's Small Appliance Repair.

After a moment, a few seconds and no longer, Jorj put the Roadrunner in gear and pulled away, showing a greater level of restraint with his new steed than he had all night. A mile down the road, he felt her in the car with him. A look in the windshield mirror confirmed his heart's prodding. "How'd I do, Sweetheart?" Though he said it sarcastically, the secret irony of his words caught him up short, so much so that his tone dramatically sobered. "Now maybe you can tell me why I saved the life of someone who hasn't been very nice to me."

Her own tone, expressed from the direction of the back-seat, showed little in the way of impression, though it was not entirely without favor. "I never doubted you." She went silent for a moment and then continued. "He doesn't know his own worth. You do, but you don't admit it." Then, in a move that surprised him, she brought her face closer. "Do you know where Saint Jude's Cathedral is?"

"Goddam, woman." Jorj sighed heavily. "That's on the West Side."

"So it is."

"I can get us there." He stepped on the gas and felt the pull of the vehicle against his back as it accelerated. Sure as sunshine, Frosty was right. All signs pointed to Route 17. He took it, onramp and all, west to the other side of New Jackson City. She waited until he wasn't paying attention, and then she was there, on the other side of the shift, staring at the radio and tape deck, seemingly intrigued by the fact that it seemed so much newer than the car itself.

"Play this," she said, making it clear that it wasn't merely a request.

He looked down, surprised, but stone-faced again. "Go ahead. Hit it if you think something's in there."

"No." She turned those dark eyes on him. "Your car, your radio."

"Fine." He released the wheel with his right hand, thumbing it with his left, and waited until she withdrew before clicking on the receiver, wondering why she would want to play the radio when there was no station to listen to.

Then he understood, or thought he did, and he felt confused, even disoriented in his surprise, as music flowed in, deep and haunting, faintly and elusively familiar, accompanied by both a woman's gentle but relentless singing voice, medieval in its nature, and a beat he couldn't shake free once it wrapped itself around him. Slow and steady, it put him in its spell, spinning its tale...

The Night Bird sings into the night
She listens for an answer
When none comes, she cries again
For what can come after?

[CHORUS] Who does she call for? Her music so sad.
Does her heart know the truth now, and all that she had?
Is her hope so undying? Does she know he'll be there?
For the darkness tells new lies, and the night doesn't care.

She listens, the echoing back
Distance means nothing
Her song doesn't measure the gap
With love there's no dying

[CHORUS]

[and music bridged a long, wordless gap]

From somewhere, the song bird speaks
Does he hear a word?
Though a wall stands between them
she taps to be heard

[CHORUS]

[More music spans the chasm and fades with the oncoming highway exit]

What, he foundered, had this to do with anything? But he knew, despite his fight to keep his head above the tide of it all, and it took him to the exit where he waited at the defunct light, dark and untended, at odds with the crossroads.

"Is this your way of telling me something without telling me?" he asked. His voice held a neutrality he detested, but couldn't desert. It was obvious he was trying to hold a high ground, whatever it might mean to him, and there wasn't a soul in the city, waking or asleep, who could have listened for the answer with as much mixture of dread and eagerness as he. In an effort to dispel the glamor put upon him, he rolled down his window and let in the fresh, chill air from outside.

When she didn't answer at first, he wondered that maybe he'd made a big deal out of nothing, that maybe he *was* losing his marbles. But she stared at him, holding his eyes, and he knew, more than ever before, what she had already told him not long before. Words were never enough.

"Turn left at the next stop sign," she said slowly, each syllable crafted with intent. "We need to finish our business here tonight."

As one in a fog, he did as she bid him, letting the slow, plodding nature of a machine with the vigor of a cat held in reserve, take them calmly down to the corner. Underneath the overpass, the headlights cut through the shadows, creating new ones with every passing of a stationary object. It was spooky, he noted, seeing the meaning of something determined by an unpopulated viewpoint. How many days and nights had he done this on foot, before the advent of this muscle-car from a bygone era, the Roadrunner, the paladin's steed?

His hand went to the radio's knob, turned off the static that filled the back and side speakers. "Who's the DJ?" He seemed emotionless, but it was an illusion. He knew it and so did she.

"Radio waves penetrate all worlds," she answered, cryptically as ever. "You get to know them after awhile."

By the time they pulled up outside the city's oldest, most magnificent church, the moon was tipping past the middle of the sky, and the clouds, so ragged and portentous before, were all but gone. Stars winked and pierced the membrane of the night, betraying the cagey light of heaven above. If the angels thought they had it all to themselves, Jorj thought idly, they needed to come down here once in awhile, at least on the night he died.

"Okay, Gret," he chose a form of address somewhat more familiar than he was used to, but life was an experiment after all, even here on Twilight Earth. "What now?"

"You should go inside, through the front doors." When he looked at her inquisitively, she added, "You will know what to do."

He shut off the engine, placing in his mind's eye where it was Dennis had told him he'd find a gas station with a working pump. The contrast of the silence was sheer, tightly meshed with the night's deep autumn chill. He felt a need to lighten the mood. "You won't try to steal the car, will you?" The keys remained in the ignition.

Her lips, full and delicate, pressed together. "Probably not."

"Then I'll see you in a bit." His hand found the latch and opened the driver's-side door. Their eyes met briefly, and then he climbed out, shutting the door behind him. Whatever reason she had for bringing him to this place, another church in a world too far for God to hear very well, he hadn't a clue. He only hoped he did a better job than he did with the Padre, the younger version. Leaving behind whatever it was he supposedly brought to the man in the first place wasn't setting well with him.

Fan-like, the stairs in front of Saint Jude's spread out like a great granite fan, curved and leading up to simple wooden doors, each a half of an arch. The brass handles seemed plain compared to the much smaller Concord Chapel, but they were also older, and dark with the many hands that once grasped at the Lord's sleeve through them. His own found them and he picked the one on the right. It was unlocked and so offered no resistance when he plied his efforts to it and passed through to the other side.

In it's way, Saint Jude's reminded Jorj of Concord Chapel, with one distinct exception, the sanctuary lay directly past the front entry. To the left, a door stood half open. A long, thick rope hung just past it, presumably to bells above.

He let the door close behind him, almost immediately smelling the odor of burning wax and a faint residue of incense. Beyond the door, he heard a car horn blow. Instinctively, he pushed against the bar, heaving the door open. The Roadrunner lay parked right where he left it. Through the windshield glass he saw Greta, watching him patiently. Then, overlapping the lay of the city, people strolled the sidewalks. A bus rolled by bound for East Street, its evening lights coming to life even as Jorj looked on. He couldn't help but look to Greta, who only watched him, probably wondering what he was doing. He grinned uncertainly, waved, and shut the cathedral door again. For the moment he only stood there listening to the sounds of the street, realizing just how much he missed the real thing, and how lonely this world was. The entrance to the sanctuary was open behind him, and now he became quite aware that a presence was even now approaching from that direction.

As he turned, Jorj expected to be questioned. After all, he wasn't exactly the church-going type, and his clothes, though better matched and cleaner than what he had on the other day, still screamed 'vagrant.' Consequently, he was mildly surprised when an elderly woman, no doubt a true street person, passed him without a word or a glance. She smelled of urine and cigarette smoke. Jorj's left hand went to her arm, quite unplanned, and she stopped, a look of indignation on her face, and fear. His right hand dug into a pocket and produced the only thing he had to his name besides the clothes and the car. The old woman shifted her eyes from the hand that held her to the energy bar in the other. Slowly, then with surprising speed, she snatched it from him and drew away. "Let me go." She croaked irritably. He released her and she pushed her way out the door, anxious to get away from the strange man, candy bar or no.

A numbness seemed to grip him still, and Jorj stood where he was a few seconds longer, letting it dissipate. As it did so, he realized that there was something familiar about this church, like he was here once before. His eyes trailed to a piece of paper on the floor, a discarded bulletin, black ink on cheap white paper. He walked over to it and picked it up. It was curled in the middle, like someone had been nervously rubbing it with their thumb, rolling it slightly in their hands. There was a roughness in the space. The person's hands were sweating while they held it.

Besides spelling out the schedule of the day's services, what hymns would be sung, and the complete Lord's Prayer, there was mention in the back of an autumn street festival for the following week. Though there was no mention of the holiday, it was clear that Halloween was intended to have some more wholesome competition from the people of Saint Jude's. He'd been to one or two of these. There would be food, carnival games, face painting. And if there was ever a time to move something to a safer place, one more closely under a priest's watchful eye…

He raised his face and gazed around him, a realization breathed upon him that not all of his words were ever lost, nor his chances entirely gone. Once again, almost automatically, Jorj made an entrance into a sanctuary, and not with an intention of prayer, though later he would come to wish that he had.

The candles he smelled burning were not a significant source of light, though there were a great many of them. The holy chamber was simply too big to be affected much by the amount of light, as generous as it was. To illuminate the great open chamber, ceiling lights, large hanging chandeliers very similar to those at Concord Chapel were employed. Like its less endowed sister church, there was a pulpit, and a choir loft, and large, beautifully crafted stained-glass windows, but all were larger and more grandiose. The balcony to the rear was higher, and built more deeply into the building, not merely a later addition. A door to his left as he came in most assuredly would take him there if he wished. He didn't. His business was elsewhere tonight.

From behind the pulpit, above the choir loft, within a deep recess, upon a curved wall and arched half ceiling, God sat on a throne, painted into heaven, with angels and rays of glory. Elsewhere, carved in wood, Jesus toiled on a cross in the three-dimensional world, much closer to mankind than he likely wished. To the right of this, in a smaller recess, Mary looked down upon her own portion of the chamber, her attention on things other than her compromised son, leaving Jorj to wonder at a religion that could have so many graven images in stark defiance of the book it served. But that, as he already observed, was not why he was here tonight. God could sort out that particular dilemma.

It was surprising to see that there was no one else within the sanctuary with him, no organist, no priest, no one but himself. He knew who he would find if he looked hard enough. The karma was too strong now to be wrong in his prediction, but he also realized that to meet up with this person now would be contrary to his purpose, hidden and waiting as it was. He made for the right of two doors at the far side of the sanctuary, by the choir loft, passing by Mary with barely a glance and marveling on the similarity of which these places were designed, despite obvious denominational differences.

The door gave way easily before his hand. It was unlatched, and beyond, the small, freshly painted hallway, which turned immediately right, was completely quiet. Jorj went through, found that it turned left again, where a closed door in the right wall led elsewhere. He passed by this latter but stopped short when he heard a familiar voice. It was the Padre's, and the tone was both angry and alarmed. By the one-sided conversation, it was easy to conclude that he was on the phone, but to whom was unclear.

"I'm sorry," the good father apologized, his tone firm but waning in its effect. "I never received it." A few seconds passed and then he continued. "Yes," I know what I told you, but my promises were premature. I was certain I would have it...no... no, I cannot. You know the vows I have taken. Confessions stay within the booth...yes, I understand the gravity of the situation." More silence, then: "I wish I could help you...very well. You do what you must."

Jorj found that the sweat broken out upon his face was cold. Whatever he was here for, he had only minutes, if even that much time. He faced the hallway left of the door, at the same time hearing a hand on the knob. Suddenly he was running past an exit sign towards a farther door, pushing through the latter, running down stairs. The air felt cooler. He realized he was in the basement, but that the stairs turned and descended again to an even deeper level. This was an old building, and a large one. How could he search it all in time? And how the hell, he agonized, was he even supposed to know what he was looking for?

You will know what to do.

But he didn't, at least not yet. Though, as he noted, there were stairs going down, there was still a large room ahead, supported by large pillars boxed in by painted wood. All of it, the walls, the enclosed pillars, even the ceiling, had the appearance of having been painted several times. There was a musty smell, and it was stronger by the stairs. For a reason that only his subconscious might understand, he chose the stairs going down. They were dark but he found a switch and flipped it, instantly illuminating his way in dim fluorescence. Beneath his feet, the floor was hard, concrete covered in old, discolored, green and white linoleum tile. Each step jolted him to his knees until, after twenty, he hit bottom.

Down here, two levels below the sanctuary and the street, light fixtures were not well-maintained, and the strobe effect from a bad ballast in at least three of the lights, in addition to the many more tubes that simply were spent and could only dimly glow at their ends, created a surreal landscape that caused Jorj to stop and question his surroundings.

It *was* down here. Something else too, waited for him, or rather someone. As his eyes adjusted to the weak, disrupted light, he spied the hotdog cart in the back, tucked in between boxes and old furniture, dusty from countless years of neglect. A lump, thick and powerful, stuck in his throat. Not merely because one of his suspicions was proved correct, but because some twenty-five feet to the left, at the end of a cleared path in the stored debris, was another door, metal and framed into a wall of newer, cinderblock construction. It thumped suddenly, again, then again. Faintly, so deadened by the formidable thickness it tried to penetrate, voices called out, a woman and a child. At least two people were trapped, or held prisoner. The fact that this was a church, a sanctified place of God, could not change the possibility of the latter.

At once he was confronted by a third problem, lingering and loud. Someone threw the fire alarm. In the fraction of a second he had to react to it, the Padre came to mind. Later he would understand why. Now he had to make a choice.

This was a test, intentional or not. He could feel pieces of a jumbled, dysfunctional puzzle coming together, all without the final picture, and he could do nothing but act, knowing that his decision now was on a larger scale than any he had ever known before.

But he knew one thing, or at least believed he knew it. The object in the hotdog cart had to go, and fast. Cursing himself, he ran to it, throwing boxes aside so that he could get to the rear doors of the stainless-steel box on wheels. Still the door thumped, even more loudly than before. If the voices still shouted from behind them, which he was certain that they did, they were completely drowned out by the clamor of the fire alarm. He realized that he was himself crying, for he knew who it was behind the door, and that this decision was a damnable one with no good end, the lesser of two evils for everyone else, an action demanding sentence to him, and no judge or jury but his own conscience, the most infamous of all adjudicators.

He tore away at the doors, bending them in his reckless desperation, and reached his left hand inside. Whatever concern he had before, that tampering with the object should set it off, unleashing an unholy fire upon this place of worship that God himself would not be bothered to cool for ten thousand years, evaporated, no more than a phantom created by an earlier ignorance. It came loose with considerable effort, all the way to his feet where he switched his grip to the top handle, formerly concealed by its hiding place within the cart. This case was made to protect what lay inside, and both were made to travel, though the weight of this approached one hundred pounds. Whatever the weight or purpose, the value paled to him, compared to what still pounded on the other side of that steel-cased door less than thirty feet away, but the destruction of this evil took priority over the preservation of...his head dropped for a second, the tears harsh and acrid. In the next heartbeat he was on his feet, carrying the heavy olive drab case at a run, towards the stairs, away from the receding door and the two behind it.

He ascended as one to his death, though that would have been more merciful to him, had he been asked. He was not. Yet on the way up, the priest appeared, a look of shock on his face, and he moved to block Jorj's way, his mouth working silently in defiance though nothing audible would, as yet, manifest itself. Jorj grabbed him with his left hand and pushed him aside, struggling with the Padre's flailing arms, barely able to break away. The latter, unable to either stop Jorj or keep his own balance, tumbled downstairs, using his arms to protect his head from the hard steps. His fate was his own, and Jorj, rushing back up the stairs to the top landing, left him to it. Suddenly, there he was, in the hallway on the first floor. Not ten feet away was an exit. He made straight for it only to find that it was locked.

Locked.

The implications were immediate. Some were less dire than others, but none boded well. He turned, abandoning the door, for it was heavy and would consume too much of his time in his attempt to break it down. Down the hall he ran, hoisting the military case in front of him with both hands. It was hard running, but there was so little time left He made it back to the freshly-painted hallway, and then to the sanctuary, when the shots rang out, three of them, the first two notching the tops of pews to his right, the third one grazing his tight triceps. There was no break in his stride, no panicked glance back. When he heard the Padre's voice behind him, and felt the final shot, just before he pushed through the doors into the front foyer, penetrate his chest on the right, he nearly dropped his charge, the damnable thing he had to protect, to keep out of the hands of...

And then he hit the front doors, hit them hard. They wobbled, but the lock that someone nefariously set held defiantly. His strength flowing out of him through his open chest wound, Jorj made for one last slam on the door.

"No!" The Padre fired again, just over Jorj's head. The round ricocheted off the wall and into the ceiling, exposing the bricks in the outer wall and sending plaster dust down upon both of them. "Don't make me kill you, Mr. Watchman!" His breath came in heaves. Something gurgled. "You know I can't allow you to leave with it."

Jorj hit the door anyway, took the bulk of the force himself, bounced back, and slumped against it, his efforts over. "The two in the basement...you're going to kill them, aren't you?"

"Of course not!" Father Francis took several steps forward. "They were going to go to the authorities!"

"But...Jorj struggled to his feet and turned to face his assailant, still gripping the military case in both arms, feeling it slip slightly but resolved not to give it back. "What is wrong with them—anybody—doing that?" He let his back and head lean back against the door. "What did you...did you think you were going to do with it?"

"Give it to me, Mr. Watchman." Father Francis was barely on his feet himself. "It needs to go back to safety."

"I'm taking it to safety, you idiot!"

The doors rattled. Voices outside barked orders, radios squawked in reply. And then an explosion rocked the church, at the back. Dust and debris hit them in a cloud that pushed violently through the foyer doors, bowling the priest into Jorj, knocking the latter to his knees.

"They know!" Father Francis cried, prying himself away. "They've been watching! I have to save the others...now! Oh dear God! Dear God in Heaven!"

There followed a pause, short and foreboding. Jorj pulled back just in time as an axe burst through the door, splintering the beautiful old oak around the area of the lock. It took the firemen several more tries but then they were through. Fire lit the back of the sanctuary, illuminating the smoke that continued to billow towards them.

He couldn't afford to lose his head, Jorj kept telling himself. He had to make these moments count, for he was so close, so close. They grabbed him and moved him towards the door. "The basement!" He yelled furiously. "There are people in the basement!" A fireman wearing a white helmet with facemask seized Jorj and barked orders at two others wearing black helmets. The latter moved carefully over the rubble in the direction of the sanctuary.

The man in the white helmet pushed Jorj roughly towards the front doors and then stopped him, suddenly aware of the nature of what Jorj was carrying. "What the hell's this! Oh shit!" He strove to grab it with one hand, reaching for his radio with the other, and then Jorj, still clutching the object with the last of his strength, pushed through the door. Resistance evaporated, and he stumbled, falling down the granite stairs. No more than a translucent ghost now, the fire chief's apparition registered astonishment as he yelled savagely into the radio clipped near his collar. It seemed he no longer saw Jorj.

His left arm went out in front of him, saving his head from the brunt of the first impact. He rolled once, feeling sharp pain as one of the bones in his forearm gave, and then his head struck a glancing blow off another step. When he came to rest, still three feet from the bottom of the stairs, his right hand still clutched the top handle of the olive drab case.

Between the loss of blood, a probable broken arm, and a minor concussion, Jorj struggled now with dizziness. Greta appeared at his side at once. Though his vision blurred, he could swear that her cheeks were streamed with tears, glistening in the moonlight. "Can you make it to the car, my love?"

Had he heard her right? Something, buried deep within him, strove to make itself heard. Had not his own tears...so recently...

"I'm okay," he replied weakly, rolling onto his knees, feeling his left arm begin to swell. He felt for his keys with his right hand.

"They're still in the ignition."

"Right." He lurched forward, found his feet for a few wobbily seconds, and then sat back down. "I think I'm going to throw up." Instead, for a few minutes, he lost consciousness. Whether it was her pleadings for him to wake up, the relentlessly impassive moon, or merely the chill of the gentle, pre-dawn, autumn breeze, he couldn't say, but he came to again, and he was shaking. "Have to do something."

This time he crawled, and successfully made it to the driver's seat. He removed the keys and found his feet again, this time keeping them. Leaning against the Roadrunner for support, he staggered to the trunk and opened it. His eyes tracked back to the stairs and the green case lying on the second step. It seemed like a very long way to go. "Gret..." He swallowed hard shook his head to clear it. The thunderous ache that rebounded taught him not to make that mistake twice. "I could use some help."

She was at his side again, but lent him no support. It angered him slightly.

"Please."

"I cannot." Her voice was immeasurably sad. "Not yet." She drew his eyes to hers merely by looking at him, and when he saw them, he calmed, waiting for her to speak again. "You need to make a sling for your arm. I cannot do it for you, I can do nothing for almost another hour, and before then, you must do something for me. I need you to be strong." Her lips trembled. It was easy to see that she was also frightened. "I'm so sorry."

"It's ok," he soothed quietly, even through his own pain. When he tried to touch her cheek, she withdrew. "What? What is it?"

"There's a blanket, here." She stood up, pointed into the trunk. Her pained expression could not hide her will to practicality. "You'll need to cut it with the scissors in the toolbox."

Jorj turned his head, slowly, almost vacantly. Yes, there was a brand new purple blanket in the trunk, and an old, cheap, steel toolbox. "It's latched." It was a joke—feeble, true—but the best he could manage under the circumstances. Her sober face could not be lightened by mere words, he noted. Disappointedly, he turned back to the task, and with his good right hand, he flipped back the cheap metal hasps, including the one intended for a missing lock, and pushed back the hinged lid. The top tray, its red paint chipped mercilessly in its aged past, held many common tools, but it was the black handled scissors that he sought. He picked them out and then dragged the blanket to his lap as he turned and slid to a sitting position against the back bumper. It was cold, but the sinking Moon was full and its generous light more than adequate for what he had to do. If only, he wished out loud in a murmur, his head did not hurt so much and he could think straighter.

Where she could not help him before, she could do something now. He still needed to cut the blanket, and do all of the other physical work, but she told him how to do it, and kept him awake, paying attention. At last, after almost twenty min-

utes, his arm, now swollen to nearly twice its size, was supported out of further harm's way, provided he did not fall again.
The eastern sky, by this time, was lightening. It occurred to him
what that would mean, one of many things that were to change
very soon. "Gret…" He wanted to move, but she had so little
time left. He wished to spend it with her.

"Come." She stood and crossed to the steps of Saint Jude's.
There is time to finish what we started."

He tilted his head, uncertain, and then saw it, the green case.
"I can't, not with one good arm and…" he caught his breath
and smiled thinly. "I'm a little low on type A at the moment."

"Forget that," she said, that bit of trembling back in her lip.
She seemed more fragile now, like she might flee any moment.
"Please Jorj. This I ask you, and not lightly. Please come and
take my hand."

Soon, within minutes, the sun would rise, stretch its rays
across the land again, or perhaps only for the first time. Jorj
watched her waiting and rose slowly to his feet, a strength
horded this past hour, drop by drop, within his abused sinews.
He used all of it now to cross to her, climbing to the top step before the wooden doors, doors which bore no sign of incursion,
by axe or shoulder. Tears streamed down her cheeks again, and
she took her place on his right.

"No matter what you see," her voice was unsteady, a boat
in high waves, but moored with heavy anchor. "No matter
what you see, what you hear, whatever it is you feel, or think
you feel, you must…*must not* let go of my hand." She turned
her eyes upon his, those great deep pools of the night, holding
all the mysteries of the universe within them, and his breath
seemed to run short. He realized his heart pounded, not from

fear, but rather something much greater. "Do you understand me?"

He nodded. "If you take my hand, or allow me to take yours, I swear to you I will not let go."

"Then look east," she cried, her voice quavering but strong. Instinctively he reached for her hand, small and slender, and she took his strong one, wrapping each finger tightly together so that only themselves, or the Almighty God himself could unravel them. It took Jorj a moment to realize that her hand, her fingers, all of her was insubstantial. Only by sheer force of will did they touch, and tie themselves together so. "Behold!" a voice, her voice, cried again in his head. "It comes!"

And it came, brilliant and glorious, bathing the land in gold, winding around shadows, beaming between buildings, touching the faces of man and woman with its gentle, persistent warmth.

Her scream pierced him like a spear, for it was loud and sharp, so unexpected. He turned to look and in his moment of horror, he almost let go, but the greater soul within him only caused the hand that clutched hers to squeeze more tightly. Hotter than the sun itself, she burned with a fire, holy and consuming...but it was not consuming at all! Through the incorporeal vision, tethered to him by a bond he could no better understand than what was happening to her now, a skeleton floated, in perfect synchrony with the woman. White energy swirled within it, and around it, manifesting in flesh, the ligaments, tendons, muscles. He watched, unable to move or speak. Organs blossomed within her, spread vascular tendrils throughout in a fine web, and all the while she screamed and moaned, pleading to an unseen force for mercy. And then his good right hand felt the firmament within it, strong and flexing against his own. The light was about her, enveloping her. No more did he see what lay beneath, but he saw her face again, and it was beautiful, despite the shocked pain upon it. With that her eyes clenched shut and she flung herself into his arms weeping. He held her tight with his good arm, weeping himself, unaware as he closed his eyes with her that the light, for a brief moment, caught them both up and then receded.

The day was new. On the steps of Saint Jude's Cathedral, a man held a naked, shivering women, both of them weeping, at first in the aftermath of shock, then for pain and sadness, finally they wept for something else, something brighter, something they'd both waited long for, and the tears flowed strong in their relief.

13

Morning finally put an end to the mutterings of the night, and Dennis was grateful for it. His sleep, aided by taped music, radio static, or otherwise numbing, distracting noise, could only partially filter out what were, to the night-plagued inhabitants of Twilight Earth, whispers from hell. Last night he had nothing to stop the murmured cacophony.

"Glorious," he mouthed the word with cautious surprise. There was something about the way the sun streamed through the blinds, a little stronger...pleasant even. He wondered that 'pleasant' was something not often felt anymore. But this was all of that.

His feet, touching the cold, clay-tiled floor, as he sat upright on the narrow padded lobby bench where he spent the night, felt dry and comfortable. He no longer suffered from nausea. Nick gave him something for his stomach the night before, once he returned with Jorj and got settled. The old man was good with things like that, another reason to miss him if his health went south. It saddened Dennis to think about the possibility. If Nick left them, he wouldn't be back. He wasn't like the rest of them.

In the background, he heard Frank up and around, busy with something. Most likely it was breakfast. The old fart never seemed to get tired of being the cook. That was a good thing, the young man mused. None of the rest of them could fry an egg past its own rottenness. It was a gift, and God help them if the old guy up and quit. Dennis stood, stretched, and went to the front window, lifting one of the blinds skeptically with his right index finger. His suspicions were confirmed by the vacant parking lot and equally empty street. No Roadrunner. No Jorj.

"He never came home last night." Nick stood at the entry to the common room, hands in his suit pants pockets. He withdrew a pocket watch and released the spring-loaded cover. "Seven thirty-six." He snapped it shut and returned it to its place.

"Should we be concerned?" Dennis knew it was a foolish question.

A thoughtful expression surfaced on Nick's bearded face. "I don't think we should ever stop, Dennis. Do you?"

"No. I guess not."

The old man nodded and came and stood beside the other, patting him on the left shoulder gently. "We'll give him as much time as we can. Bill is up on the top floor keeping watch out all of the windows. If anything moves, he'll tell us."

They took their breakfast at the table where they ate dinner the night before, minus two, for someone had to keep watch now. Everyone was aware of Jorj's absence, but no one said a word or asked a question about his whereabouts. He tripped into the night, and that was enough. Not even Bill questioned that. What he didn't know from their tales, his subconscious told him. Like them, he heard the night-time mutterings, and he had nightmares. Not even the priestly thunder could roll any of that away.

Fortunately for them, the sun had, at least pro tem. They broke away from the table gradually, away from their cold cereal, their instant milk, and their coffee. Dennis held a troubled expression all through their gathering, one that Nick noted with apprehension. He waited until Frank went off to clean up, and Padre wandered upstairs to take something up to Bill, before confronting him on it. Dennis, quite oblivious to the old man's attention, remained staring into nothing, deeply thoughtful and unsettled.

"No." Nick expressed his thought gently but firmly.

"Excuse me?" Dennis almost jumped. He quickly recovered himself, biting his upper lip absently and glancing out the nearest window.

"You're not going after him. I forbid it."

"You've never forbid me anything befo…how did you know what I…" He truly looked flustered now.

"Easy, Dennis." Nick poured himself another cup of coffee. "Stay put. He'll come."

"He's in trouble."

Nick sighed; then he sipped, wincing slightly at the burned taste. "Where did you guys find that coffee maker?" He held up his left hand abruptly. "Never mind that. Leave Jorj to his business. We have ours. If God chooses to unwind his path from ours, then so be it. But I don't think he has. You need to learn to have faith."

"In-what-or-who?" Now Dennis' ire was up, and his voice rose to the occasion. "God? Does *he* help me get a decent night's sleep? Is it *his* hand that scavenges for the food we eat? The toilet paper we wipe our…" He stopped up short, red-faced, realizing he was nearly screaming at a man with a heart condition, and one who'd taken care of him ever since he spilled out of his goddam truck. The words 'I'm sorry' wanted to slip past his lips, but they were closed tight, too stubborn to allow passage, even of so noble a duo.

Not a trifle of offence appeared on Nick's features. Rather, in the most disarming way, he smiled, and so saw his own effect in the relaxing of Dennis' facial muscles, the receding of wrath from the younger man. "If there's one thing I know, Dennis, it's that we are here, each of us, because there's at least one other person we need, for one reason or another, in order to move on towards heaven. I don't know much else, but that much is truth."

"Who do you need, Nick?"

"That's a simple one," the older man laughed. "All of you."

Now Dennis laughed, but it carried with it a coating of sarcasm. ""You sure must have pissed God off!"

"The Almighty only chastises those he loves, Dennis. He does not want us to be on any other path but his."

"Is that where our path is going?" There remained that little touch of irreverence, but like his wrath a moment earlier, it was withering.

"Of course, Dennis," Nick replied good-naturedly, setting his cup down and rising to his feet. "Don't be a fool. God doesn't want that either." Slowly he turned and wandered off. "I have to go shit like an old man, now."

"Long and strong?" Dennis called after him.

"You got it."

After a time, Dennis relieved Bill's watch. The big man came down, ate a little something more, and slept, for sleep during the day was a blessing. The Padre, with little else to do, and a restless feeling upon him, stepped outside. By now, he knew the building well enough, and there was almost no fear by himself or anyone else of him getting lost. He took his staff, cut, carved, and presented to him by Dennis to keep him from tripping, and sat out on the front stoop.

Almost at once he was aware of another presence. It stood there, watching him from across the street, the second floor, he thought. He twitched his nose a little, wondering if he could smell anything out of place, aftershave—an absurd thing on Twilight Earth but used nevertheless—cigarette smoke, booze… ah yes. He did smell something. Coffee, strong and bitter. For a second, very brief, he heard what might be a sniffle. His brows furrowed in thought, concentrated recitation of a long list of names, and their meteorological implications. "Freddy?" No, it wasn't Freddy. That man was not so much a surveyor, but rather a sulker. "My pardon. William."

This time he heard a distinct grunt. A few seconds more and then a door slammed, all pretense of stealth discarded. A full minute later a door slammed on street level directly across the great asphalt divide and footsteps approached, unhurried, but with an irritated quality to them.

"Caught by a damned blind preacher." The footsteps halted a dozen feet away, at the edge of the sidewalk where it met the curb. "Your nose could get you into a mess of trouble, Pops."

Father Francis smiled. Thunder rolled, building up to a crash that would never happen. "Good morning, Trouble."

"That's *Mister* Trouble to you." His breathing betrayed a smile of his own, though it was grim and tight-teethed. "Where's everybody?"

"Inside, as I'm sure you already know."

"Not the Watchman." The smile receded to an even line. "He never got back last night, did he?"

"Not that I know of. Must have been some night."

Frosty pursed his lips thoughtfully. "I guess I'll have to tell you what he was supposed to, but I only want to say it once." He started walking again, towards the stoop and the door.

An arm raised to meet him. "Help an old father up?"

"Right," Frosty slid past the arm and opened the door. In a loud voice, he called inside. "Nick! Git your posse together! Time for a meetin'!"

Everybody there but Bill knew Willie Bender by name. Some remembered him better than others. The older ones, Nick, Frank, even the Padre, knew him well enough to know that the reputation went farther than the man, though the reality was impressive enough. Dennis took a seat at the table, but kept his distance. Splitting hairs with another man's distinction was a waste of time, and dangerous. A killer was still a killer, and an experienced one like 'ol' Frosty'—he liked that name and spoke it in his head quite often now—was as bad as they got. Just because you might not stay dead, after all, was no reason to play fast and loose with the reaper, and that nasty scythe wielder had many who still did his bidding.

Then there was that little bit about shooting him in the Fischer Library. Dennis wondered how much he knew...probably didn't have a clue, he thought.

"What's your deal, Brinks?" Frosty eyed him skeptically. "You look like you see the devil on my back. Somethin' you wanna say before I have mine?" His steel eyes flared noticeably, making everyone wonder if maybe hell *had* frozen over and this man, standing there in his unzipped parka and slushy boots, was just back from a long stay there.

"I'm fine," Dennis replied, fidgeting in his chair. The 9mm in the back of his pants pressed uncomfortably against his skin. "All ears."

A toothpick appeared from a pocket and paused on its way to Frosty's lips. "Got anything between those ears, Mister Brinks? You're gonna need more than I've seen so far." He turned his basilisk gaze on the rest of them. Frank seemed unperturbed. Bill was asleep, and the Padre only smiled sightlessly.

Nick met Frosty's stare with one of his own, more gentle, but firm like an old tree. "Let's get to the business, shall we? What of Theodore?"

"What of Theodore…" Frosty's sarcastic smile shined like a dagger. "On his own, I'd say. Ain't heard word one from the man, and don't expect to. Would have by now if he wanted it that way. Tell you this much though. The dude ain't in Benedict's hands, and that's gotta be pissing someone off terrible!" The smile died almost immediately, replaced by a deadly serious flat-line façade. "There's some may wish they could stay dead, if they stay here much longer."

"I've read a paper or two as they've turned up." From behind his back, Nick produced the news edition Jorj brought with him the other morning and tossed it flatly in the middle of the table. "Interesting read."

"I've *seen* it." In the span of a heartbeat, Willie Bender snatched it up, and then threw it back down in the middle of them all. "Those damn fools got no idea what they're gonna get, and who's gonna get 'em with it! Some of them will be comin' here, and when they do, they won't just be bringin' their newspapers with 'em. They be bringin' something else, terrible nasty!"

"Radiation."

"Well Mister Brinks! The scarecrow does have a brain!" Frosty's eyes gleamed with mock pride. "You just might be able to save your lily ass yet! Just make sure you don't ever die again, cuz once you get hot…" He laughed long and loud, letting everyone fill in the blanks. When he saw no one laughed along with him, he only laughed harder, switching the toothpick from one side of his mouth to the other. "This whole city gonna be one big ground zero, boys!"

"As if Benedict wasn't enough." Nick glanced at the Padre and found him suddenly quite somber. "I thought he was our biggest material worry at present."

"Oh, I wouldn't turn my back on him still, any of you." There was something in his tone which troubled them even more than his words. "The man, from everything I hear, ain't right anymore. Got some kind of evil bug up his ass."

"He never was part of the congregation." If Dennis hadn't said it, likely Nick would have said something very similar. "Bad man."

Frosty raised an eyebrow, amused. "No lie there, Brinks. He woulda skinned you long ago, if he'd a' caught you. Now? The dude's a traveler." His smile took on a twist of sarcasm. "Even more so than Watchman, though he get's around pretty good too."

You've seen him?" Dennis brightened a small bit, his fear and distrust of Frosty on hold.

"Last night." The toothpick switched sides again. "Dude was drivin' around in the badlands."

"The Burned out district?" Nick looked truly concerned. "Why?" The question was not directed toward Willie Bender and honestly to no one specifically. He merely spoke his concern out loud.

Frank got up and went to the kitchen. For a second, Frosty eyed him suspiciously, and then let it go. His eyes darted to the windows, as they had been the entire time since he arrived at the Millhouse. Eventually, they alighted upon Nick once more, and they were somewhat respectful. "Look, I don't know what the man does out there in the dark of night. For all I know he might be one of the spooks now. I came here to warn you because Theodore looked out for you and yours. This I do out of respect for him." He looked up and saw Frank returning with a pot of coffee for the table, and some simple white mugs. "What you do now is up to you, but I wouldn't wait too long on the Watchman. No tellin' where he's off to or if he'll be back."

"He'll be back." Everyone turned towards the Padre, whose silence was unexpectedly broken. Something in the way he said it suggested that his was not merely a reactionary comment.

"Heh, maybe, Preacher Man." Frosty studied the blind man unhurriedly, removing the toothpick from between his own lips and flicking it across the room just over the priest's head. From his right pants pocket, the small watch pocket every pair of jeans has, he withdrew another and held it for a moment idly. " Every man for his own skin, that's what I say. Devil take the slow."

"Or the lone."

His smile faded, Frosty let the toothpick hang, slightly sticking, off his lower lip. "I don't think ol' Beelzebub's got a bead on me Nick, if that's what your getting' at. I got more than nine lives…a lot more." He snatched up a mug, poured himself a cup of heavy, black coffee, and took a slug before continuing. "And I plan on staying one step ahead of him now. I'm gonna finish this cup and go. If you're smart, you will too. Stay off the major routes. Pick a destination that's not too flashy."

"Like Mexico." As soon as he said it, Dennis wished he hadn't.

"Stop lookin' like I'm gonna fry you up for supper, bony. I'm all over *that*." He was, of course, referring to an unsuccessful stay south of the border some years back, if years truly existed on Twilight Earth. "Others went before me. I just had to learn the hard way…but I still learned. Go far; don't get kilt or ya come right back."

"What's that?" Padre crooked his head with an ear towards the south.

"Chopper!" Dennis pushed his chair back and ran to one of the front bay windows. Frank and Nick followed behind, their own sense of urgency before them rather than behind.

The three gathered around the window like dogs with a cat on the other side. Padre rose from his own chair and put his hands on the back of it. He listened intently but made no signs of moving further. Windows did little for the blind. Dennis broke away from the other two and ran to the front door. In the next heartbeat, he was outside in the street, his face pointed up and his left hand shielding his eyes from the sun. Suddenly he pointed. "There it is!" he shouted.

"Damned fool!" Frosty growled and made for the door himself.

"Don't hurt him, William." Nick said sharply.

Whether Frosty intended to heed him was unclear. Very quickly he was outside, dragging a feisty, cussing Dennis in by an arm and an ear, the younger man's pistol in the older man's back pocket. The helicopter got louder, making a distant pass, probably unrelated to anything near the Millhouse. "Shut up, ya skinny shit! Thank me later that I didn't just pick ya off from the door!" Frosty turned to Nick, his face angry and tight. "Get your boy under control, DeMoss! He almost got us noticed!" He released Dennis with a push into the common area.

The other man whirled and shrugged him off. "Gimme my piece back!"

"I ain't got time for this shit!" Willie Bender whipped the 9mm and pointed it directly at Dennis' face from four feet away. He watched as his target stiffened, wondered if the stick figure was struggling not to piss his pants. "None of us can afford to be sloppy anymore. Got that? Benedict don't play by Theo's rules. Or maybe you all forgot!" In a flash, he released the clip and let it drop into his other hand. The 9mm flew onto the table, followed by the clip. "Take your damn *piece*." He said the last word with mocking disdain. "Consider yourselves warned."

They watched, uncertain of his intentions as he strode to a back room. When he didn't immediately return, everyone looked to Nick, except for Bill who slept on through it all. Dennis muttered a few choice 'derogatories' and nabbed his pistol, popping the clip back in place. "Want me to...?"

"No I don't!" Nick replied irritably. Stay put!"

Dennis didn't like the way the old man moved, slowly but less so than usual, favoring parts of his body more than others. His color wasn't good, either. Thank whoever the hospital kept itself stocked every few weeks. Lord knew where the immigrants went, but they left their meds, and by now, Dennis knew what to scrounge for. One of the things he did the day he stopped by Jorj's old apartment was to visit the Veteran's Hospital. Old Earth had its faults, but they still took care of their WWII vets. And the old guys let go one by one, keeping a steady supply of necessities flowing in to Twilight Earth. Theo's men always kept it pretty well locked up tight, but it had leaks. Dennis knew one or two and got what he needed. The dark irony in it all was that it was so much easier now that Theo's men were such a bunch of filthy deserters. He was able to bring back a few things, glyceryl trinitrate being one of them. Whenever Nick felt pain, he placed a nitro pill under his tongue.

The old man did it now.

They had something else, something even knew better, but this they saved, for the supply was still short, and Dennis intended to scavenge more. Nitro-Dur patches had to be applied regularly, by the literature that went with them. Both he and the old man knew that the time would come for that, but as Nick always stressed: Timing was everything. Dennis watched, and when the time was right, he ignored Nick's directive and followed behind in stealth, shooting back a look at Frank that demanded silence. The very act was strangely funny in itself. Franklin Wells, as long as he ever knew him, never spoke a word to anyone.

The room into which Willie Bender entered was one he knew better than anyone, for in part, it was of his design. The walls offended the eye with cheap paneling, beige, artificial wood-grain, peeling from age. It was the kind of office/store-room one would expect from an inner-city corner bar. A sterile metal desk lurked. Metal shelves stored unwanted supplies. A large calendar, sent by a lost liquor vender, covered much of the wall above the desk. He chose that one special for its lack of buxom Norwegian blondes. Put the wrong calendar up, some desperate muthah might yank it down, or come here to 'wank the willy.' Believability…obscurity, that was always best.

Fact on Twilight Earth was, if it has a value, it's gone. Vultures were quick and thorough. Rip down the poster, move the shelves . . . find Willy's stash. Not acceptable.

In other times he would be more careful, move the shelves aside with the intention of putting them back. Not so now. They crashed to the floor with everything on them. Half cans of paint hit the outdated linoleum, some of them spilling their lids crazily, the white paint within dried and bouncing within the thin steel like stale pound cakes. Past issues of Deerhunter flew wide and rolled sloppily, their irrelevance on an animal-less world not lost on one Willie Bender. Records nobody ever bothered to verify, scattered to the corners, as unrelated to the Millhouse as scavengers from accounting concerns. Incidental trinkets joined them, their value as lost to the wide world as their meaning in the former; cheap, throw-away, not even worthy of the trash. What was left was a wall, inconspicuous, but pregnant with the child of need, and the father stood in grim contemplation, angry that it should come to this.

No secret door stays secret forever, and Willie Bender made no attempt to preserve its hidden identity. Without much effort, he pulled the paneled partition back on its shiny hinges, and flicked on a light. The car batteries, charged only every couple of months, gave dim life to the single bulb sun, but it was enough, enough for what William Bender planned to do.

He stepped into the chamber, all but one wall of which was of cinderblock, and assessed his horded resources, and they were considerable. He noted the chalk line on the opposite wall, made by his own hand, in the shape of a garage door. That was the safe knock-out. Leaning against it was a large sledgehammer. With intention, he started forward.

Before his brown, calloused, killer hand even wrapped itself around the polished wood of the sledge handle, oiled smooth by the hands of countless manual laborers, minimally paid but hardened to their work ethic, he spied the bike. Hand-picked from a surprising lot of their kind, this one's metamorphosis was unkind, but necessary, and in its way, irretrievably gladiatorial. Big was a word that easily described it, and it needed to be. There was more metal on it than any motorcycle dared bear, but this wasn't just any motorcycle. It was a Harley, a V-Rod, newest that he'd seen thus far, and the most powerful too, only now it was more.

Of course he had help. He wasn't the best mechanic, but the architect of this bike, the real one, had moved on, for good or bad…gone. What he did was increase the capacity of everything, and then added the armor. If this one blew, it wouldn't be from an RPG, or hardened rounds. It would be because Willie Bender pushed it too far, rode it off a cliff, into the sea…blub, blub, blub. The bike was a one-time-only masterpiece, and this was the time. All it needed was a rider who could keep his legs hugging the machine without losing them to enemy fire. To aid in that, steel wings were added to absorb unfriendly fire. The goddam thing was a bat out of hell. Willie Bender breathed a heavy sigh. 'God give him dry roads,' isn't that what Mickey said the day he got clubbed for his chicken sandwich? The man who did that got away, but Mickey's grease monkey blessing didn't. Willie made it his business to know what streets were plowed, what ones were iffy, and which were dry. Git outta town, then they're ok, at least to the south and east as far as Utica.

Studded tires, hard and insanely knobby, gave him comfort. Wiping out into whatever didn't suit him. These crazy rubbers, with their copper teeth, would see him through the worst. His only real friend on Twilight Earth thought he was crazy to go with a cycle, but he knew that it was strictly a northern prejudice. Hit the warmer climes and he'd only have to change tires...maybe. There was a lot of overland that could take his tread once the winter warlock was left behind. He almost smiled, feeling the road's imminent rumbling beneath him, his juggernaut helmet and plated leather jacket scarin' the crap outta anybody who got in his way...GOD damn! Crazy.

Someone was behind him. Nick. The sound of the old man's walk betrayed him.

"Shoulda' posted a keep out sign." He hefted the sledge hammer, feeling its weight. "Make a door and all kinds of folk think it's an invitation."

"*You're* the one who warned us about the first strike, the one on the Westside...*you* told us to come here because it's a safe house."

Steel hit masonry, a block partially collapsed in on itself, all within the confines of the chalk line. "Yeah," Willie Bender called over his shoulder, "but I didn't say follow my busy ass around. Go get your posse together and hit the road while you still can."

Nick studied Willie Bender's street machine from hell, his brows knotting together as they always did when something struck him as odd. "I know almost nothing about those things, William." He waited until the other man glanced his way before gesturing. "But I have heard those get put away for the winter, and without exceptions."

"You might have heard a lot of things, ol' Nick, but ain't nobody had *that* bike before. It'll do what I tell it to." He paused on his back swing, awkwardly restraining the momentum. His face screwed into a look of confused irritation. "What I'm still trying to figure out is why are you still here?"

"We're going to wait for Jorj. He will come."

"Suit yourself, just stay outta my way!" The hammer wound and struck again, widening the hole. On the third time, a fist-sized patch of daylight appeared, coming to the rescue of the waning solitary light bulb. No more words were exchanged. The hammer did all the talking that was necessary. Nick watched for a time, and then turned back, drawing his jacket around him.

"You didn't stay put, Dennis." No matter the stealth, Nick's ears could still hear a mouse in the cellar from the third floor. "I told you to stay put." The other only stared blankly. What could he say? "That's why I only trust you with certain jobs."

"Hey. Jorj does his own thing too." There was no noticeable jealousy, but he wanted to make his point.

"I expect that of him, and he doesn't pretend to do as I say." Nick waved him off and sat down at the table. "Get me my sweater will you? There's a draft in here." Dennis stared at him in disbelief for a minute, shook his head, and found the stairs to the second floor. A look from Frank made Nick laugh, but only a little. " "I know…I know. I take him for granted."

By the time Dennis returned, the sounds of demolition were louder, more determined. Then, suddenly there was silence, followed a minute thereafter by the roar of a motorcycle. Dennis ran to the back just in time to see Frosty riding his wide tires over the pile of rubble that once was a chalked-off wall. There was an automatic rifle strapped to his back, and a crazy gothic helmet hanging off the back of the armored machine. The bike looked heavy, but it moved easily, daring anybody to say otherwise. The next second, he was gone, without a goodbye. Dennis waited another thirty seconds, knowing what would come once Frosty hit a main city street. The engine opened up, switching gears into a high pitched whine, fading as the distance grew.

He became aware of someone behind him and he turned, looking out of the corner of his eye. "He's gone."

"I heard." Nick walked in and idly nudged a crumpled beer can to the side with the toe of his right shoe. "Nothing left behind here. Let's go play some cards while we wait for Jorj." He winked at Dennis. "Make sure you shut William's hidden door."

Three man sat at a table playing poker for pennies grabbed from the cash register. It was more action than those pieces of copper had in a very long time. While Frank drew, Dennis looked out the window with a look of depression. The younger man saw it was his turn and pulled a card off the deck absently without even looking at his own cards. "He ain't coming."

"He will."

"He's been nabbed." Dennis gestured at Nick. "Take your turn old man."

Nick set his cards down and folded his hands together, touching them to his chin in thought. "I think he's just laying low for the moment, Dennis. Remember the helicopter? Benedict likely wants to know where the residuals are. If Jorj is out driving, he'll be spotted, and if he comes here…"

"I wouldn't have been that smart."

Nick only smiled at Dennis, choosing not to say anything that might incriminate himself. He picked up his cards and drew a loose card off the top of the deck. It was the King of Hearts. "I find it very funny your religion has problems with this game."

"It's gambling," Dennis replied nonchalantly. "I'm pretty sure most Jews I knew before you had a problem with it also."

"You don't have to play for money, you know. I mean when it counts." Frank looked up at Nick. The latter nodded to go ahead and Frank put his fingers to the deck.

"Then what's the point of playing Poker?" Dennis sighed. "It's about cleaning up, getting the loot, sacking the city…you know?"

"I'm beginning to understand," Nick reached into a pocket and then realized he'd quit smoking and hadn't any cigarettes. "Shit."

"You know, Nick, I never should have taught you how to swear." He grinned suddenly. "Or smoke, or drink, or play cards."

"How are your studies coming?"

"Uh," Dennis shrugged. "I read a little before I go to sleep. It's coming along."

"Woe to the heroes of drink?"

"Um...I think I made it that far."

"It doesn't mean don't drink. That applies to a lot of things."

You're preachin' at me, man."

"Sorry, Dennis. It's habit."

Upstairs, Bill paced the floors between the windows. It meant going from room to room, but he liked it. He liked being up high, looking down on everything else, and having the Padre for company. When he took the watch, which he did gladly and more so than the others, he forgot about the nightmares, about the pain, the dark folk looking down on him, studying him like he was a laboratory rat. Mostly, he just thought about working on the Roadrunner, and how he might make it better. If what everybody said was true, strange as it seemed, he should be able to find whatever parts he wanted to find. He just needed the time to look.

But he also knew that there wasn't much time for them in New Jackson City. They all planned on leaving just as soon as Jorj returned. Everything was packed in boxes and waiting by the front door. They just needed Jorj, and the Roadrunner.

He wanted to paint it too, something better than that boring green. A nice deep blue would be nice, rich like the sky at dusk. It was funny how Jorj wanted other things done to it at some point, like he had a wish list going just like he, Bill, did. He liked that about Jorj, that the man was into cars, and that he loved the Roadrunner. What he didn't understand was why he wanted to add steel plates to all the doors from the inside. He said they had to be bullet-proof. He just didn't say why.

The others talked about someone named Benedict. And then there was that black man wearing the winter coat, trying to scare everybody. That was when he went to sleep. None of it concerned him. He was just the old wounded horse that they fed . . . took care of. Bill just wished they'd turn the television down at night. It sounded like a goddam crowd, a horde of miserable fucking people.

There it was again, that helicopter down south towards the bridge. It wasn't much more than a spec in the sky just now, but it circled. He could tell that because of the sound, and that it kept going back and forth, back and forth. Something...did he see it right? He stopped and strained his eyes, shielding them from the sun with his left hand. It shot something to the ground, leaving a faint line behind it. Something rumbled, different than the normal thunder. A plume of smoke rose in the distance, at the point where the helicopter fired something at the ground. Bill grimaced hard. He didn't like that helicopter. Not at all.

14

Once, a very long time ago, before later immigrants brought with them things like CDs and Ipods, Willie Bender remembered seeing a record album in a store on Alodi. It was the only damned thing on the entire floor. It's edges were worn, the finish chipping, the cardboard underneath split in multiple places. What he remembered most, besides the fact that the disk inside it was scratched, was the picture on the front. Some crazy white dude blasted out of a graveyard on a rocket-powered chopper, his head and upper body thrown back from the force. Behind him, stretching its wings like some bad mutha fucka, was a giant bat. On old Earth, he would scarcely have given it notice. He was sure a band called *Meatloaf* wasn't his his style. The problem was that he picked it up off the middle of the floor on Twilight Earth. That put everything through a different set of glasses, and it stuck with him all these long…years. He knew things got put in funny places sometimes like they were meant to be found. So much time passed since then that by now, in his own sort of weird way, he had it worked out that someone *was* trying to tell him something. That's why he had the bike made, because he never liked the bat, and the bat was what waited for anyone who didn't get out of Dodge when their time was right.

Despite the bitter cold of January in Willie Bender's where and when, the roads of New Jackson City were mostly dry. Otherwise he never would have considered the bike. It snowed at night, and sometimes during the day, but never enough to accumulate, and the winds blew everything to the edges anyway. That meant the wind was the bigger enemy, meteorologically speaking. But he could handle that, and in some ways, though he was loath to admit it to anyone else, the cold had its advantages. It was hard to leave tracks on frozen ground, especially with snow most would never see to pad his steps. Of course he might leave a little of the white stuff behind, but that melted awfully damned fast for the right people, if it was noticeable in the first place. So while his enemies weren't likely to hear his footsteps, he couldn't hide the rumble of his Harley, but tracking him was another matter. January gave back in her own way.

So he left the Millhouse with every intention of leaving New Jack City, leaving behind whatever evil was coming upon anyone foolish enough to stay. That's how he started out. Once, when he was small, his grandmother, old, her body twisted but her mind untouched by time, explained the simple, deadly relationship between curiosity and cats. "You, Willie Bender, are a cat," she told him bluntly, "and don't you ever forget it! If you don't learn to keep your big nose out of trouble, you'll be fillin' a cold, dark hole somewhere." When he came to Twilight Earth, he figured she was talking about someone else, a lifeless husk, vacant of any kind of soul. He didn't really think so anymore. She *was* talking about him. For the first time in his new existence, he second-guessed his own judgement.

Getting out while the getting was good had been his plan all along, knowing fully that it was a road of singular and very grave risk in itself. Angrily, he shook his head and turned the bike down a side street and into a small parking lot. Jorj's words came back to him, about that dick Benedict and their shared future with radiation . . . the bastard had himself a nuke. Maybe Jorj was bluffing, but he didn't think so. The dude knew something, and Benedict was the right kind of guy to mess with something he knew nothing about, especially if it represented power. The man was *all* about gathering power to himself.

So where did that leave him? Go after Benedict? Find out what he was up to besides kicking Theo out and making points with the larger, more organized groups? He laughed in spite of himself—to spite himself. How the hell was one man going to do any of that? Benedict had a small but otherwise respectable army, resources, and most importantly, time. A crazy motorcycle in the dead of winter and guns weren't much against that.

But Benedict was in town. Or would be soon, and where would he go first? Would he go looking for Theo? Maybe, but he'd piss on everything the man owned first, starting with his seat of power. The place would be locked up tight, but there was another place, one that not many others knew about, going back to the days when Theo and Benedict were friends with more dreams than brains. And he, Willie Bender, should have thought of it long before now. Theo surely did...had to. And that's where the man was, where Benedict would eventually come, bringing only a handful of trusted men at the most. He liked secret places. The darker the better. Things didn't stay secret by showing off.

That's why only four people knew that there was more to Mosswood, especially the pyramid near it's center, than appearances at first suggested. Theo and Benedict were in the loop of course, and a single trusted henchman each, of which he, Willie Bender, *was so honored.* The other man's name was Anthony Scalatto, a later defector to Theo after it became clear Benedict was a ruthless dictator with delusions of imperialism. Willie didn't trust defectors, and told Theo as much. The result was that Scalatto was kept on anyhow, and after a time, Willie understood Theo's reason. A watched man was better than one in the shadows. It seemed smart for awhile. But Theo still ended up with a shiv in the ribs, and oddly enough, the culprit was the lot of Theo's 'cabinet' with the exception of his one trusted man, Willie Bender, as yet killed but not caught.

He stashed his bike up by Flynn dormitory, in a small, grounds-crew storage shed up on Pantheon Hill. After ripping off the helmet and placing it on the seat, he covered the whole thing with a paint tarp. "Stay put, baby." He whispered reverently.

The path down the southern side of Pantheon Hill was rough, especially through the crusted snow and untended brush, but it was better than the road. If someone chose to get nosy after hearing his engine, all pavement in the area would be suspect. His footing, though sure from experience and practice, wasn't as quiet as he intended. Having one of his guns in hand was desirable, but completely impractical. With wary eyes, he made his way down the slope, counting on his January advantage: His was a landscape both leafless and white . . . hard for anyone to hide from him for long once he was on the lookout.

Mosswood's northern entrance, leading directly into the parking lot of the Forestry School, lay just west of his descent. His way was even less obvious than that little traveled footpath. By the time he reached the hill's wooded base, he was in a killing mood. Quietly he drew his 45 Colt.

The hills of Mosswood rolled and careened, cut through by wind and frozen water, forested by tall oaks, muscled with mud hardened into rock by the record cold. Tombstones pierced the snow frequently, a reign of organized death markers that would outlast the trees and the people of New Jackson City whether under the old moon or the Twilight. Willie eyed them with more than a little foreboding. He took a knife here once, and that was on Old Earth. The denizens were more numerous then, but he suspected the Twilight made them worse, more diabolical. Even in the day, though most folk of reason shunned this place, there was reason to fear for one's skin.

One would think that in all the years Theo's enemies tried to snare him, they could come up with just one good winter tracker, but they never did. There was something about this place that attracted a majority of fair-weather mercenaries, and a minority of foul-weather anything, with almost nothing once you boiled those down to anything useful. There was Freddy, good ol' rainy-day Freddy the techno-wiz. By now he was somewhere west of Toronto, braving the colder clime just to stay dry. That was a man who didn't deserve to die the vanishing death, but someday he would. The better ones always did, Willie mused. Too bad he wouldn't work for Theo, or anyone else. He was an independent, which meant workin' without a net, no protection. Even he, Willie Bender, had Theo's name to toss around now and then, and he did. Now it wasn't worth the ink to write it, so he only had his own, scarcely better but for his violent disposition.

The first tombstone belonged to a man named Alfred Krunk, 1857-1884. "Short life," Willie muttered. "Too bad about the name. Take my advice, dead guy. Change it if you ever reach Twilight."

How he hated graveyards...detested them actually. As if life wasn't cold enough for him, what places like this represented, real or illusionary, chilled him straight through to his testicles. It had nothing to do with ghosts either. He dealt with those before. Some were dangerous, most not, but they were more or less versions of everyone else, just detached. No, it was the finality, and the wish for warmth where there was none, the bitterness, and mostly, something he kept to himself, the inconsolable regret. Ahead and to his left was a ring of stones on a low hill, an entry-level place of power as someone once told him. That someone was gone now, passed on for good or ill, Twilight no longer. He kept it to his left, following the hollow between that and a rise to his right, the dirt road ahead buried under a foot of fluffy snow for him.

Theo was a child of late March. The man had snow in patches, but it melted every day under a surprisingly warm sun. At least that's what Willie Bender was always told. He saw none of that himself, of course, just his own frigid day, alternating between fits of freezing wind and sub-zero calm that encouraged ice crystals to form in his nostrils. He thought he would give just about anything to feel the warm sun again, that is without getting shot by a Mexican, which happened once.

The hollow opened out into a larger one, and he knew he'd reached the main road, if you could call it that. They didn't pave the roads in Mosswood. About all anyone ever did was to drive over the same paths again and again until nothing would grow either in the deep ruts or the hump in between, and then, when it rained, at least on Old Earth, they became temporary rivers, running off mud, exposing stones buried beneath. Anyone could easily trip or break an ankle if they didn't bother to watch where they were going.

But that was, as stated, under the snow for Willie Bender, making it easier in some areas, more treacherous in others. As always, he was a careful one, bound to his instinct for self-preservation and well-earned experience at never getting caught. He went right, ascending the gradual incline, following where it leveled off, and then descending down a winding way that bottomed out at something resembling a gully. All about him, tombstones popped out through the snow. On some of the hills, mausoleums stood like miniature fortresses, small stone houses for dead families in a creepy, lifeless neighborhood. It used to be a haunt for college kids once. Most just came out here to drink themselves into a coma, but others dabbled in witchcraft. Always someone messin' with things they didn't understand, Willie thought irritably. Them rich students believed they was havin' fun with the devil, but never smart enough to leave him alone. Willie spat on the snow, remembering those fuckers wandering around drunk on weekends. Lucky the devil always had business elsewhere.

The pyramid was one of those few places Willie knew of which actually betrayed special power, and Willie hated it. That Theo recognized its potential meant that Willie couldn't just avoid it like he wanted to. And Theo wasn't the only one to see its true colors, but most of anyone else who was aware of them still resided on Old Earth, or skipped on past the Twilight to destinations unknown. In the world Theo and Willie lived in, this special knowledge was shared only with one called Benedict, assuming the latter was closed-mouthed. Not even Anthony Scalatto understood that the pyramid was anything other than an odd edifice in a uniquely mysterious 150-acre tract of stones and dead people. Willie sniffed approvingly. Let the bastard live in ignorance; good for him, good for everyone else. Once Benedict's man, always Benedicts man. And if Willie saw him again he'd make him Benedict's *dead* man.

But this wasn't that kind of day. Every hill waited for him to make a mistake . . . each one a threat with scant protection. Willie Bender took in cautious stride, feeling a fair bit of apprehension. With care, he'd see what he needed when it came in range, and he was almost there. First, the cross atop the pyramid would rise, mingling with the brush on the adjoining hills. Then, as he rounded the nearest 'turtleback,' there it would be, an imposing, if somewhat diminutive version of its Egyptian counterparts, built block by block with fanatacism of a sort Willie would never fully comprehend, to house a man in an unmarked grave, rendering the dead nameless within its four triangular sides.

And then there was *The Below.*

Scalatto never saw it and Willie Bender only by accident did, probably one reason he was such a wanted man. *The Below* sounded better than it was, and by Willie Bender's reckoning, that was no understatement. A hole, the size and shape of a coffin, vomited darkness in a chamber below the main pyramid floor, accessible only through a 2 x 2' hole in the corner. He should have been out choking down a cigarette with Scalatto. If he had been, his life, such as it was, might have spared him certain difficulties. While Benedict's man worked on his lung cancer project outside, basking in his own hot sun, Willie lingered inside, which said a lot for the quality of having Anthony Scalatto as your trusted second. It was a cornerstone of his argument against Theo taking him into the fold later. But it worked well for Willie at the time, or so he thought. What he saw when his nose got too long and his eyes peered down through the hole almost made him piss himself, for not only did he see the portal-macabre, but there within, glaring up at him so malignantly he knew he was done for, was Benedict. Hauled up by a rope, Theo at the other end. It wasn't even the man's hateful eyes which changed everything. It was his grin, that baleful, lunatic grin. This was not the same Benedict that entered the pyramid. He wasn't a man possessed, but he was a man changed. Somehow, at the time, it was bad enough. That day Willie killed them both, something he never told Theo. Much more of an eager killer then, angry, afraid, and most of all, a borderline addict, Willie Bender wanted them far away, and discreetly saw to it that they went there.

Back then, far away meant across town, and though Scalatto went across the state, Benedict wound up a lot closer than Willie thought. He forgot that Theo and Benedict came in together, victims of the same fate, one that was never spoken of…ever. Benedict came back, silent but seething, no mention to Theo of his sudden fiery demise, or who he suspected was behind it. Business went on as usual, with the exception that someone had a new 'trusted man.', and that someone wasn't Theo.

Theo also remained closed-mouthed about the coffin-hole, and it didn't need to be said that Benedict going down it was not spoken of either. As far as Willie Bender knew, only Benedict saw him betray their unspoken expectation of privacy. Willie never told Theo, never saw the need. He never planned to go back, not even if Theo asked him. By all estimations, it never looked like the issue would come up again, short of watching his own ass against Benedict's guns, and that worked out too. Willie's justifiable paranoia would serve both himself and his boss, an easy arrangement.

If only it could have worked out like that.

He saw the cross now. It was time to be even cooler than a fart from Santa's ass. The possibility that Benedict might be tromping around right now, with the hired gun of his choice, was greater. His men were undoubtedly running the streets, on foot and driving iron. Very likely many of them Willie already knew, for they once took provision from Theo. Given the chance, he'd give them each at least one nasty debilitating wound . . . hobble them in a horrible way they'd survive and wish they hadn't. He was good at that. Let them limp back to their master. He knew how Benedict treated losers.

Every step up the adjoining hill gave and slipped, and Willie was a disciplined enough hit man not to automatically curse his luck, especially in the small ways. Underneath the powder, layered even further down by crusts which collapsed under his respectable weight, was a hard ground, muddy in the spring, tolerant in the summer, and muddy again in the fall. Upward he trudged, watchful and wary. Now was the time to case the area. From the vantage point he sought, no one would reach the pyramid but that he saw or they were already there. In the case of the latter, well, he'd give it a span, but his patience in the cold wasn't infinite. When he was reasonably certain none of the other hills harbored a killer, he'd see what the ghosts were up to.

Every wind carries a death knell, someone told him once. If that was so, then he'd heard every goddam whiny cry known to man. January was a cold, Devil's mistress. In the years that he walked the icy crystalline paths of Twilight Earth, the blue bitch saw his toes turn the color of pitch, watched him snap them off one at a time before putting a gun to his own head in agony. Every time he fucked up, she taught him the hard lesson eagerly and remorselessly. So when enough time passed by for her to penetrate his layers with her cold touch, he made his descent, intent upon the next climb, and the evil which lay beyond.

Before he reached the bottom, he sensed something was up. No clarity rescued his eyes and ears. Nothing struck his olfactory awareness, no sudden stench of sweat or whiff of a blunt. Without warning, he dove into the cover of a shallow cleft, pistol ready, as something flew by in the former vicinity of his head. It wasn't fast, likely a rock, but it was definitely uninvited, and that meant someone was 'beggin for a new hole somewhere they didn't expect.'

His shallow was exactly that, offering only a little temporary protection. Wait longer than God gave you Willie, he realized unhappily, and you be back in that burned-out flat in no time shiverin' in nothing but your worthless skin...or worse. Normally, anyone who knew him could expect him to come out with 'guns blazing.' That was in his head, but he held back, considering that the rock was not a bullet or a knife. He might shout a little trash, get a voice on the other end, but that wasn't good either. No tellin' who else was around. There might be a few unrelated irregulars wandering about. While the possibilities still debated in his head, another rock, small and worn smooth by years of rain and abrasive mud, thumped just above him, plowing through the loose snow, and rolled to a stop next to his thermal sleeve. Okay, he realized, close enough to drop a rock, close enough to roll in a grenade. Shootin' was almost as easy. Maybe someone just wanted to talk, and he had an idea who that someone might be.

Quite a long time ago, when it became apparent that there might be a need for easy identification in troubled places, they realized their shared circumstances could be exploited to that end. Willie waited. If the author of the rock could manage something else, it would come, and sure enough, within a minute, a crude snowball, packed from warmer snow, landed near his feet. Not too many could do that, for most enjoyed a kinder sun.

Whoever it was overlooked his position closely to the northern section of the hill. Willie Bender climbed out of his shallow around to the south on his hands and knees, feeling every bit the ass for letting someone, even the man he suspected it to be, get the jump on him. His new exposure went unmolested. No rocks or bullets flew his way, and he found cover further up the hill, keeping his pistol ready and his eyes always probing for that special someone.

When he finally saw the silhouetted shape hugging a hillside tombstone against the bright overcast of midday, he smiled barrenly and waved the barrel of his 45 just enough to let Theo know he was seen. They rendezvoused at the graves of Beatrice Reubeck and her husband Lester, both having died within the same year of 1955. For the moment, neither spoke, hardly believing that the other was still alive and free.

After about fifteen seconds, Willie Bender cocked a skeptical eye on his friend and boss, or former boss—their future relationship was something yet to be determined. "I figured your ass would be in the pyramid."

Unlike Frosty, The other man was almost sweating, for his exertion on such a fine, uncharacteristically warm day, caused his rather bearish frame more heat than he could easily diffuse, despite the fact that he was dressed only in light hunter's camouflage. Out of habit, he tugged at the stiff bristles of his graying goatee and regarded the black man with grim amusement, more than glad for the friendly company. "If you knew I'd be here then you should also know that Benedict will be too. Why would I wish to be trapped in that old tomb?"

Willie flicked his hand once in a shrug. "Alright. So what now?"

"Benedict won't go in the pyramid until he thinks I'm caught or dead. I've rigged the tomb because he'll be expecting that I do so."

"Wouldn't want to see him disappointed."

"Right." Theo smiled in spite of things. That was classic Theo, Willie noted, always upbeat, always confident. The dude almost never got down on himself. "That's why he'll bring an extra man...a red shirt."

"A who?"

Another smile, thin but genuine. "A fall guy, a future corpse, someone to spring the trap. Life's cheap to Benedict."

"Alright..."

"So he'll be looking elsewhere for me."

"Which is why you're here." Willie's confusion was plain. He kept his movements to a minimum, but his eyes were alert, and his ears even more so. "If we're going to bag the man, shouldn't we get into better position?"

"I've been working on this a long time, William."

Frosty cocked his head, gazing skeptically from under his thick eyebrows while waiting for the punch line.

Seeing that he was being too cryptic, Theo shook his head. "There's no time to explain. You don't need to stick around. In fact, you'll be in the way. And if you went into the pyramid before I could stop you..." He faked a wince. It seemed enough.

"So I should get going." His statement came off like a question.

Theo crouched a little lower, his left hand catching Willie's sleeve and pulling him lower to the ground too. "There."

Between the tombstones, two figures approached the Pyramid from the south-western face of it's formidable hill, slipping casually but not recklessly from tree to tree.

"I thought you said there was gonna be three!" Willie watched them approach through squinted eyes. "Funny, I only see two."

"Hush." Theo's hand, still gripping the man's sleeve, tugged harder for emphasis. "He's put a man on the opposite hill with a rifle...I'm certain of it."

"Then I'll circle around and take care of him."

"Nothing doing." It was clear Theo wasn't releasing his arm just yet. "I'm depending on getting shot. Not looking forward to it, but definitely part of the plan."

"You crazy, you know that?"

"No. Crazy is letting that bastard find his reward for his treachery. Now go get yourself lost. Wait for me at the..."

"Millhouse?"

"Eh?"

Frosty grinned wickedly. "We had a drink there once, got into a fight with some out-of-town dudes. Remember?"

Theo stared at him a moment and then nodded. "I remember. I got cut there. You stopped what could have gone very ugly." He smiled that thin smile again. "That's when I 'hired' you."

"I got Nick and his crew tucked in there. Told 'em to move on but they're waitin' on some fool who ain't gonna show up. Meet me there, if you can make it, but case it first."

"Sounds as good as any." Theo pushed him slightly. "Get lost."

It didn't sit right with him, leaving Theo behind, but he always trusted the man, even in the stickiest circumstances. When he found himself sliding down the back side of the hill on his ass, he realized that they'd never had quite this situation before, and that Theo didn't know what he knew, namely what he saw in the pyramid so long ago. By the time he reached bottom, his decision not to abandon his boss and friend was concrete. Maybe he wouldn't mess up his plans, but he sure as shit was going to monitor them, and cover Theo's six. What remained for him to decide, and it had to be fast, was whether to ascend this hill again, with the presumption that Theo was leaving it, or to find another with a good line of sight to the pyramid. If there was another sharpshooter out there, and the odds of that were good, then he'd already have the best place picked out...might be watchin' him even now. He'd take that chance. His decision made, he stealthily ascended the hill again from another face, not surprised when he reached the top to find that Theo worked his way down to the base and crept into the tombstones just across the road from the Pyramid hill.

Almost as soon as he did so, a muffled shot pierced the lazy silence. Willie jerked behind a tombstone instinctively. When he heard no ricochet, nor any sound indicating that he was the target, he peeked around again to see Theo clutching his right leg painfully. The two figures that were just about to ascend the hill to the Pyramid approached the wounded man now. Theo was discovered.

It wasn't time to lose his head, Willie realized, not that he would have anyway. Tight jams weren't new to him. Without any quick movements that might otherwise betray his own position, he slid back behind the wide tombstone that gave him cover, and holstered his pistol, unslinging his long hunting rifle. Carrying a second heavy wasn't what he liked usually, but he learned the importance of being a marksman at the right times. This was one of those situations.

What he wanted to see was what he knew they weren't going to do, and they didn't disappoint his sense of reality. Theo was dragged to his feet and his hands bound to a tree behind him. One of the figures talked quite a bit while this was done, and it was clear Theo had an exchange of his own, though what words passed did not travel intelligibly up the hill to Willie. All he knew was that Theo was in pain, and that his tone was a brave one, but that he was not getting the better of the others even with his wit. When the knife came out in the left hand of the one who had to be Benedict himself, Willie waited no longer. He leveled his sight on his target, breathed once to steady his hand, and gently squeezed the trigger.

Theo slumped. The bullet passed cleanly through his right temple, nicking the tree's edge to his left. Willie was a sure shot when he wished, and when he didn't. If his feelings were mixed now, his decisions were very clear. As soon as his kill was visually confirmed, he was off down the other side of the hill, his feet navigating the deathtrap obstacle course of grave markers lest he tempt their hungry mischief through carelessness. Noise wasn't an issue now. His single shot surely gave his position away to everyone there and he wasn't about to stick around. How he wanted to slam one home into Benedict, he rued bitterly. Had Theo not had a plan, he would have. Instead, he had to satisfy himself with sparing his boss torture. That was enough, had to be.

Something stung his neck, just under the ear and behind the jaw. His left hand, covered in a tight black leather glove, flew to the spot and discovered a dart, just deep enough in to ruin his day. His legs buckled under him even as he pulled the offending object loose from his skin. There was no way he was getting out of here on foot, he realized and his anger swelled suddenly. His right hand, feeling very far away now, found his hip and struggled with the hilt of his 45. The damned thing felt big and unmanageable. Finally he wrenched it out and brought his hand to his mouth, but his intention could not find purchase. The pistol lay in the snow where it fell from his numb grasp. He reached for his knife instead. If he couldn't shoot himself, he'd cut his way home, but then, against every fiber of his will, the light and cold escaped down a long, dark, narrow tunnel and he fell prone next to his handgun. His ears were the last of his henchmen to report, and what they told him confirmed his own fears. Footsteps approached, more than he could count. They surrounded him and then themselves faded, leaving him alone in the dark cell of his mind.

15

Memories ... what are they really? To believe in them, one must see the world as a purely physical existence, with even the spiritual taking the form of active particles, energy notwithstanding. For the mind, not merely confined to biological convolutions, surely at the very least exists in the congregation of photons, light, divine descendants of the sun itself, and something still deeper, more marvelous. *His* memories, *his* recollections, *he* thought were gone, erased, no more than words on the mental page, without pictures to go with them or emotions for color. Moreover, the words themselves bore little resemblance to any story but rather vague shapes, detached ghosts of someone else's life. So when it becomes clear that he sees them, know that it might as well be for the first time, yet he knows they are his, and the terror that accompanies his resulting passion literally brings him to his knees with a gravity he thinks will crush him, but it doesn't, for he is not the kind of man who is easily crushed. His callous is thick. The reason for some of this is that his purpose in the place and time that once was, though convoluted, is pure, untouched by evil, and if it is misplaced, he has managed to take the first few steps needed to realign them on the correct path. Like iron filings atop a cloth, beneath a powerfully persistent magnet, he could be no other way, for the point of existence he occupies is a simple one, and governed by laws laid down before mankind itself took root.

Much of life cannot be denied, whatever our choices. His fell crookedly along the path of others less pure, and that is where he stuck, lodged for a time between calamity and salvation. Now he sees at least the first part. The second is hidden for a time, but perhaps he will see it eventually, once other things have come to pass.

Her nakedness, though beautiful in the bold face of the rising sun, he could not tolerate for her discomfort in it. With an uncharacteristic degree of selflessness, he offered up his ragged shirt and pants to the altar of his affection, knowing she had yet to fully recall what had happened to her. Feeling somewhat foolish in nothing but a pair of socks, he gave these also, standing brazenly in his birth and prickling pleasantly to the cold, watching the sun's glow upon the woman, her new body before him in a full healthy blush as she donned his clothes.

The riddle, as he understood it, was incomplete, for only a part had he unlocked. The other two, one yet behind a door festering, and the other imprisoned by retrospect which ruled from a far shore, had yet to touch him skin to skin, or at least the one, for the other may have done so in his own ignorance, rendering him impotent in effect despite his physical battle won. The scent of incense lingered upon it all. Christ watched sadly, bound by his father's laws and divine obligations. Abraham, Muhammad, and Buddha minded their own lofty business. In all of this, Jorj seemed coldly on his own.

But if that was so, then how this? Greta shivered in his bare arms, now clothed as he was just a few minutes before, and as corporeal as the granite landing upon which they presently stood. They were not the strangers he thought, but reunited, and his guilt, though heavy, staggering even, was not without the balm of her forgiveness, and the strength of his own determination to do what he thought was right.

Not yet secure in the trunk of the Roadrunner, the green case sat cock-eyed, half off the final downward step of Saint Jude's Cathedral. It stared up at him balefully even as he glared at it, for both fates were intertwined. It was not meant for the hands which stole it, and he knew that now. He also understood that it was loose in the wide web of their overlapping existence, and that others sought it now that it was beyond the protection of the veil. Like moths to a flame, or, more appropriately, flies to a pile of dung, those who fornicated with hell were drawn to it, for it represented destruction and misery, something they fed upon, and something that would expand their borders. They were ever a claustrophobic lot, all of them.

Ergo, it was clear that the responsibility was his, regardless of who actually stole the abominable thing. He was the courier with the conscience, unable to deliver it because he ultimately knew better, and what irony it was that he should enter Twilight Earth by the same hands that enlisted him on Old Earth. In the fading memory of that, he laughed, thankful that some things were intended to remain ghosts, and that his will to go forward should not be distracted by unimportant events, decisions irrelevant but for their own place in divine purpose. From somewhere, a voice, his father's perhaps, told him to place it in the trunk of the Roadrunner, turn the key, and drive. His breast swelled, and he placed both hands upon Greta's shoulders, for she was deeply nested within the fold of his one good arm. "We need to go. Now."

They pulled apart from each other like spider web, she in a reluctantly receding dream, he awake but in physical pain and near emotional shock. There was little else they could afford but seeing to the business at hand. In her state, she could hardly be relied on yet, so it was up to him, and the pain of seeing to their welfare was not only acute; it marked the imperative nature of his actions. Though he could have stood and held her with his good arm until his bad one healed and then still held her longer, it was only a desire. Reality could not be denied, especially if his feelings for her were true.

Whether it was a renewed vigor spurred on by adrenaline, or merely a gift of the morning sun, he found the strength to finish the job of securing the olive drab case into the Roadrunner's trunk. When he was done, the pain of his broken arm resurged and he honestly believed he would kill for a handful of aspirin, and why not? Murder seemed far too easy here in the twilight of Mother Earth's soul. The thought bothered him so sharply that he turned and took Greta's hand, squeezing it warmly before leading her to the passenger side door of his green steed. She leaned forward, leading him to believe for a moment that their lips would suddenly meet, and instead lay her cheek at the nape of his bristled neck, oblivious to the rough feel of it. "C'mon," he said quietly. "You know we can't stay here." In the distance he heard something he thought he'd never hear again, and it gave him a jolt. Greta heard it too for she lifted her face and looked south, too curious in her new existence to feel the alarm Jorj felt she should. Though neither of them could see it, the sound of it was unmistakable. Away across the city, and from beyond the bridge over the Metoak, a helicopter approached, echoing it's blade's vibrations across every street and building. "Let's go," he said with more urgency and opened the door for Greta to get in.

She slipped in silently, a shadow across her face, for her wits were returning. Still she remained silent as Jorj got in from the other side and turned the key, gunning the gas with a naked foot. Vaguely she thought of her mother's disapproval of her riding with a naked man, and of the less than sanitary state of his side of their shared vinyl bench seat.

Why he thought it would be better to move than to stay in the shadows, just another marooned car in a lost part of an abandoned world, he couldn't give answer for. When he ripped down a long side street, feeling his oats struggle against the gravity of their situation, he realized where he needed to go, knowing not the why but only the need, and that it would be the only safe place for the day. Nick and the rest of his tribe would have to wait.

The highway was out, as far as he was concerned...too unsafe, vulnerable from above. When the helicopter passed overhead, it was actually several blocks over and could have missed him. Jorj placed his money on it and tore around a corner, shooting straight for the intersection that would meet up with Dansforth street.

"There's no such place as Dansforth Street," Dennis' voice echoed in his head.

"Yes there is," Jorj murmured in rebuttal. Greta didn't need to ask who he was talking to. Some things she still knew, though sifting through what was lost became more difficult with every passing minute. The trade neared completion.

Nor did Jorj need to see the street sign, but he looked anyways. He always did. "Dansforth." He forced the words through gritted teeth, themselves betraying the true spirit of his victorious grin. Only a few blocks to the left, on the right, he nodded internally, just about three before Saint Phillip's hospital, bastion of spiritual salvation and bodily hope. If god was up and around, he should be looking for them just about now, Jorj mused boldly.

Hank's Half-price Book Warehouse came up on the right and he slowed the Roadrunner to a placid pace, pulling into the parking lot. Somewhere well behind him, Thunder shattered the air. In his heart he knew something died a fiery, calamitous death, showering down, umbrella-like, on their half-lit world in thousands of fragmentary pieces. Some soul he hadn't met again, but did once, winked out and returned elsewhere. Weapons were so impotent when one got down to it. Jorj let the feeling subside, appreciative for the gift that it was, knowing it wouldn't last forever, and pulled into a space between two yellow painted lines. Habits were hard to break. With a quick twist of his wrist he killed the life in the engine and turned his face to the better of them both. "We're here."

Thunder receded, echoing wave-like as it crept below the surface. Jorj smiled, feeling that odd rush of gladness that he felt one morning a few days ago, the day he met Ogum. Greta's lips lifted slightly at the corners. "He's here, isn't he?" she asked.

"I think so," he replied and then, amidst an expression of pleasant struggle, amended, "No, I believe so."

Clouds converged overhead, but still they could not squeeze out the sun, and it was good, for their game was not so much a competition as it was play, and they did so joyously, sending long bridges of escaping light to an Earth yet retaining a willingness to receive and span them. Jorj eyed them contemplatively as he got out. Greta studied him lovingly but said nothing. Time was as relative as anything else here, and she would not waste a drop of this moment for hell or high water. In their separate but linked meditations, neither of them noticed the wondrous scarecrow of a man just outside the front door watching them both, smiling easily, not a trace of impatience detectable upon his person.

"I suppose you would both be liking to come inside?" he asked finally in a calm, good-natured voice. The woven hat he wore reflected the sun just right, sprinkling bits of it upon his tanned cheeks and straw hair. "Take your time. There's coffee, and it's still hot."

For some reason, coffee meant something different here. It was not just a drug, to ease through speed or forgetfulness the fear that burned and clawed against the harsh clime of twilight callous. Here it could only be an elixir, charging one's day with promise, and energy to fulfill it where God chose not to in other ways. Jorj smiled and glanced at Greta for support. "Ogum, Nick sends his regards."

In a back room, the break room for someone long since departed to be exact, a pot of coffee brewed nicely. Ogum led them to it, whistling a tune familiar to him all the way there. Two plain white cups sat upside down on a dry, clean, checkered towel. He promptly turned them up and swung his right hand out like a gate opening, inviting them to each get for themselves. "There you are!" he bowed once, smiling gently. "Perhaps I will see you later? I did hope you would bring the others but," he tisked, "some things can't be helped I suppose." He smiled at Greta. "Some things have higher ground."

Jorj set his cup down only half full. "You aren't staying?"

"No," Ogum replied, his smile unfailing.

It was plain that no explanation poised, so Jorj intervened. "But there's a ton of things I'd like to ask you!"

Ogum shrugged. "I can't tell you what you need to know, Jorj."

Despite their informal introduction days before, the use of his name came as a surprise. A shadow of frustration crossed the landscape of Jorj's features but quickly and inexplicably passed once Ogam continued.

"If it was that easy, I'd do so. My job would be so much easier."

"What _is_ your job." Jorj took an idle sip of coffee now, noting absently that pouring only a half cup cooled it faster. The sharp, rich taste caught him unexpectedly. "Jeezuss!" he murmured.

"Not in Kansas anymore?" Greta's voice was quietly musical, even in reserve. Her courage to try her own mug, not having tasted anything more than a memory for longer than she honestly knew, was still slow in coming, but her anticipation waited with a new, quickened pulse.

"Nick's never tasted like this," Jorj answered back between savored gulps. "Not to my Twilight tastebuds."

Teeth emerged through Ogam's hairy grin. "Then I'll be on my way."

"Wait!" Jorj wouldn't, couldn't surrender completely. He set the cup down hard, not meaning to, and winced perceptibly at the loud, abrupt noise it made. Ogam paused on his way, already out the door, and regarded the other man patiently.

Greta pulled Jorj's sleeve gently and smiled. "Let him go."

"I just want to ask him some questions. We can't come this far, through this much, just to..."

Greta's small right index finger touched his lips and silenced them. "Trust." She turned her face to the door. Ogam wasn't there anymore, but they did hear his whistling. It sounded vaguely celtic, perhaps Appalachian.

"I'm supposed to find him," Jorj pressed, taking her finger gently in his hands and smoothing it aside. "Nick put me on this."

"You've found him. It's enough."

"How can you say that? The man hold's keys to moving on. I know it...Nick knows it too." He realized what he'd said and groaned. "We have to go back, Gret. I can't leave the others behind."

"No one's asking you to." There was a passing sadness in her voice. "In fact, I think it's expected. This is just a taste." She sighed at the irony and stared into his eyes, holding them with her special magnetism. "One step, our first one, is here. We've been given a great gift."

"Then let's not waste it." He returned her finger from his warm grasp and poured them each another cup of coffee. "C'mon."

Ogam's whistling faded as had his presence. When Jorj took her hand and led her out onto the main floor, she knew they were not seeking the wise one, but rather something he said. Her memories, so vivid a single day before, were dreams and nightmares now, and her recollections of them forced windows onto a patchy landscape, incomplete, less potent. What she did in becoming, she did for herself and Jorj. She wondered now if it would truly serve them, or had she merely been selfish to want to escape the night for good? Only God, she decided silently, could answer that with the kind of honesty she needed.

Hank's Half-Price Book Warehouse was well stocked, but nothing seemed in order. It was almost as if there was an intention that people wander looking and not blow past sections they otherwise might. Marian Bradshaw's published culinary delights pal'd around with <u>Mike's Auto Manuals,</u> and Francis Scott's latest novels of international intrigue. Compact disks, outdated by Jorj's date of demise, littered in with the books, tucked in between them and resting on top of staggered rows with faux-bronze Beethoven and Mozart bookends.

"We're going to be here awhile," Jorj groaned despite his forcibly uplifted spirit.

"I don't think so." Greta looked but didn't yet touch any of the shelves' contents. Even the tactile threatened to overwhelm newly returned senses. One a shelf was a small wooden box carved by an Indian hand half a world and another time away. She simply stared at it as if prying it apart with her eyes to reveal its contents.

"You find something?"

"Maybe," she answered smoothly. "I think I knew what this was once."

He almost asked her to elaborate but then stopped. An understanding formulated slowly and he nodded once. "Okay. You want to open it or should I?"

Her hands empty, intertwined, seeking some measure of suddenly needed security. She realized, as did Jorj, that she sucked on her lower lip. It was something she hadn't done since she was on old Earth. A delicate, tentative glance his way was all he needed for an answer.

"All right. I got it."

"Say my name, please." Her request was so spontaneous and odd that it caught Jorj off guard.

For a moment he only stared gently. Then, in the next few seconds, concern prompted him to come to her side. "What's wrong, Gret?"

"Nothing." It was little more than a breath. "I just wanted to hear you say my name." She tried a smile, achieving a small one. "Go ahead...open the box."

His hand went to the wooden lid, undoing the tiny brass clasp. His eyes, on her own the entire time, now turned to the object of her find as he lifted the ornate, hinged cover. They both gazed down for a heartbeat or two and then Jorj released an expression of disappointment. Within was a deck of cards, turned faces down. The back of the top card was bordered black around a sparsely decorated turquoise center. Jorj was pretty certain what they were for his cousin had something similar when they were kids. "Tarot cards, right?"

"Yes."

"You're into that stuff...or were." Despite the fact that his question came off like a statement, the implication was there. She didn't answer him immediately so he closed the lid, managing a smile that betrayed tolerant skepticism. "I think I'll keep looking."

Later, Jorj found a tan canvas back pack and threw a small pile of items into it. Mostly he grabbed cassette tapes, wickedly outdated, and three books; the New revised bible, The Qu'ran, and the To'nach; three books, one family squabble.

During the time that they spent there, they never let each other out of their sight, not even for a moment except to use the bathroom which was in perfect working order. Jorj's own reasons were clear to him. Why she seemed so connected, aside of his part in her crossover, he could only surmise as a need for security and whatever feelings she'd developed for him. The memories he swelled with that morning were mostly gone, just a flavor now, a pleasant odor on the wind outside. He couldn't deny there was a good reason they were together. The why was the ever-prevailing issue.

Eventually, despite the rather strong coffee ala Ogam, The night's excursions began to demand payment for neither Jorj nor Greta yet had any sleep. For the latter, it was a strange sensation to be tired. In her time in the Twilight, she never slept a wink, and of the daylight hours, she had no memory at all. As a matter of fact, what memories she had before this morning were receding, though a certain few persisted like candles in the dark, some good, some worse than bad.

They finished their business in the store and returned to the parking lot. Other than seeing Ogam again, which itself seemed unfinished, Jorj felt they'd accomplished nothing but finding a safe haven in which they could not remain.

The morning being warmer than any he'd had yet eliminated the need for a blanket when they succumbed to the back seat. In other times, both might have taken advantage of it for other, more pleasurable, means. This morning they merely slept, content with the security of each other's arms. With the help of additional aspirin, Jorj went out like a light. Riding the waves of each breath, Greta fell asleep with her head on his chest, her right hand gently draped over his broken arm.

Somewhere, a wave rolled onto a far shore, gliding glass-like across dark brown sands as smooth as thousand-year weathered stone. Beneath, things slumbered, breathing oxygen through the water-logged grains until the night, when they would emerge to feed, or perhaps mate. Who would see them, as they pushed through the packed sedimentary layers, converging on life in a way few understood? And they were not all alike, no, no. Some had legs, small and scaled, tucked tight within their protective shells, hiding with heads that made one consider wisdom well, if only in anthropomorphic fantasy. Others, like miniature jewel cases, opened and closed through their lives in the pursuit of strange but necessary business, little more than an odd-shaped foot to carry them on their way. It truly was a life, troubled yes, but beautiful nevertheless. Love, you see, carries many facets, and not always defined by sentience as most higher forms come to know it. If God did not exist, neither would anything else. At least this much is truth for the taking.

They woke to the rhythm of the sea, the night not far off, but held at bay by a sliver of time under a thumbnail of moon. At first, neither spoke, for gifts were few these days, and not easily recognized. Eventually it became clear that one of them must, and so it fell to the woman to make sense of things, for the man could not. She spoke in a clear, liquid voice, harkening back to her earlier existence when memories both caressed and plagued her. The current of her eldritch spirit was not far off despite her recent transformation. "It is to come, my love." Her tongue tarried on the last syllable an extra heartbeat, taking in its warmth. The future might not be hers to share, and she knew it.

But still it might, and so she kept on going where the push of God's breath took her. "Here lies your feet at the end of things, and your hands at the beginning . . . full circle. Know that whatever comes to pass, this is for you."

"Will I be alone." It was a question well asked, for the legitimacy of it could hardly be denied.

"Of that I cannot say, but your journey here will not be without the company of others." She turned her face to his, catching his eyes and the waxing moonlight reflected in them. "I will cleave until I cannot."

There was a sudden urge to cry, but he let it grovel at his outer walls, knowing that every release was a slip towards oblivion. "I won't let you go," he replied grimly, realizing the futility in such a statement. She didn't immediately return words, merely holding his gaze in her own inky pools. Whatever would be was beyond their last control. Finality held the final card, as always.

"Yes, my love." She smiled, letting him have the moment with her. "Any gift, even such as we tenuously cling to now, bears a purpose. Let us not deny ourselves." With that she lay down, inviting him into her, and he followed, leaving the moon and all of its vast realm far behind. When next he and she woke, they were in a different place, even from before the beach. Rest had come and gone, and it was late afternoon now, time to move on.

Behind them was a parking lot, but Hanks didn't exist there, and Dansforth was just a fading pleasant memory that now called itself Alodi. The Roadrunner, gas pedal frequently punching the floor under Jorj's right foot, thundered northbound like a barely reigned-in bullet trying to reach it's destination before the spent shell clattered to the hard ground.

Neither man nor woman spoke. They were rested, more than either could remember being in a very long time, but there were still troubled waters to pass over, and what lay beneath could not possibly brook indelicacy.

So far as Jorj knew, they were not followed. If Benedict intended to flood New Jackson City with his soldiers, the only evidence he had as yet was the chopper, and that was not in sight. There still lingered that distinct low-key feeling about the neighborhoods and he had to remind himself that there were no hordes on Twilight Earth. It was a sparse, gray existence that often left one numb to the obvious detail of almost never seeing others on the street but those you traveled with.

And the realization of what was needed to seize and maintain power in such a place startled his frozen senses. The rumors he heard early on of gathering forces and mobilized organization took on a new meaning. You couldn't control one city and then spread out. There simply weren't enough people for that here. Armies would be nomadic, absorbing the conquered and moving on to find more people and resources in order to swell the ranks. Benedict wasn't simply a megalomaniacal dictator in a petty in-between dimension. He was all of that, but he was also being squeezed out, and Theo's group was in the way of his retreat, ripe for betrayal of any alliance they might have once pretended at. By the time he skidded gravel in the Millhouse parking lot, he was even more determined to get out of Twilight Earth and leave the default meat-grinder of its daily reality far behind.

They piled out to greet him, everyone that was inside, for Bill had watched vigilantly from the upstairs, and the noise of the 440 under the Roadrunner's hood was unmistakable. Jorj leaped out to meet them, eager to tell them of his meeting with Ogam, and their need to get fast and far away. His intentions fell almost as quickly as their relieved smiles, for everyone stopped in their tracks, looking not at Jorj now, but at his companion. Frank scowled and retreated back inside. Bill staggered as one struck physically by a blow, reaching blindly for the door handle until he found it and then he, too, followed Frank in a panic. Dennis swore openly, turning an icy gaze on Jorj. Whatever he intended to say was cut short by two further startling events. First, Nick advanced and displayed a gentle, even welcoming hand to the source of their abhorrent reaction. She had just opened the passenger-side door and stepped out when he came forward to extend courteous words. Despite his valiance, it was clear that he did so with grave reluctance. This, in turn, was interrupted by a thunder-wreathed, banshee wail. The Padre, hands over his face, dropped to his knees and moaned like an animal, all ground gained to his soul torn aside, leaving him gutted before all who remained in the parking lot. Amidst this, another man whom Jorj saw only once and never met, emerged from the Millhouse' front door. It was Theodore. The surreal effect of it all turned seconds into hours, and Jorj did the only thing that felt right to him under the circumstances. Almost neglectful of his broken arm or the pain it produced, he half-vaulted over the Roadrunner's hood using his good one and took Greta's hand deep into his own. She squeezed it hard, and though she stood strong before the entire scene, her tension turned both her own and Jorj's muscles into bowstrings. Unsmiling, she turned her dark eyes from Nick to the Padre. A tear created a small rivulet on her left cheek, noticed by only the one closest to her.

"Nick?" Jorj's voice was tight and demanding. An edge in it cut sharply through the angrily rumbling tempest sky.

The old man quickly went to the priest's side, squatting down and placing his arms around the Padre's shoulders. "What is it Francis? If it is the woman, I assure you she is harmless. See? She is out in the day. How could it be bad?" The moaning did not relent, and the blind priest shuddered. It was not irrational fear that drove him thus like the others, the old man suddenly realized. It was anguish, pure an inexplicable sorrow.

"Stand father." Jorj turned his face to the slight woman next to him, stunned that she should know him to speak to him this way, for the Padre wore no outer trappings of his profession or calling, save a small silver cross over his dark blue sweatshirt. "The harsh mistakes of the past cannot hurt us now unless you allow them to linger." Her own voice began to tremble, but she held on to a modicum of firmament.

"I'm so sorry," the padre gasped, his sobs threatening to make his words unintelligible. "I...I..."

Greta broke her hand free from Jorj's and ran to the priest, gently intervening herself between Nick and the blind man, replacing the latter's hands with her own arms. "It's okay." She was openly crying now, rocking the man as she might a baby and caressing his hair, pressing her right cheek to his left ear. "It's alright father, I'm here, alive."

Padre's hands found her, shaking leaf-like, and returned her embrace. For a moment, Jorj felt a pang of jealousy. It was irrational, he knew, but still it was there. The two, priest and woman of the night's shadows, clutched each other tightly like they might never see each other again, and still the blind man's babbled regrets spilled forth in an unrelenting stream.

"Hey Jorj." It was Dennis. "What the fuck's this?"

A straw snapped somewhere and the sound was deafening. Jorj crossed the distance in several uncountable strides and grabbed the scrawny man by the scruff of his shirt with his one good arm, nearly lifting him off his feet such was his anger. He barely felt the hands upon him through the blood-red haze. One set belonged to Nick, a man who hardly needed this kind of excitement, and the other was Theodore's. The latter's grasp was strong and firm, but there was also a commanding gentleness in it that reminded Jorj of Nick, and though another time might have allowed the instigation of further violence towards a stranger's presumption, it did not do so now. Jorj gradually found his head and relented, only then becoming conscious of Greta's pleas, urging him to stop, rushing forth like a tidal force upon his ears. He released Dennis and rocked back, feeling the hands roll him away even as their owners formed a wall between he and his intended victim. Dennis Brinks wheeled away, startled and confused, clearly not expecting Jorj to react the way he did.

Nick chanced a glance at the Padre, then Greta, and then back at Jorj. "Dennis!" He called without looking back at the disheveled man. "Go inside."

"What the hell did I do?"

"Go!" Nick's voice was deep and baritone, sparing none of his normally restrained powerful resonance. He still regarded Jorj with something resembling a glare, though the latter suspected, once his head began to clear, that there was still plenty of room for further fire. "*You* will not do that again. I don't care what that idiot says. Do we have an understanding?"

Jorj's adrenaline still fed the fire in his blood, drip by drip. Greta remained as she was, her arms locked around the Padre, but now she held Jorj with her eyes, pulling him in to a safer landing. "Alright," he grunted, facing Nick again. "I'm sorry. He's an asshole, but he doesn't mean to be." He considered Nick's tired expression and then blurted out, "I found Ogam." Unsure why he should pick this time to do so, he quickly reasoned that it was to change the subject. Silently he cursed.

The effect upon Nick was almost comical. He smiled in unbelieving sarcasm at first, and then did a double-take with his eyes. For a second he was speechless, but the sound of the chopper changed his mood instantly. "Let's get ourselves inside. There are things to discuss all around." His gaze snagged on the trunk of the Roadrunner, noting two round cavities, spider-cracked in the surrounding paint. Then he eyed Jorj's bad arm disapprovingly. "Just couldn't keep out of trouble last night, could you?" He looked pale, an alarming fact not lost on Jorj. Without waiting for a reply, he turned towards the door. "Padre! Now's the time to marshal yourself. Cry later!"

With some coaxing, Frank fixed a meal of canned surprise. Bill could not be persuaded to join in, nor would he descend from the upstairs. His words to Nick were secret, and they left the older man ashen. Theodore took his seat directly across from Jorj with purposeful intent. He rarely let the younger man out of his sight, and the degree to which he studied him was considerable, to the point where, had things not gone otherwise just a little while before, Jorj would have challenged him on the matter. Instead, he sat where he did, Greta to his right, and the Padre on her other side. In an odd moment of surrealism, the woman pulled Jorj's ear close to her lips and breathed into it three sweet words. He was unable to return them immediately, or ask the questions that snagged at his soul, for Nick banged his glass on the table for attention.

"I know some of you think we should leave right away, and I agree that we should as soon as possible, but if we leave now, we may draw Benedict's eyes. My intention is that we leave in the morning at the crack of dawn." He held the gaze of everyone he thought might argue, one at a time, until he stopped at Dennis who sat away from the table, barely touching his cold plate of beans. The ragged, stick of a man was thumbing off in Jorj's direction.

"He kind of blew that good idea, didn't he."

Nick tightened his lips and raised an eyebrow, peering nowhere in particular beneath it. Peripherally he regarded Jorj. The man did not stir. Good. "Okay, we're waiting for another reason…an important one. You want out? There's the door." He waited until Dennis looked away, unwilling to call his bluff, and then continued. "Let me make the necessary introductions now for three of you, so that we can get on with our business. We have a lot to discuss today, and probably into the night." He gestured at Theodore while facing Jorj. "This is my long-time friend and former benefactor, Theodore, the true, if temporarily deposed, leader of *our* New Jackson City." More of the description was political than heartfelt now, but no one needed to know that. He flicked his hand across the table as if tired of formality. "Theodore, this is Jorj, new to our band and a recent immigrant to our piece of whatever." He foundered when his eyes drifted to the woman, realizing that he'd not taken the time to get her name.

"Greta…Margaret if you like." She spoke the last part with something resembling distaste. It was clear that somewhere in the past that had been her name, and that some used it once, but that she, herself, did not. Her eyes slid sideways towards the priest, a subtle movement that was almost not taken for how she intended it. A silence spanned a chasm that seemed to forbid premature crossing by others, but it was the Padre who dared to say what she would not.

"She is my daughter." He spoke low, almost as if he were ashamed, but if that was so, it was not of her but rather of himself, and no one there had difficulty figuring it out. There was more left unsaid, and he did not try to conceal the fact, but further words concerning the matter he did not, would not, offer. He stared at his plate with unseeing eyes, unwilling to expose the fullness of his face to their own confused gazes even in his unbetrayable blindness. It was not so long since he'd regained his composure, and the flesh of the concealed wound he bore, never truly healed, lost nothing of the tender vulnerability each exposed nerve felt.

It came as a blow to most of them, for the fear of the night folk was hardly doused with the presence of one of their own number in such a seemingly benign gathering, even given Greta's newly revealed relation to the priest. To Jorj, the revelation was twofold, for he was both relieved and alarmed. Inexplicable memories pierced him like arrows, and there was another name he could not prevent himself from uttering in time. "Richie," he exhaled, suddenly aware of the slender hand gripping the top meat of his right thigh and the dark pools of ink imploring him to speak that name no more.

It seemed the Padre did not hear, and in the background of it all, Nick coughed uncomfortably. "Then one less secret separates us, my friend." The old man glanced at the woman and smiled sparsely. "Padre's family is always welcome under my roof, wherever that roof may be." Even with these words said, Jorj couldn't help but wonder at the hesitation, however slight, at which they were offered.

Theodore and Jorj nodded curtly. Few shook hands on Twilight Earth. The practical nature of old patterns burned down to necessity in many cases, and for men like these two, not cut far from the same cloth despite their own ignorance of the fact, such ways sufficed.

What things were communicated from that point on need not all be drawn out here. The important matters were, in short, addressed almost immediately. Theodore arrived shortly past noon bearing news that Benedict's forces had crossed the bridge over the Metoak, and that he, himself, had taken a bullet in the head that very morning. His henchman and friend, Willie Bender, was to meet him at the Millhouse. It was unsettling that the man had not, as yet, presented himself.

"Maybe he got nabbed." Dennis ran a finger along his throat in a subtle motion. "Wouldn't that suck." He glanced at Theodore and suddenly felt a chill. "It would, you know, really suck."

Theodore hadn't told anyone of his doings at Mosswood cemetery, or his running into Willie Bender. What his henchman used to call 'cat's eyes' regarded Dennis with a coolness that betrayed none of what raced through his mind at that moment, but he did consider the other man's words, foolishly uttered as they were. "Didn't like him, did you?" He phrased it with a sort of mock friendliness.

"He...he was okay, I guess." Dennis smiled weakly, glad that Jorj was starting to speak.

In the next few minutes, everyone learned of Ogam and the better place that was 'just past the first veil' as Jorj called it. Not that the man understood any of it at all, but he had hunches, and a loose enough grasp of religious language to be dangerous down the proper path. At times he looked to Greta for help, but she remained remotely silent on just about every subject that was raised. Whatever went on behind her dark eyes remained there for the time. Yet on one thing there was no question but that they agreed: Ogam intended to be follow. How they might do that, especially when they needed to leave the city, was more the question in the dark. He made it clear that he wasn't returning to Hank's, even if they were able to find it again. On old Earth, Jorj knew this would all be madness. Here, as always, nothing could be ignored nor taken for granted.

And he didn't tell them everything. It was easy to leave out Greta's transformation, and he neglected to inform them of the terrible thing in the Roadrunner's trunk. It wasn't that he didn't want to. The right time never came up, and at times when he thought it might, his mouth grew cottony, and his memory congealed to the point of zero navigation. As things turned, he was relieved of the burden that telling them would create. The unseen hand of God pushed him in another direction…that of Willie Bender. He'd saved the man's ass, after all, something that, once he'd unloaded the relevant parts of the tale, it became inevitable that Theodore would take considerably more interest.

In his discourse with Benedict that very morning, something more than his own imminent torture had troubled him. You never lost your sense of someone, no matter how much time passed, unless you forgot them altogether; he was convinced of that. But there was something in the way that Benedict spoke, and the malign with which Theodore was regarded, that bespoke of a change beyond what could be reasonably expected. The humor was absent, unless one considered hideously descriptive threats funny, and Theodore didn't. Benedict's accompanying henchman was visibly on edge, frightened even, and that was another alarm bell. Events had ratcheted up beyond the mere politics of war. How much so, or what its actual nature was, escaped him, but the chill he felt prodded him out from the trench he'd dug for himself here. He would have to break not only with his air of self sufficiency, but also with his revulsion to paranormal belief, an armor he was loath to discard.

When a window of silence presented itself, for Theodore was, trained of necessity, a polite man, he addressed Nick respectfully, transferring something of his own leadership mantle to the elder, more deeply embedded, patriarch. "I thought to go with you in the morning with the expectation of returning once William and I had gathered enough resources and men. Now I think I will take my leave and look for Mr. Bender, who I'm certain is in a fair amount of distress. A man of his means is rarely late for anything, especially to those he has always shown such unrelenting service to in the past."

"Theodore, old friend," Nick seemed to have aged in the last three seconds by ten years. "How could you possibly know where to find him? The best place to be is where you agreed to meet in the first place, and we all will have need of his strength, as much if not more than we do what is already gathered here and now. You're leaving will only weaken yourself...and us."

It was a grim, stifled laugh that replied. Theodore smiled not unkindly and glanced out the window, noting the lengthening shadows. "I thought to weaken us all a bit more, Nicolas." He knew 'Nicolas was not Nick's *true* full name, but it was a formality he imposed often in the past as a personal honor, disliking the informality of 'Nick.' "My skills in night travel are novice at best, and it is apparent now that there are two here who regularly navigate the dark, and its 'unholy denizens.' His teeth bared a little at the last two words as if to mock what they all feared. He was not a superstitious man, but only a fool did not recognize the perils of the night. Long ago he ceased ordering night patrols, for men had a way of disappearing, and too many 'good men' vanished to explain it away with mere desertion. Eyewitness stories, fantastical and horrific as he considered them, could not simply be dismissed. Even Benedict's men stayed in after dark. It took someone special to spend so many nights out of doors and return every morning. "If you would have myself and Mister Bender join forces with your group, and if there is any loyalty to me for my past protection, I must insist upon a rescue."

"No one here is under orders," Nick said firmly. "And loyalty is not in question here. You know everything that we know now. A calamity is on the way in Old Earth, and when it happens, the effects of it will manifest here forever. Think of it! Slow suffering that worsens every day until you eventually die of it. And when you do, it starts all over again! That is why we are leaving, to get away from the first effects. It is the only way to avoid it entirely. I am not from this city. When I die, as you all know by now, I will not return. The invisible fire that will soak into the ground of New Jackson City and everything attached to it, can only burn me once, for I will not be drawn like a magnet back to it. You, on the other hand," and here he waved splayed fingers across the room at them all, will never be so fortunate. Staying another night is one thing. More than that is foolishness!" He stopped, allowing himself to catch his breath, feeling it difficult to do so. Slowly, his hand shaking, he reached into the inside breast pocket of his suit jacket and withdrew a small, flat, metal box. He glanced down at his glass, dry but for a few residual beads of moisture, and addressed the most faithful of his servants. "Dennis, a glass of water, if you would, please."

In moments, Nick's empty glass was refilled. From the small box he took several tablets of aspirin and downed them with a full swallow of water. "I read somewhere that aspirin can save your life." It was a joke, told with a feeble smile, but no one laughed. Concern registered on each face to the measure of the man or woman, and to no greater degree than on the face of Dennis Brinks. Nick patted him on the shoulder and thanked him with his eyes, for words wasted energy. Like the old man he was, he sat back down. He 'shot his wad,' as Dennis so crudely and often said, and now he was pretty much done. Let the others do as they wished. When another spoke, he subtly placed a nitro pill underneath his tongue, resisting the urge to press his hand to his chest.

"What makes you think you know where to find him?" Jorj saw that Theo was moving his chair back and braced himself to do the same. "I mean, this is a spread-out city. He could be anywhere, and if he's not dead, but captured, which I think we both agree is the more likely, he might not be in New Jack at all."

"I know where to begin my search. Regardless of what I find, I'll know where to go next." Theodore smiled like a wolf now. "Think you I got to run this town simply by being a bureaucrat?"

"Probably not." Jorj's eye's were steely, but respectful. This man he exchanged words with was, in his opinion dangerous, for the trouble he was inevitably dragging him into, but he was also right in doing so. Of that he was increasingly becoming convinced. Greta's hand bit more deeply into his thigh. He could not ignore it now. At some point, very near, he knew he would have to do so.

"Probably not," Theodore huffed with minor sarcasm. "You said yourself that Benedict had a connection to this upcoming disaster. How he could when he's stuck here like the rest of us I don't know, but you did say that. Wouldn't you like to deny him the opportunity to see his plans through?"

That was what Jorj was waiting for, and dreading. That was the button. Theodore was a true leader, for he knew just where to push, and at that point, Jorj felt Greta's hatred of the man, and the threat he represented. In his own mind, Jorj also recognized that every time they came close to leaving, something prevented them, or at least forced a choice. This was the worst so far, for it was the most dire and the biggest gamble. "My arm's broken," he pointed out, "how much help can I be?" He knew the answer as soon as he spoke the words. When Theodore merely stared back, knowing nothing really needed to be said, he nodded. "Alright, we'll need a few things." His right leg burned with pain and he almost looked to his right. If he did so, he might lose his resolve, so he only placed his good hand over the woman's taut one. It didn't take a genius to know she was crying.

Sometime later, while the sun submerged and the moon lay poised beneath a dark curve of pregnant horizon, Theodore disappeared into Willie Bender's back room, now cold from it's outer breach. Jorj meant to follow but turned his feet to the front door instead, intent now upon clearing his head by the dependability of the Roadrunner.

The chopper was silent now. No one but a very few went out past sundown, even now. Some held on to their bad habits though, and ignored the informal curfew of superstition. From the moment that Jorj stepped through the front door and into the main parking lot of the Millhouse, he knew he wasn't alone. One had followed him out with a silence that alarmed his compromised sense of awareness, and another sat out on an old microwave oven near the curb like a gnomish lawn ornament, taking short pulls from something in a paper bag. The latter looked his way and grinned fiendishly. It had been awhile.

Before speaking, Jorj waited for Greta to slip to his side, acknowledging her with a caressing nudge of his elbow as she lent her warmth to his against the indifferent chill of the night. "Does everybody know where I'm going to be before I get there?" He didn't sound so much annoyed as grudgingly reconciled. "I need a quiet place to think."

The imp laughed silently and looked away.

A thought occurred to Jorj and he voiced it suddenly. "We could bring him over...like I did you." He said it with a trace of uncertainty, as if a second thought warned off the first. Greta did not respond, and that only reinforced what another side of him was trying to communicate. "Richie..."

"Ferget it." Another toke off the bottle incognito followed by a sleeve wiping across a small, smirking mouth.

"Just came by to see how Gret was getting on, that's all." The man's voice was off to their right. A curious sadness tainted it without diminishing the reliability of its strength.

Jorj turned but saw no one there. He never liked it when they did that spook stuff.

"I'm fine." To prove her point, Greta pulled her hair back on the one side, revealing a smooth, perfect cheek.

"Ha! Good then!" The imp snorted irreverently. He still looked elsewhere, and it seemed to Jorj that a bridge between them, or more specifically between the lad and Greta, lay in ruins. "I guess Jed can come back now." He chuckled again, following it up with a swig. "Not that he ever really left."

"You don't need him," Greta's words came forcefully. "You don't need him, Richard."

"Richie," he corrected her. "Keep it up and you'll be calling me Dick."

The woman seethed but bit her tongue. Emotions that coursed through her disturbed Jorj, for they were deeper and more massive than his own, and her being so new to the chemistry of them again, he feared for her loss of mastery.

Whatever," Jorj cut to the chase. The kid was his responsibility now, though exactly why he couldn't remember, but he also knew he was near the end of his own patience. "You want to hang with a guy who writes creepy poetry and hangs them on stranger's front doors? Go ahead. Tell him to fuck off for me." He started walking up the street away from the intersection where he picked Greta up two nights before. Greta, tense and tired, watched him uncertainly, feeling pulled between the two.

"Goin' to burn another house?" Richie twisted his syllables with a mischievous dexterity. "Can I watch?"

"He never burned the other one, you know." The man was back again. He had a knife scar across his face. Jorj thought his name was Sid. He stopped short when he heard what was said.

"What do you mean by that?" Jorj growled irritably.

"I'm not sayin'." The imp pretended to zip his mouth shut, then, in mock horror, unzipped it enough to make an opening for the bagged bottle. Jorj caught none of this, for he was walking again, approaching the litter-strewn gutter.

"Did you set the blaze, Richie?" Greta found her voice again. She didn't sound angry, but deep inside she was furious.

"It was *his* candle, not mine."

"But you influenced him." She would not relent. "You tampered."

Now he looked sharply at her, his face reddened with anger. He'd practiced at that, for blood didn't do the job anymore these days. "What the *hell* do you care?"

"Did Jed tell you to do it?"

He sniffed and turned away again. "I don't take my orders from Jed."

The lie blazed, a bonfire in the night, and Greta glared now at every facet of it's undesirable brilliance. Almost immediately a fire blossomed across the street in an old waste can full of rubbish. Its smoke coiled skyward, dense and snake-like.

"Showtime!" Richie yipped.

Gravity shifted under the soles of Jorj's sneakers. He stumbled and fell, got back on his feet, and cursed. The Millhouse scuffed his backside and banged his shoulder blades as he righted himself. His walk was for nothing. He opened his mouth to extend his displeasure when Sid appeared, leaning on the brick wall to his right, on the corner of the building. "You don't want to go down that way, actually."

"Oh yeah?" Jorj stepped forward and the imp laughed hard from the street, distracting him.

"Aw go on! Make it a party!"

"Don't listen to him, Jorj." Greta stood by the lad, her hands at her sides. "Go inside. I'll deal with this."

"I think we need an understanding here...all of us." Jorj advanced halfway to the street when Greta came to meet him. Her eyes were wet, and her hands went immediately to his chest to pause his steps. He stopped, but it was involuntary, for she was in the way. I've got things to do tonight," he grated through clenched teeth. "Why all of this? Why now?"

"Part of the night's peril is in confusion," she replied softly. Her voice trembled, but not so much that she seemed weak. In fact, there was an unexpected strength in it. "Sid looks out for you. Richard is under another's influence. Can you remember that from now on?"

"Ri-chee." The distant correction sounded almost sing-song, but with scraping impatience.

Her dark eyes did not waver from Jorj's. "There are other forces at work now. They don't want you to sort things out. Richie is here to distract you."

"And Sid?"

"To protect you, as best he can."

It was becoming too much for him. "Why? This makes no sense to me."

"I don't know anymore." Her sincerity cut through him. "In joining you, I've left them. The night no longer speaks to me in the way it once did. It was the price."

"Of course if he bites the big one, and skips on out of here, you'll be all alone." The imp rocked back and forth, as if enjoying his game. "You think Nicodemus will take you in, Gret? He's afraid of you too."

Her silence built a bridge for what he had to say next. He shrugged and continued.

"Ol' Jorj here ain't going to save Willie Bender. He's plannin' on sending the Benster all the way to hell." He waited while she considered his words, knowing that truth, wherever it came from, could never be righteously denied.

"Benedict?" For once she was unraveled in incredulity. "That's the focus of your endeavors?" She waited for Jorj to protest, to negate the words spoken, but he did not. He simply watched her with sad eyes, realizing how things had just betrayed him. His intentions were pure, and he never thought his reasons damning. That her reaction should be so visceral surprised him.

Her eyes, deep and dark, were nearly wet with tears. "His only importance revolves around the damnation of others. If you want to fear something, fear that! Not his guns!"

"So we...I should just let him have his way with things? Burn the ground slowly and everyone stuck to it?" Jorj spoke slowly, almost calmly, but not quite. Inside, he was far from calm. "You know what will happen if he's successful, and it'll happen over and over and over..."

"Stop it!" She *was* crying now, unable to hold back what he knew was in her all along, but what he could never see the face of. "Wanting to stop it is not enough! I want to stop it. Dear God! I want to stop it, but we can't! Don't you understand? There are reasons, other reasons why even if we could...we can't." She stared into his eyes with her own watery dark ones, deep pools of endless depths he feared to fall into, and feared more not to. "This...is...not...us."

Jorj suddenly felt awash in a feeling of anchorless-ness. Yes, he lamented, this is how it feels to be cut loose, cast adrift, left completely at the mercy of a truth you can no more understand than escape. And still he struggled, flailing for mastery of his situation. He shook his head, slowly at first, then quite violently. With great effort he tried to speak, wanted very much to say something sharp, refuting that which she so adamantly proclaimed, but his eyes were fixed, and his tongue stuck in place, his jaw set in an iron weld. He found he could not even look at her, and that pained him most of all.

"How could you not, is that it?" It was Sid. Jorj turned suddenly, for the voice was behind him.

"Boooy, you gotta lot to learn!" The imp's sarcasm was thick, but behind it lay that inescapable gel of truth and seriousness, spread over every tar-babied crack and joke. "That's why she doesn't come out and tell you everything at once. You over-react."

"Wanting to stop a catastrophy is over-reacting?" Jorj took several steps towards the boy and stopped. What was he going to do, punch a kid?

"See?" The imp smiled. "Get on your knees. It'll make you feel better when you take your first swing."

"You have to pick your battles, Jorj. Stick with the ones you can win."

How the hell did this guy keep getting behind him? Jorj fumed and did a 180. From behind him someone small and irreverent laughed. To them, he was as stupid as Dennis, but that was about to be tested, for he had a good idea he was being played, and how. "Which one are you?" he asked soberly. "The boy or the man?"

Again the laugh, just as godlike in its amusement as before.

"Spell it out, Gret." This voice was different. It was older and sadder, as one sitting on top of the ash heap, having alone survived the fire of the previous night.

When Jorj looked her way, he saw that she sat on the asphalt, hugging her knees. Her face was turned away, and he thought she might still be crying, for her shoulders and ribs shook rhythmically. Slowly, her voice began a chant, as if she were alone, with no one to talk to but the breeze and the moon.

> Slip down the slope
> each finger lets go
> behind you Elysium
> ahead is the hole
> with each one released
> two more to the beast
> insideous change
> Median's troll

Her voice trailed off on the breeze as if no one else was there to hear it. Of course there was. Jorj approached her cautiously for she seemed a creature possessed, and indeed she was, though of a prescient spirit. At the last he knelt behind her, offering no physical contact. Patiently he waited for her to finish what she had to say, for there were yet words to come.

"If you continue this path of violence, it will lead you away from Ogam, and he is the key." She paused and bowed her head for a moment, her face unseen, and then raised it."

"Sometimes violence is necessary." He honestly believed this to be true, no matter how much he wished it was otherwise.

She turned, gently, and faced him, knees touching his. Her petite right hand raised to his unshaven cheek, now under the threat of a gathering beard. Her dark eyes, even in the corporeal, never lost that inner gravity. Her expression was sad, and he knew she would say more if he asked, but that there was nothing she could do to stop him from the path he had chosen.

"If there was another way," he coaxed. "Christ! Valhalla has more honor, more love than this place."

"There is no Valhalla," she replied. "But there is heaven, when you choose to find it."

"Have you seen it? Even from a distance?" It seemed an absurd question, but one that needed to be asked.

"No, my love. You bar my way, even as you helped me bridge the chasm."

"I still don't understand."

"Nor will you, until you let the gun fall from your fingers forever."

And then she was gone. Her touch, her fingers gently caressing his face, became as sand, and then as smoke, blowing away on the night's autumn breeze. The last thing he saw was the deep ink of her eyes staring into his soul.

All things became turned upside down then, in the spiraling crush of his panic. Did he come so far just to lose her again? "Greta!" he shouted, again and again, but only the laughter of that hideous imp-child followed him, for now he ran, and to his horror, he was far from the Millhouse.

He stopped, closing his eyes. Maybe it was all just a dream...a bad one. Night on Twilight Earth played tricks, and he knew this well by now. Sounds opened up around him and he listened intently, saving the reemergence of his visual centers for last. He was surrounded by people, half creatures of light and shadow, gathered here for some reason he had yet to discern. There were adults and children, men and women, all but the occasional glimpses of detail obscured by the veil that kept them from seeing him, for his senses were better than theirs, and their circumstances more distracting.

Someone fired a gun...no, a truck backfired. The alarm that broke out momentarily died a quick, uneven death. There remained an edge to everything, for what began as a public gathering, with all or most of everyone's attention turned towards a speaker far to Jorj's right, now took on the air of a mass execution without bullets. He didn't need to understand the words—and he couldn't—to know that this was power seized and centralized in the form of a single man, one whom no one served willingly, but those that did knew the consequences of resistance. The distance to here was not covered bloodlessly.

It was an age of giants again upon the Earth. The angels, or devils now, if you will, had learned no good lessons of their original fornication. Instead they adapted, so that what offspring sprang from their loins, into the women who would die during childbirth, grew in the stature that matters most. Now, one of their kind held humanity by the throat, knowing that mankind's oblivion was not in a fireball at the end of things but was ultimately the event horizon of failure. The race could only absorb so many missteps, tolerate so many acts of negligence, before succumbing to eternal death. To this giant among cockroaches, their sins damned them to slavery before their inescapable demise, and he considered this without a fleck in the eye of his conscience, even in spite of the fact that his own sin was larger than their many small ones. Such as he ever had blind spots befitting like distinction.

That Jorj immediately felt hatred for this individual escaped his awareness. It simply existed on its own. The separation from Greta still weighed him down, though he wondered that it might be he who had left and not her.

A bright spot appeared, carried in by four others to the center of the platform from which the giant addressed the large crowd. Someone ran by Jorj, leaving a trail of afterglow in his wake. Only when it dissipated was it clear that others were breaking away, uncertainly at first, and then more determined, as if they realized the lateness with which they now acted. Through it all, Jorj found himself walking forward towards the source of the burning singularity.

It was as if someone had pierced a black paper with a needle, allowing light from a burning sun, just on the other side, to sear through, obliterating visually the edges that defined the needle's breach. Jorj found that he could not look at it directly, and even he felt the urge to run, but he also knew that there was no running, no escape, not so long as this thing remained where it was.

The giant continued his arrogant, abusive, demands, formulating his acrid words into a fiery denunciation of how they had lived and how he intended that they die, that they might serve him even still. His loyals, if such could be called that, departed now, for all colors were unveiled, and no one remained in a sanctuary, real or imagined.

In the chaos of flight, many of these creatures fell, and like bugs under a monolithic shoe, burst the light of life, the crush of others' fears robbing the singularity of its full glory before it was itself released from its unholy ark. Jorj stepped over them, careless of their plight such was the demand of his own possessed intent. He stopped before the singularity, its light blazing hot and white, unable to burn him yet, but eager to escape and consume all it could touch. The Watchman, as Willie Bender called him, regarded it balefully for but a heartbeat, and then lifted it with his good hand in the way one lifts a suitcase, for he knew this thing. The giant's words spilled to the ground, so much gravel falling unmastered from his suddenly mindless mouth. Then, caught in the furious realization of what was transpiring before his eyes, for they pierced many veils easily, the giant uttered a deep, throaty roar, and tumbled off the platform towards the man who dared to take what was not his.

Taking possession of the object was unplanned, at least Jorj had no premeditation in the matter. Now one approached who intended not only to reclaim this artifact from him, but to take his own life, perhaps his own soul, in reparation. Where could he run? Jorj began moving immediately, not at a run, for the singularity dragged at him with the gravity of a small moon, but at a hurried pace nevertheless.

The distance between him and the giant began the process of shrinking, and although it was considerable to start with, the latter possessed the advantage of the lesser burden. Jorj did not know exactly why he turned events the way he did, only that he must not deviate from his chosen course, and so he hustled forward, vaguely aware that his broken arm throbbed, and that his thoughts of Greta grew larger, until they filled him and all he wished for now was to return to her.

And like once before, her voice whispered to him. At first he thought it just the wind, the same that floated the ragged clouds above, upon their course, night after night. Then, as his perception of it improved, he heard her words of encouragement, and he followed them, for he was now at their mercy. She had come looking for him. He, lost, ran the race of one pursued, the wolf behind breathed hotly upon his haunches, nipped at his heels. Another time, Jorj would have turned and faced the fight. Now he was chained to his fate, or more aptly, his destiny. One cannot fight and win bound to a millstone.

They ran from Jorj now, this crowd of cacophony. He carried with him the source of their fear, and so he became it. Yet their painterly streaks of neon existence turned pastel in the night, and then became sunspots where there was no sun to be found. They were fading from him, or he from them, and he knew at least one veil was past.

He was denied a sigh of relief, and he half expected it. The wolf, this giant son of reckless angels and seduced humanity, pursued still, though the gap between them was evening, despite their closeness. Jorj chanced only once to look back, never letting his feet hesitate or stumble, and saw him, a ghost static shaped like a man, the hint of a business suit flailing at the edges. Hard shoes impeded him from his quarry, and the sound of them on the asphalt created an echo that every building nearby sang to in dissonant chorus. Hands, or the lit silhouette of them against the darkness, reached out, extending farther then they ordinarily should have been able to, and Jorj felt them touch his back, icy cold and screaming with the shivering horde voices of hell. There was no more speed to summon, nothing more for flight. The fingers began to close.

Another shape, more human, distinctly detailed, leaped from the darkness, throwing itself on the Nephalim born again, bringing it unexpectedly to the ground. Greta's voice urged Jorj on, leading him on a winding path of streets while behind Jorj, Sid and the giant struggled for supremacy.

He passed by the Westside Tavern now, whole and untouched on his left and lit dimly within by a small, flickering fire. A glass broke to his right. Harsh, drunken laughter exploded from the side of a building. "Keep going," Jorj muttered to himself, even as Greta pressed him to do the same. At the corner of…the street was named differently here, and it hardly mattered, for things were always in the process of changing, shifting. The night was an ocean and its currents strong and dark. Jorj clung to Greta's voice so that he would not be swept up, and in time, he came to find himself standing at the curb before the Millhouse, staring at Greta, listening to the drunken snorts of Richie, and keenly aware of what he must do now.

Setting down the green case that he carried, he fumbled for the keys to the Roadrunner. He wanted aspirin for his arm, and most of all, he longed to hold the woman who waited for him, but this thing at his feet needed to be attended to. In moments he had the trunk open, and unsurprised, he saw that it was empty. Slowly, with a strained one-armed heave, he returned the cursed item to its place of hiding. The price of this thing was climbing, he realized. How much longer, he wondered until he could no longer afford what it would demand of him? With a tired, staggered exhalation, he closed the trunk and turned, leaning back against it. Greta was walking towards him now, crying, reaching for him silently as if he were slipping away.

16

He undertook the risk with full understanding, knowing that what had to be done outweighed the chance of getting caught. His hopes hinged upon the low odds of someone seeing him with a good mixture of his own naked stealth. Now was a bad time to realize his lack of preparedness, for he should, days ago, have placed a parcel near the overpass, well hidden in one of the catastrophically heaped vehicles. At least then he would have some clothes. It could have been done before the his neck broke, but one trip out this way in the dark was enough. The last thing he heard before the sharp twist and the mercifully abrupt snap was Theodore's voice saying, "I'll make this quick." What a way to mend a broken arm. All those scientific advances in medicine and all a man had to do here was die.

It was a short bit of travel to a house which bore supplies, for Theo opened up his city's hidden larders to Jorj, and the latter chose one silently, still unwilling to give up his 'Kamaloka Crossroads.' By the time he made his exit, he had camouflage, guns, bags of ill-willed goodies slung on his back, and night-vision. This might have been fun, he mused, were the circumstances different.

Giggling smote the silence of the night and Jorj cursed. The imp found him as easily as ever. He wondered how many other denizens there were lurking about. "Hey Dick." Jorj thought he'd start things off on the right foot.

"Hi George." This voice was different, completely different. It came from directly behind him and Jorj spun, pointing one of the assault rifles he carried in the direction he thought it came from. A man emerged from the darkness, really no more than a shadow against the ambient night glow. He wore a trench coat, and his hair was almost to his shoulders. Boots, probably more stylish than practical by the sounds of them, clicked on the pavement of the street. There was a casual swagger, nothing obvious, but leaking a trace of the arrogance that carried each step. "Got your message. I see you got mine."

"You're the poet."

"And you…" there was a small laugh, "…are quite the little soldier now."

"What, did you kick Sid out of the group? I was starting to warm up to the guy."

"Sid's gone. Dead." There was a measure of bitterness dispensed. "He saved your bacon at the expense of his own. Fair trade, huh?"

Silence, and then, "Sid's not dead. No one dies here."

"He didn't die here, George. Did you forget that?"

"Jorj. The name is Jorj. And I didn't know the rules changed like that."

"Now ya do! A little late for Sid, though. He's in a very bad place right now." The imp walked on ahead, popping a cigarette between his lips. "Jed! Got a light?" He smiled when the end of his blunt ignited. "Nice! Thanks, bud."

"I know your game." Jorj started walking again, changing his direction to depart from the two, for he remembered Richie's intention to distract. "it's called Schizo. Ages five and up. Three to however many players. Not much fun though, is it?"

Jed appeared beside him, matching his stride. "Don't mess with the kid, George. You have your own problems now."

"You?" Now Jorj laughed. "You write creepy poetry, but that's just an annoyance."

"Don't get cocky. We just met."

"Not my fault." He almost stopped, but kept walking, wondering if his diverting from his intended route was anticipated. He switched directions again, deciding that maybe he might try playing their own game without them catching on. "What's your deal, anyhow? Rogue? Merc?" He grinned, his words a reconnaissance of malice. "Or are you playing Schizo too?"

A sigh. The moon came out and its first light revealed a man slightly older than Jorj, two days bristled growth on his chiseled face. His trench coat was made of black leather, open to reveal more black leather underneath. A big silver belt buckle on a steel-studded belt added a curious cliché to his otherwise Euro-stylish appearance. If the man had a gun, Jorj didn't see it. "I'm not here to answer questions, George. But I might some of them. That is not one."

"Mysterioso." Richie spoke the word from the shadows, out of sight. Jed smiled, saying nothing.

When he did, it was to cut Jorj off. "Have to tell you, taking Margaret out of the circle was a good thing. She was a bad influence on things, especially the kid."

He wanted to strike the man, for the woman was holy ground. Jorj wondered if there was anything substantial to hit. Then he remembered what the imp said earlier, that he over-reacted. They would tempt him to do so every chance they got from now on, he guessed. His self-control marshaled, he smiled back, the smile of a killer. "Those who can't do, teach, is that it? Or is it actually, 'those who can't do, fuck with those who can?'"

Without breaking stride, Jed switched to a backwards walk so that he faced the other man. "It's going to be a long night for you, George. Are you ready?"

It was another forty-five minutes before he returned to the Millhouse. Theodore met him out front, and so did Greta. Nick was not well, and was tucked in for the night with some soft, battery-powered, music. Dennis watched from the front window and Bill from the upstairs with the Padre. When Greta saw Jed and Richie, her face darkened. She was already unhappy. Their presence only worsened things.

"I'm coming with you."

"No, you're not." Jorj tried to ignore her but she gripped him by his formerly broken arm.

"*They* will, you know, and you can't stop them."

"All the more reason to leave you here." It was surreal being out of doors after dark with so many people, real, familiar, or no. He handed half of their equipment to Theodore and they commenced sorting it out. A thought came to him and he went to the trunk, opening it with a key from his pocket. Wisely he'd had the foresight to strip naked so that when Theodore killed him, he'd lose none of his belongings. Now he cursed, for the trunk was empty. The reasons for travel tonight never seemed to end.

"What?" Theodore didn't like the sound of Jorj's tone.

"Nothing," Jorj answered curtly. He didn't need to tell him anything about the blasphemous piece of military hardware he kept stealing. The gears turned deftly in his head, raising new questions. Eventually he would have answers to them, one way or another. Richie appeared in the space where the olive-drab case was and waved like a smart-ass. Jorj grimaced and slammed the trunk shut.

Greta was right there beside him. "I can help you. Theodore knows it. I'm better at the night than you are."

"I've made it through on my own."

"No you haven't. I was always nearby."

Jorj stared at her, stone-faced. He looked away before cracks could splinter his resolve. "I won't lose you again."

"If I die, I'll return to…" She paused, and then continued more softly, more subdued. "Our place."

"But the bad guys might not kill you." The words burned his mouth to speak them. "They might do worse."

"And they might to you." Her own words took on a venomous taint, for she didn't like the double standard. This body of hers, this new one, presented fewer options than she was used to.

"That's what I like to see." Jed said with a grim smile. "Everybody getting along, one big dysfunctional…."

"Shut up!" Greta and Jorj yelled in unison.

"…family."

Theodore looked up sharply from his pack, confused and irritated. "Wind it up. We have business here and the clock's ticking. I say the woman comes along. Jorj?"

"I need the Padre down here." He thought about it a second, and added. "I want Nick, too."

Despite Dennis' protests, and it very nearly came to blows between himself and Jorj, the latter woke up the old man and got him outside. Nick was dressed in pajamas and a robe. His face was tired, but some of the color was back in it. Rest had done at least a little good. Francis was there too, standing near the car.

"What's this about, Jorj?" Nick was still waking up.

"I need a blessing. It's important."

"Very well, come here."

"No." Jorj walked over to the Roadrunner. "I want you to bless the car." He stood with a small can of paint, and a brush with bristled about an inch wide. "I'm going to add my own and hope God understands."

"What's this about?" The Padre helped Nick over to the vehicle and stood by the front headlights.

"Insurance." Jorj replied. "You're a priest. He's a rabbi. I want you to do your jobs."

"I'm not a priest anymore." There was a wounded character to his tone. "Any so-called blessing I might offer would be pretty impotent about now."

"Father," Jorj replied, his impatience piled up almost to the second floor, "I brought you're daughter back. You can do this much." He glanced at Greta who regarded him back with a quizzical stare. "Nick? How about it?"

His voice was weak but he managed a thin smile. "If the Lord still listens, I'll give it my best shot."

"His ears work fine. Let's do this."

It took a moment, for Nick wanted the right words. Not just any would do. When he began, it was in a language no one else understood, for his lips moved in ancient Hebrew. To Jorj, it might as well have been Greek, but he smiled thinly, satisfied and confident. The Padre, less convinced, only watched at first. Eventually, when he saw how committed Nick was, that his spark of faith not only returned but was igniting into something greater, the Padre joined him in Latin, chanting whatever came to his mind. Jorj pried the paint can open and dipped the brush into crimson. Now was the time, he decided.

Next to him, Jed appeared, almost unnoticed at first. He shook his head disdainfully, his arrogant smile intersected by several ropes of stray hair hanging down across his face. "Wasting time while Benedict doesn't. Tick. Tick. Tick."

It was difficult, but Jorj ignored him, tracing the reddened brush in the path of a rune some called Elhaz, others Ihwar. It was Norse, and represented protection. Once he knew these symbols better. With the aid of Ogam's personal library, he boned up, restoring some of what he'd forgotten. Others might wonder that he mixed religions so, especially pagan beliefs, but after all, he decided, all things were from God, whatever God was. Let him sort it out. It was the focus he understood. If he was a hypocrite for taking this path after turning up his nose at Greta's Tarot cards, he'd sort that out later too. This mattered now.

The praying continued. Men such as Nick and Francis didn't say meaningful things in just a few words when talking to God. They went on and on, something their training well prepared them for. Jorj traveled around the Roadrunner, painting symbols that meant things to him, like the one for Christ, the 'P' intersecting the 'X', the Anhk, and the symbol for eternity. There was also the Chinese 'Yung' which bore similar meaning. And then other marks, petraglyphs as alien to him as anyone else in the lot, flowed out through his brush by spirit, for he opened himself up to it willingly. The outer skin of the car became a vast, confused network of lines and curves even he didn't understand. For a moment trapped in the span of a single pulse, he was not Jorj, not anyone, just a motivation in action. Later, on the road, he would struggle with this in confusion, for up until now, he was content to be a simple man, regarding the world at face value. His ideology, ever before, lacked proper firmament on which to stand because he trusted no one else's. There were no good examples, just defective men in the trappings of wont. Every search he ever made for God always ended up at that place. And then Greta changed it all, broke through the stone that imprisoned him, opened him up to the fire, and in doing so, showed him that if one believed truly enough, that fire would not harm him.

Ogam's diary, with its single marked page bearing nothing more than a circle, came unexpectedly into his thoughts. He painted the symbol's twin on the Roadrunner's hood, and on the top of the trunk, just below Ihwar, the rune of the splayed hand, he added that of his own right one, painted and pressed to the car's original finish as if to say 'I am the gate keeper; go no further but by my consent.' Whether imagined or not, he felt a tingle before he pulled it away for good. When he was done, he stepped back and found that all were regarding him warily. Nick and the Padre were already finished praying. Dennis watched from the front window incredulously. From the floor above, Bill stared in horror.

"You are nuts," Theodore said simply. "But...whatever."

Behind him, Jed walked around casually, smirking slightly to himself in some private thought. He didn't need to say a word as far as he seemed concerned, and he made it very clear.

Jorj suddenly felt a mixture of embarrassment and anger. "Let's go," he grumbled, tossing both paint can and brush into some bushes to be rid of them quickly.

"I'm still coming." Greta positioned herself between Jorj and the driver's side door.

Theodore looked up from the other side, impatient. "Let her in, Jorj."

"This isn't up to you." Jorj's voice was steady and heated. "Bud out."

"Jorj, the fucking clock is ticking!" With that the other man pulled the handle and opened the passenger door. For a moment he almost leaned an arm on the top, then, seeing the wet paint, he caught himself just in time, frowning like it was all madness to him. "Let her in. If she's lived in this darkness as long as everybody says, she's more valuable to this job than either of us, but only while the sun's down. Do you understand that we have an advantage here if we don't waste any more time?"

A slender hand rose up to Jorj's lips and pressed gently against them. In a slow maneuver, Greta opened the driver's door with her other hand. "I'm safer with you."

"Don't bet on it," Jorj replied, his adamantine resolve succumbing to her feminine alchemy. "I'm not Superman . . . not even Jimmy Olsen."

The gap between door and car widened enough for her to sit back and fall into the front seat. "No," she whispered, drawing her fingers away from his face. "You're Jorj. Do what you have to do." She slid over the seat into the back while Jorj watched from his place of self-imposed defeat. He could have stopped her, but some part of him wanted her to be right. Whatever his desire, and the thought gnawed on him, it didn't make it so.

"You getting in?" It was Theodore, all business.

"Yeah." Jorj sighed, catching a glare that Jed seemed un-intended for him to see. He smiled back, a bit of gloat escap-ing, for he suspected where lay the source of the other's covert malice. His gaze shifted to the others, and his smile became more sarcastic. "Don't wait up." In two more heartbeats he was in the seat turning the key, firing up the engine with the lion's hungry roar. Quickly, in a snag of conscience, he rolled down his window and barked thanks to Nick and Francis. The next moment he was tearing away, bouncing over the curb and rip-ping down the street to the corner where he barely paused, only to turn right with a loud, lingering squeal of tires. From above, unnoticed by anyone, Bill watched in concern and foreboding. Jed gazed up at him, they locked eyes for a brief second, and then the latter grinned maliciously. Like Jorj, he disappeared into the night, only more abruptly; there, and then not. Bill stepped back from the window and gazed in dumb horror at the breath mark he left on the glass. Written in it by some un-seen finger was a single word.

'Fear.'

17

Darkness superceded everything else in Mosswood. The moon hid behind a large shred of cloud, barely highlighting its edges with faint luminescence. In a few minutes it would emerge again, resurrecting in the way of Lazarus the long shadows formerly cast by every tree and mausoleum in the cemetery.

For now, travelers through this haunted wood were forced to depend on their ears, and the spread of gooseflesh over the less traveled parts of their bodies. It was a place of hills and ravines topped by stone, solitary blocks or collections placed neatly one atop another in the mockery of houses. There were more places to hide, for good or ill, then one could ever count, and in the deepest shadows of the night, things lurked, for the barriers were thin and breached in places. This was a land far from heaven. If angels watched it, they were surely fallen ones.

The Roadrunner was parked blocks away, squeezed between two ancient wood-frame houses and left in the back yard of the larger beneath a red maple tree. The three, two men and one woman, were without its wards and glyphs, protected now by only their wits and the steel they carried. The possibility existed that they needed none of the latter, although it also remained to be seen whether such earthly measures would serve them at all.

Theodore shifted his night goggles to a more comfortable position, briefly surveying the areas ahead of them from the first hill on the southern side. It was a different entrance they chose, knowing that the ones closer to the campus, specifically the Forestry School, would be watched more closely, if at all. He was glad Jorj found a cache of his equipment, and that he brought extra camos. Greta blended better now in the darkness than she would have otherwise and there was no time to look for anything else.

Things looked still and cold, but there lay the deception. The graveyard at night was a new thing to him on either side of the veil. Further, it wasn't so much the physical dangers that he suspected roamed among the granite and the marble. That he could deal with, such was his confidence in that regard. What he feared was getting lost, descending into another place, or the threat of losing his mind. Everyone of them was vulnerable, even the woman.

"C'mon," he whispered, clicking off the goggles and pulling them back skyward. His path descended the low hill to within fifty yards of a florist shop at the edge of Calvin street. Rolling before them were gentle hills, more densely populated with small, modern tombstones than trees. They were entering the newer section. Towards the north and west everything would get older and more interesting from this point on. It would also become more dense, more claustrophobic, and hostile to the emerging moonlight, though it would never shut out the pale eye from above completely. The shadows, already reaching out towards them with scraggly, arthritic fingers, could only grow darker, more stark. Who else would see the moon was a mystery, but for the three of them it held good and bad, for it might betray them; but its light was pure, untouched by the evil of this land. Neither point went unheeded.

Ahead and to the right, a stag made of moonlit granite watched them approach and slink off towards the center. It was only twenty yards away so when it moved, the sound of stone sliding on stone caught them all by surprise. Jorj, having let his paranoia out on a longer leash, paused and alerted the others, but it hardly seemed necessary. They were gazing intently at the direction from which the noise came.

"Move on," Greta whispered. Some memories were with her again, reawakened by the thick oppressiveness of Mosswood at night. "Guns won't help us. Distance will."

Theodore nodded and pressed ahead, his nerves on edge. A road went almost straight ahead to the northeast and then branched left and right in a wide, cupped, shallow 'Y' around a raised hump of land. The graves were a mixture of low square stones and bronze markers set on marble pads, the latter flush with the ground. Someone cut the grass here recently, and tended this place regularly, though no one ever found out who. Theodore wondered idly at this while he ascended, always keeping his ears attentive should that something follow from behind, or something new approach from another side. And they still had to deal with their first goal. He had yet to properly inform his companions as to the nature of it. He knew though, that it was best not to until they were there. He didn't quite know what to expect himself yet. Things *might* go bad. Things *might* go worse than bad.

At every summit, he surveyed the area with night vision. It wasn't good to use it too much, for the green light of the goggles could theoretically be seen and he didn't want to compromise their position any more than necessary. When they dipped into the next hollow, entering into the older section finally, he knew the dark shape ahead of them and to the left was a cannon. Despite the fact that the barrel was likely filled with cement, he skirted away from its cyclopean stare. This was Twilight Earth at its darkest. If a cemetery was going to harbor a live cannon, it would be Mosswood.

The moon broke out completely now. Tearing away temporarily from the clouds, leaving them shred-like in its wake. From the shadows sprang every tombstone, mausoleum, and monument in veiled white brilliance. Greta ceased her advance, suddenly tense. Before them was a statue of a nameless angel, head bowed and hands out, open-palmed in supplication. It raised its head slowly towards them, each fold of its robe scraping stonily. Eyes without detail, the same color and texture as the rest of its body, regarded them without emotion. Its mouth opened as if to speak, and Greta found her voice. "Run!" she cried, trying desperately not to scream. "We must not hear its voice! Run!" She caught Jorj by the hand and tugged. At first he only stared in disbelief, but then he let her take him away, chasing carelessly around the bend of the road, without looking to Theodore's welfare. There was no time. He followed them closely, for he was more attuned to Greta's fears here than was Jorj, who seemed not to realize the fullness of their situation, nor the degree to which the woman's senses worked here.

It could not be helped. Though they put considerable distance and hillside between themselves and the statue, its voice carried dully, finding its way to them through the darkness. What the words were, that much they were spared, but the sound itself pulled at them with a gravity that grew with every second.

"No!" Greta's grasp tightened harder, pressing Jorj to go faster. "Fight it! Fight it both of you!" And then Theodore stumbled. An ancient root, exposed by years of wind and run-off, tangled his right foot, perhaps not entirely by accident, bringing the man heavily to the eroded tracks of the road bed. Jorj hesitated and then stopped, offering his free hand to help the man up. In that instant, they were all caught. The voice became a drone, a chanting exhalation of the deeper planes of existence, drawing them away from the one they knew and into a place somehow darker, more sinister.

The effect was such that when it was over, the only thing telling them that it was so was the yellow moon, the color of cigarette tar on a heavy smoker's fingertips, and the pale straw color of its ambient light, poisonous to the soul, a corrosive acid to one's sense of hope. Greta sat in a sprawl, crying softly, her left hand covering her face, her right one barely clinging to Jorj's own left. Theodore rose dazed from his hands and knees, managing to collect his loose equipment which un-slung to the ground during his fall.

"What the hell just happened?" he asked. No one answered. It seemed like a rhetorical question. An odor of decay, worse than before, permeated everything.

"We should move on," Jorj mumbled. His lips felt numb. A shroud of fatigue more bizarre than any mere need for sleep covered him. He had an unsettling desire to find a mausoleum somewhere, enter within, and rest with the dead.

Gently, with a sliver of his former resolve, he aided Greta to her feet, and Theodore, standing straight but somewhat weighed down, studied her carefully. He appeared less directly affected than the other two.

"You'll have to undo what's been done to us," he said simply. "You know how."

She gazed at him, glassy-eyed and angry. "You won't walk that path," she replied, her voice composed a sudden firmness."

His smile, slim and sardonic, was out of place under that evil moon-haze. A thick mist was taking root, coiling among the tombstones, reaching out towards them with non-corporeal tendrils. "If I don't see it, how can I walk it?"

"You won't." She started walking, loosely clinging to Jorj's sleeve. "Violent thoughts led you here. The warden of the southern gate used them to open your souls and push this plane into us. His job is easy."

"What?" Theodore stood his ground from behind for three heartbeats and then began walking, catching up to her. "Why didn't you warn us such a danger existed?"

Stone scraped again, quite near. To their left, just off the road and at the foot of the nearest hill's slope, something dark, the size and silhouette of an ancient tombstone, turned and clicked. Away, deeper into the darkness in the direction of their journey, a loud, long wail released itself, anguish and agony indistinguishable. The three stared at it and then all around them, paranoia sprouting from a tiny seed and entangling insidiously with each vital organ. The eldest of their party considered the pyramid, and what lay, possibly still intact, within. The door there, at the heart of that horrid place, went one way. Suddenly he didn't want to go there, at least not on this fallen version of Earth, or whatever one wanted to call it. He knew they no longer walked in the Twilight. It was imbecilic to think otherwise. Theodore felt the descent as did the others, the sudden elevator drop, the lurch of his insides, and the stark sensation of regret; bitter, despairing regret. This was not where he would find Benedict, unless as a fellow inmate of the same endless prison, spiraling down into another one worse with every inevitable misstep. Another sound brought his thoughts back to the razor-line of their situation. Theodore advanced to the dark object, gun raised absurdly as if it would help him here. And then he realized that such steel was more psychological security than reality. Almost automatically, Jorj raised his own and flanked to the left, shrugging off Greta's voiced reservations. She, unlike them, refused even a knife with which to protect herself and stayed slightly behind her man.

It was a tombstone, turned perpendicular upon its dark marble footer like a key. In the mind of each person there was the same question. Had something been released, or imprisoned. If they proceeded, would they find it? Would it find them?

Jorj swore under his breath, but all heard it. The night was too unsettlingly silent for even the stealthiest sound to go unnoticed. "Over our fucking heads," he growled. He turned his face towards Theodore, his jaw set tensely. "You talked about wasting time? I think we're all about *that* now. We'll be lucky to get back at all."

Ever pragmatic, Theodore pressed his lips together tightly in thought. "If we can go down, we can go up," he said finally. "It's simple physics. This goddam supernatural chicanery is nothing more than that. Whatever its guise, its laws are ours and we can use them to get back." He glanced at Greta in the darkness. Her eyes glittered under the sickening moon. That she disagreed, or at least considered his interpretation of things overly simplistic was self-evident. "It makes no sense to go on until we are on the level we started at. Therefore, we need to return now...somehow."

"Where, exactly, were we going?" Jorj demanded angrily. "You told us the place, but not the why."

Theodore bristled but forced his initial reaction to pass. "It's the last place I saw William Bender and Benedict."

"Why there? What's the significance?"

Silence served neither to calm the waters between them nor to offer up a satisfactory answer. Theodore broke it with reluctance. There's a door going down within the pyramid. Perhaps it leads to here. I don't know. Where this version leads to you may imagine if you dare." How had he regarded it? A one-way door? He almost shivered at the implication for them all. No, he decided resolutely. If down existed, so did up. "We won't find what we need now within the confines of that structure."

Concerned suddenly with Greta's silence, Jorj took her hand. It felt cold. "What do you remember of this place?" he asked softly. "I know you've been here before; I can feel it. Try."

The pain of return was bad enough. Her eyes betrayed now the further suffering of her displacement, and the retracing of old, lost steps. Yes, she was here once, not only in the Twilight, but in this nether existence, pulled through a sinkhole of past ignorance and all the accompanying fears. How had she returned? Her hands went to Jorj's chest, mingling for the anchor, or rather the float. It was easy to flounder here, far simpler than in the Twilight. An urge to vomit, an old forgotten one, surged. She suppressed it barely. Somehow she made it out. Her head shook from side to side. "I don't remember." Her voice quivered. Like a lost child, she buried her face in Jorj's chest.

"Now's not the time to be weak," Theodore chided. "This is real. Think!"

Jorj grimaced angrily, for his words bore the paint of heartlessness. Yet the brush was not so, and he saw this. Theodore's words were undoubtedly never more trult spoken. This land sought ways around your strength, gnawed at your resolve. For only a second he pulled her close. Then, gently but firmly, he pried her away. "Work on it while we wander. We should stay on the move. Maybe something will prod your memory."

It was exactly what she feared, though this she kept to herself.

Wretched souls roamed a place like this, twice removed from even this dementedly tilted realm. There was a sense of imbalance, and though Theodore wrote it off as a physical manifestation of their forced crossing over, an adjustment yet unmade, Jorj sensed it was quite apart from his body, and Greta knew it was so. It made one tend towards stumbling, though they never actually did since Theodore's first misstep. The rough terrain, greater in gravity, steeper in climb, and deeper in ravine, left them little in the way of a conventional stride. The further they progressed into the heart of the oldest cemetery in any version of New Jackson City, the more difficult their travel became.

"Reciprocal." Greta said the word so quietly that they almost didn't hear her. When both men stopped, Jorj first, then Theodore, she repeated the word, more certain this time.

"Go on," Theodore commanded, waiting with scourged patience.

She shook her head, lack of doubt condensing like the thick mists they clung, pack-like, within. "They are interchangeable. It doesn't belong here...isn't here, but its roots penetrate to this side."

Jorj took her by the arm, realized that his strength was not under proper harness, and relaxed his grip if not his intention. "What is it Gret?" His tension steeped itself in the yellow fog, undermining the last shreds of mental clarity.

"It's all I have," she breathed, wanting to cry, holding herself tenuously at the edge. "Please let me go."

He did, sorry for his carelessness. "Give us a direction at least." He wanted to say something more, sweeter words for both their souls, but not in this place, *never* in this place. There were hells created out of many things. He'd not offer this up for one of them.

Her eyes closed, and her hands reached out until they found Jorj's arms where she clung like a child. "In a grove, near a road...not the direction we chose."

"Then we go another way," Theodore stated with renewed determination. "Towards the city or the highway?" The cemetery was sandwiched between Route 89 and the lower east side, just south of the college's main campus. When she didn't answer, he made the decision for them. "The highway."

Stockton Avenue," she blurted out defiantly. Her eyes were wide now, and more desparate.

"That's better." Theodore regarded Jorj knowingly. "That's why we brought her along."

It was true, and the younger man couldn't deny it honestly. Whatever his personal feelings were for Greta's welfare, one thing was clear. Without her, both he and Theodore would be doomed. The thought made the skin of his back prickle. He nodded and yielded to their current leader, letting him take point. The distance between them restrained itself to no more than seven feet, closer than comfortable should they be attacked, barely near enough to keep from losing each other in the pallid yellow mist.

But for the trees, and the monuments, all of which rose above the fog and betrayed paths and avenues among them, negotiating a path towards the city's edge would have been impossible but by sheer chance, and not one of them trusted their luck anymore.

Rising out of the mists, lit in the weak light of a compromised moon, an obelisk dominated their view, for it stood as sentinel to a crossroads, warding openly. At its base was a solid stone urn, wreathed in decorative carven ivy, a draping of stone cloth covering one side. A loud crack split the air and the urn tipped, tumbling from view to be lost in the morbid pea soup that rose to their chests. Another sound, hissing like many snakes, heralded an evil spirit worse than that which triggered the urn's demise, and Greta cried out, caring not for what other denizens might hear and be drawn to them.

What collected itself now beneath the surface of the boil beneath, could not hide its malign, nor would it. Theodore considered his gun and then deftly abandoned the idea for a better one. "Flee! Go!" He pushed Jorj and Greta ahead of him, choosing the way of the right. "Call up every holy name you can think of! Utter the names of your ancestors!" His feet moved rapidly now. They were practically running like dogs. "If any of that crap you put on the car means a thing," he commanded to Jorj, "speak it now!"

It is a curious thing how, when faced with sudden struggle, abrupt need, the mind freezes. Men and woman react in separate ways to some extent, but there is no one immune from the specter of paralyzation, or the salvation of clarity. Gender matters little if at all. It fell to Theodore to push them on, to buy precious seconds, for there was no physical means by which they could defeat that which now turned a baleful eye upon them. That they might escape it merely by running was laughable, for where could they go that it could not follow once released to serve as it was intended? He had not the tools to bar the creature's way. His job was done. In his mind, in those heart-stopping seconds, it was his belief that if anyone could save them, it would be the woman. She was the 'witch,' the 'night shaman.' But though fear held her not in a stranglehold as yet, the ferment of her reasoning could not be forced. Her soul was several shades deeper than either man, and time looked unkindly on such richness now.

Every symbol so far felt impotent to Jorj, and he realized the shallow nature of his abilities, and the arrogance with which he disregarded his own ignorance. This thing behind them, now swimming forward, leisurely but with growing persistence, was beyond them all. How could he, or any of them, cease its advance, entice it to look elsewhere? He could not, he decided, and looked despairingly upon the failure that would bring them down, consuming every last bit of humanity within them. A word escaped his lips, and he knew not why, though most assuredly it was a word of meaning, not merely the name for which it stood. "Ogam," he uttered, his breath ragged and harsh. Then, in anger and frustration, he gave voice to it again, crying louder so that it seemed unclear whether it be death-throw or battle cry. He turned suddenly, gun lowered but eyes raised defiantly, and faced the oncoming thing from the urn. In that moment, as Jorj let Greta slip around him, and dodged a startled Theodore, he yelled the word again, stressing both syllables as if they were colossal twins, invoked to fight in the trio's stead.

Indecision seized the urn-creature, this nether spirit, and it hesitated, swimming around them instead of into their midst, as if seeking a weak place, something they, or it, had not yet noticed. Theodore drew back to Jorj, finding Greta already there. He wished to speak, indeed, almost did, but wisdom cleaved his tongue to his mouth. This was not for his meddling, he being but a spectator in an unholy arena. It was a test of wills, a battle between two primeval forces barely cognizant of their own existence. Even Greta stood as stone, her eyes wide and ghostly in the dark.

No more did he utter that word, that name. It would do no more good than it did now. By a strength he did not quite comprehend was this glyph propped up. It neither wavered not grew stronger, being a monolith of stone itself, lending its protection but too large for anyone to control or move.

A groan of disgust escaped the surface of the brume. With only a momentary, last attempt at penetration, the creature let out a hateful gasp and drew off towards the obelisk and the urn. For an abominably long time, the three waited, breathing tensely. At length, Theodore pulled on Jorj's arm, and then at Greta's own. Wordlessly he tracked on, barely believing they yet lived. To make a sound now, anything at all, might break the spell that was woven about them, real or no.

Each branch of road, often little more than a washed-out streambed, brought them higher than and farther away from the center. No longer the pale yellow funk of sickness, the fog drifted translucently about their knees, revealing hints by the troubled moon of the sod underneath their feet when they finally felt confident to break away from the paths of other men. The markers that drifted past them, cut and polished more for the living than the dead, marked the more recently departed. Greta searched among them, her mind calling up ghosts that never lived, never took a single breath. "There are no coffins here," she announced, her quiet voice somehow blending with rather than disparaging the silence they were, until now, loath to break.

Thoughts reflected upon her words, each man wondering at them. "No bodies," Jorj remarked. His statement invited further explanation.

Her answer came with an unanticipated revelation. "Something close." She stopped suddenly and studied their surroundings. "Here."

It was a grove they entered, though in the dark, it passed unnoticed at first. Theodore decided this was the time to bring out his flashlight and Jorj did likewise. Damn what would come, they agreed, though neither spoke of it. A feeling of cover permeated this area. It was not quite sanctuary, but as close as could be attained in such a place.

His spot of light, changing size with each deviation of distance it traversed, flicked among the stones, hopping the dewy grass between. Decay, not merely of bones but of age, of civilization itself, condensed in places. If one stepped upon particularly spongy ground, the rankness rose more prominently. No earthworms, Jorj thought absently, surprised that such a pedestrian thought felt safe to re-emerge.

But why should there be. Not even the Twilight harbored sinless spirits.

A large stone, flat and smooth to the ground, caught his eye. Once it stood upright three feet above its deep-earth colored marble footing. Someone, in an act of blatant disrespect, personally directed or no, pushed it over some time years before. Two words at the top boldly proclaimed the name of the person whose grave it marked. Samuel Henry. Engraved less deeply below his name was the description, interrupted by purposeful, reckless chiseling. Born 1959. Died 1999. It was here the chisel did it's dastardly work, ending with a single word.

"Iceman," Jorj whispered, his thoughts distracted by the advent of a puzzle. The 'I' was actually lower case, not the complete word. The effect upon him, trapped in this nether world, was unsettling. Something gnawed at him quietly. He looked up, satisfied that Greta was nearby and that Theodore kept a better watch than he. His eyes darted down again, first at the last word, then at the name above the chisel's devil work. "Samuel Henry," he uttered. Would the name invoke its owner, he wondered? And his mind worked the words, and many other things, reversing them, playing with the sound and rhythm of each syllable. "Samuel Henry. Henry Samuel. Sam-u-el Hen-ry." A light aroused within him, and he followed it. What had Greta said earlier, in the depths of their realization of how far they were in? Still his mouth formed and reformed the words, back and forth, forth and back. "Gret," he called to her, his left hand reaching out until she took it in her own. "Is this it?"

She came close and stood by him. "It is."

"What do we do?"

Her head shake gave him nothing, pointed in no direction. But this *was* the place. She did not deviate from her claim.

Jorj bowed his head into his free hand. From his squatting position, he sought a little respite from frustration, the cold disappointment of having come close, but not close enough. "Some bastard knocked off this guy's information," he grunted angrily. "It might have helped us."

A twig gently snapped on the other side of the stone. Jorj looked up with a start. It was Theodore. The latter studied it a moment and then pointed at the last word. "Policeman."

The former dropped his gaze from his companion to the stone, understanding rising to meet the puzzle piece as it clicked into place. Something akin to his earlier fury kindled within him. "Stand watch, Theo." He made the name informal with intent, offering in this way his trust. "Please, Gret, you too. I need some time."

Questions poised on Theodore's lips but he withheld them. This was Jorj's purview. "Alright," he ceded, nodding to Greta and stepping away towards a tree. The thought that something might be in it did not worry him, because he knew that there was nothing here that would threaten them, nothing as yet.

Only when he smelled the burning gunpowder some minutes later, and the orange light upon the ghastly tree next to him, did he turn to look. Jorj stood a few paces from the stone, lit in an afterglow as the powder spent the last of its potent chemistry. "What did you do?" he asked, unable to contain his alarmed curiosity any longer. Without waiting for an answer, he approached to look for himself. The word was restored, burned with rough but certain letters upon the chiseled stone. "Policeman," he murmured approvingly. Perhaps it was his sense of order that made the difference, but his respect for Jorj grew considerably at that point.

"Help me with this," Jorj said, moving around to the head of the stone and working the soil underneath the edge to find purchase.

"We'll never lift it," Theodore responded, taking his place next to Jorj and searching for a serviceable handhold. He found one and together they heaved. At first they felt only the strain of their backs, for the stone was of considerable weight. Then, as if unseen hands pulled with them, or pushed from below, the head rose, inch by suffering inch, until, to the disbelief of both men, it righted itself upon its foundation block. But it was not only this feat that stunned them. Where the stone once lay, what should have been flattened earth was not at all. Steps, uncertain in their composition but sure in their direction, descended to a flattened space, walled by a single circular wall of bare soil.

"Down?" Theodore exclaimed, disappointment and fear commingled.

"Out." Jorj stopped staring and went to the landing below, scarcely acknowledging each earthen step. From his belt he drew a long knife of the style marines used in WWII. Without looking up, he commenced digging.

Above him, Greta and Theodore watched the work below, no longer keeping vigilance. If the creature from the urn, or any other enemy of light, should seek their end now, there was nothing within their means to stop it. Jorj dug the earth with his knife, and removed it to the side with his hands. And then he screamed, but it was not the blood-curdling scream of a victim. It was the naked cry of victory.

18

Several things happened when Jorj pushed through the last yielding layers of dirt and into open space. First, he felt the change in gravity as the other side sucked him through. It turned within him and, despite his initial urge to vomit, he encountered no ill effects. What felt quite the opposite was that a great weight was lifted from his shoulders, indeed his soul. It was not heaven, but neither was it hell. In fact, he knew he was another step away from the devil now, that wherever he was, it was better, much better.

What Greta and Theodore saw was a dark span at the bottom of the steps with a hand reaching out from it. It reminded Greta of 'Thing,' that stalwart five-fingered servant on *The Adams Family.* It was, of course, somebody quite different. It beckoned them down. Beneath it, Jorj's voice summoned them also, with rejuvenating urgency.

"Go!" Theodore held his rifle ready, a psychological security at best. ""I'll follow."

She touched his arm briefly and descended the steps, noting the hard-packed earth every time she put weight on a foot. How odd, she thought. Some memories borne were alien, despite their successful recollection. She took the hand and it grasped her own firmly. In seconds she was through, gasping in surprise. Though she did remember this grave as she emerged from it, the twist and turn at the end was either new or it was another bare patch in her mind's eye.

No sooner was she through then Jorj helped Theodore pass from the other side. "Twilight?" the older man asked almost happily.

"Feels that way," Jorj replied. "Never thought I'd want to kiss the ground here."

"I don't." Theo remarked, adding, "It is good to be back, though." He wished he had a watch, but that was impractical. Watches never worked, hadn't since he first died. One learned to tell time by other means or not at all. Theo lived by the numbers, a bean-counter by nature, and so his calculator sense was that the sun should not be far off. They spent far too much time on the other side. "Our job isn't done here." He looked hard and long at Greta. She seemed cold . . . tired. "Any more of those damned angel statues about?"

"No." She watched the trees now, at the level of their trunks. "There are other things though to be concerned with. Had we traveled farther down there," she pointed to the grave of Samuel Henry, it's marker unscathed and upright on this side, "it would be far worse. Still, what waits here is bad enough." She noted Theo's quizzical expression and shook her head. "I only have feelings for the dangers, nothing more."

"Then we'll have to trust those feelings." Theo scanned around them until he saw something he recognized. "We're near the northern entrance on Stockton Avenue." He pointed. "There's a small parking lot over there." His thumb jerked to the left of that. "The internal road there is paved for a bit, if

I remember right, at least until we get into the heart of things. That will take us in the right direction." He looked from one companion to the other. "You both ready? We can't stop now."

They each nodded. Jorj eyed Greta as if to remind her that he cared a great deal about her, for on the other side, all things were tainted. She returned his gaze with one of her own, warm and strong. The man readied his rifle and jerked his head. "Want I should take point this time?"

"Stay by her," Theodore gestured towards Greta. "I'm better off not being distracted right now.

The road ran west, away from Stockton and within sight of the Forestry School. Unlike the nether world they just escaped, the mist here was lighter, and gray, hanging in the air blanket-like, sometimes at their knees, other times at waist level. Each of the travelers noticed that it grew thicker the deeper into Mosswood they continued. They passed a tall, narrow, two-column Greco-roman structure, perhaps forty feet tall. It was but a taste of the architecture that was to come. Soon after there was a similar construct, only it was much grander. Jorj counted a dozen columns in its half-ring, supporting a horizontal semicircular slab, all of it white marble. Apollo or Zeus could easily have sat there once, or might still again. But that, Jorj decided, would demand that such gods would care about this place, and that, he noted, was unlikely. Glimmers of light appeared at its base, vaguely human-shaped. Slowly they began a dance around the columns. On the breeze came a chanting, drawing their attention to it, yet not against their will.

Theodore stopped suddenly, turning again to the woman. "You referred to the Angel Statue as the ward of the southern gate. Is this another? Are there ones guarding other gates?"

She thought a moment, staring with some distant focus at the dark asphalt of the east-west road. "There are, she said finally, "though this is not one of them. The gate I referred to represented that between the veils...the layers of existence." Her voice wavered as if she was unsure. When she looked up again, she spoke surely. "You will not find them on any map. I cannot show them to you. We will just have to be careful. We need not fear the dancers. They are not truly here . . . halfway so."

It didn't ease Theodore's spirit to think there were more sinkholes out there, but he merely shrugged. What could he do but be vigilant, he asked without words. One more curious glance he offered to the ritual partiers, and then he led on.

It took several minutes to reach the point where the road branched off. After taking the left hand way, it branched in three places. Ahead and to the right was a low hill and a higher one beyond that. "View over the city," Greta murmured so only she could hear. She remembered this place well. It was where she went to rest after escaping the dark place once removed. High places were good for that.

Mausoleums began to spring up in earnest now. Castles warded both hilltop and glen, mostly impregnable, though some few bore signs of vandalism in the way of broken stones and damaged portcullis. No doubt graffiti covered much of the walls inside. A shadow crossed from one towards them, and Theo raised his rifle to greet it. Its gait was human and casual, as if the weapon trained upon it was considered with little or no regard. Jorj pulled Greta to the side and then himself flanked to the left. As the shadow stepped into the moonlight, he saw that it was a woman.

She stopped less than twenty feet away from Theodore, everything below her knees immersed in the rolling moonlit fog. Her dark red hair, all curls, was mostly concealed by a wrapping of black silk. What spoke most prominently of her stature, though physically slender and wrapped loosely in dark black, was her eyes, iris' the color of green jade, even in the pale silvery light. Small bells, tied to stray pieces of her body wrap, jingled quietly when she moved, though one had to be close to hear them. While Theodore waited, his impatience prompting his trigger finger, she regarded him impassively at first, then with purpose.

"You are trespassers, seeking the Arch Fool." Her voice was deep and rich, suggesting a woman of later years.

"Oh God," Jorj moaned, lowering his rifle. "New Age Sorceress. Watch out. I think I smell incense." Suddenly he felt his body stiffen, leaving even his ability to speak impaired. She turned her face towards his, an expression of disdain pressed upon it. Jorj struggled but could only manage a strangled moan. Like a statue suddenly bereft of a foundation upon which to balance itself, he fell over into the leaves of the roadside with a painful crash. Theodore's gun clattered to the road also, the man's hands flexing in an attempt to regain what was lost.

"Your witch woman wisely swims the shadows. We have encountered one another before, though she forgot that I existed." The woman frowned. "She remembers very little. Perhaps it is best." Her regard turned upon Theodore again, all business. "If you proceed towards Langstrom's door, you will find your work only partially successful. You will, no doubt, go and see for yourself. I caution you to fear more the folly of the one you seek than any strength he believes he has gained." She paused, her eyes, now in shade as the moon went behind a cloud, narrowing to glittering slits. "You wish I should tell you more. I cannot, for a darkness covers him, not of his own making nor choosing. Know that it is not with warmth that I help you, for if you all perish to the lower planes it would trouble me not at all. I wish this other trespasser gone from my night. If you succeed, do not return after the sun sets. Mosswood will be less kindly disposed." A breeze picked up and her bells tinkled gently on it. For the first time, she smiled, but the lips formed a cold, thin curved line. Even as Jorj felt his body come under his own mastery again, and Theodore slowly stooped to recover his weapon, the woman faded, her wrappings blowing away on the wind, through the trees, and into the shadows. Greta stepped out from behind where the woman once stood, her eyes dark and deep with some of her old mystery.

"Who the hell was that?" Jorj nearly shouted, checking the volume of his voice at the last second. With his left hand he wiped the dirt from his face that falling down nearly forced past his lips.

"A New Age Sorceress," Greta answered calmly. "And yes, she does burn incense."

"She knows *you*," Theodore remarked irritably.

"Agnes Wren Steep, owner of a small bookshop on the edge of the north side…when she was alive." Greta stepped closer, seeming to gather herself again. Something within her reawakened, and though it would serve her, she feared it just the same. "I've never seen her here, and she was never a nice woman."

"Forget her," Jorj grumbled. "What was she talking about, Theo. What's Langstrom's door."

"Why the Pyramid, of course." Theodore regarded him grimly and then started walking. "Stuart Langstrom was a vain S.O.B. with delusions of his own importance. Too bad he wasn't a good enough boy to get a door into Heaven. His goes down."

The road degraded to a washed out streambed barely traversable by automobiles. To either side, tombstones lurched drunkenly, some from age, others from vandelous hands. Higher to the right, a beehive mausoleum, massive and dark in its silhouette, watched the travelers pass with its many-windowed eyes. Jorj eyed it distrustfully.

"Leave it be," Greta murmured, touching his left sleeve.

Jorj nodded, replacing it with another contender for his attention. Just off the road to the left was a small statue, headless and sitting with its hands upon its robed knees. One arm, the left, suddenly rose with a loud crack and pointed diagonally to the right. Just as abruptly the arm collapsed into rubble by the statue's left foot. Theodore, not seeing any of this at all, turned quickly. Jorj stood, leveling his rifle at the source of the noise, cursing low but angrily. "Jeezuss!" The former slowly let his arms relax, pointing to the sight at the ground.

"There's a fork ahead," Greta advised. "It wants us to go right."

"What the fuck do I care what it wants?" Jorj closed his eyes and let out a breath. "It's a goddam statue. Just a hunk of spook-rock."

A flashlight appeared in Theodore's hand. He sparked it to life and lit the statue first, and then the ground next to it where was an outstretched arm. "Did it do *that?*" He seemed a man no longer capable of being surprised.

"Yes it did." For one so normally unmoved by trouble, Jorj realized he sounded a lot like Dennis. He let his eyes shift to the woman at his side. "Or else I'm going nuts."

"You're not." She soothed. "And it won't do that again."

"Not with *that* arm, anyways." Jorj considered it a moment, thought to add something further, and then wisely changed his mind. He turned to Theodore impatiently. "Are we almost there?"

"Only if we keep moving."

There was no question but to veer right. Another statue loomed to the left, high-standing and dark against the light-etched clouds above. The moon was several heartbeats from coming out again and when it did, the statue would be reborn in great detail. Something about this looming stone giant disturbed the three badly enough to take advice from a headless statue and go around. Reluctantly Jorj conceded credit where it was due. Decidedly, liking things much better when weird was just the taste of an off-brand beer.

A patch of open sky revealed the moon in its fullness. A hill rose between them and the left fork, offering cover from what stood sentry on the other side. If a malign eye glared balefully now, it did not discover Theodore or his companions.

Twice more the road branched, drawing them into more open land dotted by more tombstones than trees, though the hills were higher still, and the valleys deep and broad. Two such hills away, dead ahead, was their destination. Creeping like a slow titan in the shadow-bathed, wooded horizon, a pyramidal structure poised in solidly dark silence. Theodore climbed the hill in between to the overgrown mausoleum there, just thirty feet from where he and Willie Bender parleyed two mornings before. While Jorj and Greta crept up behind him, he placed his night goggles over his eyes and switched them on.

"Somebody left the front door open," he stated with no small amount of sarcasm. Despite his tendency towards getting down to business, his irritation at disorder came out quite often in what Dennis referred to as, 'Advanced Smartass 101.' "Bet the wrong man went away. Oh well, serves him right, if so, for following such an asshole." He was well aware that his remarks left Jorj open to asking more obvious questions, but he ignored any that came up, clicking off the goggles and pushing them back up along his well-receded hairline. "Let's go see if there's anything worth looking at." Three steps away, his foot kicked something small and hard. The object gave and flew free of a pile of leaves and debris. Theodore crouched and picked it up, carefully studying it in the uncertain moonlight. "Willie's pistol," he murmured, more to himself. "He was definitely taken alive. The man's too careful to just lose something like this." After popping the clip, Theodore put both in his small backpack and continued down the hill towards the next.

Langstrom's tomb sat on a high hill, buried now under so much rubble that the front door could not be passed. Miraculously, whatever brought about the internal destruction spared the outer blocks, a testament to the builder, Trenton Cornelius, architect of more than one Mosswood structure, and many of New Jack's oldest buildings. Jorj whistled, caring not at all for who heard him. "You did this," he laughed, the sound harsh and grim. "Was it worth it?"

"Probably not," Theodore conceded. "A for effort, F for outcome, more than likely." He sighed. "That means we have another stop. If I'm correct in my estimations…" here he looked skyward, confused that the sun had not yet risen. "…this will decided whether Nick burns a candle in the window or in the middle of the street." He noted Jorj's skepticism and added. "He has his own rituals."

Above them, silhouetted against the full cloudless moon, the pinnacle cross of Langstrom's pyramidal peak stood stark and almost unreal. Could Jesus have hung from that, Jorj wondered? It could easily have been the Star of David or a crescent, for all he cared. Symbols were meaningless unless there was a beating heart behind them. A taste of bile rose in his mouth, for he knew what was next.

Greta accepted the capsule from Theodore, tucking it into her right breast pocket. Jor had one too. "Last resort," The oldest one reminded them. "Benedict doesn't play nice. If you get compromised, don't wait for him to throw a wrench into things. Bite and swallow. If you make it back to the Millhouse, Ask Nick where you can find the Holiday Bakery. They don't bake bread there anymore, but you'll find virtually everything else you might need." He lowered his head slightly and pressed his lips tightly together, a subtle sign of respect. His eyes locked with Jorj's. "Don't forget. No heroics. If I go down in any way at all, that bloody bastard is still the goal. He won't return here, not with the places he takes his soul. The last thing he wants right about now is to be killed, so don't take him for granted either. He'll play dirty until the end."

To the southwest, not far from the old western entrance, was the Mortuary Chapel and receiving vault, a masterpiece of cobblestone and nineteenth-century masonry. Its tower, short and wide, blended with the choking trees which grew almost on top of it, overhanging the slate roof. During the winter months on Old Earth, bodies were stored at the back of the primary floor in what amounted to concrete shoeboxes, open at the ends. Once, when Theo was just a young lad of 19 years old, he came here on a lark, armed stupidly to the teeth with men...no boys really, who craved more adventure than modern society had to offer. It was, in his opinion, a wonder they were never arrested.

They approached it from a remarkably well-paved road which wound its way around from the north, then took a tight curve from the east. On the chapel's eastern side was an additional attached structure of the same cobblestone. It led into the basement, another place Theodore remembered well. One a youthful dare he entered it, returning with a used candlestick. Despite the fact that there was little, if anything, to be afraid of, at least on that night, his courage was never questioned again by the group he caroused with.

The former master of Twilight's New Jack City was hardly surprised to see the front doors removed, ripped off their hinges and caste higgledy-piggledy on the asphalt before the main entrance. In fact, he even smiled. It was something *he* would have done, were their roles reversed. Intimidation was always a tasty temptation . . . and a necessity.

Did he know they were there, ready, or almost so, to enter and turn his world upside down?

Of course he did, just as Theodore knew Benedict would be in the chapel.

Jorj walked easily over to the wreckage, still beyond sight of whatever lurked inside the ancient church. He stooped casually and picked up a flyer that lay atop a jumbled stack of its brethren.

A Walking Tour of Historic Mosswood
New Jackson City, New York
Est. 1789

The moonlight was that bright. He smiled tersely, walked back to the woman he swore to do anything for, and handed it to her. "There's a map in there. Go home now. Your work here is finished."

She regarded him coolly. "Okay."

"You're not leaving yet, are you?"

"Nope." Her eyes remained dark and absolute.

"What do I have to do to get you to leave?"

"Come with me," she said simply.

"Alright then." His shoulders seemed to slump a little. "Have it your way. Find a safe place...please."

"Okay."

He watched her a second, the next question on his lips, and bit it off at the first vowel. Silently he turned and joined Theodore. The latter nodded his readiness and they entered under the pointed stone arch, taking in the candle-lit scene before them with general acceptance.

"Welcome gentlemen!" A smiling blond-haired man in an expensive charcoal/pinstripe suit approached to greet them. He was middle-aged like Theodore, and as neat as the head of a pin. Both newcomers raised their weapons in response. This much, at least, surprised them greatly, and Jorj no more than Theodore. The host stopped short, his smile faltering as if this was totally unexpected. He was ever an flamboyant actor, and the fact that people knew this never affected the amount of charm this man could invoke. "Please! Let us not begin the wee-hours as anything but friends." He waved a hand behind him. There was a table with several bottles of wine, all shades well-plotted, embedded in a foundation of fruit and cheese. Past the table, seen only through the space where the table cloth could not reach the floor, a brown arm moved, bound at the wrist.

It did not pass unnoticed.

"I think I might sample a glass of something," Theodore declared, holding Jorj's eyes for a second, blinking twice. He smiled easily, turned back, and walked casually on into the chamber. "What's good tonight?"

"It's all good, my old friend." The host regarded Jorj with a warm smile. It was almost disarming. "I did not get your name."

A coolness played back, returning wavelike to the one before him. "We can't all be so lucky. Guess you're stuck with Benedick."

Again, the struck confusion of a good host. "Very well." The smile never once faltered. "Please! Do come in."

"I think I'm fine," Jorj responded with perhaps more confidence than he felt. In the backdrop of the host's shoulder, Theo poured himself a glass of golden Niagra.

"A sweet wine!" Theo declared in surprise. "You never were the type."

"No!" Benedict whirled in a flourish. "But this is not all about me, is it?"

Theodore cocked his head. The smile he bore was polite, but belonged to a seasoned killer. "No," he answered, friendly enough. "I guess it isn't." He sipped once and then drew the slim glass back from his lips. "Exquisite."

"Only the best," Benedict replied with a healthy measure of pride. At least here he exhibited complete, unabashed honesty.

"And no poison."

"Please!" The host could not hide his hurt feelings, a debatably honest venture. "You do me injustice."

"My apologies." Theodore took another sip and set his glass down, drawing his fingers next to a small, succulent cluster of grapes. "You have a friend of mine at a disadvantage. Could you be persuaded to release him?"

Here the host paused dramatically, waving his hand in the air finally to dismiss the very notion. "That is the entertainment, Theodore!" He tisked loudly, noted the overbearing quality with which he did so, and tisked again less forcefully. "Such arrangements cannot so easily be cancelled. You know how these things go!"

"Yes," Theodore nodded with some disappointment. His acting skills were not entirely bad in themselves. "I'm afraid that I do." His eyes drifted to William Bender, laying within a circle of silver just on the other side of the table, naked and bound hand and foot to the floor with iron spikes. The two men, Boss and loyal henchman, locked eyes meaningfully. "What if I was to fill him with lead?"

"Ha!" Benedict glanced knowingly at Jorj, as if the entire charade was a beautifully, well-orchestrated joke, and then faced his old acquaintance. "That would not please you, for then the bouncer would come in and throw you out."

"Oh," Theodore murmured with little surprise in his tone.

"Yes!" Their host held his index finger up to Jorj, priming the man for one more point. His grin was exaggerated, like a madman. The charm, however, could not be denied. "Maybe you'd like to move him out of his...unfortunate seating arrangement."

"No he wouldn't," Theodore answered for Jorj. "And neither would I." He tried the Brie, taking his right hand away from his gun so he could manage the spreading knife. "Where is your man, by the way?"

"Buried in his work," Benedict answered abruptly, his smile somewhat downcast. "He took an interest in Langstrom's pyramid and hasn't come out since." His expression turned more appeasing. "I'm sure you understand how wrapped up in things good men can become?"

"Quite." Theodore found a napkin with which to wipe his mouth. He did so with the most elegant of manners, folding it once after each pass. "So you host this gathering all by yourself?"

"Of course!" Benedict smiled broadly. "For such esteemed guests as have honorably graced this hall, would you have..."

Light flashed in a staccato of brilliance and deafening noise. Gun smoke spanned hazily between Jorj and the man who he'd had enough of. The wall to the left, as Jorj understood it, became a masterpiece of Jackson Pollack's ghost in crimson. The man belonging to the vandalized body stared in happy disbelief for a second, and then collapsed to the concrete floor. In three more heartbeats, this vessel, too, was gone, leaving behind only the artwork as arguably the best impressionist adornment to ever grace the hallowed chamber.

The fading echoes of spent cartridges clattering to the concrete floor were quickly replaced by an awful, underlying silence. It took a full minute before one voice broke it, the voice of he who, until now, had remained uncharacteristically silent himself.

"You stupid asshole!" Willie Bender raised his voice high enough to rouse the bats who still hadn't left following the gunfire. Several found the front door and swirled out past Jorj's head. "Couldn't leave it to your goddam betters, could you?" In the foreground, Theodore held his head in one hand, unhappy.

"What?" Jorj stumbled into the chamber, unabashedly at a loss.

"He wanted one of us to do just what you did," Theodore explained, his voice tired now, haggard even. "You fell for it as good as he could hope."

"But you just told me a little while ago to kill him! You even said that the last thing that loudmouth wanted was to be killed!"

Another sigh. "That was before I saw what he had going on here. Plans change." He tapped his own rifle sharply with his index finger. "I had the first clear shot. If I wasn't firing on the man, what made you think that it was a good idea for you to?"

Jorj was speechless.

"Guess I'm still your number one then, huh Theo?" It wasn't really a question. It was the truth. "Course I gotta get out of this mess first!" His tone cast fire on Jorj. "That ain't gonna be easy!"

"He wouldn't shut up!" Jorj pressed, oblivious to the fact that he argued what some might consider fine points to a man without clothes or freedom. "The whole thing was going nowhere!"

"He *never* shuts up!" Willie exploded. "I knew that! Theo knew that. Apparently *you're* the only one who didn't, asshole!"

His head in both hands now, Theodore tried to pull it all back together into something manageable. "Let's cut the bullshit. We need to figure a way to get you out of there."

"Why not just let him walk out on his own . . . or shoot him." His last words spaced themselves carefully. No one noticed Greta's appearance in the chamber at first. They did now.

"Because that dumb fuck worked some Hoojoo over me, that's why!" Willie stopped short. "Who's that?"

"She's our guide," Theodore said tiredly.

"The Watchman's witch woman?" Frosty damn near choked over his own play of words. He couldn't see her but he recognized her voice from more than one night's outing. "Hey you! Get me outta here! Undo that stupid, superstitious joojoo of Benedict's!" The echoing irony of the words seemed to escape him in his fervor.

"I thought you said it was 'Hoojoo.'" After an unaffected silence, Jorj added, "I guess this isn't humor appreciation day."

Greta, incredulous, regarded first Jorj, then Theodore, her expression betraying her as believing she was the only sane person present. "Benedict didn't do anything. He never does. The man's a fake."

"Not this time!" Willie was beginning to master his temper. "I seen a man get eaten by this thing he called up! Ate 'em whole!"

"Anyone can invite a demon to the party. Wards and glyphs are another matter entirely." Greta walked to the other side of the table. Once there was an altar here. She kicked the silver filings away in one spot, then pushed the opening wider with the toe of her right foot. "There! You can get out now." She paused when his disbelief became unbearable. "Presto? Hocus Pocus? Alakazaam?" In a flurry of fingers, she emphasized her point and walked away, peering at her man. "You really shouldn't have shot him, you know."

"Why?" Jorj murmured back. "He's dead now...Theo already said the bastard ain't coming back."

"Theodore was wrong. He's knows that now, and he regrets all of this very much."

Chains clattered. Grunts and groans filled the spaces in between. "Iron spikes don't come out by themselves, funny lady!" When there was no immediate response, Frosty toned down his voice to something more respectful. "Theo! It is Goddam freezing! How 'bout helpin' me cut here!"

"What you're saying is hard to accept." Jorj hopped the curb, turned right to the stop sign, and made another hard right, gunning the Roadrunner's 440 engine north on Stockton. To their left was Mosswood. He wanted to swear he'd never go back into that awful place, but the easiest way to curse yourself was to swear to or by anything. Wisely, he stayed with the subject. "He'd do this willingly?"

"Benedict is ignorant…or was." Greta looked out the window, then focused on Jorj's reflection in the glass, each detail caught by the faint glow of the dashboard lights. Her tone was somewhat more subdued than before, for the adrenaline that coursed through everyone's veins was almost depleted. "By now I'm certain he is fully aware of what he's done, of what his deal has purchased for him. If he can even scream, it will be a mercy to his soul."

Jorj shivered. Not much did he give in to terror, and very little creeped him out. Possession did both. "So he thought he was to become a demon…or in his warped view of things, a rogue fallen angel. And he thought he could just waltz out of hell without so much as a goodbye or a Thank-You." He phrased it like a statement. The question in the sentence prompted Greta to elaborate further.

"Nothing from the Underworld would ever deal squarely. They consume, use, exploit. Their sustenance is misery…just as Heaven's is love." She turned towards Jorj, twisting in her seat, and watched him silently until his eyes briefly met hers before turning back to the road.

"What?"

"We exist to feed one or the other. You know that."

"I don't feed anyone," he corrected, or thought he did.

"You feed me."

His silent response punctuated the difficulties he had expressing what he felt for her. Twilight Earth was an unkind place. The soft patches she exposed on his underbelly could invite a thousand arrows if he wasn't careful. It might only take one to undo him.

Theodore and Frosty parted company with the others, once everyone made it out through the old Forestry School entrance. The sun was not yet up, but would be soon. Jorj and Greta agreed to meet them at the Millhouse after recovering the car. From there they would depart for wherever. Ogam hadn't left them a clue and Theodore might not even care. Willie Bender would follow Theo's lead, although they seemed equals in loyalty. Their relationship suggested more partnership than anything else now.

It only took minutes to reach the storage garage and retrieve Willie's 'Bat Outta Hell.' Theodore regarded it skeptically, marking Frosty's breath and the man's uncontrollable shivering. Despite Theo's sacrifice of pants, shirt, and Jorj's shoes to

Willie's cause, January's prisoner was near hypothermic. Fortunately he was tough, and as used to it as anyone could get.

"You're the passenger," The older man proclaimed.

"Uh-uh!" Willie shook his head violently, more so because his ability to move gracefully was frozen out. "M-my b-bike!"

"Look," Theodore explained calmly. "You're in no shape to even piss a straight line, let alone manage getting it out of your pants in the first place. I'll leave you out here to freeze and then wait for you at your...what's that red-haired moron call it?"

"K...k..."

"Kamaloka Crossroads. Thank you William." He spoke casually, allowing time to drag at his companion's resolve. "As I was trying to say, Once you freeze solid, say, in three, maybe four hours, I'll pick you up at your usual place and we can go on from there." The first pink rays of the sun crept through the square garage door, wondering what Willie's response would be. "It's not my fault," he added, "that Benedict burned all your nice clothes."

"F-fuck you, Fish-B-belly!" Hate never infiltrated those sputtered words, only desperate anger.

"Fish Belly?" Theodore cracked a slim smile. "That's new."

"I b-been savin' it!" Even chilled to the bone, Willie had another one ready immediately. "Cock sauce!"

Theodore tisked. "That's piggish. You used to call me ghost when we first met. I liked that better."

"Cow fuck!"

"I'll build you a fire, O.J. It should only take another half-hour...after I find some wood first." Theodore walked out of the small garage, whistling contentedly. Willie was a stubborn bastard, but he could break. And he wasn't letting the man drive him anywhere on that death machine…not in *his* weather.

"Alright, you Po'bucker!" The force of Willie Bender's words pushed all stuttering momentarily aside. "You win this one!" In an act of defeat, he collapsed into a fetal crouch, intent on preserving his dwindling body heat.

He stood outside Saint Jude's one more time, determined that it should be his last. Greta wasn't coming in. She seemed restless, moody. Since leaving Mosswood, she'd been this way. Whatever troubled her she kept to herself, and Jorj, curious and concerned as he was, respectfully left her alone to it. His business this morning, or night—he always hated applying the word 'morning' to hours of darkness—remained unfinished. It only took a minute to reach the basement, and another to find and uncover the hot-dog cart. What he lost, if he truly ever had it to begin with, was inside, ominous in its potential. The monstrous little invention, military in nature, kept getting lost or misplaced. Jorj made it his intention to make sure it was put away for good before newspaper headlines appeared, heralding multitudes of poisonous new arrivals into Twilight's New Jackson City. He appropriated the olive green case immediately, glaring inwardly for his role in the whole affair, and lugged it back to the open trunk of the Roadrunner. When he shut it in tight, his eyes fell upon 'Ihwar,' and his own splayed handprint beneath the rune. "Don't fail me," he muttered, and returned to the driver's seat.

Alodi stretched ahead in darkness but for the white embrace of the Roadrunner's headlights. Every stop sign and traffic light was meaningless without traffic, so Jorj blew through them all, hoping all of Benedict's men were sleeping soundly or too afraid to go out. Peripherally, shops and side streets alike existed only as ghosts, fleeing his future as they laughed in mock smugness, clinging transiently to his meteoric wake. Nothing seemed capable of stopping the onslaught of a loud engine in the early hours of morning. And then one unexpected appeared, zooming up on him from a total standstill.

The moment Jorj recognized the confident arrogance of Jed's smile, he gunned the engine harder, murder in his eyes despite the lack of potency in the action. Faster than the autumn breeze, the car whisked through the non-corporeal form. Greta turned to Jorj in alarm. "Don't do that again."

"It's just practice," Jorj replied sarcastically, ignoring her demand as he plowed through Jed's newly reconstituted spirit a second time. "...for when he's the real deal."

"Jorj!" Her tone sharpened.

As he came up on Jed a third time, Jorj swerved wide into the opposite lane, abruptly aware that something was amiss, too late to discover its nature. Two of his wheels struck spilled oil. By accident or malicious intent, it spread across the road but did not entirely cover the width of it. He fishtailed while Greta screamed, and then the Roadrunner spun in a 360, miraculously recovering itself just in time before otherwise hitting a fireplug. Pointing the car's nose in a more desirable direction, Jorj deftly skidded the car to a stop in a stench of smoking tires.

She didn't have to say a thing. Upon Greta's face was an expression Jorj found crushingly educational. "I'm sorry," he apologized. He glanced out his side-view mirror and grimaced.

Before Jed could approach near enough to speak, for assuredly that was his intention, Jorj's left middle finger bade him good-bye. Thunder smote the air and after a brief, disrespectful spin of its rear tires, the Roadrunner was gone, its color changing in the first rays of the new morning sun.

Breakfast was Spartan that morning at the Millhouse. Bill ate without pleasure, his thoughts still struggling with resurrected memories he wished to forget. The cold cereal, drowned in the terrible taste of old, powdered milk, passed his lips unceremoniously. Nick and the Padre, bowls pushed away for the last fifteen minutes, discussed theology to pass the time. Neither really had their minds fully focused on the topic, for everyone seemed stuck in that old pattern of waiting. Only Frank was unmoved by their circumstances. He collected their dishes without complaint, as usual, a cold cigar stump loosely held between his yellowed teeth. Vaguely, as if debating on making a dentist's appointment, he considered suicide. A new cavity added itself recently to his teeth, bringing the total count to six. New, or almost new, teeth would be good before they left on their trip.

Above, keeping a solid, anxious watch from the roof, Dennis lit a cigarette with nervous hands. Never likely to admit it to anyone, he regretted his antagonism the previous night. It didn't matter that the woman was a witch, or that she dwelled, past or present, with the creatures of the night. She was Jorj's girl. A man was supposed to respect that.

No chopper this morning, he noted gladly. That thing was trouble to them. Just as he did the day before, he hoped the damn thing crashed in a fireball. Good riddance.

He almost hopped the roof edge when he heard the familiar rumble, still several blocks away. Without waiting to confirm visually what he already knew in his heart, he was plummeting down the back stairs, yelling to the others, once inside the first-floor confines.

Jorj pulled into the parking lot, never so glad to be back. There lingered, though, that gray pall, worse than the stale feeling Twilight already imposed upon its squatters. The graveyard was left behind physically, if not entirely in effect. Something else had haunted him ever since he left the backyard, east of Mosswood. Ignoring everybody, those who spilled out of the Millhouse to greet him, and even Greta, he walked a dogged pace to the trunk, unlocked it, and lifted the cover.

"What's up, Kemosabe?" Whatever the hostilities one day before, Dennis seemed oblivious, a pretense that paid off, for Jorj's face relaxed considerably, even became amiable. "What's that?" The skinny man piled up another question, peering past Jorj into the Roadrunner's storage compartment at the olive-drab case stashed above and just past the spare tire.

"Just luggage I thought I lost," Jorj lied. "Nothing important." He lowered the lid and pressed it firmly to until he heard the latch catch. "Miss us?"

"You need to ask?" He hugged Jorj suddenly like a lost brother, stiffened uncomfortably, and pulled back. His face reddened with embarrassment.

Jorj smiled, a trace of skepticism mixed in with genuine affection. "You going 'girlie' on me?" He rapped the back of his right hand against Dennis' chest, producing a hollow thud. "Get your shit together. We're leaving just as soon as Theo and..." The humor drained out of his eyes. What he had to say next pleased neither of them. "...as soon as Theo and Frosty show up."

"Who's in charge of the operation now?" Jorj made sure he asked the question before Theodore and Frosty arrived on the scene. He could hear a motorcycle coming and guessed it was them. Regardless of who his *official* choice was, who he would *personally* follow was plain.

Unprepared for this kind of question, Nick shrugged and offered a surprise answer. "You?" His hand absently massaged his left shoulder.

"Me." The sun was yet low, and shadows played with stripes and patches of new yellow light across the street in a slow, steady game. They walked on a few paces and turned, idly studying the Millhouse.

"Theo will humor you, and still do as he sees fit." Here Nick laughed, albeit with hidden difficulty. "William Bender won't even humor you."

"I'd follow your lead." Jorj knew he didn't have to say it. "Why change a good thing?"

"Because you already do as you see fit." The old man shook his head. "Your nose for trouble is stronger than my good sense." He sniffed, scratching his nose casually. "God may pick losers much of the time, but he always turns them into winners."

"That's complimentary." Jorj listened as the bike approached closer. Soon it would roar into view, come up Alodi, and turn the corner at Thurber.

"It's the result that matters," Nick replied with no attempt at appeasement. He grew thoughtful and then added one more thing just before Theo broke onto the scene, Frosty riding shotgun. "The rest *will* follow you." Jorj didn't say anything in response. Freedom and leadership didn't mix. He was too long used to the former.

They found a place for Willie Bender to bed down, once he had enough coffee and hot soup to burst his bladder seven times over. Sleep took him almost immediately as it always does following long hard exposure to cold. While he recuperated, Jorj packed their few supplies himself, mostly food and fuel, in the trunk of the Roadrunner and on a newly acquired roof rack.

Above them all, on the Millhouse roof, Bill watched Dennis stop short as Jorj pointed him back towards the Millhouse. Whatever was in the box the skinny man carried wasn't going. He could hear the cursing easily. Mike used to curse like that every day. Sometimes he swore at Bill, and the bigger man, underneath a car, or face stuffed under a hood with a leadlight, just ignored him. It never paid to react to anyone's foul mouth.

The one thing Bill never did was swear. His old man had a mouth like a mule-tender, as his mother called it. She died believing her son to be wholly honest and fair. Bill let her believe it, though it was far from the truth. He robbed Mike blind, but never so much that business suffered. There were no good reasons, he admitted as much to himself and God, not even his former alcoholism. He just wasn't good at anything else but fixing cars and stealing. The latter, easy as it came to him, was only a distraction from the former. Since waking up in Twilight Earth, he hadn't stolen so much as a can of soda. All he did was eat, find a hot car for Jorj, and stand the watch. So why did emptiness still eat at his insides? And that face...that woman's face. He knew it in a thousand nightmares, but he'd swear on a stack of bibles that he'd never met her in person...until Jorj came home with her. Then he got so scared he nearly wet himself. And she was the Padre's daughter. Dennis told him as much, and then the good father told Bill so himself. The Padre, Bill conceded, was his most trusted friend now, even more than Jorj who saved him from . . . the better-to-forget-place. The Padre cared about him the most, took the time to ease his unsettled nerves. Padre was a good man. Why then, did his daughter strike such fear into him, Bill wondered painfully?

Something warm spread across the front of his underwear, wet and heavy. Muscles contracted, sounding alarms that he hadn't heard since he was a toddler. His hands, shaking in fear, still struggled to fend of embarrassment, folding themselves between his legs. Things were yet dry, but it hardly registered. All he knew was that she was here, watching him again, just as she did in his nightmares. He turned slowly, his lips quivering in what most anyone else would call irrational fear. His eyes plummeted to the gravel base of the flat roof, focusing nowhere. "Dunna you come up here."

It was the sadness in her eyes that broke him every time. Her face, beautiful and horrible at the same time, scarred, timelessly lovely, consuming in every aspect of motherly love, and yet she did nothing to help him. She couldn't; he knew that in a vague way. When he was at his worst, she was helpless before him, in as much agony as he.

Bill fell to his knees, and then to his elbows, bawling like a baby. His hands, now just things of clay, clawed mindlessly at the loose pebbles. He wanted to die.

In the street, Nick stood quietly, his eyes opened but unfocused. God whispered in that still, small voice, and the wordless message could not be resisted. The man swayed, oblivious of all else, and for that brief moment in time, all else went on heedlessly of him. When the last breath of the Almighty spent itself, Nick's eyelids fluttered. His iris', brown, almost golden in the quality of their color, drew back behind heavy, sage lids. The man, older than anyone else in the Twilight, collapsed where he was.

From half a block over, Dennis suddenly felt a panic grip his heart. Icy cold, it was, and that which he feared most climbed his leg to his back, and then to his shoulders where it stopped, it's head low, hooked beak waiting for the inevitable. The box he carried slipped from his fingers, no longer cared for in the least. Glass shattered within the confines of the cardboard but Dennis' thoughts were elsewhere. His eyes scanned twice and then he ran, shouting, screaming, and ultimately sobbing.

"Terminus." Jorj's voice was soft, but his words were clear and direct.

"Yes," The old man smiled, his hand weakly gripping the other man's own. "The riddle is worked out." He lay on a bed in a small upstairs room that was once an office. Now it served as a place of rest. God knew where these children found the mattress and frame. A small light glowed warm and yellow nearby. The comfort was glorious, and yet the distance from it was growing, light on a farther horizon, warm, familiar. "Jorj…"

"Nick, I figured out what Ogam was looking for." He unfolded the piece of paper he'd almost forgotten about, reading each word singly.

Time

Elysium

Reality

Manna

Immortality

Nirvana

Utopia

Shangra-la

Old fingers slipped from the young man's hands to the paper, taking them easily, and dropped the words to the floor. "It's nothing, Jorj…a make-believe place." His eyes closed for a second, and then opened. Behind Jorj was Dennis, Frank, Bill, Padre, Greta…even Theo. Every fave registered needless concern. Were Willie Bender awake and well, he would be here too. His feeble fingers abandoned him with the exception of his index. This raised itself to Jorj's chest and tapped thrice. "In here. You, every one of you, never needed anything else."

"Rest," Dennis pushed to Nick's left, opposite Jorj. "Save it. We'll get some more nitro."

"Please," Nick gently chided, squeezing Dennis's arm with his left hand. "Be true, child. Don't waste words pretending." His eyes shifted to the ceiling, an expanse of eggshell white.

Breathing was more difficult now, but he held on a little longer. "The river is too wide now for me, its current too strong. Take yourselves across it. Follow your hearts. He waits on the other side…" The words trailed into silence. He swallowed once, or did he? His lips, barely moving now, spoke a finality on one side, but something quite different on the other, even as his eyes widened suddenly in awe. "Jerusalem…"

They waited tensely for him to resume, but more never came. A wooden statue, Jorj witnessed for his first time the 'fading' of one departing the Twilight. To his right, Dennis hardened like he never did before. No tears flowed, not here. He stared for three seconds and stood. His eyes regarded Jorj suddenly and seemed to gain a color of mixed respect. Then, abruptly, he left the room, the tallest one there.

Jorj placed his right hand, now empty, splayed fingers and palm down, upon the place where Nick lay less than a minute before. The blanket was still warm from the old man's body heat. He half turned then, eyes not trained on anything or anyone in particular. "Alright. You all heard the same thing I did. Let's finish what we started." They all watched him intently as he walked out, Theodore no less so yet with a curiosity the others lacked.

Everyone seemed stricken, bereft they were of their long-time friend, and some of them, their adopted father. It was clear to them all by now that he would not appear later; not today, not tomorrow, not even the following year. Nick A. Demoss, as he ever introduced himself from first day to last, was as close to his true home as he could be now. Only by the grace of a God everyone thought abandoned them did New Jackson City come to find him within its troubled folds.

After a minute, they filed out in ones and twos. Theodore was the last to leave. For awhile he simply stared at the bed, his thoughts a collage of memories good and bad. Their little patch of Twilight Earth was not only colder now. In his estimation, it was about to become considerably more difficult than it ever was before.

They left the Millhouse just past noon. Willie Bender still slept like the dead. Theodore looked him over, determined that his frostbite wasn't worse than anything the man had gone through before, and helped load him into the backseat of the Roadrunner between Frank and Bill. Greta sat up front with Jorj and Dennis, riding the middle, and Padre rode irony, seated behind Theodore on the 'Bat Outta Hell.'

Once on I-90, picked up just north of the city limits, the Roadrunner thundered away to the east, trailed closely by an armored, Gothic motorcycle. Jorj made the decision to reach The Mass Turnpike by nightfall, quipping that he needed change for the booth. Dennis laughed alone, which made it even less funny, and so Jorj resolved to be more serious. It was going to be difficult, because sarcasm was one of his main ways to deal with stress, and the loss of Nick made his burden such that the smartass remarks just came out whether he wanted them to or not.

A rest station popped up in Oneida and Jorj pulled in, lured by the potential for gas and supplies. He found neither. Long ago, it appeared, someone else got to it first. "Not even a crumb," Dennis cursed, dejectedly. Deaths occurred on the Thruway, but not so frequently near the plazas. The inconvenience was a selfish, infernal, damnation, Jorj noted darkly, and one that needn't be repeated often if they were going to get where they were going.

And that was another matter entirely. They could go anywhere they wanted to. No one was a hostage. Yet Jorj wanted to go to New Hampshire, to Rye Beach exactly...or thereabouts. Maybe Hampton. All he knew was that his nose smelled the sea. Dansforth Street ceased to exist the moment he and Greta woke up one fine morning in the back seat of the Roadrunner. Ogam, or something higher than he, called him to the coast with a crying seagull in his mind. No one protested, though Theodore seemed indifferent, distracted really, and Willie Bender still slept. By the time the man woke up, he'd have to make a decision for himself whether to go on, or ride the 'Bat' elsewhere, quite possibly alone, though Jorj suspected Theodore would ride with him.

Indian Castle and Mohawk were the same way. Only when they reached Guilderland did they find a few drops of fuel at the abandoned Sunoco. They entered the hexagonal building and split up, some to the rest room, others to the sub shop.

Dennis managed to pry open a cash register but came up empty. "Died after closing," he groaned. "For crying out fucking loud!" With Nick gone, his language was growing more gratuitous.

Greta re-entered the lobby from using the toilet, something she did not take at all for granted, and sat down on a wooden bench to wait for the others. Jorj and Theodore had a map out and were pointing fingers rather heavily. She turned her attention back to Dennis, for his voice carried even into the rest room minutes earlier. "Try the gift shop," she suggested. Vandalism never was the best thing, in her opinion, but the man needed a release. If he didn't turn a valve, he'd burst a pipe for sure.

"What?" He looked up, saw who it was addressing him, and struggled not to let his face darken. He was behaving for Jorj but the woman was still a witch, and she spooked him. "Oh…yeah, sure."

He picked up a small, misused crowbar, scavenged from a maintenance building out back, and climbed over the sub shop's front counter. His weak smile, awkwardly hoisted like a protective shield as he passed Greta's patient stare, faltered when he watched Frosty stalk through the front entrance, looking like he was spoiling for a fight.

"Theo!" The black man yelled. "Where you at?" He caught sight of his intended quarry and closed the distance like a drunken man. Only forty-five seconds ago did he wake up to find himself somewhere very different than he remembered. "Couldn't be bothered to tell me we were leavin' New Jack?" He stopped barely two feet from the map and the men who, up until now, busied themselves plotting possible supply stops.

Jorj scratched his head absently, regarding the newly-awakened William Bender. "You needed your rest."

"Was I talkin' to you, Watchman?" Frosty sniffed once, the fingers of his left hand playing with his chin whiskers, now three days past a recent shave. His eyes narrowed coolly as he leveled his gaze back on Theodore. "What's this, huh? I fall asleep in a bed and wake up all alone in that crazy, painted-up shit box!"

"Shitbox?" Jorj stiffened. Outside he carried himself unhurriedly. "And you felt out of place?"

It was automatic that Theo should step in between the two men. It's what made him a leader in all times, if not to all men. "You know," he remarked, his voice light but cutting, the right cat could bury you both in the litter...and I will if pushed. Think you can just go back now? Forget why we left?"

Frosty grunted disrespectfully. "Ain't nothin' happened yet." He peered over Theodore's shoulder at Jorj. "You worried?"

"Actually," Jorj replied, his face, contrary to the rest of his body, relaxed into a smile. The rest of him was all business. "*You* should be just as worried as *us*.

"What?" His face screwed up into disbelieving skepticism. He spilled some of the expression towards his friend. "Theo. You buyin' this corny crap? We out, sure. But we don't need them. They're sandbags."

"I'll split when the time is right." Theodore applied enough pressure to Frosty's chest until there was room enough to study the map again. "For awhile, anyways, there's strength in numbers. Your bike's heavy, especially with a passenger. It sucks gas pretty good." He smiled at Jorj, for there was little he revealed that the other man didn't already know. "The car carries food, fuel..." His smile grew colder and sharper. Something smashed and there followed the sound of change spilling all over the floor. "One of Benedict's toys is missing, isn't it Jorj?"

Silence rose up like a wall. From the ramparts, a man watched uncertainly, surrounded on every side.

"That's what I thought." Theo folded up the map neatly, casually.

Eyes narrowed to almost paper-thin slits. "What game you playin', Theo?"

Good nature, or the semblance of it returned. The oldest man there remembered the other man who stood by him at night in the graveyard. Despite the rookie trigger finger attached to him, the man was okay. No need to upset the apple cart yet. "No game, William." Theodore offered the map back to Jorj. "Have we wasted enough time here yet?"

Jorj nodded, strangely reserved. "We should go." His eyes found Dennis and he gave a yell. The other man held up something shiny and silver, big enough to be a dollar. Greta was already walking out to the Roadrunner.

For the next fifteen miles, William Bender rode the 'Bat,' then even his stubbornness fell before the sword of a higher force. From the northwest, a weather front moved in, dark and low-hung, heavy-laden with *his* ol' man winter. Reluctantly, he switched places with Theodore who rode behind him. Soon his own roads would be white and deep. Theo's, perversely, were dry as a bone.

The cold effected him worse now, for what winter clothes he had didn't do a good job at keeping the wind out, and the spare helmet was shit...pure shit. 'Mustah,' in Frosty's jaded estimation, 'fell off the corpse's head immediately after the accident.' The visor was cracked. Even the strap had to be worked through a new hole, for the rivet was sheered clean off by whatever forces had their unholy way with things. Needless to say, Frosty struggled with the temptation that asshole car offered in terms of protection from the elements. By the time they reached the New Baltimore rest stop he'd had enough. The bike hardly stopped when he nearly fell off the seat, stumbled up to the front entrance, smashed the glass when he discovered the door was locked, and clambered in on his hands and knees like a cripple. Theo watched him, sad and amused at once. He parked the bike on the sidewalk under cover of the massive front court roof and dismounted just as the Roadrunner swung into a parking space almost twenty yards away.

People spilled out of the car. Dennis' voice rose from among them, chastising Jorj for parking so far away. Someone else remained in the back seat, apparently sleeping. Bill. The rest approached slowly, barely a regard for the large squat building that harbored, among other gardens of delight, Starbucks and TCBY. If they were lucky, really lucky, coffee was still brewing. Then again, if it was, so could be...

Three shots rang out suddenly from inside the building. Trouble. Theo swept low to the overgrown hedge bordering the building's edge near the entrance. A pistol filled his right hand in one slick motion. Someone inside had a low-caliber rifle. Whoever it was, it wasn't Willie. He looked right, confirming the hasty retreat of some to the Roadrunner, and the flanking for cover by those closer. Jorj belonged to the latter group. He was growing old, Theodore chided himself, old and foolish. He could have parked in a less conspicuous place, certainly not up next to a strange building in an even stranger location. The consolation of knowing that William Bender also pissed all over his own seasoned veteran status comforted him very little, but it did just a bit. What the real question was at the moment remained obvious. Did any or all of the three rounds fired trace a path through Willie's compromised body? A second chastisement was in order. The man never should have been allowed to enter the building alone in the first place.

Deftly seeking redress for his own negligence, Theodore peeped above the edge of the hedge and surveyed the possibility of another entrance close at hand. He knew from experience that there would be one on the other side, near the gas pumps. If possible he wanted to avoid a firefight there. Gas pumps tended to turn all fireball and shrapnel if given the chance. Since one never knew what others brought to the battlefield until often it was too late, prudence demanded alternatives.

Across the small plaza from him, Jorj waved hard to get his attention, now he had it. His right hand flashed a 9mm while his head jerked back towards the side of the building, along the main parking lot. The younger man held up five fingers twice: Ten seconds. Theo smiled thinly and without humor, nodding once. Once Jorj was on the move, he called out. "Alright! We blew it this time by not announcing ourselves. Now's your chance not to make a bad situation worse. Throw your gun out and we can all make nice!"

Silence. He counted to five.

"Hellfire on your backside then!" he barked angrily. "If our man is gone, then you'll wish you joined him!" His American-made 45 caliber Luger, an extremely rare relic even on Old Earth, raised above the hedge line and began systematically removing glass, as much for creating a new entry as for distraction. He kept his fire angled up for Jorj's benefit, and for Willie's if the man still lived.

Glass showered and it was a full three seconds before he realized he was not the only one firing. He changed clips and worked towards the door on his belly. Each round spent slid into a neat category within his mind, painting a picture of how many people were involved and what they brought to the fight. There were at least five, he decided, mostly small caliber and inexperienced. It gave him a little more confidence to get inside.

He made his entry much in the same way Willie had, finding that there was blood. Then he saw the body of his friend, breathing but prone on the tiled, glass-strewn floor of the lobby half in, half out of the men's restroom. Once, on Old Earth, the lavatory had been smaller and unisex, but this only vaguely tickled his memories. In half a second Theo reached him, determined that the man's head was grazed, and dragged him into the large room, but propping the door open with the man's foot. "Sorry, William," he whispered. "Be useful." He turned suddenly, aware that there was another close by. His Luger, raised and poised to fire, never did. Standing just inside one of the toilet stalls, peeking around the edge of the gray-painted steel separation, was a small Asian girl hardly more than seven years old. Theo, stunned, lowered his weapon. He was, after all, still a decent man. "Best get up on the toilet seat, honey, and stay there. Don't come out for anything." There was a lull in the gunfire, and the distraction of it turned his head. When he looked back, she was out in the middle of the floor, a very small pistol lofted between her tiny hands, two fingers tugging on the trigger. "Jeezuss Christ!" Theodore mouthed. Did everybody have a gun these days? Before his legs could carry him towards her with the intent to disarm, she managed to pull the trigger all the way back. It was not a great shot, but it found unbelievable purchase. Theodore fell with a 22-calliber hole above his left eye, piercing the neat hairs of his brow with alarmingly significance. He gasped for several more seconds before fading, leaving Willie Bender unconscious and the little girl alone to ponder the success of what she'd been taught to do. Very carefully, and as quietly as she could, she returned to her former place inside the stall, up on the toilet seat. Theo was only the third person to tell her to do just that.

From Jorj's perspective, things were as messy as they could get. Not only was he shooting at strangers, but they were shooting at each other. It seemed that the timing couldn't have been worse. Then he recognized one of Benedict's boys from another fight and questions mixed with possibilities he lacked time for. Within fifteen minutes, two bodies lay bleeding on the main floor. Another, slumped over a restaurant counter for the past five, met the reaper and left quietly with him. All became terribly quiet but for an old man's groans. Another shot barked once and the old man, his hand feebly grasping for his lost .38, left the building. From the gift shop, Jorj watched Willie Bender lean heavily against the doorway, blood dripping from a savage graze on his left temple. He held his pistol as a drunken man, darting his eyes left and right with a frightening disorientation that made Jorj himself want to fall down. Even in as bad shape as he was, the man was still a dead shot.

"Willie!" Jorj called out. "That's three, counting the body in the…" he paused, then corrected himself. "Three gone! How many…"

When Willie answered, his words were slurred. "Benedict's men…two of 'em. That's them, died." He careened onto the main floor, wagging his 45 left and right. "The old man was protectin'…he stopped, trying to recall something important. "Where's Theo?" he asked abruptly. "God my head hurts!"

"Outside, I thought." Jorj eased out from the shop, stepping gingerly over the broken glass. "Theo!" He called again but there was no answer. "Who was the old man protecting?" Jorj slid towards the front entrance, glancing out one of the shattered windows. "You saying there's still somebody left?"

"Don't know," Willie answered curtly, his breath exiting in short puffs. He staggered, catching his balance on a defunct

ATM machine. "Think the old jackass was crazy. Kept yellin' in some other fucked-up language."

"Like 'get out'?" Jorj frowned. On the sidewalk was a spent clip, undoubtedly Theodore's. In the distance he spied the road-runner. Beneath it he saw several pairs of feet. "I think we'd better check on the others. If Theo isn't with them..."

"Shut your mouth, Watchman. I can figure that out for myself."

"Hey Frosty," his smile grated with unwilling force. "Let's just get one thing straight. We work together, or you work alone."

"I already work alone, white bread. And you can shove that 'Frosty business' up your ass!" He shambled to the door. Jorj shot off the lock before he got there and pushed hard, making an opening so neither of them would have to crawl. Before going through, he turned and looked back. "Somebody *is* watching us." His numb fingers barely held the grip of his pistol, let alone any command over firing it. He was cold, so cold his teeth chattered mercilessly. "Hate leavin' with my tail between my legs."

No more was said until they reached the car. Jorj made a decision before they got there, in fact made it inside the rest stop building. For now he kept his long-overdue revelation to himself. Theo wasn't there, and no one needed to guess why. Even Willie knew not to go looking, even if he was in the shape to. If the man wasn't dead, he'd make himself so soon. The badly wounded didn't fair well in the Twilight. Doctors, if any existed, had yet to announce themselves.

Willie had his own ideas too. His silence, though, the others mistook for his condition. Crammed as he was in the back seat by the driver's side window, he plotted. He wasn't goin' to no damned beach in January. Let Dennis ride his bike now, as long as the moron didn't wipe out. Until he got his own head back so things weren't actin' all crazy, someone had to bring the 'Bat' along. Might as well be that skinny, good-for-nothing freak.

Jorj, in a show of generosity, cranked up the heater once they were on the road. Warmth flowed over Willie Bender, eventually calming the uncontrollable shivers that racked his long-abused frame. Bit by bit, he began to piece together facts and hearsay. Theo said some things he was just now remembering. He needed time to decipher them. The heater helped, and that was good. His head hurt like hell, but that witch had a way with taking care of things like that. Though he refused the bandage, he let her clean the wound, and the aspirin he accepted willingly. Another day, he decided. One more day.

Left behind, small feet tiptoed out onto the main floor of the damaged rest stop facility, alone and uncertain. They carried their diminutive owner to the front door and then to the parking lot where all the big people no longer parked. The pistol was no longer in her hands. She hated the thing and what it did. Three times she called the name of Petri, the old man who gave her food and comforted her when she cried.

In response, a horn blew and she turned. An old maroon Buick rolled to a stop diagonally across the white, evenly-spaced, lines. "Petri!" she screamed in delight.

A man opened the door and got out slowly, as if arthritis bothered his joints. His near-white hair, like his wrinkled skin, betrayed great age. On his bland-green laborer's shirt was stitched the name 'Ardon Farms'. A sweat-faded, brown foam trucker's cap lingered loosely in the fingers of his left hand. His eyes regarded her kindly, relieved that she was alright. "Are they gone?"

She nodded, speaking words he didn't understand.

"Good." Somehow she understood him. She always did. "Come!" He stooped and offered his big, open arms. She ran into them gladly, laughing even. "Let us go someplace safer, little one."

20

Everyone was a little quieter now, a bit more distracted. Nick was gone. So was Theodore. The rest just got lucky. Any one of them knew where carelessness got you. The problem was that it was becoming stock and trade now. Everyone was burned out, tired as the restless dead.

Deep down in Willie Bender's soul, well past the deep throb of his glanced-off skull, was a thread of guilt for which he had no knife to cut. It was his fault that Theodore wasn't with them anymore, and that the man was in more danger than was fair. In hard rationalizations, he also blamed everyone else. It wasn't his fault he got dragged out this far, away from his supply lines and his chosen route. That Theo could take to his grave. It was a thought that eased his conscious for a few more miles, but then, as these things always do, guilt crept back into his belly like a snake and coiled up within his ribs until he could think of nothing else. He, Willie Bender, was the careless one. No one else got out first, went straight up to the door, and shot out the glass. Only a fool would sit inside the damned building and not shoot back, not ambush the intruder. The whole firefight might not have happened at all if not for his own mistakes. And so it fell to him to attempt rectitude.

January hated motorcycles. It hated still more those who rode them without the proper protection from its icy soul. Willie thought long and hard on riding it back. It was clear to him that he would never make it. Either the cold would get him or the cold would, he mused darkly. And as far as he traveled with Theo, his core was about as worn out as he ever felt it. He was a pussy now, plain and simple. No tough guy attitude would work now. That left only one other option.

The next rest stop he checked out personally. No more accidents. No more mistakes. What he did, he did alone, because as far as he was concerned, no one did it better.

Every window stared at him suspiciously now, and they had good reason to. He was an angry man, and one in a hurry. He also knew though that these things weren't to be rushed recklessly, and so he proceeded with caution. So too, he also wanted a bit of drama. It would help him later. A door in the rear, a service entrance, offered him access to the inside where he found the building utterly empty. Maybe, he conjectured, the fatality just saw it on the highway. He didn't pretend to be an expert in these matters. All he knew now was that it was a damned good thing he had other skills besides killing. Silently, he began counting to himself, idly watching the others through a window at shrub level. When the time was right...

The least patient among them was Dennis. The pending all-clear signal couldn't hold back the forces of his bladder. Braving nothing but the waning autumn sun, he ran to the nearest bush, almost two hundred yards away, and relieved himself with a sigh. No Twilight severity ever managed to erase patterns of modesty, programmed from an early age into an inescapable discipline despite his other, later-learned, undignified behaviors. The entire operation took him all of three minutes, and he walked back slowly to stretch his legs without a hurry. The parking lot was as barren as a desert. No cars, besides the Roadrunner, no trucks, buses, trailers, nothing. It was strange, and the first one they came across so empty. When he saw the white circle, four feet in diameter and perfectly painted with a spray can, it surprised him, for it looked freshly done, or at least within a couple of days. He stopped to touch it and held back his hand. It was plainly dry, no need. This wasn't official, he decided. Who painted a circle out in the driving lane between the long rows of spaces? Nobody serious. Even the Department of Public Works gents just marked of a rough 'x'. Nothing fancy those. This was deliberate, but it described no plain purpose that he could see. "So what do you care, jerk-off?" he asked out loud. He reached into a pocket, took out a smoke, and lit it up with one of his few remaining matches from a frayed-cardboard matchbook. "Hafta get some more once ol' Frosty's done in there." He puffed twice, inhaled once, relished a long, drawn-out exhalation, and started back towards the others.

"What now, Jorj?" The Padre bummed a cigarette from Dennis, and a light. On old Earth he hardly smoked at all. Now he did so quite frequently. Most everybody did. One could easily jump to the conclusion that the low-grade cough the good father acquired was directly connected to this small vice. More likely though, it was simply from nerves.

"As soon as the man's at the window waving, we go. You heard him, Francis." He addressed him by his given name more often now, as Nick always had.

"No, that's not what I meant."

Jorj grew impatient, both with the confusing triviality of the subject and with Frosty's extended absence. The man *had* insisted on going in alone. "What's really on your mind? We're waltzing around here."

"We're just going to the beach?" His dark glasses reflected Jorj's irritated expression back perfectly.

"Father..." The old patterns always re-emerged in times of stress. Jorj glanced to the Roadrunner's hood. Greta lay sprawled across there, her back to the windshield. Was she for real, he wondered?

"Look," the Padre stared blindly away as if studying appreciatively the horizon they'd just fled. "Maybe God's conferring with you on a steady basis, but all I have, truly have, Jorj, is logic. I may be a sham as a priest, but not as a thinking man." He sighed, folding his arms before him, leaning against the rear passenger side of the Roadrunner. "I knew Ogam for awhile. Smart, if not entirely a deductively cerebral man."

"No crime in that."

"No," The Padre agreed. "He was intuitive." His words dropped off into a silence that communicated on a more tactical level.

"Get to the point, Franc."

"Francis."

"Okay..."

"You've a good heart, Jorj, but you don't follow it. You bungled the drop on purpose, but the real bungle was in trusting me." He smiled widely and patted his own shoulder maliciously. "Most of my memories are crap these days, Jorj, but nightmares serve to remind us of key events, if we pay attention."

Stunned, the other man nodded hesitantly. "You got me there. I kind of forgot all that, and when I remembered, it was just to...to get it back." He shook his head. "Hey! I follow my heart more than you think."

"And look where it got us, Jorj."

What?"

"Abandon those you love, even if it's for a greater cause, and there's a price." He took a last drag and threw his stubbed brand to the asphalt. For a second he debated, and then old disciplines, ancient guilt really, won out. His sneakered foot searched for and crushed the last life out of that tobacco fire.

Shame pierced Jorj's ribs like a hot blade. Quickly, the emergency crews responded to his conscience to put out the fire and staunch the flow of blood. The next emotion he felt was anger.

"All clear!" It was Dennis, and the skinny scarecrow of a man already was off at a run. Even here, in such a desolate existence, Mammon had his hold.

The dream evaporated, each purple cloud of darkness grudgingly releasing its sticky grasp. Jorj jingled the keys. "Gas first."

One pump alone had fuel, but only the minimum octane, and that itself smelled a little old. Cut it with better from their dwindling stock, Jorj decided, and hope it didn't gum up the engine. After getting what he could, he paused, considered the windshield, and grabbed a squeegee from its place next to the pay booth. The reservoir was dry. He turned and started walking towards the side entrance to the building, up the sidewalk with untended shrubs along the left next to the facility, the red cedar chips faded with age. Maybe inside he'd find some water to clean off the glass.

It was a hollow sound that greeted him. His own footsteps echoed on the tiled floor, mingling with complaining voices, the most of which belonged to Dennis.

"Nada!" His bark was angry. "We should have just taken an exit back in Scranton!"

"More risk than we need," Jorj reminded him tiredly.

"We need food…" Dennis paused, his eyes almost crossing in frustrated revelation. "…I need some entertainment! I'm bored, Jorj. I crave…" He turned suddenly, aware of a presence that always seemed too watchful for her own good. "What?"

Greta smiled, but the mood behind the expression was grim. "Cravings are worse below the twilight, Dennis. Learn to control them before it's too late."

"Right…" He stumbled backwards, the words as much a blow to him as her creepiness. He had no idea what Jorj saw in her, except she was kind of pretty, and smart.

"Enough." Jorj did a quick survey himself, moving around quickly from room to room. "You cased it all?"

"Down to the last nothing."

"Alright then. Let's stop wasting…"

The roadrunner's engine rumbled to life. In the few seconds it took for Jorj's confused expression to suddenly turn to suspicion, and then to full, furious understanding, the rumbling picked up and then slowly faded in volume.

"No!" Jorj ran to the side door, Dennis and Greta at his heels. He pushed on the bar, shoved past, and ran into the lot. Only when he saw that the gas station was vacant, and that green car traveling away from them westbound on the eastbound lane of the Thruway was none other than his own, did he stop in defeat. From his lips came resurrected every vulgarity from its ancient primordial grave.

Even Dennis stopped cold in his tracks, impressed with his friend's remarkably broad vocabulary. "Where the hell did *you* go to school?"

"Shut up, alright?" Jorj ran the fingers of his right hand through his greasy hair in frustration. "Stupid, stupid, stupid! I fell for his fucking trick! You'd think that once I saw the damned place was empty…"

A small, pale hand found his shoulder and started massaging the muscles around it, working its way gently up to his neck. The owner seemed quite calm, even a little amused. "He won't get far, you know."

"Huh?" It occurred to Jorj that maybe she referred to their gas situation. "He has enough fuel to…"

"…get himself into trouble." She finished for him, her smile, this time, genuinely pleasant.

"I don't get it." His face was thunderstruck. Did she not see their predicament?

Her lips curled just a little bit more. "He kept a newspaper from the day he died. It lay on a table waiting for him when he crossed over to the Twilight." Her voice stressed the next sentence as if it were a punch line. "He never bothered to look at the weather forecast down this way, only at the southern tier and below."

For the first time in minutes, Jorj started to relax, even to smile. Then it fell away all at once as he realized another implication. "If he bangs up the Roadrunner, I'll kill him!"

CROSSING the two red wires was the easy part. Getting at them took a little more time. Let Watchman complain later, Frosty smiled bitterly, his hands stiff from the cold. If the man ever got his car back, that half-wit mechanic could fix it up for him.

When the engine turned over, it almost immediately took to its new life. Willie "Frosty" Bender put the Roadrunner into gear and gave more gas to the cause, enough to turn the sudden forward push into a momentary sense of weightlessness once he reached the highway and relaxed his foot. Tiny flakes of snow, no larger than the head of an eraser in their crystalline matrix, began to fly towards him like stars. He grunted and cranked up the heat, determined to get warm and cheat 'Ol Man Winter.' The effect of the snow, as sparse as it was, was gently mesmerizing, and so, against his will, also possibly enabled by the rush of warm dry air from the car's heat vents, Willie slid into a lethargic, melancholy groove.

How long had he known Theo? Longer than he could count by any measure. From the first day the man offered him a job, not long after Willie's arrival, they encountered trouble, and every opportunity to trust each other proved true. As Theo rose up through the ranks, and gathered strength, so did Willie Bender. Now? Frosty nearly laughed. All gone, everything but for a few stashes, dwindling safe houses in a city where things were heading towards a slow burn. Only a fool went back there, he chastised himself, but he knew his duty. Sometimes a man had to be a fool. There weren't many people Willie respected, much less liked, in any version of Earth. Theo hit both marks dead-on in all of them.

The fact that it was a mutual relationship cinched the decision to go back. He wasn't going to leave Theo to burn, not if he could help it.

There was something else too. It nagged him quietly, but with growing irritation. Theo and the Watchman shared a secret, and if his own nose was true, it was a dangerous one. The man had something in the trunk. For a minute, he debated, and then he pulled over onto the slim shoulder of the highway, the one the signs say doesn't exist so no one will be tempted to do what he just did. He soaked in the heat for a time, the engine idling with his foot on the brake, and then threw the car in park. Against his will, he opened the door and stepped out, closing it behind him and going to the rear of the car.

It hit him as soon as he got there. No keys. Cursing, he got back inside and shut the door to conserve heat. Awkwardly, for he was a big man, he climbed around, searching under the seats, and in the back, for a tool of some kind, but found nothing useful. Dennis' stupid books, kid stuff, littered the back seat. Spent food wrappers, half packs of cigarettes, other odd garbage, made a disheveled mess. He didn't find the crow bar he was looking for. That, very cruelly, was likely in the trunk, the very place he needed it to open.

Of course he could rip out the back seat.

He made it cleaner than he expected. All of Dennis' crap tumbled onto the floor, half stepped on by Frosty's wet shoes. The back cushion pulled away finally after Willie's fingers pried their best, and behind it was revealed something the man never anticipated exactly, though it fit Theodore's cryptic comments to the Watchman. And Willie knew what it was, knew it well. He did a stint in the military, enough to see some of the more exotic tools of ground warfare. If the contents matched the olive drab case before him, he was in an unfortunate position.

"Damned SADM," his lips moved in near silence. "Watchman found himself a bad, bad toy to mess around with." His breath took on the vibrations of voice as he felt the full mixed weight of fear and grave curiosity. His eyes scanned what no non-military personnel should have in their possession, or should carelessly lose once they gained it illegitimately. He didn't have to open it, or jiggle it to check its weight. His heart spoke truthfully. It would weigh 163 pounds and have a minimum yield of .01 kiloton; W54 Special Atomic Demolition Munition, the mother of all landmines. Where that Fish belly found it didn't matter anymore. The question now was what to do with it, and did it have a wire.

Frosty's head fell into his right hand tiredly. If he dropped it off on the pavement now, right fucking now, would it blow and burn before he got away? Was it leaking slow fire even as he considered this option? Would suicide, the magical reset button of Twilight Earth, cease to work in the same way ever again for him? He cursed quietly, a gnawing sense of defeat not far away, and let his eyes wander through the rest of the visible trunk. Nothing of interest to him. Slowly, almost automatically, he pushed the seat back into place, noting absently that it would not sit firmly again until fixed. Too late for the radiation question. What remained was the why.

A memory, hardly difficult to raise, stood before him. Was this what the newspaper led up to? The possibility that this Watchman took it away from someone else elbowed him deep. The man had a tendency to get into situations, and hang with travelers on the wrong side of the sun. And there was something else. Once, some days or weeks back, Frosty couldn't remember anymore, the man tried to stop him from tormenting his old back-stabbing partner back on North State Street. That ridiculous white dude didn't even know why the man was getting' shot in the knee, and still he had to play 'good guy,' not even guessing what the 'bad guy' was. Such naivety disgusted him, but it also made sense. Someone bad was surely missing this piece of ordinance and would be lookin' to get it back. That's why the man put those funky, superstitious symbols all over the car. A light bulb burned bright over Frosty's head for a second and then exploded. "Benedict," he mumbled. "Ol' Tall and Crazy got robbed."

His narrowed eyes became slits, and he smiled. New Jackson City was safe from fire, but he wasn't, not so long as he traveled back there. If the nuke was wired, he should be going the other way. With an effort of will, for the heat lulled him into cottony arms of warmth, he climbed back into the front seat and cracked the driver's-side window for air. Time to go.

Snow fell languidly, promising nothing, offering little to the highway. Willie Bender grimaced and put the car in gear. He squeezed the gas pedal to the floor and spun the steering wheel, ignoring the slick slash of tires on wet pavement. In earnest, he took the Roadrunner back the way he came, knowing he wasn't going to stop at the nearest exit, nor the rest stop just before. In fact, he didn't know where he was going, only where he didn't want to be. Theo was on his own.

21

Sixteen miles into the drive, Willie Bender hit whiteout conditions. His previous speed of 90 miles per hour abruptly dragged back to 40, then 20, then 10. Reciprocally, the vulgarities which poured past his lips increased tenfold. Within ten minutes, he was suddenly forced off the road, fishtailing into the high bank well off the shoulder. Every prayer that could bubble up past his lips did so as his foot pumped the break pedal. The roadrunner skipped up and over and there it lodged, both headlights pointed forty-five degrees into the snow-filled sky. In a fit of rage, Frosty exited the vehicle and kicked it, kicked it hard in the back panel just behind the driver's side door. With a last spiteful heave, he slammed the door to, watched in furious disbelief it didn't catch and returned, and slammed it again. This time it stuck. The glare that threatened to erode the rest of his face into so much melted wax, turned with his body and assaulted the highway east and west. Up and down Interstate 99 the way was completely obscured. Snow descended in unbridled, primeval laughter, and there was nothing he could do about it. The thought that all of this was for nothing, and that the others, now much disabused as to his motivations, would eventually come upon his misfortune, and that, even worse, in their greatest weakness, and their highest strength, they would forgive him, not even realizing why he did what he did.

Setting his jaw hard, anger brimming past the high water mark, he yanked on the car door only to find that it would not give. Shouting more words his mother never taught him he staggered and slid around to the other side and tried the passenger side door. It was locked. His fist balled up before he even knew what he was doing, and he hit the window, shattering glass over the front seat. Pain erupted in his knuckles but he ignored them, as he did the snow that now found itself free to enter where before had been forbidden. A quick release of the lock and he was in, pulling away the back seat without even the slightest pause or consideration. For a single breathless minute he stared furiously at its contents. "Watchman!" He yelled it out, vaguely aware of the absurd notion that it might carry on the wind all the way back west some fifteen plus miles to where the others must, by now, be walking. "Goddam you Watchman!"

His chest heaved with labored breathing. Many times he'd been angry. He'd been shot, stabbed, tortured, abandoned, betrayed...but every time, he had an enemy other than himself. This time was different. He was the bad guy, the stupid muthah fucka. Willie Bender stepped in his own pile of shit, dragged others into it, and they would still take it on the chin! Bunch of goddam martyrs! Bullshit! That's what he called it. Plain and simple! Then he saw something no one had noticed before, and it changed everything. He peered into the trunk for a closer inspection, his shivering subsided. Then he began to laugh, at first just in spite, then uncontrollably. No one had looked at the one piece of information that mattered, and at best, only two of them would have understood the significance. Let them come. They had a 10-ton TNT yield of nothing! Zero. Zip. Now all he had to do was decided whether to tell them or not.

Nothing lasts forever. Ogum, the bum from Maple street that took up in the old Language Hall, and later in the New Jack campus library, told Willie Bender that when the old man was a beggar. Theo always said the man was original to the place. Truth was another matter, something no one ever knew for sure. What was clear was that at one time the man wore a placard that read 'Will work for food' over his chest. It was a time of few immigrants. No one ever starved physically on Twilight Earth, but not eating regularly was a misery. Pleasure, if you could call it that, was as rare as a clean wipe after a turd. You took what you got, and if you could get a little of the old something every day, well, then you called that a win, plain and simple. Even an old man stuck in his own philosophical bullshit knew that. But whether one offered him food, or kicked him in the stomach—and Willie saw that happen once or twice—he always had a word or two back, and just about every damned time it pierced something.

"Whatchoo mean, old man?" Willie retorted, faking his pigeon English like he did when he wanted to mess with people. "I ain't died yet."

But the answer to that question meant listening, and though Willie heard the words, he didn't catch them and they sank too deep. Now they returned, drawing blood, though exactly why, he couldn't say. "You don't exist anymore, you just don't know it yet."

The odd thing was, somehow Willie did know it. Goddam it, but he did. It was alright, the old one reassured him, as if he needed the comforting words of a bum. It wasn't possession of time and space that mattered. It was the endless chain of existence that really made it all worth it, and if you were really patient, and listened carefully, your chain could escape ignorance and find a dwelling better than here.

'Here' was getting cold. Willie considered restarting the car to turn on the heat, but he put it off for now. Gas was scarce. He would wait until it got a little colder. Watchman would be along by morning. Best not to waste what they didn't have much of. Slowly his body curled into the fetal position that conserved warmth. It would be a fight not to sleep, he mused, shivering and unaware of the leaking tank inches below him.

When the Roadrunner zinged by going east, Dennis rolled his eyes and swore silently. He was through pissing in the weeds, and just in the process of zipping up his pants. No one needed to tell him what the sound meant. All their walking was for nothing, and the day was getting long in the tooth. At the moment, everyone seemed content to inspect a recently jack-knifed tractor trailer off the highway where it folded a chain-link fence as sweetly as a napkin. Oddly, and in a strange twist of fortune which would matter later, the cab was mostly upright, if not untouched by damage. But the doors still closed, and that was something worth noting. That the windshield was only spider-cracked and not shattered also seemed beyond reason. Nevertheless, it was so. The torn-up earth around the accident was as fresh as you could expect. Somewhere, quite possibly nearby, a guy in a trucker's cap wandered the world, but he wasn't at his Kamaloka Crossroads now. Practical as always, Jorj had the back doors of the trailer pried open and was examining the contents with wordless old Frank. Near the highway, Padre stared sightlessly at the deep blue sky, oblivious of the interruptions each cloud made in his panoramic darkness. Dennis noted cynically, and yes, even a little sadly, how Jorj's girlfriend watched him. "God," the man whispered in melancholy disdain, "If I had my mom here, you can bet I wouldn't be..." He stopped, making a face. "Who am I kidding?" He asked nobody. What exactly he meant, he kept to himself, for something new drew his attention.

A hubcap, just a plastic ring really, hung on a fence pole a few lengths up from the derelict tractor trailer. Why it caught his eye, or held him past the initial glance, escaped him, other than the fact that it faced him exactly, forming a perfect circle inside and out. He stared at it a moment longer, shook his head, and started back. What was in the rig, he wondered?

Because the trailer was on its side, they never saw the company of the hauler. Had they, it's quite possible they might more eagerly have gained entrance to the insides. Someone, somewhere, was moving, changing residences. Their possessions never made it to the new home, at least on the day they were supposed to. Instead, like the truck and the driver, they took that long tumble, breaking past the barrier of many a 'god' to land on the desolate shores of Twilight. By the time Dennis reached the big open doors, Jorj and Frank were up to their hips in broken furniture and burst boxes of someone else's lives. Frank smiled, tossing Dennis something that looked only dark in the shadows. The younger man wheeled out of the way, suspicious to the end, and then watched as a playground ball hit the grass at his feet and bounced off beyond him.

"Nice!" Dennis hollered, climbing in to wade through the debris of goods. "Find any food, you losers?"

"Go eat the kickball," Jorj remarked without looking up. He had his pocket knife out to slice open a determinedly resistant cardboard box.

"Funny."

"Frank," Jorj glanced at his older companion and thumbed towards Dennis. "Tell him about the food we found."

"Even funnier." Dennis made a face at Frank, but the old man had his attentions elsewhere. "Guess I'll just look myself." His face brightened suddenly. "Let's stay here tonight."

"I was actually considering that," Jorj mumbled, holding up a Barbie Doll and grimacing at it intently. "It may take that long just to find more than toys and goddamned knic-knacks!" He let his eyes, and his frown drift out past Dennis' long, greasy hair. "Day's waning."

"We won't catch up to him by nightfall, even if he really does put it in a snow bank."

Jorj sighed heavily. "He'll blow through all our gas trying to keep warm tonight." From his cascading mountain of someone else's junk, he surveyed the immediate boxes without real expectation of finding something useful. "Look for a gas container...please."

"Aye-aye, El Capiton!" Dennis spat himself out the back and was gone, into the sun.

It took awhile to make the search a methodical one, for the Twilight lends itself more towards chaos than it does order. Fortunately most of this small group of people still retained enough of the latter in themselves to be more than mere vultures, and that was good, for it was by this shared nature that they not only managed to find needed items, but also a few extras, and a good fire besides to ward of the night.

To say it surprised Jorj, after he had time to reflect upon it, that Dennis was willing to brave the night with nothing but a tractor trailer for shelter, was an understatement. Sure the cab was built for long hauls, complete with a bunk section behind the two front seats, and there was battery power for a little white noise if Dennis couldn't stand country music CDs, but it wasn't what he was used to. Besides, the man, distinguished mostly by his crude sense of chaos, shamed himself into giving it up to Greta in a singular show of mannish nobility. Fortunately for him, she was far beyond such things, and reminded him, for his own benefit, that the night was still her turf, if no longer her real home. He wasted no time in claiming a bunk after that. And quietly, for he still feared the dark now, he coaxed Frank into taking the other one. Given the alternatives, he was the obvious choice. A fallen, blind priest would never see demons come. Bill lacked the smarts, and Jorj would be sleeping with...his rudimentary analysis stopped there at the borders of uncomfortable land. He still couldn't figure that one out, and didn't want to.

They ate gummy bears that night, stale ones, but nobody noticed. There wasn't a one of them that liked the stupid, colorful little gelled blasphemes of God's green planet, but since that was another place entirely, and this was all they had, they shared and nibbled without complaint.

All the tables and chairs that could be brought to bear with fire saw them through the dark hours, and long dark hours they were. Despite the half quart of Jim Beam Frank found, there was no cheer, and talk was subdued. No one shook the gibbering voices of the night on their road trip that day. Twilight Earth was thin, and there were hordes to hear just on the other side, welling up from dark haunts below. At night they were loudest, or perhaps the world was just silent enough not to obscure them. Whichever it was, the dark was full of their noise, just loud enough not to be ignored, not quite severe enough to be properly understood, and perhaps that was for the best, though it unnerved everyone around that fire, in the crotch of the jack-knifed rig. What everyone noticed, with the exception of Bill, and possibly the Padre, was that even Greta was afraid, and that made it all a little worse.

They left the lion's share behind them when they left the following morning. What they brought they took turns pulling behind them on a red, plastic wagon, a hollow mockery of the Radio Flyer. Jorj hoped the wheels would last long enough for the miles still ahead of them, but he knew the limits of cheap plastic. Most of what they towed was gasoline from a car they found, saved in any vessel able to hold it. In all, they had no more than seven gallons, but they also knew that they could return here with what they brought and get more, provided someone else did not scavenge it first.

By midmorning, they passed the rest stop where Willie Bender tricked them. Still not a car in the lot, and Jorj saw no reason to take another run through the building. He was anxious to get the Roadrunner back, and to see that it, and its contents, were all safe and sound. The night before he had dreams, no, nightmares really, of finding it upside down, the man inside a hopeless cripple. What told him that it bore no honest portent was that Frosty would never let himself stay in such a bad condition. The man would end it somehow and start fresh back in

New Jackson city, probably taking his car with him and losing it in the ether. That, Jorj decided, would piss him off more than anything so far that the man did to him. You don't mess with someone else's wheels, much less lose them for good.

Before the sun rose to zenith, they neared their goal. Dennis, with the exception of the priest, the one with the worst eyesight among them, was the first to spot the Roadrunner. At the distance he saw it, it resembled only a blurry spot of darkness against the distant sky, like a bird hovering just above the ground. By the time they all reached a better vantage point, the car shape was obvious, and Jorj took off at a run, oblivious at first that the car floated, its headlights aimed skyward.

The moment he placed his hand on the door handle, the car plummeted to the Earth, bouncing the shocks alarmingly. Inside, Willie Bender's head rebounded off the ceiling and then joined his falling body in a tumble from the back seat to the floor in a pile with Dennis' abused personal possessions.

"You bastard!" Jorj yelled, nearly ripping the door off its hinges as he opened it and throwing back the front seat. With both hands, he grabbed the man inside and dragged him out, ignoring the snowflakes which appeared on the man's curly hair and black skin like tiny white flowers. As he raised one hand in a fist, intent on bringing it down full on the man's face, he stopped, realizing that Willie was barely conscious. The skin in his grasp was very cold, evidence supporting the fact that the car was not running. "Aw shit!" He noticed that a bluish character had mingled with the Willie's color. Cold, Carbon Monoxide poisoning, either or both, Jorj figured.

Quickly, he pushed Frosty back into the back seat and got in the front after pushing things back in place. He heaved the door closed and fumbled for his keys, locating the ignition key and inserting it in its place on the right side of the steering wheel. As soon as he turned the key, he knew he lost this battle. The battery was dead and there was no gas left in the tank. Willie Bender was not dressed for the cold like he was used to, and he had already been compromised. Only one option was left if he wanted to save the man. Jorj climbed in the back, measuring his distaste against his inconvenient sense of compassion. He would do what needed to be done, but he wouldn't like it.

Dennis stood outside the Roadrunner, his face in his hands. It was unclear whether he was moaning or laughing. When Greta joined him, she grimaced and opened the door to get inside. "Jorj!"

He realized then, when he heard her voice, that he was alone. A mixture of relief and sadness warred within him, with the former taking the lion's share of the battlefield. "He's gone. Maybe the cold, maybe the exhaust; I don't know." He sat up, still feeling the frigid spread along his body that once belonged to Willie Bender. "I tried."

22

Several women screamed. The intersection of Terrence and Newcastle became a study of local chaos. The immediate cars stopped abruptly while those behind them and to the sides swerved around and away. Many on the sidewalk stopped also, some dropping packages. Crack addicts, and there was more than one, changed whatever they were singing to new words reflecting the experience without missing a beat.

No one helped the man up, no one dared. For only a moment did he lie there, and then he was on his hands and knees, glaring first at the road beneath him, then at the onlookers, witnesses to a phenomenon few ever got to see with their own eyes. "Whatchoo lookin' at?" He growled at a fat youth standing next to what was probably his younger sister. "I know you ain't lookin' at anything you ain't seen before. Mind your own damned business!" He pushed himself to his feet and stood erect. This was new. People, life...he was insanely hungry.

Not the Twilight.

He pressed his lips tightly together, an angry expression set to repel nosy types, and quickly surveyed his surroundings. He knew this place, but it wasn't New Jackson City, not one stone of it. Still, he knew where to go.

It was wise to run, though he didn't really want to. Where there were people, soft and such easy targets, there were strongmen keeping the peace. Probably they wouldn't care much for a naked black man running around, even in a black neighborhood. No one barred his way, though some of the earlier alarm did give way to laughter, as he thought it might. That was fine, just so long as no one got in his way.

His knuckles rose and fell on the door he knew he would find. When the youngish woman he was sure would open it did so, her scream hardly surprised him. Keenly aware of the fact that others, out on the street and the side walk, still watched him, he sized her by the elbows and pushed her back past the front door, releasing her immediately and closing the portal behind him. "Get me some damn clothes, woman!"

She was as black as he was, and her face bore an uncanny resemblance to his own, though she was slighter and better complexioned. Her voice went silent, but her mouth hung open. The scarf which half-wrapped her hair was half off, dangling akimbo from her head as she backed to a wall at the far end of the foyer. "Willie," she breathed. "I saw you lyin' in the morgue!"

"No you didn't!" He shot back, "and don't ever say that horseshit again! Now get me some clothes!" The next thing she did surprised him. Her arms flew around his shoulders, even as his own rose to stop them, but it was too late. He was locked in a weeping embrace. Jeezuss Christ!" His hands went to her arms, pressed gently, and then switched sides, wrapping around her in defeat.

23

It was her intention to reach her father, to soothe his soul some-how, and if possible, save him from descent. From the moment of their reunion, she knew the difficulty of this, for her own soul still bore the frozen burn-scars of despair. Yet nothing was impossible, even for the Twilight-bound daughter of a fallen priest, and so she spent what time with him she could, when he would let her.

The late-morning sun shone through a gossamer veil of rippling storm clouds, each rumble of thunder in the back-ground hardly noticeable to her anymore. Greta Ursala Rad-stone sat in the grass, remembering her full name for now, wondering also if she would forget it later. Memories of Old Earth came and went, as most good things did in the Twilight. Her delicate fingers split the stem of a daisy, its flower long since dormant from the late season temperatures, and exposed the wetness within. Idly she smoothed one thumb along the waxy insides, letting the chill breeze raise prickled bumps de-liciously along the flesh of her arms. The Padre sat some few feet away, half-turned from her. What he listened to, or for, she thought she knew, but he was quite silent, and very still. The breeze picked small strands of his hair and whisked his forehead gently, barely touching his dark glasses. His mouth was a thin, straight line, unmoved by the forces of nature, perhaps even unmoved by anything at all today. Though he neither smiled nor frowned, something troubled him, something besides their predicament. Greta sensed it. What it was gnawed a little deeper every day. Soon, she knew, it must break through to the surface. Should she attempt to draw it out, she wondered? Could it be serious? More so than everything else touched by the Twilight? She brooded over this silently, a shroud of concern settling over her heart.

By the Roadrunner, Bill picked through their new toolbox, more than content to have something close to him that he knew well and could use. Even though his small collection was far from complete, it was a start. Let something go wrong with the car. He was ready now. The man Dennis called Frosty was gone, and he felt better for it. No one needed the violence that man brought with him. It made Bill angry that the man was so mean, and so cocky. Whenever he was around, Bill remembered what he was like a long time ago, when he used to get so drunk he'd pick fights. He hated those memories, and the way he was. Though the world was changed, he lived with good people now. Helping them helped himself.

With a dead battery, the Roadrunner went nowhere without a tow, and Triple A wouldn't send a truck this far. Jorj and Dennis left an hour ago to retrieve the battery from the tractor trailer, and Willie's motorcycle from the rest stop. Though Frosty sabotaged it before his ill-considered theft, they planned to wheel it back by nightfall and use it as a charger. If Bill could put things back together, they could be on the road again the following morning.

Noon came and went. It was another couple hours after that before Jorj and Dennis returned. The good mood Dennis left with that morning, presumably influenced by Frosty's demise, was now eroded by fatigue, thirst, and a general sense that they didn't really know where they were ultimately going. They wheeled the armored bike up to Bill, put the kickstand down, and collapsed tiredly in the grass. Dennis was the first to speak.

"So I ask you again, how do you know we're even going the right way? There's no messages on the road signs, no arrows, nothing."

"I already told you." Jorj lay flat, staring up at the clouds, and the translucent cellophane covering of Padre's storm clouds. God, he wished he could do something about those things. "I had a dream."

"Oh, that's right." The sarcasm was subtle, but not overly so. "I have nightmares just about every night. Should I be worried?"

"Yeah. I think they're all going to come true, Dennis, all at the same time."

"Funny."

Jorj smiled. "Did I say I was kidding?"

Now Dennis frowned. "Look. Don't play with me. We left the only place of real security to come out this far and all you can give me is that you had a dream? I've yet to hear what the dream was about other than it involved the beach. You always dodge that one."

"I think Bill's made a breakthrough over there. He just smiled and patted the seat of the bike."

"He smiles when he's had a good bowel movement, dude. The man's a...see? You did it again!"

"I had the dream too, Dennis."

Dennis turned his head. Greta walked slowly over through the grass and sat down near him and Jorj. "You both had the same dream." It sounded like a statement and a question, mostly because of his immediate skepticism.

"Uh huh." She smiled gently. The memory of it was the most pleasant one she knew since passing away from Old Earth.

"Alright," Dennis leaned up on one elbow and looked her square in the eye. "Was I having fun there playing in the ocean?"

Here Greta's smile dimmed. Jorj remained silent.

"I see," Dennis remarked, not lost by the implication. His expression turned both bitter and afraid. "Brinks buys the farm, parties with the worms, snorts the dirt, becomes the woody…"

"We made love."

This stopped Dennis cold in his tracks, skidding into a full 180-degree turn. "Huh?" Deer caught in the headlights of a redneck's pickup truck stood a better chance of getting away than he did at the moment. "You? Me? Uh…" something akin to terror seized him and his muscles coiled instinctively in the 'flight' half of 'Fight or…' He glanced at Jorj suddenly to see which was worse, the act itself or the pummeling it would invoke.

"She meant with me, stupid." He wasn't even looking at Dennis. The sky seemed so much more pleasant right now.

"Oh." Relief washed over him. He wondered if she sensed that and felt vaguely ashamed because of it.

A wrench banged clumsily under the Roadrunner's hood. Jorj jerked his head in the direction, recalling Bill's original torment back in Mike's Garage and the sound of the accompanying slide of a tool across the garage floor. The man under the hood poked his head out awkwardly, locked eyes with Jorj for a brief, uncomfortable second, and then retreated to the engine again.

"What's he doing?" Dennis asked. "All he has to do with the Roadrunner is connect the jumper cables.

"Got me," Jorj replied easily, setting his head back down in the grass. He was very tired and didn't feel inclined to speculate.

Dennis rose stiffly to his feet and yawned, spying a convenient escape. "I'll go see if he needs help."

Greta waited for him to go and then moved closer to Jorj, sitting next to his chest. Gently, she took his left hand and stared at the palm.

"What's my fortune?" He asked her with less than serious intention.

"Got me," she mimicked. "I just wanted a look."

"They're dirty, sweetheart." The endearment came off sarcastic, but there was an obvious note of well-masked sincerity.

"I can see that. You might clean under your nails later. Would you like me to..."

"No," he interrupted, his tone laced with microscopic urgency. "There's the stink of death on them."

"There is everywhere, sweetheart." A more pleasant sarcasm dripped from her lips. "None of us can help that."

"Listen. I never killed anyone before I came to this place. I never hurt a fly...well, there were a few guys, but they deserved it."

"Did anyone you killed not come back?" Her eyes met his unabashedly.

"No."

"Then don't agonize. Ogam didn't lead you on a trail of breadcrumbs because he saw a bad man." Her hand squeezed his. "You're not, you know."

He didn't answer. At best, he couldn't honestly say that he was a good man, and when he thought about it, she hadn't said he was either. Gently, he returned the squeeze, trying to remember what it was like to feel the other half of the sun.

True to Bill's reputation, one which grew considerably with every day on the road, he not only raised the Roadrunner from flat-line, but repaired the "Bat" also. Like a boy with a new toy, and perhaps something of a trophy, Dennis claimed the bike. What he did not tell the others, wisely, perhaps unwisely, is that he discovered a small, James Bond-like grenade chute under the seat, armed and ready. There was also a sawed off shotgun mounted ingeniously in the crotch of the handlebars, with the stock truncated and an electronic trigger connected to a thumb button next to the grip. Instead, he merely smiled his goblin smile when Jorj shrugged, calling it the war machine, seeing only the armor. It wasn't quite that, but ol' Frosty certainly thought of a few contingencies.

They camped another night, by collective, mutual agreement. No one cared to travel once the sun went down, though at least two of them could have been persuaded to go along with the idea. Under no circumstances did Dennis intend to. Of all the group, he was the most afraid of the dark. With the passing of Nick, though his insecurities manifested in a forced sense of independence and bravado, he was still, in essence, a scared, over-age kid.

That is not to say he did not grow once away from the shadow of that grand patriarch. In fact, he took more responsibility for his actions, and actually read the books that Nick gave him with renewed focus. And if anyone mentioned the old man, in name or no, he remained distantly silent, closed-mouthed in a way he never before seemed capable. Jorj noted this more than the others, for he was, perhaps, the one who knew Dennis best, though he had not known him nearly as long.

Shortly before nightfall, they built a fire with what remained of the wood. It was not enough to last the night, and no one had the heart to attack the surrounding scrub trees for additional fuel. Life was cheap enough in the Twilight without burning green wood. It smoked like crazy anyway.

Sleep for Jorj came in the arms of Greta, and for her in his. They spared a futon from the flames for their own comfort within the trailer, and on this they lay in unsettled comfort. It was not easy showing affection in this plane of existence. Breaking down walls was not something one did easily. It wasn't that either of them lacked trust in the other, merely that being soft was not safe, and disappointment hung over all . . . their personal Damocles' sword. Jorj feared the weakening of his own shell. At his core, he vowed not to strip his defenses bare so long as there were dangers yet before them. He never counted on the consequences of his feelings for the woman in his arms, or the shaking his own foundation took as a result. She seemed perfectly at peace with the arrangement, and that was good. Let her find what he could not, as yet, make peace with. She was an anomaly in a land of anomalies. His eyes, weighted down by his fears and uncertainties, closed finally, carrying him off to another place far from his trailer full of other people's junk.

He walked the path of a dark, narrow river, along its banks to the right going east. The sun, long since tripped into Hades, regarded the low-hanging, orange moon with a jealous glare. The humidity was high, but, thanks to the same circumstances that released the stars into the punchbowl ocean above, the air was considerably cooler than just hours before. The man gave the scene a cursory smile, believing it illusory. A dream, after all, was nothing else, no?

If it was truly fata morgana, he soon found that it carried a very real touch, for something quite hard, a brick perhaps, struck him in the back of the head and broke in several pieces. He reeled for a second, half turned, and collapsed onto the dirt beach adjacent to a warehouse dock, his eyes blurred with pain. Another man might have been rendered unconscious by the blow, even slain, but he always did have a hard head. No one who ever knew him would argue that point.

It wasn't over. These things seldom ended so easily. Three well placed kicks robbed him of his breath and his resolve. He couldn't stop them from rifling his pockets, or kicking him again several more times when they found nothing of value on him. Not even his pocket knife was deemed worth the trouble. They cast it aside where later, when he struggled to his knees in a despicable condition, his hand would fall upon it. Under the crèmecicle moon they left him to die, but he did not. Toughness crossed all worlds, and these thugs had no idea the time they wasted.

When Jorj picked up his path again, it was walked in pain, but he knew where he was going. Dennis had neglected to tell him of the circles, certainly marks, sigils, glyphs, all left by Ogam. That he saw more than his mind registered was hardly a surprise. Jorj would forget everything about them later, but for now, he knew enough to sleepwalk into the next in line, one Dennis would see tomorrow and maybe, just maybe, point out to another, possibly himself. The fact that they called who they would was lost on him, and Jorj, even with his present knowledge could not circumvent that. Ogam wasn't stupid, and the forces he served were both bound and blessed by indomitable laws. In his way, the old student of mythos was the same. He performed as Pan, leading them all on with pipes that promised nothing, yet brooked no refusal.

They played a song of confusion now, not for him; for another.

Did he know the face? The name? Even the neighborhood? The curtain was down, the supporting veil thick, so that even if his hands parted the outer folds, only a gossamer web, vague at best, filtered out the recognition he was sure must be there. He found the next dock, a crumbling mass of concrete, and clambered up onto it, freeing flakes of rust from the once-protective steel that lined the decrepit edge. Waters lapped against the outer wall to his left, but he ignored it. His way was right, towards the driveway next to the building, and the dull, lamp-lit street it led to beyond.

Each successive street grew worse before the neighborhood improved. Winos, crack heads, crack whores; they all stared at him, for he was as out of place here as they were in his world. Even dirty and clobbered, he didn't carry himself right. The air of someone who could handle himself was overshadowed by his lack of local street sense. But for his poverty, he was ripe for the picking.

It was fortunate for him, though not for a hurried cabbie, that an accident took place. The woman whose car ran into the yellow Chrysler survived, but would be a long time regaining the use of her legs. In the interim, cops and other emergency personnel filled the corridor within minutes. Someone had a cellphone and knew how to use it. Jorj, however out of his element, passed through easily and unmolested. Another migrant, he mused, watching but careful not to rubberneck. Where exactly was anyone's guess. Several blocks later, the knuckles of his right hand came down three times on a fine wooden door, it's green paint holding adamantly against the harshness of the urban atmosphere. The neighborhood wasn't bad, and Jorj had certainly seen worse, but if someone bet him the cops only came around when the news crews did, why would he throw his money away?

Of course, first he would have to find some coin to so endanger.

Through the wooden barrier, a testament to better times and more noble architecture, he heard footsteps and two voices, one unhurried, the other urgent, demanding. The former belonged to a female Jorj never met, so it was hardly surprising when the door opened and the eyes on the other side displayed nothing but stealthy caution. When Jorj saw her face, at once beautiful and fiercely suspicious, he understood why he was here. She lifted one eyebrow, a dark line on skin the color and texture of good, rich coffee. "Can I help you?" The tone neither implied genuine courtesy nor was it particularly inviting. In fact, it was clear she wanted Jorj to go away.

He smiled, his disarming good nature at war with his arcane mission. His words produced themselves slowly and deliberately. "Maybe, but I think that I am here to help you."

Her frown heralded the closing door. It slammed in his face without a Ms. Manners' 'No thank you.' Jorj knocked again to the tune of her yelling "Go away or I'm calling the cops!" Immediately an exchange took place on the other side and the urgent voice, the one belonging to an angry black man, barked an oath, instigating footsteps, hers, on a return path to the door. Jorj waited patiently. It opened in a quick, casual lurch. "Come in." She offered no more welcome than before, but the door was open and she did not bar his way.

Three steps past the door he had a gun to his head, the right temple, pressed firmly enough to leave a flesh indent for minutes afterward. "Before I withdraw this lead spitter," a familiar voice demanded, "tell me why I should."

"Why spoil a winning pattern?"

The gun pulled away. Jorj chanced a glance to his right. Out of the shadows, Willie Bender emerged, the pistol, too small and smart for a man of his stature, now leveled at his midsection. The man tilted his head quizzically, almost in disbelief, with the beginnings of a stunned smile burning fiercely through the dim ambience of light from a room further down the hall, probably the dining room or kitchen. "What," he exclaimed, as if even this confounded his own weird day, "are you doing here?"

"I need you to come back."

Laughter came slow at first, but it did come. It was harsh, acid, and full of denial. "Watchman! I never figured you to be stupid! Why start now?"

"That's not my call. You drew me here." Jorj turned to face him more directly, eyeing the deadly caliber with due respect. "Shoot me, I'll go back; that simple. The choice, I believe, is entirely yours, but I don't go back until you send me or we go together."

Willie turned his gaze sidelong, his smile still wide and toothy white within his dense facial hair. "Fine line between brave and stupid, Watchman. Which is it?" He waited and then cut off any further chance of an answer with a short, stifled sigh. He turned his head towards the woman, backed tensely against the wall next to the front door, and made a request. "We need some coffee." His smile, nothing more than a fading bit of frost in the sun, held on a moment longer. He squinted his eyes in a short visual slang, communicating an inside joke lost to Jorj. "Creole, if you would please, dear?"

"Shut up, Willie." She sled past them in a hurry, as if they might grab her, or catch her skin on fire. In another two seconds she was in the lit room down the hall. The pistol shook twice in the same direction, commanding Jorj to follow in the woman's wake. Venting a short puff of air from his nostrils, Jorj complied, curious that the gun should matter to him now at all.

Like the rest of the house, the kitchen typified lower middle class America during the eighties, complete with dingy, cigarette-stained, hold-over wallpaper from the decade before. The woman, middle-aged and thin, filled a glass coffee pot while staring out through a window that looked upon the dim siding of another house less than ten feet away. In the center was a matching, out-dated table and chairs. It was towards the table that Willie wagged the gun, and Jorj, smiling sarcastically, picked a chair on the wide side of the oval and sat down before the remnants of the night's dinner. All that was left on the plate in front of him was a piece of gristle. Once it had been a steak. "Got anymore of this?" he asked. His mouth watered. The temptation to eat the gristle surprised him.

"Don't you have money, Mister?" The woman, still not short on introduction, half turned with one eyebrow raised disapprovingly. "I don't run a diner here."

"This is my sister Darlene," Willie introduced her to Jorj, his face trimmed with a sarcastic cut. His hand lowered the barrel of his weapon more casually. He stared at it a moment, frowned irritably, and raised a withering look at the woman. "Fix the man a bagel, D." Next to him, against the wall under a cheap, plastic clock, was another table, small and with a drawer. He slid the latter out and placed the pistol in it, shutting the drawer afterward. His stare leveled on Jorj, one eyebrow raised with a slight, humorless smile. "Guess I don't really need that at the moment."

"Why don't you fix him up?" Darlene slid the coffee pot onto the hot plate of the maker. "Can't see I'm busy?"

"Woman, your as much a pain in the ass as you were before I got . . . " His mouth puckered and he glanced uncomfortably at Jorj. "Bagels are in the Fridge," he grunted. His hands went up to cover his face in a frustrating rub.

"Willie tell you where he's been?" Jorj asked, a determined intent underlying the mock playful tone in his voice.

"He don't tell me nuthin. Man mind's his own business." A wall hid what she really thought, but Jorj saw through it. Things were easier on this side, and harder too, but for different reasons. Three steps carried him to a refrigerator prowl, no time or patience to be an overly formal houseguest. "Onion bagels…nice!" He grabbed the margarine, knowing it was bad for him, hardly caring. "Knife?"

"How 'bout I stick it in your back?" She looked like she would do it, but he rightly judged the skill with which she bluffed. He followed her eyes to a drawer and made for that.

"He'll just come back," Willie groaned, his hands still across his face. "He's like a fucking cat."

"Well he ain't my cat." Darlene glowered at the strange, hungry man trespassing in her kitchen. "Food costs money. I don't need to be feedin' your underworld scum."

"Hey!" Jorj whipped around, butter knife in hand, balancing the bag of bagels and the margarine in the other. He was well aware how his clothes reflected her well-guided but inaccurate opinion. "You don't know what we're messed up in, but I guarantee you, it ain't crime. Don't judge me!"

"Mmm!" She smiled for the first time, but it was high and without an ounce of trust. "My brother don't hang with nobody but that they're dirty."

Jorj suddenly grinned, and it had the affect of both startling the woman, and nearly disarming her with its psychotic genuineness. "Change always comes first with a knock, and then a crash. Sometimes they're so close together you don't see it, but when you finally can't ignore it anymore, take a good look, 'cuz there's nowhere else to go at that point but bullshitville. He's a better man than you ever knew."

Now it was her lips that pouted. Her eyes, suspicious but caught in the spider strands of doubt and wonder, rolled towards her brother who still covered his face. "He been actin' funny, I'll give you that." Then, quite easily, she turned her gaze back on the strange white guy in her kitchen. "You talk crazy."

Her finger clicked the coffee maker on and out of the room she walked, just like that.

"I should kill you." Willie splayed his fingers so he could look at Jorj. "I should."

"But you won't." Jorj found the toaster and pried the first bagel apart so he could stuff the halves in the slots. "No one kills a hungry man 'til he's done eating unless he's a complete asshole." He stopped, shrugged, and then continued. "You ain't that anymore."

"Don't tell me what I am." The hands came away from the face. His expression turned testament to an old patterned indignation. "You don't know nothing about me, Watchman."

"I'll know even less tomorrow, but tonight, I know all I need to." The toaster popped up. Bagels were ready. Jorj plucked them out gingerly and slathered them with hard, salty, yellow vegetable oil. It was a deliciously disgusting pleasure. "Juice," He exclaimed with a full mouth. "No! Milk!" The one thing that was hardest to come by in the Twilight was cow juice. However brief, Jorj was not going to waste this trip into the blessed lands of Old Earth. He grabbed the fridge door and swung it to.

"You have no right."

"I'm not here on my own recognizance." In fact, it was true. No pledge had he uttered before crossing over from a troubled sleep in the arms of a troubled woman. There was none that could be enough, but he had come anyway, knowing that this was the only way this night, and that there was no one else to do it. One could say he was sent with an unspoken agreement he could not refuse. Whatever God was, It sure knew its business. "The right of which you speak belongs to a longer, stronger arm than mine. Count yourself honored. Someone took notice."

"Yeah!" Willie stood up, forcing the chair away. "And I'm getting' sent back down the river! No fuckin' way, whiteboy!"

"The path up leads back for just a little while." He finished the first half and started on the second. Willie raised his hand to slap it away and then let it hang there, all malign retreating back into the bones within. Jorj hardly acknowledged it. "Stay here, it's a dead end. Die you go down."

"Not fair."

"Don't talk to me about fair," Jorj mumbled between hard chews. "I want to stay here too."

Willie regarded him with pathetic disdain, as much for himself as not. He considered Theo, still scraping old haunts for a foothold. Outside, a siren eased into audibility, getting steadily louder. "That's for me, ain't it.?" There was defeat in his voice, but it was a good kind though he knew it not.

Caught in mid swallow, a glass of cold moo-juice raised high, Jorj shrugged innocently. When he finished, and the glass was lowered, the sirens were much closer. "Make a decision."

"Damn you, Watchman."

"Decide, William."

Lights pressed through the edges of drawn shades, red and strobe-like. The walls and ceiling marbled where the urgent light bathed in the unfriendliness of cold, impersonal authority. Darlene came rushing into the kitchen to find it empty of the men once there, but not their wake. The margarine still lay on the counter next to the sink, uncovered with the butter knife impaling the hard yellow slab within. Bagels built a nice tower out of their bag as if waiting turns at the toaster. At the front door, someone knocked, loud and intentional.

24

He woke in her arms again, just as he left them. She seemed not to have noticed, though he was sure she must have. No sooner did he come to this conclusion then her fingers tighten. She was glad he was back.

"Did you find what you were looking for?" she whispered, half asleep. The darkness still ruled, and she was loath to tempt it from where it crouched by the lingering coals of their once vigorous fire.

"After a brick and a good meal."

"What?" She was more awake now, fingers moving to rub sand from tight, packed corners.

"Never mind. Go back to sleep." He certainly wanted to. His stomach didn't feel filled, but his spirit did. He smiled quietly. "Winter's over for awhile." He wasn't sure she understood, but it didn't matter. Gradually he drifted, as did she, but not before a finger tapped him on the shoulder. At least he thought it was a finger, and what bothered him about the matter entirely was that it was not his own nor did it belong to Greta. One eye opened. Outside, at the edge of the coals, an imp crouched on the grass, puffing a fag with a determined, troubled presence. Jorj rolled his eyes. "I'll be back." She shifted, releasing her hold on him. Perhaps she thought he needed to piss. Just as well. He probably did.

"What are you doing here?"

The imp regarded him callously, his former sarcasm either deceased or in exile. "The question *is*," he grunted, what are *you* doing?"

"Trying to sleep." Jorj squatted by the coals and ran a stick through them. They smelled of impurities. The wood they burned came mostly from coated furniture.

"No, stupid. Why are you out here? Where are you going? What's the grand motivation?"

"Which question should I answer first?"

"All three."

He heaped what coals were left into a pile and watched their glow brighten. Satisfied for the moment, he threw the stirring stick on top. "None of your business."

"Really?" The imp named Richie stared at him in disbelief and then glanced at the remains of Jorj's burning pile. "Save one of those for your head then."

"Huh?" He had the urge to hit the child, for child this was truly not, at least it was not in the strictest sense of the word.

"Something's waiting for you that you're not going to like. Keep going down this road and you'll see."

His interest caught finally, Jorj refocused. "What is it?"

"Who is it? An old friend, and he's pissed."

"Jed? Benedict?"

The imp smiled coldly. "Would you change your mind if I told you? Turn back with your tail between your legs?"

"I think not," Jorj replied stiffly. "Why the half-warning?"

"Greta deserves something. She was good to me."

"You can cross over, you know." Jorj extended a hand.

"Kidding, right?" Richie's sarcasm threatened to reignite. There were so many things he could say. "Isn't it enough what happened to Sid?" He turned away, frowning. The cigarette in his small fingers, mostly neglected, dropped a load of ash to the ground.

"Sid was a good man, smart and practical." He stressed the next part. "Few words." Richie turned sharply on him but said nothing. Jorj continued. "Don't even tell me he can't come back. We both know better than that, don't we Richie?"

Again, silence.

"Just like Jed? And how about the old man...I saw him once or twice."

"I gotta go."

"Just like that? We're just getting started."

Someone coughed to the left and Jorj flicked his attention away, realizing it was Dennis in the Cab. When he turned back, the imp was gone. Old trick, that. For a moment, he stared down at the last of the night's warm ashes. No light was left in them save the stray flecks of red which died one by one in the chill breeze. He shivered, turning slowly away towards the trailor and the woman within. What was he taking them all into? Richie avoided that. Only a malign existence, vaguely indicated. He was correct to ask him if it would stop him though. It would not. There was only one way out of this place, and though he could not see the eye of the needle yet, thread it he must. If he was unable to do that...

Morning came with dwindled food supplies and a general return of the native gray pall on the senses. Dreams don't last forever, and neither do their effect on things. Jorj walked up to the highway, elevated from the trailer havoc below. The sun made everything brilliant. Even the clouds above were edged in sharp white fire as they voyaged across the great azure sea. Thunder welled up, slow and gradual. There was no need to turn, for Jorj knew who was coming up to see him. "Good morning, Father."

"What's good about it?" The Padre released himself from Bill's guiding hand and stood up next to Jorj, judging position by the sound of his voice and deftly covering the three feet of uneven ground without tripping. It was an acquired skill.

He sighed. "Don't make me think so hard so early." Off in the distance, the shadow of a passing cloud stretched across the highway, pouring out a sharp border between illumination and non. Jorj studied it silently and the Padre listened to the sound of his breathing. When the shadow passed, Jorj turned abruptly. His eyes scanned the area of their temporary habitation below. Something was missing. "Bill?"

"Yes, Jorj."

"Where's the Bat?"

"Gone."

"I can see that. Why is it gone?"

"Because Willie took it."

"Willie's dead," the Padre interjected.

Not having an argument for the obvious, Bill simply repeated his answer.

"When did you see him, Bill?" Jorj cast his gaze back up and down the highway, and at the chain link fence on both sides. No breach in them, as far as he could see. "And which way did he go...and why the hell didn't any of us hear him leave?" The last question blurted out in an almost angered pitch.

Their mechanic stumbled mentally, tripping over each interrogation. It seemed impossible not to stutter.

"Easy, boy," Padre found him and took him by the arm.

"N-no," Bill shook his head. "I just remembered, he used to watch me too, in the shop…" The big man turned away. "He made all kinds of noise this morning, just after first light. I tried to wake you all up but you just lay there like you was dead."

"Jeezuss!" It was too much for Jorj to accept. "I woke up <u>with</u> the sun, Bill. I even…" Something came back. There was a roar, a bike bursting away, breaking free with a rider down the way they would be going. "Alzheimer's."

"It's coming apart, isn't it?" Padre sniffed the air as if it would confide something to him the others could not hear. "Fraying thread by thread."

Jorj looked at Bill. The big man only stared at the ground, numb from the neck up. When he looked back at the Padre's scarred face again, he thought he saw the trace of a smile.

"Nick warned me this might happen," the priest went on. "He said that this world was held together with nothing stronger than scotch tape, and that it wouldn't last forever."

"You lost me, father."

"Slippage, I suppose." He regarded Jorj sightlessly. "You can't depend on firm boundaries anymore. If things made not much sense before, they'll make even less from here on in. Hell is a madness of the soul, and our twilight might be crumbling into it as we speak."

"Hmm." Jorj considered this, and then spat on the asphalt, two feet from the dotted white line. "Guess we'd better get going then, huh, Padre?" He started back down the shoulder of the highway to the grass, nudging Bill as he passed the man. "Saddle up, bud."

Broken egg that it was, the trailer gave up its rotten yolk to them and was left behind. Little satisfied by its offerings, the five men and one woman took to the road in a path following Willie Bender, unaware that their next meeting with the former right hand of Theodore would be their last in this world, and that, for good or ill, the final chapter of their Twilight existence, indeed in their collective company, was almost over.

It came up over the horizon of a miles-long stretch of highway, blended at first with the distance, but then obviously an unnatural span of all lanes, east and west. Jorj pulled the Roadrunner over onto the right shoulder after the next exit was found to be blocked, keeping the engine running. He stepped out casually, but his demeanor was one of deadly seriousness and suspicion. "Dennis," he called behind him. You and Bill come out and watch both sides of the highway as best you can for anything out-of place. Everyone else stay in your seats." In the trunk, he rummaged until he located his binoculars and then carried them to the front of the car. Bill held vigilence over the north, Dennis the south.

What blocked the highway could best be described as a large fortification built with concrete and wood. Several cars, their condition impossible to determine, pointed their noses at the western wall, parting in the middle where the highway on the other side could be accessed through a square gate, open and large enough to accommodate a tractor trailer. Jorj cursed under his breath. Richie could have just told him the details, saved them the back-tracking. ""Okay, we turn around and find another way east. "I don't like the looks of what we have ahead of us."

"What is it, chief?" Dennis asked the obvious question for everybody.

"Toll booth," Jorj replied.

"No kidding?"

"No kidding." He lowered the binoculars, keeping his eyes leveled ahead. "Get in, both of you."

One hundred and eighty degrees burned a black arc against the pavement. In the span of a heartbeat, what was ahead was now behind them and growing smaller. "We'll get off at the next exit..." Jorj's words stopped abruptly and his foot went to the brake, lurching them all forward.

"What the hell is that?" Dennis leaned even further to the fore and gripped the top of the front seat so hard the vinyl squeaked between his straining, bony fingers. His stomach, now trespassing into the territory of his throat in warlike fashion, threatened a solidly unsatisfying vomit. He knew what it was, or at least that he had seen it before and knew as much as any of them did. The vinyl cried noisily as his nails dug in deeper. "Jorj?"

Any answer that welled up immediately lost its grip and fell away. The man at the wheel, his gut urgently warning him of an old familiar, seemingly irrational fear, spun the car around again under a protest of screaming tires and gunned the engine. Suddenly, the fortified barrier grew before them.

"What's happening.? Anyone?" The Padre turned left and right, hoping for a sign. Bill answered him, his voice strangely monotone. "It's Soulstealer."

"Who? What?" Jorj yelled now, racing towards the barricaded exit, debating in seconds the unlikelihood of their survival should they attempt to run through its cinderblock wall. At the last, for it was quite close, he slowed quickly and then skidded to a stop. His intent was to abandon the car, have everybody hop the barrier, and run like the devil himself was after them. Perhaps the old bastard was, he mused.

Before he could speak, Greta grabbed him by the arm. "Drive," she pleaded. It was clear she was not immune to the fear he felt, but something below the surface waters of her voice demanded that he do as she demanded. "Drive straight to the end of the highway as fast as you can. Do not stop for anything…" When he stared at her as if she was crazy, even though he knew she wasn't, she slugged him in the shoulder with her small fist in desperation. "Go! What are you waiting for? It gets closer every second we sit here!" Her face, a shadow of heaven since her rebirth, was contorted in a way Jorj never saw before. His foot hit the gas in response, even before his eyes saw where the Roadrunner was taking them.

They could have gone off the road at that point, further than the shoulder and into the grass, maybe even the chain link fence down the incline, but luck treated them to a 'gimme' and the tires brought them up onto the road in a thunderous roar. One glance in the mirror confirmed his worst fear for the moment. That thing, that horrible thing, was almost on their bumper.

A little girl screamed from the back seat, terrible in the high pitched lack of testicular fortitude. Frank, himself too frightened to slap Dennis, clung to Bill. Mike's Mechanic simply stared dumbly ahead.

Where were the wise words, Jorj wondered in his adrenaline crazed, near panic? Why didn't Ogam's elfishly mischievous voice, or Nick's gently compassionate one, speak now in his head, encouraging him where he could find no courage at all? Only his heart hammered within, a cold, merciless accomplice to the terror in their wake. Above the roar of the Roadrunner's engine there mingled, tentacle-like, a belled dissonance, fever-dreamed, hallucinogenic tones promising ice cream summers, but offering something else entirely and very darkly different. Frozen were those unsung words, with no hint of sweetness in them at all.

One by one, to the perplexed dismay of everyone in the muscle car, Jorj's runes peeled away, each ripping the air in their release with a strangled cry. The fortification, now plainly visible by every eye that could see, flew up to meet them; three hundred yards, two hundred yards...

Only the circle and Jorj's hand struggled, anchored to the car but rippling in the wind. A moan, eldritch and appalling, rose up from them. When only one hundred yards remained before sure annihilation, with everyone's screams silent or bleedingly unstoppable, the sky dimmed, darkened, and suddenly they were through, passing where should have been their catastrophic demise. Whether by instinct or something more divine, Jorj's hand flicked the headlamps on, grimacing when he saw the legion of potholes hurtling at his tires. In motions that surely would have sent the car into a roll had another been at the wheel, the first five pavement craters were narrowly avoided. The sixth shook them, the seventh, like a seal broken, snapped something beneath them and the car went out of control. It bounced horridly and landed in a sideways skid, spinning the night around them in a wide semicircle and then backwards down an embankment. The Circle, and his handprint, resettled themselves, their voices dying to silence in the new night. They had come to a dead, dark stop.

Knowing it mattered hardly a jot, Jorj found a pistol, shoved down between the door and the seat, and exited the vehicle. Almost immediately a searchlight felt around blindly from above. The whir of chopper blades joined it like locusts. Jorj knew beyond a shadow of a doubt that such blindness could not last forever. "Where the fuck is Willie?" He found himself saying, counting heads as the others got out. Why he asked he couldn't say, though he thought he knew the answer. No way the man got out the way they did. Instead, he switched to another, hoarsely shouted question. "What just happened here? Gret!"

She took his arm and they found shelter in a marshy, foul-smelling stream below, about thirty yards to the east. It seemed everyone was in tow. "We're in the netherworld," she answered finally, as if it needed saying. "It was the only way."

"You did this?" Jorj was incredulous, and it was difficult not to shout now.

Something rose up between them. It was her shame. "I said it was the only way! Did you want to face that…"

"Of course not!" He barked sharply. There was something more than adrenaline at work here. The place leached evil into one's soul. Quickly, defiantly, he exhaled. He had to resist what it was already trying to do to him. "Why is it dark already?"

"It's always dark here." She was crying. The words came wet and despairing. "It is shunned by the light."

"Then we leave." Jorj watched above. The beam was from a helicopter alright, but not from the like he ever saw before. It moved with a serpentine fluidity, and there were arms attached to it. Technology, twisted, had found a place in a nightmare world, and it hunted them now, a predator with a new scent to follow.

"Where's the Padre?" Dennis started out of the weeds. Jorj gripped him by the belt and pulled him back into the fragile hiding place. "Goddammit Jorj!" He fought desperately to loosen the vise-like hold. "The Father's gone missing!"

Strong and sure, Bill wrapped his arms around Dennis. "Padre said to stay down!"

"What?" Jorj pulled himself closer to the two men and glared at the big one severely, aware that the beam searched them out, closer...closer. "When did he...?"

An engine turned...turned...and then chugged enough to pick up a crooked rhythm. It was desperate at first, like the cough of a cancerous lung, but then it built momentum, and with each piston feed, each one that would undoubtedly be among the last, the headlights found the juice to blaze on, challenging the creature above to a final showdown.

His horror took hold, horror at the return of choice, choice of living or dying, and who would receive the results of each. Within the trunk of the Roadrunner, an unseen fire burned as it had for countless millennia. Quite possibly only he understood what was going to happen next. "Go!" He shouted, dragging the two men to their feet and pushing them east down the stream. Not waiting to see if they would keep going, he found Greta, hoisted her to her feet, and forced her by the elbow before him in the same direction. "The slow don't make it out of here! Get going! Mother of God! Run like hell if you want to live!"

When she resisted, it was for her father, and she called out to him now. The Padre, bathed in lights both ambient and directly brilliant, hesitated momentarily in his smile, and then fumbled to put the car in drive. It's complaints were many, and its ability almost gone, but it creaked forward, at first slow, but then faster, clunking down the road like the derelict it had become. He steered it away from the sound of her voice until he could hear it no more. "That's it, child. I'll do what should have been done a long, long time ago."

Fire spat from the starless sky. At first, it merely punctured the hood and the roof, spilling blood and oil, slowing, and then bringing both tragic heroes, machine and man, to a defeated halt. Then, as if it sensed something far more dangerous, it focused its rain of death on the trunk, and as it did so, fire erupted from within that small space, shooting skyward in a pillar of white plasma to meet the aggressor above. In a pulse, everything in between, and for a considerable distance around, vaporized. What did not fall into this sphere of fiery oblivion wished that it had. Beyond that found luck like no other before, and what good there was in it spanned the impossible, breaking asunder the bridge of time and space behind.

The darkness that lay on the land was less than a moment ago, as if the sun, still crouched below the treeless horizon, had advanced a bit farther and stopped cold. All around them felt like a mortuary. Were it not for the tall grass they found for shelter, the illusion would be complete. Jorj lurched with each regurgitation, his stomach's sidewalls slapping together in a most horrid fashion. Several feet away to his left, Greta did the same. There was no sound of the others, and that, somehow, made it all worse.

"You led us out." His words scraped by dry chunks of vomit, acid in his throat. His skin blistered with a midnight burn. It might kill him. Then again, it might not.

She nodded twice, shakily. Much more she could not manage. Life had blessed them, but at great cost to her.

"Dennis! Bill!" Jorj recovered himself just enough to shout one more name. "Frank!" Greta's hackled coughs answered him, but nothing else did. "Didn't make it..."

Her head shook and she sputtered. Grief always agitated sickness. She collapsed on her side, weakness finally claiming her and forcing upon her an insecure rest.

Death walked this land. Each felt it as much as they did in the nether-Mosswood. She took them too far, and both knew it. That she could guide them through a veil, not only once but twice since her rebirth, came as a shock to Jorj, and he wondered that she could not, or chose not to lead them out of Mosswood's nether shadows when Theo was still with them. It wasn't a question for the asking now. Instead, he struggled to marshal himself. They would need every bit of strength they could summon, and he feared most of it would be his own.

His hands found his love and gathered her to him. A coldness lingered in her response, though she clung to him loosely. Something between them had changed, as if in her sliding through existences a portion of her soul was torn away. Still, he caressed what was there, knowing that he must save her, and that it wasn't her fault. "We must get back home," he whispered, his voice shaking. "You're the only one that can do it."

Almost imperceptibly, her head shook. "Cannot…" she managed to murmur.

Jorj held her a little tighter. "Then show me. Use my strength to get us there."

A wind picked up of a sudden and the moon, a big, bloated, yellow tooth, broke through whatever passed for clouds here. Jorj looked up in alarm, for it watched them with malice, and if it did, others did also. He lay low, covering Greta with his body until the leering blob fell behind cover of its own. It would be back soon enough.

"Greta," His chest quivered, the moorings to his heart in disrepair. "You can't give up…I don't know what happened, how you did it…what you used to do so easily, but you have to do it again."

"Nooo!" She moaned like an animal, her soul caught in a snare, broken and hopeless. "I can't! I can't!"

"We can't stay here," Jorj pressed. "Ogam gave us the way out, but it starts on the twilight side. One more good push and we're there." He studied her tormented features, searching for the words that would trip the lock within. "I'll be with you, Greta. Take my strength."

"You know how," she answered, sobbing. "You always have."

"No Gret!" His urgency welled up harsh. "I don't! I'm lost here. I've always been lost. That's why I need you. Can't you see that?" He realized as the words spilled out, that what he was saying meant many things beyond their immediate need, but he didn't care. Damned the logic, or illogic, of the situation. His heart pumped forth antidote to the poison around them, if only for the moment. This, he felt, was his...their only chance. "I'd give my life...my true life for you."

"Don't say that!" Her face buried itself in his chest and she clutched him with a stubborn passion he feared was gone. Her cries heaved out of her, muffled by his body, and for awhile, it's all she could do. When she pulled away, a shadow passed and Jorj felt the waters draw back from the shoreline of the present, portending a terribleness he could not stop. Her eyes, glazed and blind to all but a purpose born out of sacrifice, regarded nothing he could see. Her fingers found his lips and touched them softly. Jorj's heart flew into panic, his body too paralyzed to obey the warning command it cried so urgently. Ghostlike, her words floated to him as the world brightened to full day. "Come back for me, my love."

He was alone. The wind, fanning the tall grass in daylight near I-90, caressed his own long hair in mockery of her fingers, and though the dark weight upon his spirit was lifted away, another burden replaced it. Like an animal, he threw his forehead into the dirt and groaned in anguish, rending the soil with his fingers. Only a few hours before they had all been together. Now, he was bereft of her also. What had he done? What did he ask her to do? A voice, the darkest, most personal one we fear, whispered that he could not go on, and he caved to it. Had someone walked up to him then, and for hours to come, they could have killed him and he would have done nothing to stop them.

No one did.

Night came, but with it the moon and stars. No bloated bag of puss was this orb. It was a step removed from the old one, and the strength within it, the haunting link to what men call divine, called to him. Heavy-hearted, he rolled over and stared at it, finding a steady, numb stability in the focus of it. Several times he broke down, yet each time his well refilled a little higher, until finally he could hear that other voice, the one deeper in, where all things live and breath the stuff of gods. His road went on when he was ready for it. In no way could it be denied. All who fell to get him there demanded that he walk it to its end.

Once, what seemed ages ago, in fact only weeks, the night meant different things to him than it did Dennis, Nick, and Frank. Even Greta did not see it the way he did, and perhaps it marked a difference between all of them, and why he was considered so pivotal. Dumbly, he stared at the stars, and then the grass, seeing no more meaning in what brought them together than he did why he was here in the first place. He rose to his feet and stood against the wind, gathering strength in opposition. That was what he was about, he supposed: opposition. Every turn, a shackle presented itself in his life, each new thing threatened to sucker him, imprison him somehow, exploitation and stagnation of the soul. For that reason, no religion ever held sway, never gained the ground he himself claimed. His was a bleak land, but in a sense, pure, waiting for the right thing that never came. Now he scanned the line where land met sky, wondering if it was there even now. Slowly, ever so slowly, his feet started walking, dragging him along on a dark gray path.

A watcher appeared, manifested as a shadow, a silhouette against the silvered landscape. It followed at a distance, staying just close enough to not be missed. Jorj knew he would not be alone. It was why he walked now, for he needed not to be alone in his thoughts, even if he was not among friends. With a mix of sadness and relief, he wondered if it was Richie, or maybe one of the imp's 'friends.' Almost any one of them would do right about now.

The night held a mix, monsters and lost ones, failed souls of different fashions. He learned that from the start. And although others recoiled at the terrors of the night, fear was not a presence for which Jorj was particularly vulnerable, especially now. What he found he could not ignore, or be numb to as he was other things this night, his personal darkest, were the mutterings, for they were louder, more demanding of his attentions. It was true what the Padre said. The Twilight was on the verge of collapsing into hell, or at least the next closest existence. Would they all crush into that evil place like falling dominoes? Cratering down into the depths of darkness, leaving a cloud of dust and smoke made up of every regretful, shameful soul ever to be caught in the cataclysm? It was impossible not to care, if for no other reason than that one very close to his heart would be its eternally damned prisoner, never to see even the ambient light of heaven again. That he could not, would not tolerate.

Ghostly headlights approached from behind, and he turned to watch them, offering no other response. As they passed, pushing no wind before them, leaving no in-sucking swirl of air in its wake, he saw no car behind those wavering, illuminated disks, and no visible driver in tow. It was not surprising. The overlap here fluttered in a non-corporeal breeze, and travelers would slip in and out all night with unequal effect. All of it, scarcely of interest to him, served as a shallow distraction.

Overhead, the great wheel turned. The moon rose and fell, dragging stars in its great net back down into the deep blue sea, away from that nigh-immortal slayer of darkness, the warrior of gold named Sol. That he was forced to confront feelings of emptiness again, triggered by his first morning alone under an obliviously smiling sun, need not be described. Jorj may not have seen what others saw, but it was his spiritual constitution that made him a survivor, and it was this that kept him going even now on the path he started weeks ago.

Away west he saw the line of fortification across the highway, and he cursed it darkly. It was the cause of his pain, the reason his circle of companions lay broken and scattered. He wanted to vow destruction upon it, to raze it to the ground someday, but such wishes were fairytale musings. He was not returning, and he had nothing now to knock it over but a small pistol with one clip. His attention turned to the weapon, still stuffed in his back pocket, and he drew it out. What had Greta said concerning guns? He couldn't remember exactly, but she had warned him. And what she said to Theo in the graveyard: "You won't walk that path ... Violent thoughts led you here." There was a stonily honest echo reverberating now, however indirect. He threw the pistol as hard and far as he could towards the great concrete wall a mile away. In the distance it clattered on the hard pavement. Let them have it and choke on it. He'd finish this as he started it, depending only on himself.

Before noon his feet, tired but resolute, carried him to the top of a long rise. From that vantage point, the highway stretched southeast for miles, and about three quarters of the distance to the horizon, a dot broke the light gray of the narrowing asphalt. What it was he couldn't tell, but it was the only thing there, and the highway dipped just before it. The absence of his gun struck him then. His senses were returning, despite his heavy grief. Ths was too soon to have his mission threatened. Any time was too soon.

"You over-react," he chastised himself, his voice wedged with grit. Face it when you get there."

The next exit sign he passed told him nothing, having both number and location blasted down to the bare metal. What a shotgun started, wind, sun, and rain finished. Escaping where he could not, the off-ramp veered away to its home, leaving him to his own business. Away left, beyond the endless chain-link fence, woods and neglected farms ruled the landscape, small kingdoms without lords or ladies. Round bales of hay, swept up in the torrential growth of forgotten fields, waited for the horses that didn't, and never would, come to this place. 'Silly rabbit,' Jorj heard Dennis' voice in his head, 'Twilight's not for animals.'

A small stream trickled to the right and Jorj, thirsty, hopped the fence and descended to it. The water ran clear here so he drank, tasting nothing at all but appreciating the coldness of it. When he was satisfied, he climbed back over to the highway and continued on his way.

He reached the place where the highway dipped. The way was long, and it took him a full twenty minutes to span it. When he emerged, he saw that ahead of him, maybe no more than a good ten-minute walk at his own unhurried pace, was a black man on an armored motorcycle. Willie Bender tipped his head once. It appeared he was waiting.

Some might have called them enemies, others distantly respectful comrades. Whatever the appearance, the uneasiness they once felt before seemed rather petty now to them both. Truth and awareness were bitter teachers, but what they taught could not be ignored, and neither man was so stubborn that he could deny what was his lot in it all. "Get on," Willie said plainly, his tone betraying nothing of either malice or benevolence.

Jorj climbed on behind him, noting with surprise that the leather of the man's jacket was warm from the sun, and that when the other man spoke, he exhaled no steam. "They're all dead, you know."

"I know."

He wanted to ask the obvious question. An anger welled up, threatening to flow out the recent breach in his soul, but he shored up the rift and recovered, knowing that such feelings now were unfit, too small for the larger matter both men were here for. It didn't matter how Willie Bender made it past the road block fortification. Here he was, better for the wear. As they took off just south of the sun's wake, one thing was clear to Jorj. Everything that he'd been pushed towards was almost over. By the end of this day, or possibly the next, salvation or damnation would stand alone on the battlefield, declaring itself the victor.

The rest was a blur of farms and woodlands, towns and shopping malls, intersections blown through without stopping for traffic lights, incredibly long stretches of neighborhoods, granite cobblestone walls, and ultimately the smell of the sea. The seasonal tourist town of Hampton hit them cold and gray, the sun playing hide and seek but mostly hide. Each wave carried itself forcefully, born on a stiff, off-shore wind. Willie and Jorj rode the Bat through the once crowded ocean-side town, grateful only for the change in scenery. Anything different was a relief, and the sea cast its own spell on all who came within its well of influence, moving them to its own ceaseless rhythm.

Late afternoon straddled evening when Willie pulled the bike to a stop, dead center of Route 1A. He kept the engine running and turned his head to the side. "End of the road for you, Watchman. I have another appointment."

Numb in both body and mind, whipped mercilessly by the long wind, Jorj dismounted, swaying with a dizzy step backward. "One day we'll need to settle up on a few things," he remarked. ""If secrets matter anymore, I'd like to drag them out into the open and let the sun put an end to them."

Willie smiled. It wasn't the wicked one he usually offered, nor was it a false one. In it, Jorj thought there was a cold respect, and fatigue for what was their lot. Also, and most importantly, there was hope in it, that there might actually come a time when they would stand again as comrades and measure their shared past with the yardstick of truth. "Good seeing you again, Watchman." He pulled away, turned the bike around, and then lit it up, tearing the southern road with a blaze of deafening fire. Jorj watched him go and then studied his surroundings, unsure where to go next.

North, something moved within him, as a voice might. His feet, in response, began walking, dispelling slowly the effects of the long motorcycle ride. Another couple hours and he would find the end of the road, his road. What lay there he didn't know, but it pulled him towards it like a swirl of gravity, an in-suck of water he could not, would not swim out of. Destiny, he knew well, would not be denied. If it was hell, he'd stand against it forever. If heaven, well…he'd see.

25

He arrived on the shore at sunset. On another coast, the view would be breathtaking in about three hours. Here it was still beautiful, but not quite the same. Yet there was a special quality to it, if one could call it that, and most of that could be blamed on the sky, one new to him, if only for his having changed locations.

Rye Beach attracted the more philosophical souls on Old Earth. It was a place of rock and stones, outcroppings which defied the ocean tide, and harbored hordes of tiny crustaceans. In the Twilight, only their shells dwelled among the clefts and hollows. Seaweed, green and thick, formed large patches of slimy carpet. By late evening Jorj found his way here and walked down to the water's edge. The tide was up, following the moon in its irresistible gravitational net. When Jesus approached the first of what were to be his disciples, Jorj mused, he must certainly have felt the momentum at work here.

A sailor's delight, some used to call it, for crimson portended fair weather for the next day's morn. Jorj found little joy in what he saw. He was alone, and that could not be paid for with anything of value as he saw it. She told him he would come here, and that his fate would be thus, or might be. Somehow those words she spoke, whether in dream or distant reality, never sank their full weight onto his shoulders, and maybe rightly so, for could he have carried on otherwise? He thought not. On the waters, cut like moving glass, lay mingled across on those dark waves the blood of the sky. A single tear, unbidden, unwanted, and certainly unwelcome, found a path down his cheek as he stared out into what he was sure must be the oblivion of his soul. What had any of them done, he asked creation, to deserve the evil that befell them in the days leading up to this?

Into his hovering despair, a vision intruded, as displeasing as the tear he presently wiped away with the back of his right hand. Like the tear, the vision seemed very real, and some thirty feet out from the shoreline ahead of where Jorj stood. It rose from the waves, man-shaped, and did not stop until its feet were melded with the unsettled surface. Details, cloaked in shadow and distance, betrayed nothing, but a voice resonated from the thing that Jorj knew well, and with it came memory of destinies intertwined in darkness.

"Such a long way to come for nothing." The vocal chords belonged to Benedict, but the master of them was someone else entirely. This much could not be hidden. When Jorj refrained from a reply, it continued in its malignantly sonorous note. "On a sea of blood come I, also from a distant place." This broke Jorj's silence, for his patience for drama was never robust.

"It's curved sunlight, you asshole. The light gets broken and you get red." He paused, frowning deeper. "Not biblical enough for you?"

It was impossible to be sure whether the body was human, or a mere construct of water. The creature that occupied it seemed as unmoved by Jorj's words as by this missing bit of clarity, for the latter it alone knew the answer to. "Less than an academic explanation," it went on with obvious slight of respect. "But one would expect ignorance to be a prime suspect in your intellectual inabilities."

"Sure," Jorj verbally shrugged, his body as motionless as his confronter. "What do you want?"

"To gloat."

"That's it?" a slight twitch of Jorj's hand incriminated it, for there was a strong desire attached to the idea of finding a stone to throw at the water creature. Though the desire did not diminish, the involuntary nature of the action did, and Jorj, as oblivious of it as he was fear at that point, did not lose his tongue. "Gloat away. While we're at it, Go away too. I expect you won't though so why don't you let me talk to the one you stole the voice from? Is he still in there somewhere? Or did you eat him for lunch?"

The screams that immediately followed were terrible on a level or two beyond shocking. In fact, they had the effect of sending Jorj into the cover of a granite outcropping where the water had eroded many large clefts. He wished then that his request were not made, for Benedict's voice climbed to a hair-raising crescendo. It was the gibbering wail of a tortured man with no hope of succor. When, after what seemed an over-long span, the screaming ceased, the former voice returned, hoarse and gritty, but quite capable of talking through what, to someone, must have been a formidable amount of physical pain. "I am afraid his vocabulary is rather limited these days. His preoccupations do not lend themselves well to the verbose."

Jorj gathered himself together and stepped from the rocks, ashamed that he was so quick to run and hide. If he was expected to wait here for something, if this was in fact that something, then all excuses for encumbered behavior were his for the taking. With the glare of a man who had no more to lose, he approached the water's edge. He remained silent, for there were no words yet fitting what he felt inside. His hands, now at his sides, resisted balling into fists, though the urge to do so was strong.

Slowly, in a move that surprised Jorj, the creature in the guise of water closed in on the shore until it stood just five feet out. It raised an accusing finger, on an arm that seemed to be just a bit too long. The accompanied sound of twisting ropes suggested to Jorj that there was a real body within that circulating sheath of water, and that it was likely Benedict's after all. He doubted, though, that tendons, stretched to the point of nearly snapping, had anything to do with the possessed man's screaming. Inwardly, he shuddered. Benedict was a ruthless asshole on his own, and he certainly asked for his circumstances, but did he deserve them? Did anyone?

The finger did not waver. Benedict's voice croaked for a tone of condemnation. "Oh, Jorj Tory Watchman, I own all of your demons. They give up their secrets willingly, for the wrongs you have committed, and I drink them like sweet wine."

"Keep talking while you drink. Maybe you'll choke on what you don't really know at all." Both of Jorj's middle fingers rose to the occasion, an emphasis that did little to assail the truth he felt dangled from the other's utterances in talismanic fashion. He had to hear this, listen to all of it. This was why he was here.

"Her long torment was your fault, you know." The creature, a demon of the underworld whose soul was now so lost that love and hate had effectively trading places within it, began a movement on the surface of the water that resembled a ritualistic dance. Though the body itself remained motionless, the arm outstretched, the branding finger leveled at the man on the beach like a poisoned sword; as an object, it traced a path over the water, connected only by the soles of the feet, that Jorj was slow to recognize, for the entire spectacle was odd in itself. "The child? His path is ruinous, and all because of you. I will see him soon. He shall join my legions."

Anger and immense sadness churned up a pressure within Jorj's heart, and his eyes welled. How could he argue. Though his hatred of this thing, and even of the man it held in a grasp so blasphemous as to trigger undeserved sympathy, caused his hands to ball into fists, and his arms to tighten, each muscle a tight cord of braided steel, he was essentially disarmed, for he knew the monster spoke true. This was his prosecutor, and the Earth all around, though it be Twilight or no, was judge and jury. As each chain clasped around his limbs, linking him to the drowning stones that were his misdeeds, his mistakes in another life, he felt his strength ebb. In this state of voluntary helplessness, he observed the path which led to his end.

"All dark roads begin with intention, and yours, though it bore the trace scent of nobility, could not escape the stain of misguided good will." There lingered within the words a relish, as if the demon was taking sustenance from them, and perhaps it was, for such beings do not take on the same nourishment as do creatures of the light. "Did you think a change of heart would cleanse your soul? Or that betraying those whom you first took up arms with would undo what had already been set in motion?" The words and laughter that rasped out past Benedicts tortured lips described vocal chords that were nearly shredded. This evening was not the first time the body had been given over to the former owner. "All it did was to set you on another course, one on which you could betray others closer to your heart. Had you not traded your love for something you thought more urgent, neither she nor the child would have fallen into the night, and the priest's soul would have been spared that which caused him to send her there. Do you not see your folly? What is done cannot be undone. Your deeds are empty. Where you sought to achieve good, you have only brought down ruin."

His lips trembled. All of it was his fault. Not all the memories were with him, but enough to incriminate. The men who were behind the bombings, not only in New Jackson City but across the east coast, preached a litany in opposition to corporate enslavement, against the greed that prevented the golden age every human was entitled to. In desperation, men like Jorj, honest, simple men with noble intentions, joined their ranks, seeking the ends with little true consideration of the means. An 'American IRA' the newspapers called their organization. No Robin Hood color, no romance of the French underground in the eyes of the general public. To those who belonged to the organization, they were partisans in a war for the soul of mankind. It took the deaths of innocents for Jorj to see that they were wrong. By that time, he was a courier in possession of something not even the Middle Eastern terrorists had yet been able to acquire. His change of heart, when it came, drew him to the only man who could help him.

"When the good father set fire to his cathedral, did you feel remorse?" The voice was positively death-like now, barely able to produce a semblance of Benedict at all. "Where was the urge to run back inside, to save the woman who was pregnant with your child?"

The memories smote Jorj hard, each one cutting deep, each spilling blood. He dropped to his knees, his hands wringing the air now in his stunned surprise and sorrow. Almost unaware of the creature defiling the water less than ten feet distant, the man covered his face with wrenching fingers. The words were a hypnotic spell of nightmarish telling, and he was helpless against the reality of the path he once walked.

"Think you that she is saved? That your sunrise brought her back to hope?" If one listened to the horrific sounds, evidence of a physically abused prisoner, blood could almost be heard seeping through the raw flesh where no healing, save to draw out the agony, could find purchase. "The night, Master Watchman, was reclaiming her even before she died, as far back as your drive with that preposterous vehicle you thought would protect you. She is quite worse off now, thanks to you, for even the illusion of hope you dangled before her was wrenched away. A taste stolen, you must understand, is more cruel than the one never had in the first place. Now she craves in a very dark place that which she can never have. In fact, I think I can hear her weeping."

"Don't listen to him, Jorj!"

Crouched on a rock, not far from the line where water met sand, the imp Richie took one last drag of the cigarette he'd been smoking and threw it disdainfully into the water. In one smooth motion, he hopped down and ran through the lapping waves to the man who once he loved as a big brother, and did once again. "Don't fucking listen to him! He weaves lies in with the truth!"

Jorj woke as if from a horrid dream, noticing with an unnatural clarity that Richie left footprints in the sand, big, sloppy, cake-like clumps dug out in the wake of each step. His heart was still wretched, but there was life again, at least enough to kick away at the water that threatened to drag him under the surface. The boy reached him with a minor impact, threatening to bowl him over, and hugged him around the waist, uncharacteristic of his previous incarnations. That the sun was down, and the moon was up now, only vaguely occurred to the man to which the boy clung. Delicately, the man put his arms around his hugger, ever aware of the horror that walked the water in mockery of Jesus just three feet out from the shore. Now he saw the path it traced too, a five pointed star, the head of a goat, with the base point aimed directly at himself.

"He'll speak again, Jorj!" The boy yelled, angry and defiant, but urgent in his intentions. "Shut it out! I live! Greta lives! They all do, every last one!" Without hesitation, he added breathlessly: "It will be ok. You turned on the path."

The last wall came down. Every soft place in Jorj's soul suddenly found itself exposed, and in that instant, the arcane atrocity advanced from the water, intent on seizing the moment of weakness it had long waited for. But it did not find that for which it clawed. Richie stood on the beach alone, grinning fiercely, his arms empty but still warm.

"He's gone," the boy said, the broken lance of victory extended before him. The pennant of his words flapped in the breeze that suddenly blew in from the ocean. "You can't have him!"

Rage seethed just below the surface of the demon as it considered the imp's words. With a gentleness that masked the darker intentions of untold depths, it made its reply. "Then I shall have you instead."

"No." The voice was Sid's this time, not Richie's. "You won't have anything at all."

"Heaven is a perfect circle, no beginning, no end. It is our naturally intended state and should not be seen merely as the end of a long road. It is not for those who would quit the work upon finding it but rather that they should continue the way in which it took to get there in the first place. Only then is one worthy of Heaven. Enter the sweet center, the sages say, but do not tarry there, lest it make you unworthy."

—OGAM'S NOTES

Two rivers flow in opposition, neither halting the other's advance. Jorj cannot see them, but his immersion in their turbulent waters makes any attempts to ignore their presence impossible, not that it was what he truly wished to do. He was as much led here by a higher force as by himself. Mighty currents, permeating all things in all possibilities, these rivers are energies, one positive, the other negative. Only in the middle, the lukewarm region one great prophet of antiquity warned his followers of, were their eddies and swirls, a trap of stagnancy for the unwary or ill-advised. The same force that pulled the man away from the bank wrenched him into the undertow, an irreversible situation once set in motion. The speck he knew, and the God he forgot, faced each other like old friends, one in joyous terror, the other in patient waiting. Union was only just begun. There was still confusion, and unasked questions anxiously sought the surface. In so much light as this new ocean drowned him, Jorj seemed blind at first.

But he was not alone.

In a way, they were like half brothers, as in a sense we are all siblings. For now, what made them different drew on common recognition while the rest gathered into itself, waited for the loose threads to untangle. In the moment that the current was at its strongest, he was swept up in a euphoric peace. All existence filled him, and he it. This was the incredible unification he sought from the beginning, though he never once recognized it until now. In the same singular instant of timelessness, Jorj was reborn, or rather, as he finally knew it for what it was, healed. Within that measureless span he floated free until he found himself cast up on the shore of another when, and another where. Light mingled here, producing, or perhaps revealing, shapes, perspective, and then an endless horizon. The soles of his feet touched wetness and he looked down to see water.

A voice spoke now, familiar and pleasant, and the slightly squeaky nature of it could not help but produce humor in the ears of whoever listened. "What would *old* Jorj would say?"

The high was wearing off. In its aftermath was a strength that was almost immeasurable, and a relief. Jorj did not look troubled, but his confusion was evident. "I'm not sure it would be appropriate."

"A river always moves, Jorj. It can't stay at the source for long. You know that."

His expression must have spoken for him, for Jorj considered the answer as if he had already asked it.

"Many heavens, but this is not one. Your water returned to the fountainhead and flowed on through. Heaven is a place of work, after all. It kicks each of us out into where we will be most useful." The tone evened slightly. "Damage and pain are the price. Some pay more, others less, but the work goes on."

"Work? Heaven's supoosed to be about rest."

"Did you think that your water would retire to a sedentary existence . . . a shallow pool? Is that what you wanted?" The voice seemed to come from one side and then the other. All things were truly possible. "Heaven is not a vacation. It is the horizon you saw yesterday and will see again tomorrow."

Jorj sensed disappointment, his own. "It is elusive then."

"Man's soul is elusive. Souls lose their way. Our work is to find and lead them back, as I was found, and in turn found you."

"And God? Why does he let them get lost in the first place?" Suddenly he realized how quickly he was slipping. "Oh."

"It takes time for the child to see the adult within., Jorj."

"I don't understand."

"You will in time. What some call 'God' is the only reality. We are just the bits of it's learning, it's evolution, and if it knows all, sees all, is all, well . . . the 'all' keeps expanding. Frankly Jorj, it makes me dizzy just thinking about it, but there is no contrary truth. *God* does not stagnate."

Up until now, Jorj walked the waters, feeling neither tired nor in any sense of hurry. It was then with a sort of clinical perspective that he considered his next words, but deep within him, growing at an alarming rate, a fire burned, the fire of true life. Old drives, suppressed by this taste of Heaven, began to re-emerge. The time would come, and very soon, when he would swim the dark waters again...his river had to return along its former path. "My friends wander in darkness."

"You must go find them, Jorj. Die again so that you and others may live."

"Will you be here?" He seemed uncertain, unwilling to release what he assumed to be his lifeline.

Ogam smiled behind his disembodied voice. "I already am."

Jorj understood now why the return meant death, for a part of him died that could not be replaced. The virgin soul, innocent in its ignorance, was innocent no longer. Forever he would feel this pain, this utter revulsion, and it would taint the bliss that would suffer with him for eternity, at least the eternity he understood, making it bittersweet, ever-present. To they who dwelt on the long, dark road stretching the distance between heaven and hell, he became a guide. It was up to them to follow or no, and he had been warned. Intent is one thing, disregard another. The acuteness with which he felt everything now made his final state of existence a mixed refuge from the cold gray he never realized was all he had ever before known. A delicious agony, both prize and price.

One last time he looked upon the graffiti sprayed on the highway overpass support column. *Dead Again*. He understood. He understood it now so very well.

But, he conceded, and he did so with a mixture of stubbornness and submission, how could one face the universe, the master of all creation, the great collective of all that ever was, is and will be, and simply exist? Reaching what he once regarded as the finish line should not carry a blasphemous disregard for sacrifice, nor for the horrible fallen, degenerate state of those still in the swamp of creation. How could he simply float? An anchorless spirit? Caring nothing for others, relishing in the comfort of separation, spared only because the cries and screams of collective misery cannot rise high enough to reach his ears?

It was his own choice now, ever would be, and he stood well upon it, feeling the stone of it, and the holy steel. He made manifest what he was, no more first feeling the cold of asphalt, or the frigid autumn air upon his newly-knit back. He was warm, in spite of everything else, and his new life blood coursed within him, forever a fire unquenchable. What was warmer still was the knowledge and purpose he embodied. He knew where to find them, and what to do. The well-spring called to them all. He would lead them there.

END